THE FIREBRAND

BY

SUMANA SHASHIDHAR

&

SHASHIDHAR BELWADI

THE FIREBRAND

By Sumana Shashidhar and Shashidhar Belwadi

Copyright **Sumana Shashidhar and Shashidhar Belwadi** ,
6420, Grand Meadow Lane, San Jose, California – 95315.
Email: sumandeep2k@gmail.com

English Edition 2017

Pages **492**

Paper

Size

Price:

E-Book Link

Printed At:

"Each soul is potentially divine. The goal is to manifest this divinity within by controlling nature, external and internal."

Swami Vivekananda

From: "Advaita Ashrama" <advaita@vsnl.com>
To: <sumandeep2k@hotmail.com>
Sent: 31 October 2003 11:50
Subject: Message for (Smt.) Sumana Shashidhar

Dear Sister Smt. Sumana Shashidhar,

Please refer to your e-mail dated 12 September, 2003 and my e-mail letter dated 22 September, 2003 addressed to you from our Mayavati centre. I have also now received your e-mail dated 28 October, 2003.

The permission wanted by you to consult the following books and to quote from them in your proposed book on Swami Vivekananda to be written in "Historical Fictional form, highlighting the travel of Swami Vivekananda to the USA, with special emphasis to his explosive appearance at the Parliament of Religions at Chicago, his efforts to establish a Mission in the USA, his travels through USA and Europe, and other incidental matters," is hereby given to you on the following simple conditions:

1. You will suitably acknowledge that we have accorded you our permission to reproduce portions from those books;

2. You will kindly see that while making use of these books or quoting from them the facts and ideas of are not distorted in any manner;

3. You will please send us a complimentary copy of the book when published for our information and record.

The books are:

1. Swami Vivekananda in America, New Discoveries ... Marie Lewis Barke;
2. Life of Swami Vivekananda by his Eastern and Western Disciples .....volumes 1 and 2;
3. Life of Vivekananda ...... Romain Roland;
4. Life of Ramakrishna ......Romain Roland;
5. Complete Works of Swami Vivekananda ..... Volumes 1 to 9.

Please acknowledge the receipt of this e-mail letter as well as the letter being sent to you by postal mail through your father as per your instruction.

With good wishes and namaskar,

Yours sincerely

Swami Mumukshananda
President
Advaita Ashrama, Mayavati

ADVAITA ASHRAMA • 5, Dehi Entally Road • Kolkata 700 014 • INDIA
E-mail: advaita@vsnl.com • Website: www.advaitaonline.com

To Smt. Sumana Shashidhar
C/o Sri B. N. Shashidhar
1135 G & H Block

THIS BOOK IS DEDICATED TO

SISTER GARGI – MARIE LOUISE BURKE

TABLE OF CONTENTS

	Page
ACKNOWLEDGEMENTS……………………………………...	8
PREFACE……………………………………………………..	11
CHAPTER 1. THE FIRST MEETING………………………….	18
CHAPTER.2. THE MONK…………………………………….	27
CHAPTER.3. A SHORT AUTOBIOGRAPHY…………………	41
CHAPTER.4. MAGIC AND MIRACLES… ……………………	54
CHAPTER.5. CHILDHOOD…………………………………...	69
CHAPTER.6. THE GREAT REFORMERS…………………….	82
CHAPTER.7. MY MASTER…………………………………..	98
CHAPTER.8. MASTER AND DISCIPLE…………………….	126
CHAPTER.9. LOVE AND TEMPTATION……………………..	144
CHAPTER.10. DESPAIR AND RESURRECTION……………..	153
CHAPTER.11. LIFE WITH THE MASTER……………………..	167
CHAPTER.12. THE WANDERING…………………………….	181
CHAPTER.13. THE DECISION……………………………….	197
CHAPTER.14. THE VOYAGE………………………………..	209
CHAPTER.15. THE PREPARATION………………………….	227
CHAPTER.16. THE RETURN………………………………..	243
CHAPTER 17. THE PARLIAMENT OF RELIGIONS………….	254
CHAPTER 18. THE FLASH OF INTELLECTS………………...	275
CHAPTER.19. PLANNING FOR THE FUTURE………………	289
CHAPTER.20. THE GREAT BATTLES……………………….	312
CHAPTER.21. THE AMERICAN LESSONS AND MISSION…	339
CHAPTER.22. THE AMERICAN DISCIPLES…………………	361
CHAPTER 23. MEETING THE ENEMY……………………….	390
CHAPTER.24. THE CHRONICLER AND THE DISRUPTOR…	408
CHAPTER.25. FRIENDS AND PHILOSOPHERS…………….	428
CHAPTER 26. A CONTINENTAL INTERLUDE………………	455
CHAPTER.27. HOMEWARD BOUND………………………..	481
ABOUT THE AUTHORS………………………………………...	492
CONNECT WITH THE AUTHORS…………………………….	494
AUTHORS' THANKS…………………………………………..	494

ACKNOWLEDGEMENTS

Our heartfelt thanks to the Advaita Ashrama, Mayavati, for granting us permission to freely use the material in the books published by them, even to the extent of quoting the words as they are. Of course, this book being partly fiction, some literary liberties have been taken, but it has been ensured that there is no distortion anywhere.

Heartfelt thanks also to the Ramakrishna Ashrama, Mysore, which gave us access to so much literature on the subject. It also gave us peace in the meditation hall, and great devotional pleasure in listening to the Arati songs in the evening.

Our deepest thanks to Frank Parlato Jr., of Niagara Falls, Canada, for giving us free access to his website www.vivekananda.net. The material in the website, and the photographs, are priceless. The work of Frank is amazing, and his generosity the hallmark of his country. Suitable tribute to him will be paid later in due course of time.

Our thanks to Ed Coxe of Andy Barr Productions Support (http://www.carl.sandburg.com) for giving us ungrudging permission to reproduce the poem "Chicago" by Carl Sandburg.

Thanks are due to the Archives of Historic New England (www.historicnewengland.org) for according permission to use the photograph of Sarah Ellen Waldo.

It was kind of www.ridgely.org to declare that the photograph of Frank Leggett was in the public domain, and could be freely used.

For the various photographs used in the book, thanks are due to:
The Vedanta Society of Chicago.
The Vedanta Society of St. Louis.
The Art Institute of Chicago, especially its fantastic research section and research team.
The Indian Railways.
The website www.ramakrishna.eu

Our thanks to Ms. M. Girija for providing us the portrait of the Bhairavi Brahmani. Thanks also to Ms. Deepti Shashidhar for freely giving us her poems, and Ms. M.N. Rajeshwari for her critical insights on many aspects.

The authors' failure to obtain a necessary permission for use of any other copyrighted material included in this work is inadvertent, and will be corrected in future printings following notification in writing to the Publishers of such omission, accompanied by appropriate documentation.

Our thanks to Ms. Sajni Doddannavar for gifting us rare photographs and material on the Swami. Last but not least, our thanks to Ms. Meenu Lalwani, for her painstaking proof-reading, and suggestions in grammar and other language aspects.

****

PREFACE

Undoubtedly, Divine powers guided and helped Swami Vivekananda in enthralling a continent. It is equally true that it was America which helped in making the Swami's mission move forward, and Americans who helped in establishing the Belur Math.

America was considered a thoroughly materialistic nation. Nevertheless, its men and women, supposedly worshippers of Mammon, flocked in the thousands to hear the Swami speak. They came to hear him repeatedly, hardly the behavior of mere money-minded people. The Swami earned a relatively small amount in America. This was not due to the lack of generosity of the American people. The Swami hated money. He gave more importance to free lectures. He charged a pittance as admission to paid lectures. He never took money given as donations if he did not feel like it.

If he had left it to his American admirers to handle the financial part of affairs, he would have got thousands of dollars. That was an age where even a hundred dollars was big money. It was an age where a medium-sized Indian family could have lived comfortably, even luxuriously, on a paltry thirty rupees (50 cents by today's rate) a month!

To my mind, the American men and women, who assisted the Swami, were not any less than the 'Ishwarakotis (souls who are ever perfect),' the devotees born to aid the Swami's Master, Shri Ramakrishna Paramahamsa. The ladies treated the Swami like their son, their brother. They took care of him financially, and were always sensitive to his smallest needs. During his frequent ill-health, they nursed him as lovingly as a mother or sister would.

The families that opened their doors to him treated him as a close family member. They loved him as much as they would their own children. The Swami was more at home, and at ease, in American households, than he would have been even with his relatives in India. An attempt is made in this book to give rightful recognition to these affectionate men and women of America.

If the American people had been wholly materialistic, the Swami would have shunned them like the plague. He would have returned to India soon after the Parliament of Religions, inner voices notwithstanding. Instead, he was captivated by the American people. He stressed their innovative skills, their genius, their industry, their adventurous spirit, their receptiveness to new ideas and their organizational skills. He admired their dignity of labour, their clean towns and cities, their systems, the American women and, not least, their ice cream!

A totally spiritual person, the Swami was very taken with the deep vein of spirituality in the American psyche. He voiced a hope to weld the Eastern and Western cultures, taking the best aspects of both. He hoped to bring about a fusion of spirituality and practicality, religion and industry, faith and genius and bring into existence a new breed of men, able to stand on their own feet, facing all odds

In the triumphal march of the Swami through America, the role of the American Press is outstanding. Much of the deep research on the Swami's travels by researchers was done by following the newspaper trail that he had created! Many of his lectures exist only because they were reported by the Press. It is startling to find reporters writing fairly accurately on subjects that must have sounded Greek and Latin, if not Sanskrit, to them. The Press was generous enough in reporting in their news columns the programs of the Swami, and the times, days and dates of the next speech.

True, many of the newspapers stirred controversies that caused tension and anguish to the Swami for several months. This was, however, a part of the game. Controversies ensured increased circulation, and more attendance for the Swami's lectures! The newspapers did not create the controversies; this was done by the Swami's enemies. When the truth about any controversy was revealed, the newspapers were as generous in printing the truth as they had been in highlighting the controversy. They need not have done this. After all, one poor colored Indian, teaching an eldritch philosophy, was as nothing to this powerful Fourth Estate! Truly, the Press was, and has remained, the bulwark of democracy in America.

No one can sum up the work of Swami Vivekananda better than Sister Nivedita (Margaret Noble). She says:

"These then - the Shastras, the Guru, and the Motherland – are the three notes that mingle themselves to form the music of the works of Vivekananda………These are the three lights burning within the single lamp which India has by his hand lighted and set up, for the guidance of her own children and of the few years of work between September 19, 1983 and July 4, 1902, And some of us there are, who…..bless the land that bore him…..and believe that not even yet has it been given to us to understand the vastness and significance of the message that he spoke."

This book seeks, in this first volume, to present the highlights of the life of Swami Vivekananda from the time he left for America in 1893, till his first return to India in 1896. The historical fiction mode of narration has been chosen so as to flesh out the details. It gives the reader a direct look at what presumably happened, good or bad. The Ramakrishna Math and Mission have been very transparent in all their publications. Following Oliver Cromwell's injunction, this book impartially follows the "warts and all" method.

This book is meant mainly for the general reader. However, devotees of Sri Ramakrishna and Swami Vivekananda may also find something new between these pages. It has been attempted to contain in this one book the facts, episodes and research contained in many volumes. It is a primer, from which one can go on to serious research, if one wishes to. Above all, being fiction, this book takes some liberties with some details, but in a totally non-objectionable way. There is no distortion of facts.

Assuredly, this book is a tribute to Swami Vivekananda. Equally, it is a tribute to America, the American way of life, and the American people.

Sumana Shashidhar and Shashidhar Belwadi
San Jose, California, U.S.A., and Mysore,
Karnataka, India.

*****

The World's Columbian Exposition was held in Chicago in the year 1893.

The World's Parliament of Religions was one of its Congresses.

The Parliament of Religions was held in the Art Institute at Chicago on September 11, 1893.

194 official delegates, and 41 different religions, from England, France, Scotland, Sweden, Switzerland, Germany, Greece, Egypt, Syria, India, Japan, China, Ceylon, New Zealand, Brazil, Canada and the United States of America took part in this Parliament.

150,000 people attended the 17 days of the Parliament

A brass plaque outside the Fullerton Hall in the Art Institute, Chicago, commemorates the Parliament of Religions.

It reads as follows:

> ON THIS SITE
> BETWEEN SEPTEMBER 11 AND 27, 1893,
> SWAMI VIVEKANANDA (1863-1902),
> THE FIRST HINDU MONK FROM INDIA
> TO TEACH VEDANTA IN AMERICA,
> ADDRESSED THE WORLD'S PARLIAMENT OF
> RELIGIONS, HELD IN CONJUNCTION WITH
> THE WORLD'S COLUMBIAN EXPOSITION.
> HIS UNPRECEDENTED SUCCESS
> OPENED THE WAY FOR THE
> DIALOGUE BETWEEN EASTERN AND
> WESTERN RELIGIONS.

Only one delegate from one country is mentioned in the plaque, tacit acknowledgement that that one delegate represented the true spirit of the Parliament of Religions.

*****

CHAPTER 1

THE FIRST MEETING

It was a windy evening in Chicago on August 12, 1893. The overcast sky and light showers contributed to the chill in the wind that blew in from Lake Michigan. I had completed my night shift at the Grand Central Station that morning, and it was my day off. After resting through the day, I did not expect to go out for the evening. I was now sitting cozily in my warm room with my Engineer's handbook and other sundry technical literature. They dealt with the new electrical systems proposed to be installed in the rail coaches and locomotives by George Westinghouse.

Around 7.30 pm there was a knock on the door. I was surprised. Hardly anyone visited me. I had very few friends and only one relative, my Uncle Joe, the loco driver. I opened the door, and found one of the cleaning boys from the Mechanical section. He said: "I was going home, and the Boss asked me to give this note to you."

The Boss was our Station Master (SM) Bill Schumpeter. I took the letter, thanked the boy, and sent him on his way. I opened the note and read: "Dear Jock. Both Flanagan and Pulaski have called in sick. A lot of freight from Nebraska is lying piled on the tracks. I'd be obliged if you could help out tonight. You can take your day off whenever you want. Collect your gun from the Office. Thanks, Bill."

Technically, as Electrical Supervisor in the Mechanical Section, I reported to the Mechanical Engineer. The station and track staff was directly under the SM. But Bill Schumpeter was a powerful man in all senses of the word. One crossed him at one's own peril. He was, moreover, a powerful ally. Favors done for him would fetch rich dividends in the future. Besides, I was young, strongly built, eager to learn, and ambitious. I did not refuse any duty that came my way.

I finished my dinner around 8 pm, and dressed warmly for the night ahead. There were no Security men, or Policemen, to patrol the railway stations during the night. Incoming freight trains would pile up their goods on the platforms. These would be stacked in manageable piles, waiting their turn to be taken inside the Freight Office. Some of this freight was valuable, and pilferage was common. The Track Supervisors and Inspectors had their work cut out for them. During nights, they also carried guns to protect themselves from armed robbers; hence the SM's direction to me to collect the gun from the office.

It was a short walk from my room, in one of the alleys of Polk Street, to the Grand Central. The station was at 600 South Wells Street, at the Harrison Street South West corner in the Loop neighborhood of Downtown Chicago. The Grand Central was a magnificent piece of architecture designed by the famous architect Solon S.

Beman. It was completed and opened for the public in 1890.

JOCK MCCLINTOCK

STATIONMASTER BILL SCHUMPETER

It started with a modest train shed span of 119 feet. It fronted 228 feet on Harrison Street, and 482 feet on Fifth Avenue at the South West corner. In the front was the beautiful square-topped bell-tower. It rose to a height of 242 feet, and held a clock-bell weighing nearly 6 tons. The fore building was 100 feet high, with 7 stories and basement. It was constructed from Connecticut brownstone, brick terra cotta and steel.

There were 3 elevators. The station was made the hub of almost all the railroads like the Michigan Central and the Chicago-Burlington & Quincy Railroads.

The main concourse contained a number of pillars supporting a high roof, and was golden-yellow in color. It was well-lighted with Thomas Alva Edison's recently invented electric lamps. The seating capacity of the waiting rooms was 1800. 77 tracks carried 10,000 passengers daily. The 560 foot long open train shed covered 7 tracks, each accommodating 7 coaches and the locomotive. To serve the depot, and not close off Fifth Avenue, the approach to Polk Street Bridge south of Harrison Street was turned sideways, and made architecturally a part of the Grand Central.

THE GRAND CENTRAL RAILWAY STATION, CHICAGO

WAITING ROOM OF THE GRAND CENTRAL RAILWAY STATION, CHICAGO

The Grand Central Railway Station was an architectural delight, a railroad man's delight, and my only love for a long, long time. Before coming here, I had worked at the Old Union Station. I came here at the beginning of 1893.

I reached the station and went first to the SM's office. Bill had left, but the Night Clerk, a jolly man named O'Brien was in the seat. We chatted for some time and he told me a few good jokes. Then I signed for the gun and belt, and strapped the belt around my waist. I next went to the Freight office. I checked out with the staff the location of the various parcels on the tracks. I started my patrolling of the tracks to check out the goods. The station was closed to passengers as the last train from St. Paul had pulled in about an hour ago. The waiting room was closed and locked.

It was windy on the platforms as I covered Tracks 1, 2 and 3 from end to end. As I was going along Track 4, I heard a peculiar humming sound, like the rumble of an approaching train. I halted. The sound stopped. I moved forward, and after some time the sound started again. It was an open-throated sound gradually descending to a hum. It was very regular, musical and puzzling.

I unbuttoned my holster and put my hand on the gun butt. The sound seemed to be coming from the middle of a heap of bundles stacked around a wooden bench. "Must be a hobo, or a drunk," I thought. I cautiously moved towards the packages. The stacking of the bundles was incidentally such that it stopped the wind on the windward side. The other side was slightly open. I peeked in through the opening and saw a strange sight. In the middle of the packages, on the bench, sat a man!

The man, obviously from a foreign country, was seated on the bench in a peculiar way. His legs were crossed one over the other, and tucked under him on the bench. His steel baggage trunk and a large cloth carry-bag were by his side. His head was covered with a conical woolen cap. He wore a long coat of maroon material over dark trousers. He wore socks, and his shoes were below the bench. His hands were on his lap, with one palm lying over the other. His eyes were closed and he was making this strange sound. Still keeping my hand on the gun butt, I called out to him: "Hey, mister! Who are you, and what do you think you are doing?"

The man opened his eyes and looked at me sharply. Then he smiled. He uncrossed his legs and came to his feet, sliding his shoes on in one liquid motion. With his left hand he removed his cap and bowed slightly, looking at me all the time. He again smiled, and said: "Good evening! My name is Swami Vivekananda. I am from India. I have come here to take part in the Parliament of Religions!"

-----ooooo-----

THE DOOR OF DESTINY

Strolling along the corridors of time,
By chance you randomly open a door.
Suddenly, an experience sublime
Ensures that you are changed forevermore!

This chance may occur once, ne'er to repeat,
You may be least prepared, your problems rife,
But lo, this golden chance will make you meet
The greatest Person to enter your life!

Who stands your knowledge on its head, and scans
Your heart, raises the tenor of your soul,
Alters your whole life with its humdrum plans –
The highest plane of God will be your goal!

But then, you see, it is just Luck that can
Conspire with Fate to smoothen full your road,
And if the gods be kind, this person can
Put you right on the path to God's abode!

SUMANA SHASHIDHAR

CHAPTER 2

THE MONK

Lost in my observation of the stranger, I scarcely heard what he said. He was a striking figure of a man. He was about 5 feet 9 inches tall, square-shouldered and broad-chested. He was heavily built, and weighed around 170 pounds. He looked more muscular than fat. He had parted his hair at the center. He was of olive complexion. He had a full, handsome face with a vast forehead and strong jaw.

His eyes were his most striking feature. They were magnificent – prominent, large, dark, with heavy lids and piercing gaze. When he spoke – even those 2 sentences – in his rich, deep baritone, it was like hearing splendid music. The harmonics of his beautiful voice had the vibrations of a sonorous gong. Such was his majesty that I involuntarily thought: "This is no hobo! This is a King!"

I recalled myself with an effort. I took my hand off the gun-butt, and bowed in turn. "Hi. I'm Jock McClintock of the railroad. Please call me Jock. Sorry, I didn't catch your name?"
"My name is Vivekananda," he said, and continued with practiced ease: "It's pronounced We-wake-awe-nun-daah. If that's too hard, you can call me Swami for short."
"Glad to meet you, Swami. Which part of Indiana do you come from? Our Union President Eugene Debs is from Terre Haute."

"No, no," he exclaimed. "I'm not from Indiana. I come from India in the Asian continent. I am from the province of Bengal in the east of India."

"Oh, I'm so sorry," I said. "I've read about India. But how did you reach here?"

We had been standing till then. Swami indicated the bench and said: "Shall we sit down?"

Both of us sat on the bench, and Swami continued: "It was a long and tedious journey by ship and train. I started from Bombay, India, on May 31, on the Steam Ship 'Peninsular' and reached Yokohama, Japan. From there, I embarked on the SS Empress of India, and reached Vancouver BC on July 25. From there I traveled by train and reached Chicago at 10.30 pm on July 30, via Winnipeg and St. Paul."

"Oh, my goodness! That's a journey of 2 months! What countries did you travel through?"

"I traveled through Ceylon, Malaya, Singapore, Hong Kong and Japan."

This was indeed a fantastic voyage, and I said so. "You have seen countries I have only read about! Are you a businessman?"

He laughed loudly, shaking all over with mirth. "I'm very far from being a businessman. I am a Hindu Monk, and a wandering monk at that! That is why the Swami is added to my name. It's the equivalent of your priests in the Catholic faith being called Brother or Father."

"Didn't you say you had come to Chicago for some conference?"

"Not exactly a conference. You see, the Chicago World's Fair is hosting what is called a Parliament of Religions. Representatives from all religions will attend from around the world to explain the basic tenets and advanced theories of their respective religions."

"So why are you at the Grand Central?" I asked.

"Oh, Jock (he pronounced it somewhat like joke), it's a sad story. You see, I came to Chicago knowing only that the Parliament would be held here. I did not know the date, or the month, of the meetings. A few days after reaching Chicago, I went to the Information Bureau of the Exposition. There I learnt that the Parliament was to open sometime in September! So I'm stuck here."

"That's bad!" I exclaimed.

"No, Jock," he replied, "That appears to be the good news! The bad news is that not only is it too late for registration, but no registration will be accepted without references. I have none."

"Oh, my Goodness!"

"Still worse is the fact that I'm running out of money. Chicago is an expensive city. Also, as a foreigner, I've been cheated badly a number of times."

"So what are your plans?"

"I have contemplated the problem deeply. I have decided that I must go to Boston, and come back here in September."

"But where will you stay, and what about your references?" He smiled and said: "God will provide, Jock, God will provide!"

"Well," I said, "Boston is a cold place, but the weather will be fine till September. Tell me, do you belong to any particular Order of monks?"
"Well….broadly, very broadly, I belong to the Order of Ramakrishna. Ramakrishna was my teacher, my Guru, my Master!"
"In India, did you have a formal education before you became a monk?"
"Yes, indeed. I studied Arts at the Presidency College, Calcutta, and also Law. My college subjects were physics, chemistry and mathematics. I also studied English and Sanskrit literature, philosophy, astronomy, languages and Hindu religious scriptures."
"And your parents….?"
"My father was a very famous attorney in Calcutta when he was alive. My mother is looking after the family, which has my brothers and sisters. We are a large family."

I asked him: "How come you are sitting here on Track 4?"
"I knew that the train to Boston was in the morning. As in India, I thought I would come to the station in the evening, and find a place to wait. I found the waiting room closed. I asked an official about it, and he said it would be locked till morning. Before I could ask him anything else, he hurried away. So I just wandered in through the gate to this

platform. I found this place an ideal buffer against the cold wind."

"Well, you're lucky," I said. "By the way, what was that humming sound you were making?"
"Actually, I was meditating. I was uttering the word 'OM' in a particular way. Doing so helps concentrate the mind, control the senses and relax your body for meditation on the Lord."
"Oh yes." I said, "I have read about 'OM.' Without any offence meant, Swami, how do you make a living? Does your order support you, like the Catholic Church supports its priests?"
"No offence taken, Jock. My order does nothing to support me. Shortly put, I beg for a living."

He saw my face and laughed. "Jock, in my country a man who becomes a monk gives up fame, fortune and progeny. He is entitled to beg for alms. It is the duty of the householders to maintain him."
"But, Swami, are you sure every day that you will get enough for that day?"
Swami smiled and said: "Our needs are very limited. During emergencies, God provides."
"That's the second time you have said that. Does God really provide in times of need?"
"Jock," he said, "Let me narrate my own experience. At one time, I had the same doubts you have. I was very vocal about it. I never took anything for granted. My doubts were cleared in this manner."

As a young monk (said Swami), I was traveling from place to place in India by train. One scorching summer, I caught a long distance train to a distant place. I reached the starting station late, just managing to catch the train. So I had no food with me for the night, not even a water pot. I took my seat in a coach. Opposite me sat a merchant, who we call a Baniya in India. He was a middle-aged man. He seemed to dislike monks, or at least have scorn for the saffron robes I wore.

We traveled all night and I grew hungry and thirsty. The Baniya was well-stocked with food and water. I had no money even to buy water from the water-carriers at the railway stations on the way. I requested the Baniya for some water. He jeered at me and said: "Does not God provide for you? Sorry, I have just enough for myself."

He had enough food and water to provision a small household! By late night I was deathly hungry and thirsty. All the while, the Baniya ate well, drank water copiously and made fun of my starving condition. He was more odious, if possible, while eating sweets. I was in agony, but determined to present a bland face to this miserable creature.

The next day, at scorching noon, we had to change trains at a station called Tari Ghat. In the station, seeing my empty-handed condition, the station porter mistook me for a beggar. He did not allow me into the station shed. So I sat down on the ground, in the burning sun and leaned against a post. I was half-dead from hunger and thirst. I closed my eyes for a while.

TARI GHAT RAILWAY STATION

When I opened them lo, my tormentor was again sitting before me in the shade! He said: "People like you deserve only to sit in the sun! Look here, what nice sweets I am eating. You do not care to earn money. Be content with a parched throat, an empty stomach and the bare ground!"

I forced myself to look at him calmly and impassively, not moving a single muscle in my face.

Suddenly, a local inhabitant appeared on the platform. He traversed slowly along it, looking at the faces of the passengers. He was carrying a cloth bundle and a water-glass in his right hand. He had a bamboo mat and an umbrella under his left arm. An earthen water-pot was in his left hand.

He looked at me, paused, and then moved on beyond me to a vacant place. He cleaned the spot and spread the mat there. He put the water and the bundle on the mat. He removed the cloth covering of the bundle to display a covered plate. He opened the umbrella and leaned it on the ground to cover the articles on the mat. To my utter surprise, he came up to me, prostrated on the ground, touched my feet and said: "Come, Babaji. I have brought the food for you." Monks and Saints are called 'Baba' in India, and 'Ji' is an honorific like 'sir.'

He kept insisting that I come and eat the food. I kept wondering what this meant, who this man was, and what he wanted. I suggested to him that he had made a mistake and that the food was meant for someone else.
"No, no," the man cried out, "you are the very Babaji I have seen!"
I was even more astounded, and asked: "Where have you seen me? I have only just arrived here for the first time!"
By this time, seeing this drama going on, some of the other passengers collected near us to hear our conversation. The man had this story to tell.

It seems he was a sweets-vendor, with a shop of his own in the town. He ate an early lunch due to the heat and then had a siesta. This is the normal custom all over India, more so in summer. The next thing he knew, his household God Shri Ramji was pointing me out to him. Shri Ramji told him to prepare some pancakes and curry for me, and take them to the railway station. He was also to carry a mat, sweets and cold water!

The man woke up with a start, saw that he had been dreaming and promptly turned over and went to sleep again. Again he dreamed, and this time saw a visibly annoyed Shri Ramji appear. The god berated the man for his laziness and repeated his instructions. He actually pushed the man off the cot, so that he fell on the floor with a thud! The last recollection he had was of Shri Ramji telling him sternly not to forget the sweets! The man ran helter-skelter to obey the command. He woke up his wife, and got the things prepared fast. Then he took the items mentioned and ran to the station, where he recognized me!

Saying this much, the man again prostrated before me. He entreated me: "Now do come and have your meal while it is fresh, Maharaj!"
I could not control myself. Tears of love flowed from my eyes. With a full heart and choked throat, I thanked the simple soul for his hospitality. The kind man protested, saying, "No, no, Babaji. Don't thank me. It is all the will of Shri Ramji that I had the good fortune to serve you."

While he was speaking, more and more people from the shed had collected near us. The good man had spoken in the normal loud voice used by the rustics in the north.

All of them heard the story in pin-drop silence. Suddenly, there was a shrill devotional cry of: "Bolo Siyavar Ramachandraji ki jai (Proclaim victory to Shri Ramachandra, consort of Shri Seeta)!"
More and more people fell at my feet, especially the women. My tormentor, the Baniya, led all the rest in this! He appeared stunned, and repeatedly begged my pardon for all his behavior with me.

It all ended with the crowd leading me to the mat, and watching me eat the food there. One of the women fanned me with a hand-fan she had. The porter who had pushed me out of the shed held the umbrella over me. The Baniya plied me with his own sweets in addition to those on the plate!

Later, when I continued my journey, I was well looked after by my co-passengers. Believe me, Jock, after this all my doubts that God would provide vanished. I go about my work without any worry. Of course, sudden problems do perturb me. After I grow calm, I come back to God's will!

I was still thinking about this story when Swami suddenly asked: "Jock, what is your date of birth?"
Surprised, I asked: "Why?"
"Jock, you are very tall and well-built, and you carry a gun. There is, still, an innocence that shines from you. Speaking spiritually, you have a special aura, pure like a child's.

Your aura is also very familiar, as if your soul and mine are acquainted. That's why I ask you your date of birth."

Bemused by all this, I said: "Well, for what it's worth, my date of birth is January 12, 1863."

Swami looked at me for some time and then a slow smile spread over his face.

Puzzled, I asked: "What?"

He said: "I knew there was something special about you! Can you believe it, Jock, that you and I were born on the same day of the same year?"

Before I could react to that, he went on in a rush: "What a wonderful thing it is that thousands of miles from my country, across the wide oceans, in a foreign land, I have established a karmik connection! It is like finding a soul-brother! Now I no longer feel like a stranger in a strange land. I will no longer feel lonely, without a soul to frankly talk to. I foresee that whatever I achieve in America, you will be a part of that adventure. In future, you can call me by my given name, Naren."

With his slight accent, it sounded like No-rain.

I thought he was reading a lot into a chance encounter, and the coincidence of our dates of birth being the same. He was in a strange land, lonely, and had not really talked to anyone, let alone his own countrymen. A railway platform, and a stranger to chat with, is something many people look forward to. Especially if you know that you may never set eyes on that stranger again!

I was a good listener, and if my listening made him happy, so be it. He was obviously an emotional person facing innumerable odds. He had very little money, no credentials, and no chance of registering himself in the Parliament to which he had come. His hope and faith in God was touching, but I didn't think anything would come of it. As for his achievements in America, and my part in it, well, the less said the better! Only his God knew what lay ahead!

Naren said: "Tell me about yourself, Jock, if you don't mind."
"I don't mind at all, but it's not a very interesting life," I said.
"Still, I would like to hear about you."
I leaned back on the bench, thought for a while and then began my story.

******

THE RIVER OF LIFE

*Life is like a flowing river, joy and sorrow are its banks,
All are caught between these two, and never mind titles or ranks,
Who can say that this is my bank, and that other bank is yours?
The river flows on regardless of the clamor on its shores.*

*Joy between two sorrows lies; what's there to be happy about?
We'll suffer sorrow after joy, of this fact can there be doubt?
Joy and sorrow, after all, alternate like the night and day,
In this darkness of the night, who shows the lamp to light our way?*

Know then that we ourselves are the lamps to illumine our road,

Joy and sorrow are but states of mind, they have no fixed abode,
Share joy, in sorrow be patient; if you accept this notion,
An easy life you'll have before the river joins the ocean!

DEEPTI SHASHIDHAR

CHAPTER 3

A SHORT AUTOBIOGRAPHY

I was born in Toledo, by the shores of Lake Erie, on January 12, 1863. My father, Patrick McClintock, of Irish descent, was Professor of Mathematics at the University. He was of the Catholic faith, though not a practicing Christian. My mother Lara was from Canada, of Russian ancestry, and of the Jewish faith. She taught in a children's school. My father used to mention only one relative, his cousin Joe, who was a locomotive driver in Chicago. My mother had no relatives, either at Canada or in the States. From my father I inherited my love of numbers, mathematics and science. My mother taught me to love languages. I was quite a prodigy as a child, reading my father's text books and asking him a lot of questions.

When I was fifteen, both my parents died in a freak boat accident on Lake Erie. I was an orphan with no relatives to look after me. Fortunately for me, my father's best friend, Tom Humphrey, Professor of History, came to my rescue. He and his wife Eve, Professor of English, were a childless couple. They took me into their home, published notices in the newspapers, and waited for any relative to appear. No one did. Tom and Eve settled my parents' financial affairs with the banks. They sold my parents house. They put all the funds into a Trust for me, and looked after me as their own son.

I continued my studies. In spite of their busy schedules, Tom and Eve gave me a lot of attention. In addition to math (I had gone into calculus and other advanced math), Tom roused my curiosity in History. Soon the Greek conquerors and philosophers, as also the Roman emperors, thinkers and demagogues became my heroes. Reading about Alexander the Great, I also became interested in India, its thinkers and philosophers and its great civilization.

Eve dunked me into English, both literature and grammar. I read most of the classics with great pleasure and curiosity. Eve also made me learn three languages, French, German and Spanish. She said these were common all over the world, and a working knowledge would be very good for me. They were no difficulty; I became quite fluent in them within a year.

Seeing my proficiency in math and science Tom, with my assent, enrolled me in Engineering. Till the age of 21 I studied Engineering, specializing in Mechanical Engineering. Of course, with it there was some knowledge of Electrical and Civil Engineering also. I was always curious, and so progressed well into the world of mechanical engineering, lapping up all the handbooks and magazines I could lay hands on.

Taking after my father, I was more than six feet tall, with the build of a football player. However, sports never captured my attention; only books of engineering and mathematics. The one thing I was blessed with was a photographic memory. I just had to glance at a page and it would remain imprinted in my brain.

During all this period, the memoriam notice of my parents' death was published every year, on the date of their death. The leading newspaper, the 'Morning Clarion' carried the notice. It was a mark of remembrance and respect by Tom. One morning, glancing out of my room window, I saw a man standing before the house with a newspaper in his hand.

He would look at the newspaper and then at the house. After a while, he moved towards the front door. I was surprised to see him lurch from side to side as he walked, as if he were drunk. Later, I would recognize this as the trademark of a locomotive driver. The driver spent most of his life compensating for the pitching movement of the locomotive. Like the sailor, the railroader could never get used to the fact that the ground could be steady beneath his feet.

This, then, was my uncle, Joseph McClintock, the loco driver from Chicago. He had found me through a sheer accident. A cleaning lad had found this paper, with the memoriam notice, discarded in one of the cars of the Chicago-Boston Express. Glancing through it, he saw the name McClintock and took the paper to Uncle Joe, who read for the first time about the death of his only cousin.

Uncle Joe did not know about me, either. When he talked to Tom and Eve, he was very insistent on doing the right thing by his nephew. He said that I should come to Chicago, stay with him, and get a good job in Chicago. Tom and Eve were reluctant, but they recognized the right of the family over me. The long and the short of the meeting was that I left for Chicago with my uncle. The Trust Fund was allowed to remain in Toledo till I reached the age of 30.

My Uncle Joe and Aunt Debbie were kindly people, living in a small house in the outskirts of Chicago. It was decided that we should look around before selecting a suitable job for me. I spent a week exploring Chicago, and seeing the various wonderful things there; things which I had never even imagined in Toledo.

Two days later, my uncle thought he would show me the Union Station where he was employed. The first glimpse of the Union Station was breath-taking. It was a large Victorian structure, with a high roof looking like two great chimneys. There were 5 tracks in the station and the loco shed was at one end. The Station Master was Matt Carpenter. Uncle Joe took me to him.

Carpenter's large office was in the center of the station. At one end of the office there was an ornate table for visitors, surrounded by couches and a sofa. Seated there, drinking coffee with Carpenter, were two impressive men. One of them was lean and lanky, with a serious face, which would break out into a dazzling smile from time to time. The other was a giant of a man – big, jovial, and healthy, with a red-cheeked face and a hearty smile. Carpenter was a roly-poly little man, obviously deferring to both the visitors.

My Uncle Joe pushed me towards Carpenter and said: "Boss, this is my little nephew, Jock McClintock."
I was taller than my uncle, so there were smiles around the table.
The giant murmured: "Not so little!"
"Your nephew?" asked Carpenter. "I never knew you had one! Where were you hiding him for so long?"
Uncle Joe related the events leading to my coming to Chicago. All of them became grave, and Carpenter said: "Sorry, Joe, and sorry, kid. We're sorry to hear about this. What do you plan to do with him, Joe?"
"He has almost finished his engineering. In fact, his guardian told me that he has gone much ahead of what is normally taught. He is a genius in mechanical engineering. I was thinking of searching for a suitable job for him," said my uncle.

Carpenter interrupted: "By the way, Jock, let me introduce these gentlemen to you."
He motioned towards the lanky person and said, "Meet Mr. Eugene V. Debs, President of the American Railway Union. And this is Colonel Robert Green Ingersoll, the famous attorney and atheist. He is delivering his famous lectures around Chicago."

I stepped forward and shook hands with both of them.

Debs looked at me and said: "How old are you, son?"
I told him. He nodded and said: "You look older and you're strong and healthy. Your uncle says you are far ahead of the subjects taught in your course. My advice to you would be to forget about ivory tower learning. Get a job, and study during your free time.

"Know how I studied? I dropped out of school when I was fourteen. I went to work for the Vandalia railroad car shop at fifty cents a day. I painted cars, and scraped paint off the cars that stood in the yard. After a year, I got a temporary job in the same railroad as a temporary fireman. I did a good job in keeping the steam pressure up in the boiler.

I was given a permanent job, assisting engineers. Most times, my run would end around midnight in some godforsaken place. All the others would hit their bunks. I would light a candle, pull out the book I carried in my knapsack and read all night. They called me the Mad Frenchie! I slept very little. I was always studying whenever I could."

Carpenter chimed in: "And they *were* tough times too, Gene. I remember that there was danger all the time. Accidents every day, trains flying off their tracks in icy conditions, freight cars and whole rakes derailing, couplings snapping! But they were exciting times, too."

Ingersoll laughed and we looked at him. He said: "I remember Gene when he was a younger person. He was an intellectual even then. But he was naïve, and believed everything the newspaper wrote. Once, he invited me to deliver a lecture to a society of free-thinkers or something in Terre Haute. He could not trust his eyes when I detrained! He saw me as I am now, only younger. He had expected a broken and beaten man. The newspapers said that was because God had punished me for my blasphemies! I had a hard time convincing him that I had *no* son at all, let alone one who was locked up in an insane asylum! And that my daughters were not alcoholics, cowering in the bosom of Mother Church! That they were still devoted to me!"
Ingersoll laughed again, and we echoed him.

EUGENE V. DEBS

I had occasion in the near future to go to a few of his lectures in Chicago, and what exciting affairs they were! To start with the audience would be laughing, chatting and waving to friends. At the same time they would be whispering as if the end of the world were around the corner! Everyone would be very tense. When Ingersoll came to the podium, the audience radiated palpable hostility at his handsome, erect, bear-like figure leaning across the footlights.

ROBERT GREEN INGERSOLL

He couldn't have cared less about the hostility. Against their will, the audience would be impressed with his confidence, amiability and goodwill. Then Ingersoll's hypnotic voice would roll out, rich and mesmerizing. He would challenge all the sacrosanct precepts of his age, debunk all superstition and speak of the glory of the free and open mind. His audience would be captivated because he was totally without fear.

My Uncle Joe turned to Debs and asked him: "Gene, what do you think I should do about Jock?"
Debs asked me: "Would you like a job in the railroad?"
"If it's possible, I could give it a try," I replied.
"Well," said Debs, "It depends on how much you know. Matt, Joe says Jock is very good in Mechanical Engineering. Why not test him, and see if he is fit for the railroad?"
Carpenter said: "Ok, and I think the best person to test him is Lenglen." He pronounced it Long-law.
"Oh God," said Debs, "That Frenchie is madder than me!"
All of them burst into guffaws, including my uncle.

I was asked to wait in a chair outside Carpenter's office. My uncle went in search of the Chief Mechanical Engineer, Henri Lenglen. After a while he returned with a man who was athletic in build, with long hair, sideburns and a pencil mustache. They went into Carpenter's office. Then my uncle called me into the office and directed me to a chair opposite Lenglen. In a typical French accent, he asked me: "They tell me that you are knowing lots of mathematics and engineering. So tell me what you know about cam-shafts in the piston rod assembly?"

For about a half hour he questioned me on various aspects of math and engineering. In some fields I knew more than him; in others I was quite ignorant. Finally Lenglen said: "Not bad at all. I can use him in the new section dealing with electro-mechanical devices."

Debs broke in: "Look, Henri, I want you to give this boy plenty of time to study, too. Not just engineering but whatever he wants to study. I never want him to think that his job destroyed his thinking power."

"No problem," said Lenglen, "There will be plenty of time. I'll get him membership of the library also. Let him try to specialize and earn more."

Debs turned to me and said, "So what do you say, son? Want to work for the railroad?"

Ingersoll's measured drawl broke in: "Forgive the pun, but don't you railroad the boy, Gene! Let him come to a decision after sleeping over the matter. I'm sure Joe will also help him reach that decision."

Debs said: "I agree. Think over the offer, son. Right now the railroad is a tough place to work in. But our union is fighting on many fronts regarding safety, personal security and death benefits. By the time you are thirty five, the railroad will look after its employees and families from cradle to grave."

How right Debs was! He was to hold epic battles with James Hill, President of the Great Northern Railway, and Charles Pullman of the Pullman car fame, and acquaint them with the power of the workers' will! He was to have friends like the famous attorney Clarence Darrow. He would persuade a number of philanthropic tycoons to truly make the railroad a beneficial organization.

Well, the long and short of the matter was that the figures of Debs, Ingersoll, Lenglen and Carpenter, and the authority they personified, dazzled me. In addition, I developed a young man's love for the steam engine. The fiery boiler, shining controls, gleaming wheels and pistons and ear-splitting whistle fascinated me. This was how I started to work in the old Union Station.

Lenglen was a good, though impatient, teacher. He could not tolerate slowness and delay. He got me books from the library. He posed theoretical problems in metal fatigue, electro-mechanical problems and designs for good air circulation. They were tough, but very interesting to figure out. Meanwhile the Grand Central station was steadily moving towards completion. Three years after it was completed, Lenglen was transferred to the Grand Central. He pulled me there with him.

And that was how I happened to meet Naren on Track 4!

*****

THE GREATER MIRACLE

In France, in Lourdes, at Massabielle – most wretched place on earth,
The place of shingles, swine and snakes, where the swirling river Gave
Washed up the bones of beasts; there, one day, inside a filthy cave,
Bernadette, a peasant girl, simple of speech and religion,
Did behold the Lady of the Immaculate Conception!
In white dress, white veil, blue girdle, golden roses on bare feet,
The Lady created a spring that healed incurable ills,
Does so e'en now in thousands! The girl was canonized a Saint.

Great miracles these, but don't forget a greater miracle,
That teen-aged virgin Bernadette, naïve, less lettered than most,
Did force the might of France to fulfill her Fair Lady's fiat
To build a chapel near the spring, and let processions come there.

Faced bent police, biased Judge, cynic Prefect, venal Mayor,
Jeering Doctors, jaundiced Churchmen and most cunning Bureaucrats,
Brought them finally to their knees (some quite literally so!),
Made the Emperor to intervene in person and declare
Lourdes holy! What arms did she use for these unequal battles?
Simple logic, direct words, unending and unbending faith
And loyalty to her Lady. Pomp, show, wealth she never craved
Till her dying day. Does not this miracle inspire us yet
To put aside religion, and sing the Song of Bernadette?

SHASHIDHAR BELWADI

CHAPTER 4

MAGIC AND MIRACLES

Naren heard my story with great interest and sympathy. Then he said: "It is God's will that you have arrived where you have, and yet remain so balanced and cheerful. For many people, the death of their parents would have been a very traumatic experience. Recovery would have been very slow. By God's grace, the love showered on you by your friends and relatives has sustained you. Did your faith play any part in your recovery?"

"Naren, though my father was Catholic, I never saw him go to church. Neither did I. The Humphreys', real intellectuals, did not treat the church as a part of their lives. Then Robert Ingersoll showed me that blind faith in religion is like being superstitious. So I am neither a theist nor an atheist, not even an agnostic. I just don't pay attention to religion."

"At least you are frank in what you say, Jock. My Master used to say that an atheist was better than a religious hypocrite. The atheist was at least sincere in his beliefs. In that way, the Hindu religion is a very tolerant religion. It allows any person to do as he pleases. It does not place any restrictions, except ethical and moral ones. Even atheism has been recognized as a school of thought, and its followers are the Charuvakas."

I changed the subject and said: "I have heard and read that India is a land of magicians and illusionists. It's famous for black magic and the Indian rope trick. Is there really a lot of this in your country?"

"Hardly," said Naren, "I have wandered every nook and corner of my country as a monk. Wherever I heard about such a person, I would make it a point to visit him or her. I would examine the so-called miracles or tricks performed. In most of the cases, I found the tricks to be just that, cheap tricks."

"In most cases? Does that mean there were some exceptions?"

"In my experience, some people do possess powers of the mind which are inexplicable from the scientific point of view. I myself have experienced such incidents. I'll tell you about some of them. But first let me tell you what I consider to be true miracles."

When I was much younger (said Naren), a long article appeared in our Calcutta English daily newspaper. A Frenchman wrote it, in a very impassioned tone, but very well. This is what he wrote.

In February 1858, at Lourdes, in France, there was a wretched place called Massabielle. A peasant girl, Bernadette, saw a vision of a Lady in White at the mouth of a cave there. Only she could see the Lady and communicate with her. Word soon spread that Mary, mother of Jesus, had spoken to Bernadette! Bernadette herself never identified the Lady in White as Mary at any time, then or later.

ST.BERNADETTE SOUBIROUS

At the Lady's direction, Bernadette scraped out a hole in the floor of the dirty cave. Some muddy water was revealed in a puddle. Later, quarrymen dug deep at the spot. Out rushed a stream of pure, cold water! It was totally different in nature from the waters of the river Gave flowing near the cave. And it was this spring water that started the miracles at Lourdes. All the miracles are recorded, and even churchmen don't understand them. These are the first three miracles.

The wife of a slate-miner, Bouhouharts, became desperate when she saw her baby-boy dying with a fever that turned his face brownish-yellow. If he survived, he would be a helpless cripple. Many prayed for a merciful early end. One day, death seemed a matter of minutes. The mother ran with the baby to the grotto, unclothed him and dipped him into the cold water up to his neck. After fifteen minutes, the baby stirred and cried. The mother wrapped him in warm clothes and rushed home. The baby slept for the whole day. Waking up, he drank two glasses of milk, something unheard of! After some time, the baby sat up in its basket for the first time in its life!

THE VIRGIN OF LOURDES

This first miracle was noted by the Church. It was shrugged off as a natural cure due to a variety of circumstances. The Church also defined any medical miracle as "the instantaneous cure of an irremediable or irreversible disease." Then it sat back to wait for this definition to fail!

The second miracle was the cure of Marie Moreau. This teenage girl was diagnosed as totally blind due to retinal detachment of both eyes. Her sight was covered by a purple veil. A hundred cures were attempted and failed. At Lourdes, a handkerchief drenched in the spring water was applied to Marie's blind eyes, and left for some time. When the cloth was removed, the girl uttered a piercing cry that riveted everyone. The purple veil was torn; she could see! She could read printed matter held before her eyes! This miracle also caused a big tear in the purple veil covering the Church's eyes.

The third miracle was even more remarkable. The father of the boy concerned was an atheist! A disease closed the boy's food-pipe gradually. Only a few drops of milk and soup could pass through. The boy read about Lourdes, and begged his father to take him there. The father would do anything for a cure. He loved his son, and was anguished to see him gradually dying of this dreadful disease. At Lourdes, a few drops of the spring water were trickled down the boy's throat, with great difficulty. After some time, the father handed the son a biscuit. The boy ate it normally! Not only that, he even asked for more biscuits!

"Now these are real miracles, Jock," Naren said. "The grace of God touches a person or place and miracles take place there. What I have seen are inexplicable incidents, not miracles."

"What are these remarkable incidents that you have seen?" I asked.

"Shiva….Shiva…." said Naren, looking up at the ceiling, "I shall tell you. Then you can seek your own explanations, give any name to these phenomena and draw your own conclusions."

The first incident (said Naren) concerns a man in Calcutta. He was reputed to be a mind-reader and adept at fore-telling the future. My friends and I each wrote down a question on many slips of paper. Each of us put a slip with a question in our pocket and went to see him. The man greeted us and made us sit down. Then he addressed each of us, repeated the question in that person's pocket, and gave the answers!

If this was amazing, consider what happened next. He took a number of pieces of paper and wrote something on each piece. He called us one by one to sign on the back of a paper piece. We did not know what was written there. Then he told us to put the paper in our pockets without reading them. For half an hour he foretold the future for each of us. Then he said: 'Think of any sentence from any language you like.'

I thought of a long Sanskrit sentence; one friend thought of an Arabic sentence from the Koran; another a German sentence from a medical tome, and so on. All these languages were unknown to the man. He said: 'Now take out the papers from your pockets and read them.'

The sentences in Sanskrit, Arabic and German were written there in their entirety! These sentences had been written half an hour before they had even entered our heads! I visited him again with other friends. This time also he came out triumphant!

Another time, as a monk, I was told in Hyderabad of a Brahmin who could produce a number of things from the air. I went to see him. He was not well, and promised to come and see me as soon as he became well. Some days later he came to where our group was staying. He said he was ready to show us his tricks. To forestall trickery, we removed all his clothes. I gave him my own blanket to wrap around himself. 24 pairs of eyes were boring through him!

He then said: 'Each of you can write on a slip of paper whatever you want.'

We discussed as a group, and wrote down the names of fruits. Some grew in this country, some did not. We handed him the papers one by one. He looked at each slip, then reached under the blanket and produced that fruit! And in what quantities! If all the fruits he produced were weighed, it would be twice the weight of the man himself! We suspected hypnotism. He told us to eat the fruit, eating them himself. We all ate them; the fruits were absolutely

fresh and delicious! To cap it all, he produced a huge mass of roses. Each flower was perfect, with dew-drops on the petals and intoxicating smell! When I asked the man for an explanation, he said: 'It is all sleight of hand.'
Even a fool could understand that whatever it was, it could hardly have been mere sleight of hand!

Again, as a monk, I was traveling in the Himalaya Mountains. At nightfall, I availed the hospitality of the hill-people at a village. Sometime later, I heard the beating of drums. My host came to me and said: 'A devata or good spirit has possessed one of the villagers. Come and see, Maharaj.'

I went with him, and saw a tall man with long bushy hair sitting erect on the ground, eyes wide open. Next to him a fire was burning. I gathered that the person could not come down from his exalted state of possession. An axe was heated red-hot in the fire and applied to various parts of his body, and even his hair. Nothing happened and the man expressed no pain. I stood mute with wonder! The head-man of the village turned to me and said: 'Maharaj, please exorcise this man."

I was in a nice fix. As I neared the man, I saw the axe lying there, cooled to blackness. Impulsively, I touched the head and burnt my fingers! With smarting fingers I placed my hands on the man's head, fixed my mind on Shiva, and did a japa or prayer. To my utter bewilderment, the man came around in ten or twelve minutes.

Oh, what gushing reverence the villagers showed to me! I was taken to be some wonderful man! Truth to say, I never felt like a bigger hypocrite! I could not make head or tail of the whole business then or later. And my smarting hand did not allow me to sleep the whole night. I lay thinking: 'There are more things in heaven and earth, Horatio, than are dreamt of in your philosophy!"

Let me relate a final incident. Once, at Madras, in South India, I was staying at my friend Manmatha Babu's house. All arrangements for my departure to America were complete. My friends were insisting on my immediate departure. One night, I dreamt that my mother had died! I was totally distracted. My friend sent a telegram to Calcutta to find out the facts. I was unwilling to do anything before getting any news of my mother. My friend suggested our visiting a man who was reputed to have acquired mystic power over spirits. He could tell fortunes, and read the past and future of a man's life. Though I normally keep far away from such persons, Manmatha's request and my mental suspense made me agree to meet this man.

The man lived outside the town. We, that is Manmatha Babu, Alasinga Perumal, and I, covered the distance partly by railway and partly by foot. We reached the place, and what a sight met our eyes! A ghoulish looking person was sitting close to a cremation ground. Of soot-black color and haggard appearance, the man was wearing only a loin cloth. His teeth were stained, with gaps, and protruding through thick, purplish lips. His eyes were blood-shot. He was chewing betel-nut and spitting out red saliva from time to time. When he talked or laughed, we could see that his lower teeth were jet-black. This man, Govinda Chetti, was a person to be avoided even in dreams!

For a long time he did not even appear to notice us. It was hot, I was impatient. We decided to leave. Suddenly, the man told us to wait. He drew some figures with a pencil on paper. He kept aside the paper, and drew some more figures with his fingers on the ground. He became perfectly still in mental concentration. Then he relaxed and looked in our general direction. With my friend Alasinga translating, the man uttered my name and my father's name. He continued with my genealogy and the history of my long line of forefathers. I was absolutely stunned!

The man then shifted slightly on his haunches and looked at me directly. He said: 'Your Guru is with you now, as he has been with you in all your wanderings. He is annoyed at your lack of faith. He wonders why you have come to a cremation-ground and its demonic keeper.' He laughed horribly through his stained teeth. 'Anyway, he says he will always guard and guide you. Your mother is hale and hearty at her home. She is not even ill. You need not be disturbed on that account.'

I felt a great burden slip from my mind at this happy news, and heaved a sigh of relief! The man then said that I would very soon have to go to far-off lands for preaching

Vedanta. He foretold some incidents that would happen during the travel. So far, all that he said has turned out to be true. After we returned to Manmatha Babu's house, we received a wire from Calcutta that my mother was indeed well.

"Astonishing and fascinating, Naren," I said, "But how do you explain them?"

"My theory is this," Naren said. "These events of a psychical nature really come under the realm of science. Students of this science find that these events, though extraordinary, are also natural. They are not freaks of nature, but come under laws like other psychical phenomena. There is nothing supernatural about them. My conclusion is that these extraordinary powers are in the minds of men. But in some, their minds are part of the Universal mind because they are adepts at this science. This science is vast and wonderful. Men can succeed in business, but very few can succeed in this."

"What did your Master say about these powers?" I asked.

"Oh, my Master absolutely disparaged these supernatural powers. He said you cannot attain the Supreme Truth if your mind is diverted by the use of such powers. Ninety percent of the sadhus or hermits are seduced by these powers. Normal people are lost in wonder if they come across such powers. My Master mercifully made us understand the evil of these powers which are hindrances to real spirituality. I am now able to take them at their proper value."

I asked him: "Naren, you are a graduate. So does your Master have a Doctorate in Philosophy?"

After a surprised glance at me, Naren suddenly burst into laughter. What a laugh it was! A great, booming laugh, the sound rolling across the empty tracks like thunder. His whole body shook with laughter. I could only sit silent and perplexed, grinning foolishly. After some time Naren regained control and said: "You don't know what a good joke you have cracked, Jock! My Master a PhD? Let me tell you, he was a rustic, an almost unlettered man. He attended one or two classes in the Primary school! Such was my Master!"

I was astonished. "This seems ridiculous! You are an educated person and an intellectual. And you say that an almost illiterate man was your Master?"

Naren replied: "In India, Jock, in spiritual education, knowledge is all that counts. We do not go by academic degrees. Of course, in their own place, degrees and intellectualism get all our respect. But in spiritual matters, the Teacher is one who shows us the Truth and the Reality of the Infinite. He removes our ignorance. He gives us a practical experience of the Infinite. The Teacher may belong to any caste, creed or race."

This was a novel concept for me. "But I have read that in India only a Brahmin can be a teacher, and only a Brahmin can be taught."

"No, no, Jock," said Naren, "Not nowadays. Maybe it was so in the ancient days. Even then, it was the teacher who decided who could be called a Brahmin. Let me tell you a very ancient story from one of our Upanishads, our sacred texts. This story, from the Chandogya Upanishad, appears crude, but the moral is clear and lofty."

A young boy (said Naren), called Satyakama, told his mother: "I want to study the Vedas. The teacher will ask me the name of my father, our caste, and our Gotra (lineage). What should I tell him?"
Now, the mother was not a married woman. An orphan of very poor low-caste parents, the poor lady had served in multiple households. She had been sexually exploited by the ruthless men-folk of those households. She had to hold her tongue due to her poverty. The child of such a woman is an outcast, not recognized by society. He is not entitled to study the Vedas. So the poor mother said: "My child, I served in different households at the same time. You were born as a result. I do not know your family name or who your father is. My name is Jabala, so your name is Satyakama Jabala. This is what you should tell your teacher."

The little boy went to the Sage and requested to be taken as a student. The Sage asked him the usual question: "What is the name of your father, and what is your caste and lineage?"
Boldly, the boy repeated to the Sage what his mother had told him. The Sage at once said: "One who is not a Brahmin could not speak such a damaging truth about oneself. You cannot not be a Brahmin, since you have not swerved from the truth. I will teach you the Vedas."

And the Sage kept the boy with him and educated him.

"So you see, Jock, in days of yore adherence to the truth proclaimed the caste of a person. Nowadays, birth alone leads to such classification. In urban areas, the reformation movements have considerably removed such differences. In rural areas, however, superstition and blind prejudices still hold sway."

Naren's narratives fascinated me. I was like a little boy listening to stories, and what stories they were! The prodigy part of my mind grasped the logic of what he said. The stories were made more interesting by his flashing eyes, sonorous voice and his gestures. He had a habit of looking up at the sky and saying "Shiva, Shiva," from time to time. All in all, he was a story-teller par excellence!

I said to him: "I have learnt many new things about your country and its customs. If you don't mind, can you tell me a little more about your life, your family, education and entry into spiritual life?"
Naren pondered for a while, and then said: "All right. We have the night before us. I'll try to tell you about my life and mission as briefly as possible. Let me arrange my thoughts."

At that moment, a freight train came chuffing in. I excused myself to attend to it. As I was leaving, I saw Naren assume his cross-legged position and close his eyes.

*****

ELEGY IN A COUNTRY CHURCHYARD

Full many a gem of purest ray serene,
The dark unfathom'd caves of ocean bear;
Full many a flower is born to blush unseen,
And waste its sweetness on the desert air.

Th' applause of list'ning senates to command,
The threats of pain and ruin to despise,
To scatter plenty o'er a smiling land,
And read their history in a nation's eyes.

Far from the madding crowd's ignoble strife,
Their sober wishes never learn'd to stray,
Along the cool sequester'd vale of life
They kept the noiseless tenor of their way.

THOMAS GRAY

CHAPTER 5

CHILDHOOD

I finished with the train and flagged it off. Then I went on an inspection patrol. I covered all the tracks and checked all the freight bundles. I was back with Naren in a half hour. He was leaning against the back of the bench and welcomed me with a smile.
"Everything all right?" he asked.
"Oh, yes. No problems anywhere," I replied.
"Good, good," he said.
There was silence for a while. Then I said: "Naren, you were going to tell me about yourself…"
"Yes. Let me start from the beginning."

I was born (said Naren) on January 12, 1863, into the Datta family of Simulia, a northern district in Calcutta. It was a rich, powerful and aristocratic family of Kshatriyas or the warrior caste. It was known for its charity, learning and strong independent spirit. My father, Vishwanth Datta, was a prolific scholar from childhood. He was proficient in Sanskrit, Bengali, Persian, Arabic, Urdu, Hindi and English. He knew astrology and loved music. His greatest love was History.

My father rose to the position of Attorney-at-Law in the Calcutta High Court. He was very skilled and earned a great deal of money. He spent the money liberally and lived affluently and ostentatiously. Very independent, he was generous to the point of prodigality. He never thought of tomorrow. Giving to the poor and needy was like a disease with him. Once, when I criticized him for giving money to a worthless drunkard, he said: "Wait till you understand the great misery of human life."

Due to his vast knowledge, my father had a broad outlook. He was a liberal Hindu, indifferent to caste. He tried to get at the essential teachings of all religions; he ended up having very little faith in any of them. He said most of them were superstition. He did not believe in a soul or an afterlife. However, he considered the great religious books as works of art. His favorites were the poetry of Hafiz and the Bible. He defended the remarriage of girl-widows. I imagine that I have inherited my intelligence, my artistic sense and any compassion through my father.

SIGNATURE OF VISHWANATH DATTA

BHUVANESHWARI DEVI

My mother, Bhuvaneshwari Devi, was not any less than my father in her own way. She managed the household expertly. Her many chores included sewing, music and the daily study of our Epic poems, the Ramayana and the Mahabharata. She is a graceful, regal, majestic lady, a true product of a royal estate. In all matters of importance, her judgment was the final one. She has a sweet voice and can sing beautifully. She is deeply religious, memorizing long passages from the Epics. I was a very difficult child to bring up. I gave my poor mother a great deal of trouble. From her, I have inherited a deep respect for religion. I have also striven to develop a high moral character.

My father held physical courage and fearlessness in high esteem. With his encouragement, I boxed, swam, rowed and rode horses. I exercised hard and became an athlete. I was never timid, and his lessons made me fear no one and nothing. I was the leader among the youth. My mother taught me the religious and devotional aspects. I became skilled in dancing the great religious dances, like the one with the burning coals in an earthen holder in front of Mother Kali. Encouraged by both parents, I studied vocal and instrumental music under famous Hindu and Muslim professors. I developed a good voice, which my Master said was 'delightful and charming to the ear.' I wrote tunes, and have published a documented essay on the science and philosophy of Indian music.

THE SWAMI AS A MRIDANGA PLAYER

I did not neglect my studies. At college, I cultivated the sciences, astronomy, mathematics, philosophy, and Indian and Western languages. I read the English and Sanskrit poets. I adored the Vedanta and hungered for philosophic discussions. Above all, I concentrated on meditation. I felt that this was the only way to realize the Absolute. I wanted to be sure that it was God indeed who made man. If I had to have a holy Guru, I wanted one who could say to me: "I have seen Him. I have touched Him. I am He."

Every night, I fell asleep in a singular way. I would lie on my chest. I would close my eyes to feel drowsy. At this point, a spot of light, changing its colors, would appear between my eyebrows. It would grow and burst, bathing my whole body in a flood of white radiance. I would then fall asleep. I thought this happened to everyone. My friends denied any such happening. Even now it happens, but is neither so frequent nor so intense. Every night I dreamed that I would become a wealthy man, with honor, power and glory. Then the dream changed. I saw myself as renouncing the world and becoming a monk. The second dream always had the upper hand.

One day, when I was in the Second year of the FA class, the regular English professor could not take our class. The noted scholar, Prof. Reverend William Hastie, who was the Principal of the Institution, took the English literature class. The subject was a poem by William Wordsworth, 'Excursions.' While contemplating the beauty of nature, Wordsworth had used the phrase, "the state of trance." The students did not understand the meaning of the word 'trance.' After trying to explain the meaning in several ways, Prof. Hastie said: "it is a result of purity of mind, and concentration in some particular object. It is so intense that you become that object. It is very rare. Personally, I have seen only one person experience that blessed state of mind. He is Ramakrishna Paramahamsa, the priest of the Kali temple at Dakshineshwar. You will understand what a trance is if you go there and see for yourself."

Prof. Hastie was about to continue, when there was a sudden commotion from the rear of the class. Prodded by the boys around him, my classmate, Bipin, stood up and said: "Sir, I have seen Shri Ramakrishna."
"Where did you see him," asked Prof. Hastie.
"Near Dakshineshwar, sir, in a villa, about 5 years ago, sir. I was with a party of Shri Keshab Chandra Sen. I saw Shri Ramakrishna go into a trance, sir."
Prof. Hastie told him: "Tell the class all the details, boy. Be sure you leave nothing out."
Bipin came to the front of the class, and told us the following story.

During the early months of 1875 (said Bipin), Keshab Chandra Sen, the head of the Brahmo Samaj, happened to be at a villa near Dakshineshwar. Bipin's elder brother was a disciple of Keshab. He brought Bipin along to the picnic. The group was sitting in the hall, discussing some religious matters.

PROF. REV. WILLIAM HASTIE

Suddenly, the watchman of the villa came in and said the Keshab: "The madman of the Kali temple has come here. He wishes to meet you. He won't take no for an answer."

Keshab asked: "Who is this madman?"

"Well," said the watchman, "He is called Ramakrishna, but we know him as the mad priest of Kali Ma at Dakshineshwar."

Keshab started and rose: "Shri Ramakrishna? And visiting me? Usher him in at once with full respect."

The watchman saluted and went out. Keshab told his group to sit in a semi-circular fashion. Whatever happened, the group was on no account to laugh or show any disrespect to Shri Ramakrishna. "Study him well," said Keshab, "You will meet few like him. I have not met him personally though I have seen him before. His reputation in spiritual circles is of the highest, though controversial."

Ramakrishna entered with two of his followers. He stood just inside the door. He looked from side to side, blinking his eyes in the comparative darkness of the room. His eyes fell on Keshab and he smiled an enchanting smile. He glided toward Keshab, stood before him, and said: "I hear you have seen a vision of God. I have come to find out what it is."
Keshab was shaken by this unexpected greeting. He joined the palms of both hands, bowed low and said: "Gurudev (Divine Teacher), what makes you think that I have seen a vision of God? Who told you so?"

The contrast between Ramakrishna and Keshab was striking. Ramakrishna was a small brown man, very thin and extremely delicate-looking. Keshab had a striking personality. He was tall and fair, his face was oval, his complexion clear; his face was tinged with the reddish color of the setting sun.

Ramakrishna said to Keshab: "I was resting in my Mother's temple after prayers when my nephew – there, that fellow – told me that Keshab Babu has come to the kotha (villa). He told me that people say that you have seen a vision of God. So I came running to see you."
Keshab said: "Gurudev, do you believe such rumors? Do you think I am really capable of such things?"

Ramakrishna said: "Of that I have no doubt, Keshab babu! Many years ago, nearly ten years ago, when you were with Deben Babu at the Adi Brahmo Samaj, I observed you. Several people were meditating on the platform of the Samaj. You were in the center of the group, lost in contemplation, motionless as a piece of wood! You were then a young man, but I remember thinking: 'It is at his bait that the fish is nibbling.' God was responding to your appeal alone!"

Keshab blushed at this praise and his happiness was reflected in his face. He said: "Surely you are pulling my leg, Gurudev! But first, please sit down, and then enlighten us regarding the nature of the Infinite, the Nirakara Brahman."

A low seat was pulled up, and Ramakrishna seated on it. His nephew and the other person sat behind him. Keshab sat at his feet. Our semi-circle drew closer to him.

Ramakrishna began: "The nature of the Nirakara Brahman…how to put it simply….." and lapsed into a short silence, head bowed and eyes closed. Then he lifted his head with eyes still closed and began to sing a famous hymn to Kali. We all knew it and sang along with him. In the middle of the song, Ramakrishna suddenly fell into a trance. He froze with his hands upraised, eyes closed, smiling.

RAMAKRISHNA IN A TRANCE

Keshab gestured to us to continue the song. After some time, Ramakrishna's nephew crept up to him on his knees. He repeated the names Rama, Krishna and Kali loudly into Ramakrishna's ears. Our singing faltered and stopped. Then Ramakrishna's eyes opened slightly. He looked around as if he were in a strange place. He looked at us and said: "Who are these people?" Seeing Keshab, Ramakrishna vigorously thumped the top of his own head several times, crying out: "Go down, go down."

Then he burst into a flood of magnificent words and examples regarding the One and Infinite God. Keshab was extremely impressed. From time to time he turned to us, and by gestures drew our attentions to some significant remark or uttering. Much later, after Ramakrishna left, Keshab told us: "Mark my words! We are dealing with an exceptional personality!"

At no time during the whole incident did our group think that Ramakrishna was mad, or feel a desire to laugh at anything he did. We were transfixed by his personality and behavior.

After Bipin's story ended, Prof. Hastie told us: "There is no doubt that Keshab Sen was spellbound by Ramakrishna. Right now, Keshab and Ramakrishna are the greatest of friends. Some friends tell me that Keshab is almost a disciple of Ramakrishna. I have read Keshab's writings. In sermons, in journals and reviews, in both English and Bengali, he has everywhere alluded to Ramakrishna. Keshab seems to have put his own fame and reputation at the disposal of Ramakrishna. Mark my words; this is what has caused Ramakrishna to become known within the intellectual circles of Bengal and beyond."

In this way, I came to hear about my Master for the first time!

*****

A PSALM OF LIFE

Tell me not, in mournful numbers,
Life is but an empty dream!
For the soul is dead that slumbers,
And things are not what they seem.

Life is real! Life is earnest!
And the grave is not its goal;
Dust thou art, to dust returnest,
Was not spoken of the soul.

Not enjoyment, and not sorrow,
Is our destined end or way;
But to act, that each to-morrow
Find us farther than to-day.

Art is long, and Time is fleeting,
And our hearts, though stout and brave,
Still, like muffled drums, are beating

Funeral marches to the grave.

In the world's broad field of battle,
In the bivouac of Life,
Be not like dumb, driven cattle!
Be a hero in the strife!

Trust no Future, howe'er pleasant!
Let the dead Past bury its dead!
Act,— act in the living Present!
Heart within, and God o'erhead!

Lives of great men all remind us
We can make our lives sublime,
And, departing, leave behind us
Footprints on the sands of time;

Footprints, that perhaps another,
Sailing o'er life's solemn main,
A forlorn and shipwrecked brother,
Seeing, shall take heart again.

Let us, then, be up and doing,
With a heart for any fate;
Still achieving, still pursuing,
Learn to labor and to wait.

HENRY WADSWORTH LONGFELLOW

CHAPTER 6

THE GREAT REFORMERS

"Naren," I interrupted, "You have mentioned persons like Deben Babu and Keshab Sen, and the Brahmo Samaj. Who was Keshab? Did he start the Samaj?"
"Let me give you a short history of the reformist movements in India, Jock," said Naren.

During the eighteenth century (said Naren), orthodox Hinduism in India had degenerated into superstition and fundamentalism. The symbolic idol worship became dogmatic. Casteism was rampant and other religions were condemned. At that time, a giant appeared on the scene. He was the first true cosmopolite. He ushered in a new era of spiritual history. This extraordinary man was Raja Ram Mohan Roy.

He belonged to a great aristocratic Bengali family. He was born in 1774. He was brought up in the court of the Moghul Emperor, Akbar II, in Delhi. The official court language was Persian. As a child, he read Euclid and Aristotle in Arabic. What a paradox! An orthodox Vedantic Brahmin was nurtured in Islamic culture! Only at the age of 15 did he study Sanskrit at Varanasi. He discovered the great works of Hindu theology. Islam had already taught him about the one true God; Vedanta confirmed that faith.

He developed hatred towards idolatry and the ritualistic part of orthodoxy. He denied the incarnation of the Hindu gods. At sixteen, he published a book in Persian attacking Hindu orthodoxy. His enraged father threw him out of the ancestral home. For 4 years he traveled in India and Tibet, studying Buddhism. His father recalled him home when Ram Mohan turned twenty. His marriage was performed, hoping that this would ensnare him in worldly fetters. This hope proved to be futile.

Two things happened now. The first was that Ram Mohan learnt English, Hebrew, Greek and Latin. He studied and was impressed with European laws and forms of government. He put aside the fact that the English were the rulers. He wooed and won them, and made them his allies for the larger good of India.

The second thing was that he was totally horrified by the awful custom of sati. He witnessed the terrible spectacle of his sister-in-law being burnt alive on the funeral pyre along with her dead husband. The barbarous sacrifice and the struggles of the victim haunted him constantly. He decided that he would rid his country of such crimes. He spoke and wrote so violently against these customs that the Brahmins forced his father to throw him out of the house again in 1799. Ram Mohan took up work as a tax-collector. His intelligence and genius aided him to be promoted quite fast. He became the Minister of the district within a dozen years.

His father died. Ram Mohan inherited his vast wealth and property. He was declared a Raja by the Emperor of Delhi. In Calcutta, he lived in a palace with vast gardens. This fortune did not turn him from the study of the Hindu scriptures. His aim was to restore the pure spirit of the Vedas. He translated the Vedas and wrote commentaries on them in English and Bengali. Simultaneously, he delved deep into Christianity. He accepted the ethics of Christianity, but rejected the incarnation of Jesus. He denounced the Trinity as vehemently as he denounced Polytheism. The result was that all temples and churches were closed to him. If the Brahmins hated Ram Mohan, so did the Missionaries.

Ram Mohan cared not a hoot for temples and churches. In 1815 he opened the Atmiya Sabha for the worship of the One and invisible God. In 1828, the Adi Brahmo Samaj was founded at his house. This was a universal house of prayer open to all, no matter the color, caste, creed, nation or religion of the devotee. Respect of all religions, and forming of strong bonds between all religious people were the main ideas of the Samaj. Presiding over this house of prayer was the gigantic personality of Raja Ram Mohan Roy, an adept in Sanskrit, Bengali, Arabic, Persian and English. He authored hymns, poems, sermons and philosophical treatises; in every field, he was a Titan!

The Emperor of Delhi sent him as an Ambassador to England in 1830. He arrived in April 1831, and was warmly received at the Court of St. James. He made many illustrious friends. He visited France. In 1833, he died suddenly at Bristol of brain fever and was buried there. Thus passed a gigantic personality. He left an undeniable stamp on writings of all kinds. In the short time that he had upon this earth, Raja Ram Mohan Roy visibly transformed India.

RAJA RAM MOHAN ROY

"I admire Ram Mohan Roy deeply," said Naren. "But I find his love for the English abhorrent!"
"What's so wrong with that," I asked.
It was quite the wrong question to ask. The blood rushed into Naren's face, and he burst out: "Our so-called

conquerors! They came to trade, and stayed to pillage and loot! The English......only just a little while ago they were savages. The vermin crawled on the ladies' bodices. They scented themselves to disguise the abominable odor of their persons! Even now, they are barely emerging from barbarism!"

    I was quite shocked at this outburst, and said: "Naren, I have met some very decent Englishmen, and....." He cut me short: "They are quite savage! The frightful cold and the want of privation of their Northern climate have made them wild. They only think to kill! The love of man is on their lips, but in their hearts there is nothing but evil and violence! He says I love you, my brother, I love you. All the while they cut your throat! Their hands are red with blood!"

There was silence for some time. I remained quiet to allow Naren to cool down. Then he sighed and said: "Shiva, Shiva.... I see red whenever our rulers are mentioned. I am sorry. Let them be! Where was I?"

"You stopped at Ram Mohan Roy's death," I prompted him.

    After Roy's death (said Naren), his friend Dwarkanath Tagore was the Chief of the Brahmo Samaj till 1846. He passed aw ay suddenly. His son, Devendranath Tagore, or Deben Babu, took charge, and really organized the Samaj. He is a great Sage, a noble figure. He is an aristocrat by birth and is physically and spiritually beautiful. His intellect and moral purity are of the highest order. He improved the Brahmo Samaj in its faith, ritual, theology and training of ministers. He hated all forms of idolatry. The philosophy of the Samaj was based on the Upanishads, and was very spiritual in nature.

PRINCE DWARKANATH TAGORE

Deben Babu's son, Rabindranath Tagore, introduced his college classmate Keshab Chandra Sen to the Brahmo Samaj. Soon, Keshab became Deben Babu's right-hand man. Younger members, who could not identify with Deben Babu, were drawn to Keshab. In 1862 Deben Babu adopted Keshab as the Co-adjutor of the Samaj. Little did he realize what he had done!

DEBENDRANATH TAGORE

Keshab had all the right credentials, of course. He was not an aristocrat like Ram Mohan or Deben Babu. He belonged to the liberal middle class, with an admiration for European customs. Educated in an English school, he knew no Sanskrit, but was familiar with the Bible. He attempted to introduce Christ into the Brahmo Samaj. He also encouraged inter-caste marriages. Deben Babu was outraged! In 1866, there was a parting of ways. Deben Babu headed the Adi Brahmo Samaj, and Keshab the Brahmo Samaj.

The Brahmo Samaj dabbled with the Koran, the Bible and the Zend Avesta. Keshab's speech on Jesus caused a scandal. With all these, none doubted Keshab's sincerity and his love of public welfare. Even the Viceroy sympathized with him. His journey to England in 1870 was a great success.

Then he toured India and was aware of the basic dichotomy of religion in the country. The majority of the population followed polytheism, the worship of many gods. The Samaj promoted pure Theism, one God. Keshab tried to bring about a compromise through the doctrine of the New Dispensation. It said in effect that the different gods were merely attributes of the Single God. This doctrine was like a lamp on the wall separating Advaita and polytheism. Keshab did his best for the social progress of India, but the thirty-three million gods of India defeated him. He died prematurely in 1884.

KESHAB CHANDRA SEN

Even during Keshab's lifetime the purely Indian Arya Samaj burst upon the scene. The Arya Samaj countered Westernization, and captured the Hindu psyche through its inherent nationalism. Heading this movement was the strongest personality India has seen, a lion among men, Swami Dayananda Saraswati. Born into the highest grade of orthodox Brahmins in Gujarat, he became an idol hater at the age of fourteen. His father was an equally unbending figure, but could not force the son to participate in any religious rite. The end of this terrible struggle came when at the age of seventeen Dayananda left his father's house, never to see him again!

Dayananda then wandered all over India in saffron robes for fifteen years. He begged for his daily bread. He searched out Vedic scholars and learnt from them the intricacies of Vedic philosophy. He practiced yoga and developed himself into a muscular athlete. He looked like some hero who had stepped straight out of the pages of Homer or the Hindu epics. He reveled in religious debates. The only problem was that he spoke only Sanskrit and was not understood by the masses. All the fatigue, insult, suffering and danger he underwent made him all the stronger.

This steel was finally tempered into a cutting edge by a blind Guru at Mathura. Swami Virjananda Saraswati was an extremely learned scholar. He was tough as nails. No one could tame or dominate him. For three years this

Guru hammered Dayananda into the final shape he was to assume. Before letting Dayananda go, the Guru made Dayananda swear an oath, on his life, that he would re-establish the ancient Vedic way of life and destroy idolatry and superstition.

SWAMI DAYANANDA SARASWATI

Dayananda was the ideal person for the task set out by his Guru. His knowledge of the Vedas could not be equaled by anyone he disputed with. His voice was like thunder, defeating any attempts to out-shout him. In five years, Northern India was completely changed. The populace saw their orthodox Brahmin scholars bite the dust before this Hercules. Despite not understanding him, the people could not deny his power, his learning and his mastery of the Vedas. A wave of admiration for him swept through the North! A new religious leader was born!

The defeated orthodox Brahmins appealed to the Vedic Pandits of Varanasi (Kashi) to challenge and overthrow this upstart. Varanasi is the holiest city in India; it's Pandits the cream of scholars in the country. The result of a Vedic battle there would decide for all time what the Truth was theologically. The Brahmins of Varanasi challenged Dayananda to a battle to the death. Dayananda accepted the challenge, and strode into the sacred temple of Kashi like a colossus in November 1869. And what a battle it was!

Even Homer would have been thrilled! It was a battle between the Greeks and the Trojans all over again, but with one difference. On the Trojan side there was an army; on the Greek side stood only Achilles! On one side was seated Dayananda and on the other side were seated a phalanx of 300 orthodox Brahmins, cheered on by a huge crowd of supporters, and backed by a million sympathizers!

The battle went on for days, and the full spectrum of Dayananda's learning dazzled the opponents. Sometimes he would compare the texts in all four Vedas to show the harmony of a disputed text. Sometimes, to resolve the ambiguity of a Sanskrit statement, he would resort to the Ghanapaatha (the bell mode of chanting where the words are repeated back and forth in a bell shape) to demonstrate that he was right and the Pandits were wrong in their interpretation.

The sledgehammer of Dayananda's logic flattened the opponents. The sharp sword of his knowledge slashed through their sophistry and obfuscation. Ultimately, Dayananda brought the Pandits to their knees and proved that his version of the primitive Vedas was the True Word, the Pure Law. The Brahmins excommunicated him; Dayananda could not care less! The dust of this epic battle spread over the whole land, and Dayananda's name became famous.

There were attempts to kill him. His response was the stuff of legends. A carriage of two speeding horses sought to trample him; he stopped the carriage with one hand! A cobra flung at him was caught and crushed in his bare hands! Three persons sought to drown him in a river; it ended in the three persons nearly being drowned themselves, saved only by Dayananda's mercy! He was poisoned numerous times; by his yogic power he threw out the poison from his body! In a much quoted story, an assassin sought to kill him with a sword. Dayananda caught the sword by the sharp edge, pulled it out of the assassin's grasp and broke it across his knees!

He declared war on Christianity, Islam, Sikhism, Jainism and Buddhism, with piercing commentaries which trampled the religions underfoot. Brahmin orthodoxy was treated with the same utter contempt. The people adored him!

Dayananda visited Calcutta in 1872. He met my Master. He also met Keshab Babu and saw the working of the Brahmo Samaj. He immediately rejected their theories and their western ideas. On the other hand, he did learn two new concepts. The first concept was that, in future, all his teachings should be in the common language of the populace. The second concept was his immediate grasp of the power of an organization. The concepts were immediately converted into practice. In 1875, the Arya Samaj was founded in Bombay. Very quickly, the Arya Samaj organized a network over almost all of India. Only Madras, in South India, was immune to his teachings.

Dayananda revealed himself to be an organizer and administrator par excellence. His reforms were revolutionary and his practices bold beyond the societal norms of those times. He taught that there should be equal justice for all men and no injustice to untouchables. He led a crusade for equality of the sexes, equal education, widow remarriage and all control by women over household matters, including finances. He advocated temporary unions between men and women for having children. The Arya Samaj took a lead in education, starting of orphanages, homes for widows and the concept of social service during natural calamities.

Dayananda's death was as dramatic as his life. In September 1833, he was the guest of the Maharaja of Jodhpur. There, he spoke out against a dance girl called Nanhi Jan. In revenge, the dance girl bribed Dayananda's personal cook to give him poison mixed with powdered glass. Before it could be purged from his system, the poison entered Dayananda's bloodstream. The guilty cook confessed to his master; Dayananda forgave him and assisted him in escaping from the palace. He was shifted to Ajmer for better treatment. There, on the morning of 30 October 1833, he passed away. He was chanting Sanskrit mantras till the very end. It was the day when the festival of Deepavali was held all over India. While lights blazed all over the country, a blazing light was extinguished at Ajmer.

"These, then, Jock were the great reformers of our country, the builders of unity," said Naren.
"Fascinating," I said, "And how was your Master compared to these reformers?"
Naren said: "Oh, my Master was a totally different sort from all the others. Outwardly, he was all devotion; soft, feminine. Inwardly, he was all knowledge, always residing in Brahman. His story is awe-inspiring. I have never told anyone about him. But let me tell you about my Master, my Guru Sri Ramakrishna Paramahamsa."

Just at that time, there was a noise from the side of Track 2. I excused myself and went quickly to Track 2. Coming to a pile of bundles, I saw that one of the bundles at the top had slipped to the floor. It appeared as if the bundle had not been properly balanced at the top of the pile. However, not taking any chances, I went all round the pile. Nothing else was disturbed. I went on a quick patrol of the remaining tracks, just to rule out any trespassers. I walked back to where Naren was sitting. I sat down on the bench and looked at him expectantly.

****

THE DIVINE ECSTASY

The sleeping Serpent stirs, wakes, uncoils, and slithers up
The Sushumna from the nether regions to the brain,
The body's racked with pain, mind in terrible frenzy,
Heart wrung like a wet rag, soul in horrendous anguish
At the thought of never beholding the Beloved!

But suddenly a great flash of lightning in the brain
Obliterates all the world. Nothing exists except
A boundless dazzling ocean of ineffable joy,
Roaring, hissing, luminous waves engulf, suffocate,
Swallowing and drowning one, and rolling all around.

The mortal coil is shuddering, there is no control
O'er body, mind, senses – another Will directs them –
Unconscious yet conscious of the lurking Beloved!
Then a veil of drifting glowing mist, dissolving waves
Of molten silver shot through with sparks of golden fire!

Through the mist is seen, hazily, a finger, hand, feet,
Breath, voice - then the whole effulgent Person appears,
Occupies totally – vivifies body, heart, mind, soul
In a Divine Possession – there is only the One,
And ecstasy in the embrace of the Beloved!

SHASHIDHAR BELWADI

CHAPTER 7

MY MASTER

My Master (said Naren) was born on February 18, 1836. His parents, orthodox Brahmins, resided in the village of Kamarpukur, in Bengal. He was named Gadadhar and called Gadai. He was a normal little boy. At the age of six years, he was, one day, following the narrow path between rice fields. A black cloud covered the sky. Gadai raised his eyes. He saw a flight of snow-white cranes pass the edge of the cloud. The contrast was so beautiful that Gadai was overjoyed. The joy was so emotionally intense that Gadai went into ecstasy and fell unconscious. Little did he know that he was destined to pass half his life in this manner!

FAMILY HOUSE OF RAMAKRISHNA,KAMARPUKUR

Gadai's father died a year later. Till 1855, the family suffered difficulties due to lack of resources. Now, in Calcutta, there lived a very rich woman named Rani Rasmoni. She built a temple at Dakshineshwar, on the eastern bank of the river Ganga. The temple was dedicated to the Divine Mother Kali. A problem then arose. The Rani was an untouchable by birth. She could not find a Brahmin priest for the temple.

OLD VIEW OF DAKSHINESHWAR

RANI RASMONI

Fate decreed that in 1855 Gadai's elder brother Ramkumar take up this duty. But Ramkumar died the very next year. Mother Kali now beckoned to the poor, innocent twenty-year old Gadadhar to replace his brother in 1856. Little did he know how the Divine Mother would toy with Her child!

Now Gadai, on account of his Karma, his fate from previous lives, was a unique person. His Kundalini, his indwelling spiritual power, was awake. In a normal person, the Kundalini is dormant until awakened by yoga, meditation etc. In Gadai, the Kundalini, since his childhood, had been high up in the Sushumna, the spiritual central channel of the body. As the priest of the Kali temple he had to follow strict rituals. He also constantly offered devotional prayers to Kali. All these raised his Kundalini still higher. The beautiful Mother Kali became a living, breathing mother, avoiding and hiding from Gadai. He used to cry like a neglected child for his mother to appear before him. Visitors to the temple were shocked to see him groveling on the floor, totally out of control! They did not know what to make of this.

MATHUR MOHAN BISWAS

Naren was shaking with laughter. "Imagine the scene if you can, Jock! There was the priest writhing about on the floor of the temple! On one side there was Rani Rasmoni bleating: "What is happening, what is

happening?" On the other side was her son-in-law Mohan Mathur, older than Gadai, plaintively calling out: "Father, father." Next to Gadadhar was his nephew calling out "Hari Bol, Hari Bol!" loudly into Gadai's ears, as he twisted about on the floor moaning "Mother, Mother!" The visitors could be excused if they thought that they had mistakenly wandered into a lunatic asylum! More of them sidled towards the door than towards the beautiful idol of Kali!"
Naren's laughter was very infectious and we both laughed for some time. Then Naren wiped his streaming eyes and continued the story.

The scandal quickly spread. People thought him a madman. His face and chest were livid. His eyes streamed with tears. His body shook with spasms. Gadai felt – he knew – that only a thin screen separated him from his Mother. He had only to tear down this screen. But how? In a frenzy, he rushed towards the sanctum of Kali to seize her sword and kill himself. Suddenly, everything material vanished! A limitless, glowing ocean with great luminous waves of Spirit engulfed him. He fell down. In the depths of the ocean he saw his Mother. He could not control his eyes, body or mind. He was filled with the Divine Mother. For days, he never closed his eyes, could no longer feed himself. His nephew looked after his needs, else he would have died. He had seen God, experienced God, and yet he lived!

But what a life it was! The after-effects of this encounter lingered. In the middle of offering prayers to the

Mother, he lost consciousness. Or else he stiffened into a statue! His body burnt as if with fever, and he oozed drops of blood. Rani Rasmoni and Mathur Babu were caught in a dilemma. Friends recommended getting rid of this mad priest; they would never do *that*! Instinctively, they knew his intrinsic worth. But his actions were disturbing the even tenor of the temple. They decided to send him home to Kamarpukur for a short time so that he could get well.

His mother thought that marriage would bring him to his senses. She secretly decided to find a suitable bride for Gadai. This was not easy, as they were a poor family. When Gadai came to know about this search, he did not oppose it. He told his mother: "Don't waste your time fruitlessly. Go to Jayarambati village. There, in the house of Ramachandra Mukherjee, you will find her who is destined for me."

Gadai's mother and brother were skeptical, but they made enquiries. Jayarambati was six miles away from Kamarpukur and indeed Ramachandra Mukherjee lived there. He did have a daughter, Sharadamani, who helped her mother in the kitchen. In those days, education for a girl was unheard of. And yes, Ramachandra was willing to give his daughter Sharada in marriage to Gadadhar.

But an embarrassing problem arose! Gadai was 23 years old; Sharada was but 5 years of age! Since no better match could be found, this problem was swept under the carpet. The wedding was celebrated in Jayarambati in May

1859. Sharada stayed with her parents for 2 more years, and then went for a few days to Kamarpukur. Thereafter, she returned to her parents' house and Gadai returned to Calcutta.

SHRI SHARADA DEVI'S ANCESTRAL HOME, JAYARAMBATI

Gadai seemed to have returned to normality in his behavior. But Mother Kali was waiting for her prey! No sooner did he cross the threshold of the temple than the Mother began to toy with him. His divine madness returned, his eyes would not close and he begged the Mother for her vision. Luckily, he appeared normal during the hours the temple was open to visitors. Still, people knew that he was unbalanced. Any little eccentricities were excused, indeed looked forward to! In this way, two years passed.

The problem was that Gadai did not know about the Kundalini. Thus he was physically and mentally assaulted, did not know the cause and did not know what to do. It was only by the Mother's grace that he was alive. He had no Guru who could instruct him on how to control the rampant Kundalini, and harness it to realize the Infinite. After two years Mother Kali took pity on her battered child and decided to send him a Guru.

THE BHAIRAVI BRAHMINI

One day, in 1861, Gadai was sitting in the portico of the temple. He was delighting in the flow of the river Ganga. A small boat sailed up and was tied at the foot of the steps leading to the temple. Out stepped a tall, beautiful woman wearing the saffron robes of a Sannyasini, a nun. She came up the steps straight to Gadai and stopped in front of him. She looked at him and burst into tears. "My son," she said, "God told me about you. I have been searching for you till now. I have a message to you from God."

The child-like Gadadhar immediately accepted her as his mother. He never even bothered to ever find out her name. To everyone she remained ever after the Bhairavi Brahmani, the Brahmin nun. Thus this highly educated lady from a noble Bengali family, very learned in the holy texts, became Gadai's first Guru.

The first thing the Brahmani had to do was to convince Gadadhar that he was not mad. All his sufferings were by-products of his stumbling along the path of devotion. She also convinced him that he had covered three-fourths of the dangerous path. He had achieved in a few years what normally took centuries to achieve. Now, as his Guru, she would methodically guide him along the balance of the road. She instructed him in Vaishnavism and Tantra. The former channelized his devotion in a controlled manner. The latter path, of sixty-four major tantric sadhanas, was a mine-field of loathsome practices. Guided by her even through this shadow of the valley of death, Gadai overcame degradation, madness, even death.

He came out of the ordeal shining like burnished gold. He was an adept in the sadhanas, the disciplined and dedicated practices. He displayed the 'nineteen attitudes' of one in whom the Lord resides. The Brahmani had taught him all she could. She asserted that he was an Incarnation of the Divine. She convened a meeting of the learned Pandits at Dakshineshwar. After long discussions, the Pandits, who would not go so far as to declare Gadai an incarnation, agreed that Gadadhar deserved public recognition. He became famous and people flocked from far and near to see this holy man who was a master of all the sadhanas.

Gadai hated all this talk of his being an Incarnation. True, the Brahmani had taken him to the summit of a mountain. But Gadai saw that there was one last steep peak which he still had to conquer. The Brahmani, her work done, departed in 1863.

In the latter half of 1864, a sterner and more virile teacher took her place. This was Tota Puri, a naked wandering monk. Before he started on his wanderings, he was the head of a monastery of seven hundred monks in the Punjab. Experience had given him discipline and leadership. As John the Baptist to Jesus Christ, Tota Puri was the fore-runner of Dayananda Saraswati. Forty years of grueling asceticism had made him adept in the Vedanta. He could attain Samadhi, where his soul would know a complete and unbroken union with the Divine. Like Dayananda, he was physically extremely strong; mentally he had a will of steel. Tall, robust, handsome, this magnificent monk towered like the rock of Gibraltar. He wandered one morning into the precincts of the temple of the Divine Mother at Dakshineshwar.

Gadai was seated on the steps of the temple. He was immersed in the vision of the Personal God. His face and body were shining with the vision. Suddenly, he was brought down to earth by a stentorian voice: "Look here! I asked you who you are. Didn't you hear me?"
Gadai looked up and started to his feet on seeing this towering naked ascetic. He bowed and said: "Namaskar (Salutation), Master. I am the priest of Kali Ma's temple."
The ascetic said: "I am Tota Puri. I have been observing you for some time. I see that you have gone very far on the path of Truth. Do you wish to go further, to the very end?"
"Go further, Master? But how?"
"I will teach you the Vedanta, and you will reach the next stage. What do you wish to do?"
Gadai looked at Tota Puri innocently, and said: "Please allow me to take the permission of Mother Kali. If she agrees, I shall become your disciple with the greatest pleasure."

Gadai got up, and went into the temple. Tota Puri was taken aback and stood gazing at the temple with a frown. Then his stern visage relaxed, as he chuckled to himself: "Taking his Mother's permission, forsooth! What a nincompoop!"
Nevertheless, he waited where he was for some time. When Gadai did not show up, he impatiently turned and started walking away. Suddenly, he heard Gadai's voice behind

him: "Master, Master! Mother has given me permission. I am now totally under your guidance."

TOTA PURI

Tota Puri turned back, and they both went into the temple. Sitting there, Tota Puri explained to Gadai that what he had been experiencing thus far was the Savikalpa Samadhi, in which the mind is conscious only of the soul and aware of the blissful experience.

What Tota Puri wanted to do was to take Gadai beyond this to the state of Nirvikalpa Samadhi, where even the mind vanishes and so does duality; the person is one with God. For this, said Tota Puri, Gadai had to learn Vedanta after becoming a Sanyasi, a monk. Gadai agreed, but requested Tota Puri to keep this a secret so that Gadai's mother, staying with him, might not be shocked. He also arranged with his nephew to look after the temple prayers and rituals till he returned.

Next morning, Gadai and Tota Puri went to a small garden nearby, with a small mud hut. A sacred fire was lit, and the two sat opposite each other across the fire. Then Gadai was subjected to stern Vedantic discipline. Tota Puri told him: "First, strip off all your clothes. You should be as free as the sky, as free as space."
Gadai complied with the order and put all his clothes to one side.

"Now," continued Tota Puri, "You have to renounce your title as priest of the Kali temple."

"But Rani Ras…." Gadai started to protest.
"Shut up," thundered Tota Puri, "And do as I say. Repeat after me, 'I renounce my title as priest of the Kali temple."
Gadai did as he was told.

Tota Puri did not leave him at that.
"Now break your sacred thread, and renounce your Brahmin caste. Throw the broken thread into the fire."
Gadai was appalled. Snap his sacred thread? "No, Master, I cannot do this! This will be sacrilege!"
"Don't you trust me? Don't you want to reach the top? Do as I say!"
"But, Master…."
"Don't go on bleating But, Master! Don't you trust your own Mother? Does She forbid you from doing as I say?"
Gadai paused, and said: "No, She does not. But snapping the sacred thread….?"
Tota Puri roared: "You do not trust me! You do not trust your Mother! Yet you want to reach Samadhi? YOU FOOL, SNAP YOUR SACRED THREAD IMMEDIATELY! SNAP IT, I SAY!"

Gadai convulsively caught hold of his sacred thread, and snapped it in two. He threw the pieces of the thread into the fire. His tuft of hair, denoting his caste, followed next. Then he performed the rituals of destroying his attachment to friends, relatives and the world. All his desires, material and sexual, were also sacrificed in the fire.

"Good," said Tota Puri, "Now, former priest, conduct your own funeral service! Your past is dead. Your ego should also die, Do it!"

After that ceremony had been concluded, Tota Puri asked his disciple: "What were you called?"

"Gadadhar."

"Gadadhar is dead. There is no longer any Gadadhar. What is your family deity, your Personal God."

"In Kamarpukur," said the disciple, "Shri Rama is our family deity, Master."

"Well, then you are now Ramakrishna! I name you so."

Tota Puri then gave his disciple a loin-cloth and ochre robe of a monk.

Then the initiation of Ramakrishna in the nuances of Advaita Vedanta commenced in a room near the temple. All the Upanishads, especially those which led to the Infinite One, were drilled into him. He was taught how to meditate very deeply in the quest for the self. This would make him go into Samadhi, and realize the Brahman.

Ramakrishna grasped all the precepts very quickly. This did not surprise Tota Puri. After all, was not the disciple adept in all the sadhanas? Ramakrishna went on detaching his mind step by step from everything material. At the threshold of the portal of Samadhi, he faltered. The Divine Mother was barring his way. Time and again, She barred the way. Ramakrishna was in despair. He pleaded with his Master: "It is no good! I shall never be able to attain Samadhi!"

Tota Puri was furious. In a blazing rage he shouted: "You fool! What do you mean you cannot attain Samadhi? You must succeed! AND YOU WILL, EVEN IF YOU DIE IN THE ATTEMPT!"

Cooling down a little, he asked Ramakrishna: "What is the problem you are facing?"

"My Mother is coming in my way of reaching the end of the path."

"Then cut Her down! Remove Her from the path!"

"I do not know how to do this!"

"Concentrate, concentrate! Forge your Will into a sword and remove all obstacles from your path."

"But I *am* concentrating fully! What more can I do?"

The impatient Tota Puri looked about him wildly. His eyes fell on an empty bottle which had contained oil. He broke the bottle with one sharp blow. He picked up a shard of the broken glass. He rammed the point of the shard into the forehead between Ramakrishna's eyes. A drop of blood oozed out. Ramakrishna did not know; Tota Puri did not care. Tota Puri then roared: "Concentrate your mind on this point, you dunderhead! Cut down anything that comes in your way."

Ramakrishna concentrated on the pricking point between his eyebrows and meditated mightily. Soon, the radiant form of the Mother appeared. The glass spear in his forehead and Tota Puri's ringing exhortations in his ears spurred Ramakrishna on. He begged the Mother's pardon, used his discrimination like a sword, and cut the form of the Mother in two. The last barrier disappeared. His spirit lost itself in Nirvikalpa Samadhi. Subject and object disappeared. Everything, including duality, was blotted out. Brahman, beyond thought and beyond words, was attained!

Tota Puri was watching everything. He saw the Samadhi stage, but thought that Ramakrishna was still dallying with the Mother. Leaving Ramakrishna to his devices, he got up, locked the room and went away for three days. When he unlocked the door and tested Ramakrishna, he was astounded. The disciple had indeed attained Nirvikalpa Samadhi, achieving in one day what had taken Tota Puri years of rigorous asceticism! The rigid corpse-like body of Ramakrishna was radiant, shining brightly with the serenity of Brahman. Tota Puri took immediate steps to help Ramakrishna's mind come down to the worldly plane. Never again would he doubt the potential of Ramakrishna.

Tota Puri's plan had been to remain in Dakshineshwar till he helped Ramakrishna attain Nirvikalpa Samadhi. For no discernible reason, he stayed on for eleven months. As a Vedantin, he considered Brahman as the only reality. Maya, also known as Ignorance or Illusion, did not exist according to him. He had no faith in Personal gods. Prayers, chanting of the names of gods, and spending emotion in the worship of such gods were sheer nonsense! Ramakrishna maintained that Maya was also God, one face of Brahman. Tota Puri rejected this theory.

The Mother decided to teach him a lesson! This rock, who had never been ill for even a day in his life, was struck by a virulent strain of dysentery. It lasted for months. He could no longer concentrate on Brahman. Disturbed and disgusted, Tota Puri attempted suicide by drowning in the Ganga. While chin-deep in the water, he found he had neither the will nor the power to even destroy himself! Coming out of the river, he discussed this matter frankly with Ramakrishna. Ramakrishna chuckled and said: "You are experiencing the power of Maya! The Divine Mother has unmanned you! Pray to her to free you from this Maya."

Tota Puri was outraged. But he had one sterling quality. If he decided that something was true and correct, he would stick to that decision, come what may. Once, Ramakrishna had teased him about his short temper. Tota Puri had vowed never to become angry again; he had stuck firmly to his decision. So he passed the night alone in meditation. In the morning he was transformed. He came to Ramakrishna and told him: "You were right. Brahman and Maya are one and the same!"

Then he went before the Divine Mother, prostrated before her, and prayed sincerely for forgiveness. The Mother responded to her prodigal son. Tota Puri's illness vanished instantly. He prostrated again to the Mother and came to where Ramakrishna was sitting. Bowing to him, Tota Puri said, "My one-time disciple, I acknowledge you as a Master! My work here is over. I bid you farewell. I shall commence my wandering once again."

Tota Puri turned and left the temple precincts. He never looked back even once. He was never seen again at Dakshineshwar.

I had listened spell-bound till now. Suddenly, a question crossed my mind.

"Naren," I said, "After your Master realized Brahman, what was his attitude regarding the Mother and other personal gods?"

"Good question, Jock," said Naren. "I once asked my Master the same question. You have attained Nirvikalpa Samadhi, I said. Then why do you run to Mother Kali for advice like a child? His reply was very simple. When he thought of the Supreme One as inactive, he called It Brahman. In the active form he called It Shakti or Maya or the Divine Mother. It is like milk and its whiteness, or a diamond and its luster. The two things are distinct, but not different. You cannot conceive of the one without the other. Brahman gave him the supreme knowledge. Maya guided him to operate on the earthly plane. Do you follow the logic?"

"Yes," I said, "It's clear and logical. So what happened to your Master after Tota Puri left?"

After Tota Puri departed (said Naren), my Master unknowingly started to flirt with death! The memory of the Nirvikalpa Samadhi was an addiction. It was easy for him to slip into that state. Off and on, he would court ecstasy and remain cataleptic for long periods. His spirit would desert his body, which resembled a deserted, dilapidated house. But for the nourishment forced on him by his nephew, he would have died.

Once, in fact, he went too far. His nephew was helpless. It looked as if the last moment had come. Divine Providence caused a wandering monk to turn up. He saw at a glance what had happened. He gave great blows to Ramakrishna's body and pulled the departing life back. It was a miracle. No wonder Ramakrishna later strictly forbade his disciples to attempt the experience!

Mother Kali decided that things had gone far enough. Her son had not been born for such frivolous activities! She decided that what had been sauce for the gander would have to be sauce for the goose too. She had taught Tota Puri the importance of Maya by inflicting on him a lowly malady. She did the same for Ramakrishna. She inflicted on him a violent attack of dysentery for six months. The malady brought Ramakrishna down to earth with a thud! Forgotten was the rarified upper stratum of Brahman when his nether regions were on fire! He stayed on a worldly level, doing his duties as a priest and caring for his Mother.

Ramakrishna's curiosity was then aroused about the other great religions in India, Islam and Christianity. He saw that each of the religions had a large number of followers. He had no doubts about the Hindu religion. But were the other religions True? Did they lead to God? He decided to test each religion. He took his Mother's permission to do so.

He started with Islam. He was initiated into that religion. He moved out of the temple. He renounced all his Gods, and did not worship them. He wore the clothes of a Muslim, and repeated the name of Allah. But for Rani Rasmoni and Mathur Babu, he would have eaten beef, too! Beef is forbidden for all Hindus; Ramakrishna was not only a Brahmin, but also the priest of a temple! Whatever Ramakrishna did, he did whole-heartedly, not bothering about the social consequences of his actions. Within a short time he realized the Muslim God with attributes, and went on to Brahman without attributes. He proved to himself that the river of Islam also led to the same Ocean!

The same proved true for Christianity. He heard the reading of the New Testament in Bengali. He then meditated on a painting of the Madonna with Child, and holy visions revealed themselves to him. It culminated in a face-to-face meeting with Jesus Christ. In a vision both of them embraced, and Jesus entered into Ramakrishna. He immediately went into Samadhi, realizing Brahman. Henceforth, he never doubted the divinity of Christ.

One thing became clear to him. He had tested and practiced all religions. He had assimilated the precepts of the numerous Hindu sects. Whatever the religion, however elementary or sophisticated it might be, whatever path it may follow, it nevertheless led to the same God.

In the midst of all these experiments, he wondered why Maya was making him suffer. He was cruising along to an ecstatic death; he had almost rid himself of the cycle of births and deaths. He had achieved what the Yogis in the Himalayan caves took ages to achieve. This was due to the grace of the Mother. This was what every person aspired to achieve.

Then why had the loving Mother herself slapped him down to a rude realization of his mortality? Where had he gone wrong? Whenever in doubt, this innocent child ran to his Mother. He did so even now. He asked her the same questions that were in his mind. The Divine Mother's answer: "How selfish you are! Are you the center of the world? Do you not see the suffering around you?"
And the Goddess Kali was silent after that!

Selfish? In what way had he been selfish? What, indeed, did he have to be selfish about? He went mentally through the list of persons he knew and came in contact with. In no way had he withheld anything from them for his own gain. He despised wealth. He hated money with such intensity that physical contact with a coin burnt him. So what was left? If the Mother had called him selfish, he must be so. And why had She mentioned suffering?

Ramakrishna pondered over Her words, meditated on them. In this introspection one thing became clear to him. The only treasure he had was knowledge. From this knowledge he had gained wisdom. Wisdom, and the experience of Samadhi, begat humility and devotion. This devotion became manifest when he served the Mother, the prayers and the rituals. What else did the Mother expect from her poor priest? What else *could* he do, anyway?

And then, in a flash, he realized why the Divine Mother had called him selfish. He had not *gone* wrong anywhere; he had *done* wrong! The word 'served' was the trigger. He cringed with shame! He realized that he had been born into this world of men not by sheer accident. There was a Divine purpose behind it. Personal salvation was not his goal. He had no right to hope for personal liberation. He had a different obligation from century to century. He had a mission!

Whichever way he analyzed this truth, he found it led to one conclusion. His mission, his supreme duty, was to help others! Not only to help them, but to serve, serve, serve them! In a state of super consciousness he murmured: "Jiva is Shiva. Who then dare talk of showing mercy to them? Not mercy, but service, SERVICE; for man must be regarded as God!"

All right. He had realized that he had a mission. He had to serve men and help them. But how? How to start this mission? He would have to learn. Who would teach him?

He was like a child in this world, and a helpless, bashful child at that. But he realized that he would have to leave all this bashfulness behind, and become worldlier. He decided that he would learn from anybody who could teach him anything.

He had no pride to start with anyway. Though intellectuals viewed him with suspicion, he sought them out. He begged audiences with eminent, learned and religious men. He met the poor and the rich. He met scientists and men of high society. Any crumbs from their table were grist for his mill. He gathered knowledge and experience, true, but could not formulate a working blueprint for action.

And then, he met Keshab Chandra Sen! Keshab was the Head of the Brahmo Samaj. At the first meeting itself, the organization and discipline of the Samaj impressed him. Subsequent meetings taught him, as it had taught Dayananda before him, the strength that an organization could have.

His questions were answered. In his mind he visualized the organization he should strive for. At the center would be an elder brother. All around him would be a spiritual group of younger brothers. Together, they would weave a basket of love to offer to the loving Divine Mother. His mission became crystallized. First there would be a nucleus where spiritual decisions would be taken.

These decisions would then be passed on for action in the real world.

But first things first! Some loose ends had to be tied up. Foremost was the thought of his wife, Sharadamani. Ramakrishna visited Kamarpukur. Sharada was now fourteen years old and mature beyond her years. Ramakrishna was delighted to find that her spiritual level was very high. He clearly explained his mission in life. She understood it perfectly. Instinctively, she also realized her part in the mission.

SHRI SHARADA DEVI – THE HOLY MOTHER

Then suddenly, Ramakrishna told her that as a wife she had holding rights over him. He considered every woman his mother, including Sharada. However, if she demanded her rights as a wife, he would sacrifice his mission! The pure-hearted Sharada rejected his offer, and renounced her rights. He had always been her guide; now he would be her elder brother. In the future he would educate her, and make her a diligent wife and a good manager.

Sharada Devi came to Dakshineshwar. Ramakrishna recognized the Goddess in her. One night, in May, he made Sharada Devi sit in the seat of Kali. As a priest, he performed the Shodashi Pooja, the adoration of womanhood. At the end of the ritual, both were in superconscious ecstasy. Coming down to the worldly plane, Ramakrishna hailed her as the Divine Mother. Thereafter, she was always called the Holy Mother. The Divine Couple sat back. They waited for their children to come to them. Thereafter the Mission would be launched!

Naren was silent for a while. "This, then, was my Master, Jock. When I think about the change in him, even now I wonder. He had always been a timid, bashful, introverted person. Suddenly he decided to lead a life of action. He conceived the thought of building a Mission, and attracting like-minded young men to join it. This behavior seems so anomalous."

I said: "Naren, you often mentioned that he used to run to the Mother to get answers to his questions. How did this behavior strike you during your early meetings with him?"
Naren said: "Initially, I thought him to be a mystic and a weakling. How wrong I was! The difference was that he knew instinctively what the truth was. He would never budge from that position. The Mother helped him to

develop a will of steel about what was the right thing to do."

"So how did you come into contact with him? He and you, from your own descriptions, seem to be of totally different temperaments. How were you attracted to him?"

"It's a long story, Jock, but your questions deserve an answer. Let me tell you what transpired."

****

A SONG I SING TO THEE

Like to the playing of a little child is every attitude of mine to Thee.
Even at times I dare be angered with Thee; even at times I'd wander far away;
Yet there, in greyest gloom of darkened night,
Yet there, with speechless mouth and tearful eyes,
Thou standest fronting me, and thy sweet face
Stoops down with loving look on face of mine.

Then, instantly, I turn myself to Thee, and then at Thy Feet I fall on bended knee,
I crave no pardon at Thy gentle hands, for Thou art never angry with Thy son.
Who else with all my foolish freaks would bear!
Thou art my Master, Thou my soul's real mate.
Many a times I see Thee – I am Thee!
Aye! I am Thou, and Thou, my Lord art I!

SWAMI VIVEKANANDA

CHAPTER 8

MASTER AND DISCIPLE

In my youth (said Naren), I was naturally interested in what was happening around me in Calcutta. The most happening thing was the Brahmo Samaj. Its star was Keshab Chandra Sen. He was famous as an orator and debater. Social and religious groups vied with each other in inviting him to their platforms. He never disappointed them. My intellectual friends and I sat spellbound through his interactive speeches. He was our hero, or idol; who was there who did not wish to emulate him, to be him? We empathized with all that he said.

The next logical step was to join the Brahmo Samaj, the new one. I was enrolled as a member. My friends and I were emotionally linked to the Samaj. We despised the caste system, we hated image worship, and we were contemptuous of polytheism. We also wanted women to be equal to men in all respects. The Brahmo Samaj promised to set right all these social and religious problems.

The burning thought in my mind since I came of age was to find out the truth of God's existence. I wanted someone, anyone, to answer the question: "Have you seen God?" But who should I ask? I thought about it deeply. The answer was, obviously, the great Sage, Devendranath Tagore, or Deben Babu. He was considered by all, without exception, as the best spiritual teacher then. He was a towering figure, also aloof and Olympian. Gathering all my courage, I had a meeting with him alone. I was excited, I was tense. Forgetting all the niceties of formal greetings and pleasantries, I blurted out the question: "Sir, have you seen God?"

Deben Babu looked at me in surprise, then with amusement. What a presumptuous question from a small boy! There was a spell of silence. Then he smiled and said: "My boy, you have the eyes of a yogi."
He would say no more. The reply was neither here nor there. I was deeply disappointed, and came away.

This was my first disillusionment with religious leaders. The disillusionment continued. All the religious leaders of the other sects also gave waffling answers. Obviously, not one of them had seen God! I was reminded forcefully of Fitzgerald's stanza in the Rubaiyat:

Myself when young did eagerly frequent
Doctor and Saint, and heard great argument
About it and about: but evermore
Came out by the same door as in I went.

I complained about this to my relative Ramachandra Datta. He first laughed, then turned serious and asked me: "How serious are you about your question?"
"Very," I replied. "If I am to proceed on the religious road, then I must know that God exists. Else everything is mere cant and hypocrisy."

"If you have a real desire to realize God, why are you wasting your time in the Brahmo Samaj?"

I flushed with anger, but merely said: "Do you have an alternative?"

"Yes," he said, "Come with me to Dakshineshwar!"

Dakshineshwar? Where had I heard about it before? Ah yes, in my college, through Prof. Hastie. I pondered: "If an Englishman, and a Christian priest, at that, was impressed with this person at Dakshineshwar, what harm can it do if I visit the holy man?"

I immediately accepted the suggestion of my relative. With two of my friends to give me company, I visited Dakshineshwar for the first time in December 1881.

My friends were normal fun-loving young men. The temple did not affect them. They prattled on about many things. At first, I enjoyed this light chatter. Then the atmosphere of the temple influenced me. I became silent and introverted, seeing and hearing nothing. I was surprised to hear a sweet voice calling me: "Naren, Naren."

I looked towards the voice and saw my Master for the first time. He had a short beard and beautiful half-closed eyes.

I got up respectfully and said: "Yes, sir. I am Naren."

"Naren," he said, "I hear that you sing well. Please sing a hymn."

Since it was the temple of Mother Kali, I sang a hymn on the Mother. I sang it with full feeling and emotion. In the middle of my song, the Master suddenly and quietly passed into an ecstasy. As I watched intently, his whole body first relaxed, then became completely rigid. The eyes were not wholly closed. His lips were parted in a smile, showing white teeth. His chest and face were suffused with blood.

After I had finished my song, the Master slowly came out of his trance. He suddenly got up and came to me. He took me by my hand and said: "Come with me."
He led me on to the north verandah, and closed the door. We were alone. Nobody could see us. Then, to my utter surprise, he began to weep! He caught my hand and said tenderly: "Ah, you have come so late! Why have you been so unkind as to make me wait for so long? My ears are tired of hearing the futile words of other men. Oh, how I have longed to pour out my soul into the breast of somebody fitted to receive my inner experience!"

Then he let go my arm. He folded his hands and said: "Lord, I knew that you are the ancient Sage Nara, the incarnation of Narayana. You have been reborn on earth to take away the misery of humanity."

To say that I was shocked and amazed is to put it mildly! I was reminded of the watchman of the villa in Bipin's story and his description of Ramakrishna. I thought: "I am dealing with a madman! Is this what I came here to see? He ought to be put in a straitjacket! Why, I am the son of Vishwanath Datta! How dare he speak to me like this?"

Outwardly, I remained stone-faced and did not show any emotion. My chief desire was to get away once this charade was finished.

And then, in a normal tone he said: "Naren, my boy, do you see a light when you go to sleep?"

I nodded. Then he said: "You see? This assuredly shows a great spiritual past. The soul has learned well to sink deep into meditation. The meditative state has become spontaneous with you."

"What unmitigated nonsense," I thought. I just let him talk. It was a great relief when he said: "Promise me that you will come to see me again, alone, and soon."

To free myself from this lunatic, I promised. Mentally, I decided to not even sleep with my head in the direction of Dakshineshwar! We went back to the common hall, where the others were seated.

My Master invited questions of any sort from the group. A few were philosophical, but most of them were worldly. He answered each question with a lot of common sense. He pointed out the scriptural sanction behind each answer. Where the meaning was abstract, he narrated a parable to make his point clear even to the simplest person. Watching all this, I did not find anything strange in his ways or words. He was strikingly sincere.

Then one slightly intellectual person asked him: "Master, can we worldly people realize God?"
The Master said: "God can be realized. One can see him and speak to him as I see and speak to you. You weep for your wife, your children and your possessions. But who weeps for God? Let me tell you a story. A disciple repeatedly told his Guru that he wanted to realize God. The Guru would smile each time. On a hot day, both Guru and disciple went to the river to bathe. Both entered the water. Suddenly the Guru forcibly held the disciple's head under the water till he struggled to get free. The Guru let him go, and then asked him: 'What did you want most when under the water?'
The disciple answered: 'A breath of air'
The Guru said: 'Do you want God in the same way? If you do, you will get him in a moment!'

"So, you see, you must have that thirst, that desire for God. Your books, your intellect and your rituals will be useless unless you have that thirst. If you do not have that thirst, you are no better than an atheist. In fact, the atheist is

sincere, and you are not! If you have the thirst, you will realize God, whether you are worldly or saintly. Otherwise, seeking refuge under the cares of the world is hypocrisy!"
While speaking he looked at each person in the audience. After the last sentence he was looking at me.

Aha! The ground had providentially been laid. I sensed a window of opportunity through which I could voice the question eternally burning in my mind. Looking directly at him, I asked: "Sir, have you seen God?"
I expected him to hesitate, and then utter some nonsense. But he said immediately: "Of course! Of course, my son, I have seen God! I see Him as I see you before me, only more intensely. In fact, if you want, I can show Him to you!"
For the second time that day I was stunned! These did not seem to be idle words. But how to reconcile this simple and serene sage with the madman I had met on the north verandah? I thought to myself: "He may be mad, but he is also great! He is worthy of respect."

I left Dakshineshwar in a pensive state of mind. The daily life of Calcutta, and the activities of the Brahmo Samaj, seemed mechanical to me. Dakshineshwar was a totally different experience. The Master had said that he would show me God! What could this peculiar person show me? And how had he discovered the fact regarding the light I saw when I went to sleep? These thoughts knocked against the corners of my brain at all times. Even my mother noticed the change in me and asked me if I was unwell. I was, but not in the way she thought me to be. A month later, alone and on foot, I returned to Dakshineshwar.

My Master was sitting on his small bed. He welcomed me with a broad smile. Affectionately, he asked me to sit near him on one side of the bed. I did so. After a moment's silence, he fixed his eyes upon me. He murmured something under his breath. He moved closer to me. I prepared myself mentally for some eccentric gushing, or some crazy behavior. Instead, he suddenly placed his right foot on my body. The contact was terrible, like a crippling electric shock! My eyes were open. I saw the entire room whirl and vanish. Everything, even my individuality, was swallowed in a nameless void. I was terrified! I thought I was facing death. Involuntarily I cried out: "What are you doing? I have parents at home!"

I heard him begin to laugh. He passed his hand over my heart and said: "All right. Let us leave it at that for the moment. It will come, all in good time."
As he said these words, the strange phenomena disappeared. I returned to normal. Everything around us also returned to normal. Still trembling from the violent experience, I remained on my guard. There were no more surprises. The Master treated me with simplicity and kindness, as if nothing had happened.

What *had* happened? Was it mesmerism? Two things militated against this notion. I was not a weak person with blind faith; I was violently antipathetic to all hypnotic action. Second, I remembered all that had taken place. So it could not be mesmerism. On my return home, I pondered over this incident. I ended up revolting against my own inexplicable vision. So when I visited Dakshineshwar a week later, for the third time, I was fully prepared. All my critical faculties were fully alert, and on the defensive.

That day, my Master took me to an adjacent garden. We strolled about in the garden for some time. I was silent, listening to what he had to say about Mother Kali. Then we sat in the parlor. Soon the Master went into a trance. I was watching the process keenly. Suddenly he reached out and touched me. I lost all consciousness. When I came to after a while, the Master was massaging my chest. I asked him what had happened. Very evasively he said: "I had some questions about your antecedents, your mission in the world, and the duration of your mortal life. I got fitting answers."

Who had he questioned? Who gave him the answers? He told me nothing more. However, from that day he gave me an honored seat among his disciples. He treated me as a privileged person.

He might treat me as a privileged disciple, but I did not accept the title. I did not want to be called anyone's disciple. My Master had powers which I did not understand. But I hated to be dominated! I would only accept from my Master whatever stood the test of reason. I detested sentimentality and tears as feminine traits. I questioned everything; nothing was to be on trust. I denied the Hindu Gods. I mocked Advaita as atheism, the Hindu Scriptures as nonsense. I was bold enough to tell my Master: "Millions of people may call you God. I will not do so till I have proved it for myself."

Far from being shocked, my Master laughingly approved of my doubts. He said: "Naren is correct. Do not accept anything because I say so. Test everything for yourself."

I remember one test that I cheekily carried out. My Master used to tell us that he hated money, gold, jewelry and ornaments. He was physically repulsed by them. During his early days as a priest, he would decorate Mother Kali only with flowers and cloth. His nephew would decorate the idol with jewelry. I found this type of repulsion hard to believe. Once, when there was nobody in his room, I hid a silver coin beneath the pillow of my Master's bed. I contrived to be nearby to watch his reactions when he returned.

My Master came near the bed. He touched it as he started to sit on it. Suddenly, his whole body reeled as if he had received a physical blow! He was bewildered and asked us to check his bed. I pretended to check it and told him there was nothing there. Again he neared the bed and flinched and stopped. He told his oldest disciple to check the bed. This time the silver coin was found. My Master looked around accusingly, like a small child. He found me smiling. He frowned and asked me: "What is there to smile about, Naren?"

I told him how I had tested him. The other disciples were outraged, but the Master approved of the test.

My criticisms and passionate arguments filled him with joy. After a particularly heated debate he would exclaim: "Look, look, what penetrative power! Naren is a raging fire. He is filled with the power of Shiva. He destroys all illusion. Mahamaya herself can come no closer to him than ten feet! She is held back by the glory She has Imparted to him."

I would be acutely embarrassed. The other disciples would good naturedly chuckle, and nudge one another. Sometimes his joy at something I said would transport him to ecstasy. But a few times my sharp criticism hurt him. I was without any consideration whatsoever. I remember one such incident.

One day my Master was visited by Keshab Babu, Vijay Krishna Goswami and other leading lights of the Brahmo Samaj. I was still a member of the Samaj, and had the greatest respect for them. All of them sat in the parlor. I was also present. My Master was in a lofty, sublime mood. The discussion was of the highest order. After the meeting was over, and the guests had left, the Master called all the disciples to the parlor. After summarizing the meeting, he said: "You know, Keshab has one sign of greatness which has made him famous. My Naren has eighteen such signs! In Keshab and Vijay, knowledge burns like a candle-flame.

In Naren, it is like a blazing sun. It dispels all ignorance and delusion!"

This was too much! I was outraged and enraged. Compare me with Keshab Babu and Vijay Babu? They were heroes; I was an insignificant person. I blazed out at my Master: "Sir, why do you say such silly things? People will think you mad! Comparing the world-famous Keshab and the saintly Vijay with a nobody like me? Please, never do such things again."

My Master seemed unrepentant. In fact, he looked quite pleased. He said: "I cannot help it. Do you think those are my words? What my Divine Mother told me, I repeated. She reveals only the Truth to me."

This reference to the Divine Mother for support did not impress me. I boldly and harshly said: "You think that these are revelations from the Mother? Can they not be mere fancies of your brain? You love me, and wish to see me great. Hence these fancies come to your mind."

My Master was upset. He got up and rushed out of the parlor. There was pin-drop silence. Some disciples glared at me angrily; some stole glances at me. I was not in the least contrite. Such nonsense had to stop, once for all! After a while, the Master returned to the parlor and sat down. He seemed at peace with himself. He looked at me and said: "Naren, your reasoning perplexed me. So I appealed directly to the Mother. Do you know what She said? She said: 'Why do you care for what Naren says? In a few days, he will admit every word of it to be true."

In the face of such unreasoning statements, what could I say? I sat silent, and said nothing.

To avoid such intemperate statements and actions, I avoided him. I stayed away from Dakshineshwar. This made him behave in a manner that irritated me still further. He began to search for me in the streets of Calcutta! In fact, he even disrupted a session in the Brahmo Samaj temple! His unexpected entry provoked a scandal. There was much scornful criticism. When I took him to task for this, my Master said: "I am ashamed of my actions. But I cannot help myself."

I cut in: "Hold on, Naren. What was this incident? Don't hurry over the details. Do tell me all that occurred."
"Oh, Lord!" said Naren, "Even now I feel embarrassed to relate the incident. Do you really want to know what happened?"
I sensed something juicy! I said: "Yes, indeed. Please tell me the whole story."
Naren said: "All right. Once, I did not visit Dakshineshwar for several days. My anxious Master sent for me. I avoided going to him. So my Master set out for Calcutta. He surmised that I might be at the evening service of the Brahmo Samaj. He came to the temple. He had often visited it before. He knew many prominent members intimately. The evening service was already in progress. Suddenly, out of nowhere, my Master made his appearance. He was in a semi-conscious state. He glided in exactly like…like.. Banquo's Ghost!"

Naren was laughing so hard that he could just gasp out the words. The image was so vivid that we could not control our laughter for a long time. We would stop, look at each other and burst out laughing again. Finally, we managed to control ourselves, and Naren said: "Oh, I have never laughed so much after my arrival in America! That felt good!"
Then Naren went on with the story.

When my Master made his appearance (said Naren), the preacher, confused, stopped the sermon. All eyes turned towards this apparition. A muted babbling broke out in the audience. Unmindful of this commotion, my Master glided slowly to the pulpit. Reaching it, he went into a trance, hands upraised. The disorder in the audience increased.

Recently a split had taken place in the Brahmo Samaj. Many leading Brahmos suspected my Master of having influenced Keshab to cause the split. They considered this visit an intrusion. The lights were suddenly turned off. Later it was explained that this was to restore order. I suspect they wanted to attack my Master physically under cover of darkness. Anyway, this added to the confusion. There was a stampede towards the door.

I was in the choir and was watching all these proceedings, horrified. I knew why he had come here. It was up to me to rescue him. Just as the lights went out, I caught hold of him. I dragged him through the crowd to the rear door. I took him to Dakshineshwar in a carriage. I was boiling with anger and shame. I took him to task repeatedly. Every time I stopped, he would say: "What could I do, what could I do?" He did not appear in the least sorry for all the disorder he had caused. My anger came down by degrees. I was touched at the same time. I knew his great love for me. But this pursuit had to stop.

Very reasonably, I told him: "No man ought to allow himself to be infatuated with another, Master. Take care. If you love me too much, the result will be disastrous. There is one great danger. You may forfeit your own spiritual greatness. You will sink to my level. Then what use will all your Sadhana (disciplined practice) be?"
I went on like this till we reached Dakshineshwar. Without a word my pure and simple Master listened to me. His face reflected all the fear and hurt that he felt. My heart was squeezed at his reaction; but I hardened my heart. Incidents of such nature should never be repeated.

As soon as we reached the temple, my Master ran into the sanctum sanctorum of Mother Kali. I followed, curious to see what he would do. I saw my Master sitting before the Goddess. He talked to Her like he talked to me. Like a child complaining to his mother, he told the Divine Mother of his affection for me, and the disorder it had caused. He repeated my harsh words to Her. It was a monologue. In the middle there would be pauses as if he was listening to Her. I felt I was intruding on something very holy. I went out of the temple. I sat on the steps, enjoying the cool breezes of the Ganga.

Shortly after, my Master came and sat beside me. He was his jaunty self again. I turned to him and asked what the Mother had told him. He slapped me lightly on my cheek and said: "You wretch! I will not listen to your lies again. The Mother told me that I love you because I see the Lord in you. If the day comes when I can no longer see Him, I shall not be able to bear the sight of you."

Later he asked me: "Naren, was the evening an embarrassment for you?"
"Yes, Master," I replied, "It was a disaster."
He chuckled slyly, and said: "But I got you back! I got you back!"

****

THE TRIANGLE OF LOVE

What is love? Where is love? How do you know for sure it is love?
The world is full of talk of love, but we find it's hard to prove!
Soon enough a man finds out there is no love in his nature,
A woman finds she cannot love no matter what, poor creature!

What then are the true tests of love? Over this question dwelling,
The first test is it's not reduced to mere buying and selling,
Love to get any profit with intent of future reaping,
Arguing, haggling, and bargaining, why that's pure shop-keeping!

The second test is that, with love, the object is very dear,
All fear is suppressed; true love transcends the barrier of fear!
A dog barks and a lady flees with screams and movements uncouth,
But to defend her child she'll jump even to a lion's mouth!

The final test of love is that it's your highest ideal,
Project this ideal on someone and lo, it's your love real!

This is why in this wide world a startling thing we often find,
Beauties love Beasts! We shake our heads; gently murmur "Love is blind!"

For all types of love these tests are the one sure measuring rod,
Whether love of parents, kith and kin, friends, ladies, love of God!
And then of course, if you love true, you never have to worry,
Never repent, never complain, never ever say sorry!

SHASHIDHAR BELWADI

CHAPTER 9

LOVE AND TEMPTATION

"Naren," I interrupted, "You have told me of your Master's love for you and vice versa. If you're sure you don't mind, can I ask you a very personal question?"

"I don't mind. For a monk, there is nothing personal. I shall answer you truthfully."

"In India, you said, children are often married off soon. Did your parents ever try to find a bride for you?"

"No, Jock. My father was against child-marriages. My mother knew that I considered women of my age or younger to me as sisters, and older to me as mothers. My destiny has ingrained this feeling deep in my heart."

"I might be over-stepping, but I have to ask you this. Were you ever tempted? Or exposed to temptation?"

Naren was silent for a while. Then he replied: "Jock, the answer to the first part of your question is NO. I have never in my life looked with lustful eyes at any woman. Once, however, in the days of my youth, I was much troubled by a fit of passion, of lust, due to a book lent by another schoolmate. I became terribly vexed with myself. In my rage, I sat upon a pot of burning charcoal nearby. It took many days for the wound to heal. It was a very radical cure, but a permanent one!"

He paused and said: "Regarding the second part, the answer is yes. Let me give you some instances."

Once (said Naren), my examinations were fast approaching. I took to studying in a room in my maternal grandmother's house nearby. There was less noise and distraction there. In the house opposite, across the lane, was a young widow. When I left my room from time to time, I used to notice her. In my room, after a hard session of study, I would relax by singing.

One evening, I lit the lamps. It had been a hot day. I kept the front door open to cool the room. I took up my books to study. Before starting, I sang a hymn to the Goddess Saraswati, the Goddess of Learning. In the middle of my song I heard a slight sound near the door. I stopped singing and looked there. The young widow was standing in the doorway. There was silence for a while. Then she said: "Babu, I am the widow in the opposite house. I have heard your songs on many an evening. I admire you. Do you scorn me because I am a widow?"
I was shocked. Her words were like a thunderbolt. I prostrated myself before her. My head was toward her feet. With great force I exclaimed: "Mother, mother! Why have you come? I regard you as my own mother!"
A moment later the girl was gone. I was alone. The next day I changed my room. I never came to that house again.

On another occasion, my wealthy friends played a joke on me. They took me to a garden party of singing merry makers. I enjoyed the singing. In fact, I sang a few songs myself. After some time, I felt tired and sleepy. I was used to rising early and retiring early. My friends took me to a room nearby. It was empty. My friends told me to make myself comfortable. I stretched out on the bed.

After some time, a young lady walked into the room. I sat up hurriedly on the bed. She sat on a corner of the bed. She told me that she was a dance girl. She said my friends had sent her to me. It never occurred to me that my friends had sent her there to tempt me, as a joke. She told me many interesting things about her life, her sorrows and misfortunes. I had never heard anything like this before. I was quite interested in her story. Many of her predicaments evoked my sympathy.

Some time later the girl said: "Thank you for your patience and your sympathy. No one wants to hear my problems. Let me reward you with a kiss!"
She got up and started around the cot. I was aghast. Looking stern, I sprang to my feet. I invoked my Master. I halted the woman in her tracks with a look. I told her: "Sister, I must go now. I have genuine sympathy for you. I wish you well. If you sincerely realize that it is a weakness to lead such a life, you will get over it some day."
I left her in the room and went home.

Next day, when I met my friends I began to berate them. They went into fits of laughter. I asked them what had happened. They told me the girl had returned to them bewildered. She told them sarcastically: "A nice trick you played on me – sending me to tempt a sadhu or monk!"

I taxed them for playing such a dirty trick on me. They laughed even harder. They said: "We had, and have, full faith in your chastity and purity."
They were not malicious souls. I had to join in their laughter.

Again, I was once in deep troubles. I was in utter poverty. Various temptations came my way. A rich woman sent me an ugly proposal to end my days of poverty. I sternly and scornfully rejected her proposal. Another woman also made similar overtures to me. I said to her: "You have wasted your life seeking the pleasures of the flesh. The dark shadows of death are before you. Have you done anything to face that? Give up all these filthy desires. Remember God!"

A final incident. It is not directly connected with your question, but may interest you. During my wanderings in India, I came to a place called Limbdi, in the Bombay Presidency. I learnt that there was a place where ascetics lived. I went to the place. It was isolated, but quiet and peaceful. The monks welcomed me warmly. They urged me to stay with them as long as I wished to. I was tired and hungry. I accepted their hospitality. I had no idea of the character of the monks. I stayed with them for a few days. Then, to my horror, I found that the monks belonged to a degenerate group of sex-worshippers. I could hear the prayers and incantations of men and women in the adjoining room. I decided to leave the place at once. I cautiously tried the door. It was locked. I knocked on the door. A voice asked me what I wanted. I was locked in with a guard at the door!

A little later the High Priest of the sect summoned me and said: "You are a monk with a magnetic personality. Evidently you have practiced celibacy for a lifetime. Now you must give us the fruit of your long austerity. We shall break your celibacy, and perform a special type of spiritual practice. We shall then acquire certain psychic powers."

I was deeply shaken. I outwardly showed no sign of anxiety and kept my presence of mind. I pretended to take the matter lightly. I evinced keen interest in the procedures. I was escorted back to my room to await the auspicious day. During the day, a few of my devotees were permitted to meet me to discuss religious matters. One of them was a boy who was very loyal to me. When just the two of us met, I swore him to secrecy. He smuggled in some paper and a pen.

I wrote a note to the Prince of the State. I explained my problem and asked for his help. The boy hurried to the palace. By God's grace, he somehow managed audience with the Prince, and gave him the note. The Prince immediately sent his personal guards to my rescue. The Prince then invited me to stay at the palace, and I accepted.

"Jock, I hope I have answered your questions satisfactorily. Love does not exist in the world for the

pleasures of the flesh alone. Love sublimated leads you to God."
"I am sorry to have diverted you from your main narrative, Naren," I said, "Please continue with your story."
"Where did I stop?" Naren asked.
"The two of you were talking outside the temple after the Brahmo Samaj incident."
"Oh, yes," said Naren.

  I continued (said Naren) to visit my Master at Dakshineshwar. I saw a subtle change on his part. Very soon, he became completely indifferent towards me. He did not look at me. He talked, laughed and joked with others. This did not bother me in the least. One of the disciples made an oblique remark about the Master's behavior towards me. It made no difference to me. I always came patiently back just to see and hear him.

  One day, the Master addressed me directly: "Naren, I have not spoken to you for a long time. Why do you still persist in coming here?"
I replied frankly: "It is not just your words to me that attract me. I need to see and hear you because I love you."
The Master seemed pleased, but said: "You do not want to acknowledge my Mother. Then why do you come here?"
This seemed neither here nor there. I said: "Is that a condition you are laying down? To come here, have I to acknowledge Her?"

He paused, and said: "No, not really. Who am I to impose such conditions? But why do you refuse to accept Her?"

I said: "I do not feel the need to do so. Formal acceptance, just to please you, is a sham."

My Master said: "Mark my words. Very shortly you will accept Her. You will weep at the very mention of Her name."

I did not feel the need to say anything in reply. The subject was dropped.

My Master was at that time teaching us about Advaita Vedanta. The teaching was that the Soul inside us is the same as the Supreme Brahman, the Absolute. In short, man is God. I rejected the idea as madness and blasphemy. At every opportunity I ridiculed the idea. One day, we disciples were waiting for the Master to join us. Someone started the topic of Advaita. Very soon, it became the subject of jokes. A disciple, Hazra, was a comedian of sorts. He soon had us roaring with laughter. We ridiculed the concepts of Advaita: "This jug is God…these flies are God.." and so on. From the adjoining room, my Master heard the laughter. He came in quietly, in a semi-conscious state, and touched me.

You will find it very difficult to believe what happened! But it is true, every word of it! At his touch, I felt a storm sweep through me. At once, everything was changed in my sight. I saw with amazement that nothing existed but God! In my house, all that I touched and tasted was God. I was like an intoxicated person. I stopped doing anything. My parents thought I was ill. The experience vanished after a few days, but the memory remained with me. Nevermore would I deny the truth of Advaita! In a semi-conscious state, my Master descended into an abyss. His touch at that time dragged me down into the abyss as well.

    A series of mystic experiences swept through me during the period. I repeated "Shiva, Shiva" like a madman. My Master looked on with understanding. He said compassionately: "Yes, I remained for twelve years in that condition!"
However, my nature would never have become what it is now had not tragedy devastated me. This tragedy kicked me out of the luxurious arms of doubt and intellectualism. This tragedy brought me face to face with the eternal problem of evil and existence.

*****

TO AN EARLY VIOLET

What though thy bed be frozen earth,
Thy cloak the chilling blast;
What though no mate to clear the path,
The sky with gloom o'ercast;

What though if love itself doth fail,
Thy fragrance strewed in vain;
What though if bad o'er good prevail,
And vice o'er virtue reign;

Change not thy nature, gentle bloom,
Thou violet, sweet and pure,
But ever pour thy sweet perfume,
Unasked, unstinted, sure!

SWAMI VIVEKANANDA

CHAPTER 10

DESPAIR AND RESURRECTION

As I told you previously (said Naren), my father was a very independent thinker. He had very set ideas about his family. He gave the entire family a very comfortable life. He insisted that his sons practice a high standard of living, and should be fit and healthy. He gave us a good education. With these three factors, he envisaged that he was equipping them for adult life. The sons should fend for themselves in the future. He had no doubt that we would do very well in life.

My father earned a great deal of money. He spent it freely in luxurious living and unstinted charity. To calculatedly build up a savings fund for the family was not part of his make-up. But we had so much that we thought, even my shrewd mother, that we had enough for any emergency. The bubble burst with a bang! My father, the sole earner in the family, died suddenly in early 1884. We were all devastated. The central load-bearing pillar of our lives was gone. We missed him terribly. His ringing laughter, his jokes, his learned discourses, and his routine which had carved the time-table for our home – all this vanished. We performed all the ceremonies to ensure a peaceful journey for his soul. This took all of almost a fortnight. These ceremonies cost a lot of money, too, for we had to maintain the standards of our clan.

Once that was done, we sat down to find out how much money we had left. I went to all the banks where my father had his accounts. I met his friends, learned barristers and attorneys, to discuss this matter with them. We looked at all his books of account to find out about any loans. The end-result was the same overall. Except for a pittance, my father had left no patrimony!

We were horrified to find that we were facing ruin! There were six or seven mouths to feed. To our further dismay, we found that my father had taken fairly heavy loans. The creditors knocked on our doors. They were polite, but it was our duty to satisfy them. Many belongings in the house had to be sold to repay these loans. Now my wise mother took charge. She asked me to start looking for a job to help the family.

I had no doubt that with my intelligence and hard work I would get a good job. The reality was terrible. Office after office, firm after firm turned me away. I could not use the influence of Keshab Chandra Sen, because the poor man had died before my father in the same year. Trudging from office to office, hunger pangs gnawing at my stomach, was an unforgettable experience.

I soon realized that this world has no sympathy for the weak, the poor and the deserted! Worse still, some of my friends, who could have helped me, deliberately avoided me. Once, I remember, I sat with some friends in the shade of a monument. It was summer and I was tired and hungry. One of my friends began to sing about the abundant grace of God. It seemed as if he was mocking me! I turned on him furiously like a tiger. I berated him for his ideal vision of the world. Not knowing the problem, my friend was hurt, but remained silent.

At home, matters were desperate. The food situation was very bad. I took to telling my mother that I had been invited for lunch by this or that friend. Once out of the house, I fasted. Sometimes I was lucky. Since I was a good singer, I was invited by rich friends to their houses to sing. This would earn me lunch or dinner. One thing surprised me. These friends knew about my misfortunes, but never showed any curiosity about it. I did not enlighten them, either.

One incident showed me how devastated my mother was by our circumstances. One thing I had never forsaken. That was my devotion to God. Every morning, I offered prayers to God. One day my mother swept into the room. She suddenly burst out: "Fool! Be quiet! Stop this mockery at once! What has God ever done for us? Shut up!"
I was severely shaken. This, from my pious, devout mother! Such words from the mother who had installed God in my heart!

Naren's voice broke. Tears filled his eyes. "My poor mother, my poor mother! Shiva, Shiva…" he muttered, and looked down. My own eyes smarted in empathy. After a few deep sighs, Naren looked up and said: "I always feel guilty that I could not do anything for my parents. If the parents are pleased, then God is pleased with that person. He is a good man who never speaks harsh words to his parents. My father had always been my friend and my guide. My mother was, and continues to be, my ideal."

Anyway (continued Naren), the words of my mother pierced my heart. I felt that she was right. What, indeed, had God done for us? Why did He make us suffer so much? Had all my appeals been lost in space? Angry, I denied God. I spoke against God openly. I became known as an atheist. Harsh words were spoken against me. I became even more hardened in my position. All thoughts of my Master were wiped from my mind. He, too, did not interfere with me in any way.

One hot summer's day, I was searching for any job I could get. The search was useless. By evening, I was hungry, bathed in my own sweat, and feverish. Totally exhausted, I sank down in front of a house. My will was shattered and I was in total surrender. Suddenly, a Divine Light surrounded and entered me! I felt refreshed and alive! My tiredness and hunger vanished. More than that, all my doubts were washed away. I could truly say: "I see, I know, I believe, I am undeceived!" The revelation had occurred after all my pride, my ego, was wiped out by my attitude of surrender. I went home and meditated. The way seemed clear to me. I would follow in the footsteps of my grandfather, and become a monk. I would tell my mother the next day and renounce the world.

The next day I was waiting for the opportune moment to make my announcement. Suddenly, my mother came to me and said, in an annoyed tone: "There is a visitor for you."

I went into the parlor and saw, to my utter surprise, my Master! I touched his feet and welcomed him. He blessed me and then looked around the parlor. He said: "I heard the sad news about the death of your father. You must have finished all the ceremonies by now. I came to pay my condolences."

I thanked him. He went on: "So how is life treating you? What are your plans for the future?"

I said: "I am looking for a job to help our family."

"Good, good. So you are presently free?"

""Yes, Master."

He smiled sweetly and said: "It has been a long time since you came to my hut. Why don't you come with me and stay the night in Dakshineshwar?"

I was trapped! A thousand excuses came to my mind. I really did not want to go there; but I could not refuse my Master, either. I agreed, got ready and accompanied the Master back to Dakshineshwar.

At Dakshineshwar, as we sat in his room with a few others, he talked of service to mankind. Suddenly, he sang a beautiful song which brought tears to my eyes. The song hinted to me that he knew my decision to renounce the world. This hint was confirmed when he burst into tears and said to me: "Naren, I know that you will not remain in this world for long. For my sake, please promise me that you will stay in it as long as I live."

I had to make that promise to my beloved Master.

I went back home, and the drudgery and misery continued. I got a job as a translator in a solicitor's office. The post was temporary, the salary just enough to maintain our family. But it was not certain how long even this would go on. Frustrated, I was struck with an idea. My Master was the beloved son of Mother Kali. Why not request him to pray to the Divine Mother for the welfare of my family? No sooner thought than done. I went the very next day to my Master, and requested him to carry out my appeal.

My Master thought about the matter. He then said: "Good idea. The Mother will certainly look after your welfare."

"I shall be much obliged, Master," I said.

"There is one small problem. I can pray to the Mother only for myself. It will not be right for me to pray to Her for someone else's welfare."

He saw my downcast face, and said: "However, what prevents you from praying to the Mother yourself? Why do you require an intermediary? I have always said that your powers of concentration and meditation are immense. The Mother will certainly grant you your wish!"

I agreed happily, and entered the temple of the Mother. I sat before her beautiful idol and prayed. Never having adopted half-measures, I prayed with all the sincerity I had in me. The Mother's love flooded me. I was filled with sublime emotion and forgot myself for some time. When I became normal, I went to the Master with a joyous heart. He smiled at me and asked me: "Did you pray to my Mother, Naren?"

"I did, Master," I replied.

"How do you feel now?" he asked.

"Very happy and very relaxed, Master," I replied.

"Good, good" he said, "And did you ask her all that you wanted to? Did she agree to your requests?"

KALI BHAVATARINI, DAKSHINESHWAR

I was dismayed at the question. I realized that I had totally forgotten to ask the Mother to remove the misery of my family and myself. I told my Master so. He looked concerned and said: "Never mind. The Mother is very generous. Go again, and ask her whatever you want."

I re-entered the temple, and prayed to the Mother. When I went back to my Master, I found that I had again forgotten to ask Her what I wanted.

The Master, undeterred, sent me back to pray again. This time, I did remember what I had come to request. I framed the sentence for my request, and said: "Mother…" I stopped, and deep shame overcame me. Here was the Divine Mother of the universe, and I was asking for stupid and pitiful things! I continued my prayer: "Mother, I need nothing save to know and to believe!"

I went back to my Master and narrated what had occurred. He looked at me with shining eyes and said, "Naren, I had expected nothing less from you."
From that day I was a new man, leading an entirely different life. I accepted my Master as my father, my preceptor. I dimly realized that he was slowly but steadily training me for some main part in a drama which only he visualized.

"Naren," I asked, "Do you have a photograph of your Master?"
Naren said; "Oh, yes! Do you want to see it?"
"Yes, if you don't mind showing it to me."
"Not at all," he said.
He got up, and put his steel trunk on the bench. He opened the lid. Between the clothes, wrapped in a cloth, was a framed photograph. He looked at it and then gave it to me.

I saw an aged person, sitting on the ground with his legs crossed over each other. The fingers of his right hand were intertwined between the fingers of his left hand. He wore a short piece of cloth around his waist. It covered his thighs. Another small piece of cloth came from over his left shoulder and lay over his chest. He had a short beard and mustache. His hair was close-cropped. His eyes were half-open; so was his mouth. He looked very other-worldly. I said so to Naren as I handed the photo back to him.

"Oh, Jock!" he exclaimed, "If you only knew the troubles we went through to get this photograph! Let me tell you the whole story!"

My Master (said Naren) never wished to have his photograph taken. He discouraged all efforts in that direction. Once a devotee, Ram Chandra Datta had a photograph taken. When my Master saw the print, he remarked: "Who is this? Am I such an angry man?"

Datta realized that the Master did not like the photo. So he threw both the print and the negative into the Ganga. Another photo was taken when he was in Keshab Sen's house. In it, he is standing in a trance, supported by his nephew. The third photograph was taken when he went reluctantly to a studio at the insistence of a household devotee, Manomohun Mittra. In this, he is fully dressed, wearing shoes and a coat. He had never otherwise worn them in his life. It is a very rare photo. My Master hated it!

STUDIO PHOTOGRAPH

This other photo, which you see, was taken with a lot of deceit. A devotee, Chatterjee, had brought a professional photographer to Dakshineshwar. He begged the Master for a photograph. The Master refused and went into the Radhakanta temple. Chatterjee appealed to me for help. I told him to keep the photographer ready but hidden. The Master came out of the temple and sat on the verandah. I sat before him, and we engaged in some high philosophy. As I expected, the Master soon went into ecstasy.

SHRI RAMAKRISHNA PARAMAHAMSA

I told Chatterjee to hurry up and take the photo. My Master had bent to one side. The photographer caught his chin gently to straighten him. Now, in Samadhi, the body becomes as light as a balloon! My Master's entire body floated off the ground. The photographer was so startled that he let my Master go. Luckily, I caught him before any damage could occur. I told the photographer to hasten. He took the exposure as fast as he could. My Master was completely unaware of this incident.

Later Chatterjee brought a copy of the photograph to Dakshineshwar. With a lot of hesitation, he showed it to the Master. To all our surprise and delight, the Master said: "This represents a high Yogic state. This form will be worshipped in every house as time goes on."
The Master went into ecstasy on seeing the photo. He touched the photo to his head several times. He remarked

later: "This photo is very nicely taken. The mood is very high – fully merged in Him. Here God is fully depicted in His own nature."

A copy of this photograph, approved and blessed by him, is what I always carry with me.

I had to leave Naren alone as I went for a patrol of all the tracks. Everything was fine. I came back shortly after, and waited for Naren to continue his story.

****

ASHRAM BY THE RIVER

Soft bells and chants preface the dawn of day,
The Prayer Hall awaits; lamps light the way,
Cymbals, flutes and drums and the morning hymns
Greet the inmates as they arrive to pray.

Long ere the eastern firmament turns red,
The Guru and disciples leave their bed,
Argue great questions morning, noon and night,
Some aloud, more by deep silences said.

The temple bells herald the break of dawn,
Flowers for the Gods from the sacred lawn
Are handed over to the priests, and they
Strive piously their idols to adorn.

The sun beats down, but from the south a breeze
Cools the pilgrims camping under the trees,
Morning worships pause with the bells of noon,
Resume from dusk till night without surcease.

Eternally a song the river sings,
And to the ears a lulling murmur brings,
The river-boats with sails flit to and fro
Like swarms of butterflies with colored wings.

Bells, conches, cymbals, hymns with sound and show,
Attract the human river's ebb and flow,
The ashram's free souls rise above this din,
And ever crave the Absolute to know.

DEEPTI SHASHIDHAR

CHAPTER 11

LIFE WITH THE MASTER

From 1884 onwards (said Naren) I almost lived at Dakshineshwar. By the grace of the Divine Mother, we won a long-dragging court case. There were awards with costs. We had enough money to live fairly comfortably. The days of pinching money and rationing food were over. I could leave my lowly translator's job. Now, I truly became a disciple of the Master.

What a heaven Dakshineshwar was! Whenever I feel homesick, it is due to the memories of Dakshineshwar. While the temple bells woke up the faithful, we devotees would cluster around the Master's bed. When he woke up, he would sing his morning prayer. There would be a short break for ablutions. We would then reassemble on the verandah by the Ganga. The Master would start a discussion on any subject. With changing topics, this discussion would go on till noon. At noon, the Master took his meal. Then he rested for a short while. Once he got up, the conversations would begin again till dark. The temple lamplighter lit the lamps. Conches and temple bells announced the evening service. Our discussions continued under the full moon.

What discussions they were! There was no harping on doctrine. Doctrine was immaterial. The Master used all methods to instruct us. His ecstasies, his rich parables, and laughing stories highlighted the comedy of life for what it was. At the same time all of us were given complete liberty to express ourselves.

He would slyly start an argument between the disciples. When the argument reached screaming pitch, he would throw in a quiet remark. This would be full of spiritual wisdom and common-sense. The argument would stop. The disciples would ruminate on what he had said. The end result was deeply-rooted enlightenment. The Master took care to see that all the disciples participated and were ennobled by such holy discussions. He never preached. A word, a smile and a touch gave men what they were looking for.

There was one more thing that he did. I did not understand it then. He postulated some particularly difficult concepts of the Vedanta. Then he would tell me, "Naren, explain to me what I taught to all of you. Mind, it should be in language, and words, which even a yokel can understand."

I thought this was to keep me on my toes. Initially I found it difficult to convert the complex thoughts into simple words. As we went on, I found I could easily make the most difficult concepts understandable. I could repeat them in simple terms. Some of these simple terms still did not make the listeners understand my meaning. My Master asked me to explain through examples from daily life.

Some of these innovations came out very well. My Master was delighted. In some cases he went into ecstasy. Much later I understood that the Master was training me to deal with the masses. Very much later, I divined that he had started the process of passing on the torch.

He felt that two things hampered his drive to transfer all his knowledge to us. The first were his ecstasies. They were taking up the time he might have given to us. He prayed to Mother Kali: "O Mother, stop me from enjoying these ecstasies. Let me stay more in my normal state. Then I can do your bidding. I can serve the people better."

The second problem was the flood of visitors to see him. There were two types. Most visitors just wanted to see the holy man and salute him. This was not a problem. Our discussions would go on and the visitors would also move on. The second type of visitor was more troublesome. These were people who had some knowledge of the scriptures. Many were steeped only in the epics and stories of God. These would ask him questions which were bothering them. The process of answering them satisfactorily drained my Master.

He never turned anyone away. He listened to them patiently, told them parables and sent them away smiling. However, he complained to his Mother like a child: "Why do you bring so many people here? My health is gone. Why don't You take care of them Yourself?"

The beautiful Mother just smiled enigmatically.

In 1884, a death saddened him. His great friend, Keshab Chandra Sen, died in January. My Master had foreseen the death. A few days before, his eyes filled with tears when someone referred to Keshab. He said: "The Rose Tree is to be transplanted. The Gardener wants it to produce beautiful roses."
This had sounded mystical to us. We did not pursue the matter. Shortly after, Keshab died, and we understood what he had meant. The Master said sadly of Keshab's death: "Half of me has perished."

In the latter half of 1884, my Master's health worsened. It started when he dislocated his left arm while in a trance. It was very painful. In April 1885, his throat became inflamed. Constant talking had overstrained his throat. His ecstasies had flooded his throat with blood. Doctors forbade both speech and ecstasy. He could not follow their advice due to his compulsions. The disease grew worse. He could not eat solid food. But not for a moment did he neglect the flood of visitors. They came to see him day and night.

Then one night the Master had hemorrhage of the throat. Doctors diagnosed cancer. A specialist confirmed the diagnosis. The Master grew worse. A doctor we trusted implicitly told us: "The Master must be shifted from the city of Calcutta. He should take rest in the countryside."

We agreed. It would stop the flood of visitors. There were beautiful gardens in Cossipore, in the suburbs. In the midst of these gardens was a house. It was far away from the din and bustle of Dakshineshwar. We shifted the Master to that house in Cossipore in December 1885. The Master was lodged upstairs. The Holy Mother, Sharada Devi, lived in a room on the ground floor. Twelve of us looked after him round the clock. We never left him alone.

All the other disciples nominated me to direct their activities and prayers. All of us prayed constantly for the Master's recovery. We begged him to join us in our prayers. He merely smiled. One day, a Pandit or a scholar and teacher visited us. He believed devoutly in the Master. In front of us, he told the Master: "Even the scriptures have given permission for saints like you. You can certainly cure yourself by an effort of will."
My Master said: "My mind has been given to God once and for all. How can I ask God to give it back?"

We would not take no for an answer. Why did he not wish to be restored to health? "Do you think," he enquired, "that my sufferings are voluntary? I definitely wish to recover, but that depends on the Mother."
We all said: "Then pray to her."
"It is easy for you to say. I cannot say the words. Naren, have you forgotten your own case?"
Desperately I said, "But you are the beloved child of the Mother! She will certainly listen to you. She cannot deny you what you ask."

The Master listened gravely, then smiled sweetly: "All right. I will try. The rest is the Mother's will."
We left him alone for several hours. When we returned, we asked him what the Mother had said. The Master said: "I said to her, 'Mother, I can eat nothing because of my illness. Make it possible for me to eat a little.'
The Mother pointed to all of you, and said: 'What! Can you not eat through all these mouths?'
I was so ashamed that I could not utter anything more."
We could say nothing against the Mother's words. Some days later he told us: "My teaching is almost finished. I cannot instruct people any longer. The world is filled with the Lord. So who can I teach?"

My Master had never hidden the fact that he regarded me as his heir. One day, he said to me: "I leave these young people in your charge. Busy yourself in developing their spirituality."
We were to lead a monastic life. He introduced us to that life by ordering us to beg. We were not to differentiate on the basis of caste, creed, race or religion. We had to beg our food from door to door. At the end of March 1886, he gave us monastic initiation. He made us all wear saffron robes. We were all monks from that day on.

Disciples at Alambazar Math
Adbhutananda, Yogananda, Abhedananda, Trigunatita, Turiyanananda, Nirmalananda, and Niranjanada
Sitting: Subodhananda, Brahmananda, and Akhandananda

Trigunatitananda, Shivananda, Vivekananda, Turiyananda, Brahmananda And Sadananda

Whenever a Master is born, it is ordained that some special devotees be also born at or around that period.

These gravitate to the Master at the right time. They become the innermost circle of the Master's devotees. Their mission is to complement the work of the Master and keep his teachings alive. The Master recognized six disciples as specially meant for him. He called them Ishwarakotis. I was one of them. Out of the other five, some had had to marry early to fulfill family circumstances. But their spiritual greatness was unquestionable. These are my spiritual brothers. I trust them implicitly.

One day, I was meditating as usual. My Master was in an adjacent room. It appeared to me as if my meditation was becoming more and more intense. Suddenly, without warning a light shone in the back of my head. It expanded gradually, and then suddenly burst. I felt myself entering the portals of Nirvikalpa Samadhi. The experience I cannot describe, except that it gave immense bliss. After a long time I returned to myself, and what a return! I felt that I had only a face, but no body! I cried out repeatedly: "Where is my body?"

The other disciples were terrified. They rushed to the Master. He listened to them with a smile, and then laughed: "Very well. Let the rascal stay like that for some time. He has worried me long enough."
My Master helped me to come slowly down to the earthly plane. The lasting feeling was one of infinite peace. After recovering, I came to the Master. He said: "Naren, the Mother has shown you everything. Now this experience shall remain locked to you. I shall keep the key. After you

have finished the Mother's work, you will experience this treasure again."

Some time later, the memory of this state began to haunt me again. I resisted as long as I could. When it became unbearable, I approached the Master. I begged him to grant me the experience again. For the first time, and the last time, the Master was furious with me. He literally shouted at me: "Shame on you! I always thought of you as a great Banyan tree. I imagined you giving shelter to thousands of tired souls! Instead, what a selfish thing you are seeking? You want your own well-being? Shame!"

I was amazed at this reaction, and begged his pardon. He cooled down quickly and said: "Don't hanker after these things, my child. Samadhi is just a one-sided ideal. You must be all-sided. You must enjoy the Lord in all ways. Do you understand what I mean?"
I thought about his statement and said: "There must be both contemplation and action. The highest knowledge must be converted into the highest service of mankind. Am I correct, Master?"
The Master laughed happily and said: "Naren, you always understand me so well."
I had felt humiliated at his angry words. But I had to admit that his severity was justified. He was preparing me for some Mission. Here I was, hankering after an experience useful only to myself!

My Master was becoming more and more detached. The fatal disease he suffered from did not erase the loving and kindly smile from his face at any time. One day, he called me to his bedside. He requested all the other devotees to leave us alone. After they left, he asked me to bolt the door. He looked at me and passed into ecstasy. It was so powerful that it enveloped me in itself. I passed into a semi-conscious state. Coming back from that state, I saw tears in my Master's eyes. He said to me: "Naren, I have transferred all my powers to you. I have given you my all. By these powers, you will do immense good in the world. You will accomplish wonders."
I felt that he and I were one. Wherever I was, he would always be with me!

On the afternoon of Sunday, August 15, 1886, he was strong enough to talk to us for two hours. At nightfall, he became unconscious, and so still that we thought he was dead. By midnight, he stirred and gained consciousness. We propped him up with pillows into a sitting position. He was supported by Ramakrishnananda, who also fanned him. I was rubbing his feet. My Master started talking to me in a low voice, repeating: "Naren, take care of these boys!" a number of times. Then suddenly, in ringing tones, he cried out three times: "Ma Kali, Ma Kali, Ma Kali!"
He then asked to lie down.

At One o'clock, there was a low sound in his throat. He fell towards one side. The doctor felt his pulse and said that it had stopped. It occurred to us that the Master was in

Samadhi. Hardly had the thought occurred, a thrill passed through the Master's body. There was a serene smile on his face. His eyes were focused on the tip of his nose. His hair stood on end. These were all signs that the Master has entered into the highest plane of Maha Samadhi. He would never return to the earthly plane again.

On the evening of August 16, 1886, all of us, his disciples, carried him to the place of cremation. After the cremation, the ashes were collected in an urn and sealed. The urn is being guarded by my brother monks. One day, by God's grace, we shall build a permanent Math or Monastery where we will intern my Master's Relics! That will be his final resting home.

Naren sat silent on the bench, looking into the distance. I was silent too, and then got up. I left him to his thoughts. I patrolled the tracks once more, assuring myself that everything was o.k. I checked my watch. The time was slightly past 2 am! Naren had held me spell-bound for nearly four hours!

Sitting with him, there seemed no unreality to what he said. When I was alone, the whole tale seemed unreal and strange. To my American way of thinking, and my own unspiritual way of life, the whole tale seemed incredible. But Naren's sincerity was apparent. His emotions and his straight-talking were absolutely genuine. And, I had to admit, it was one heck of a tale!

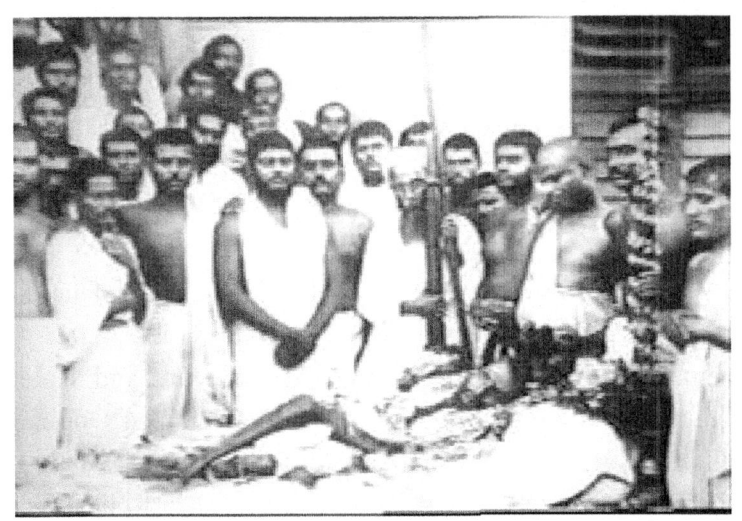

PASSING AWAY OF SHRI RAMAKRISHNA

****

WANDER - THIRST

BEYOND *the East the sunrise, beyond the West the sea,*
And East and West the wander-thirst that will not let me be;
It works in me like madness, dear, to bid me say good-bye;
For the seas call, and the stars call, and oh! the call of the sky.

I know not where the white road runs, nor what the blue hills are;
But a man can have the sun for a friend, and for his guide a star;
And there's no end of voyaging when once the voice is heard,
For the rivers call, and the roads call, and oh! the call of the bird!

Yonder the long horizon lies, and there by night and day

The old ships draw to home again, the young ships sail away;
And come I may, but go I must, and, if men ask you why,
You may put the blame on the stars and the sun and the white road and the sky.

GERALD GOULD

CHAPTER 12

THE WANDERING

After finishing my rounds, I went back and sat on the bench next to Naren. He had got over his pensiveness and he smiled at me. Not wanting him to stop at that point, I asked him: "Naren, your Master died in 1886. About seven years later you are here in Chicago. I'm very curious to know what happened in between."
"Jock, again it's a long story. Let me try to give you the highlights," said Naren.

After the death of the Master (said Naren), we were all shattered, especially the Holy Mother. Having become a widow, she wanted to remove all her ornaments. The Master appeared before her and said to her: "Sharada, there is no need for you to remove your ornaments. I am always with you. I have only passed from one room to another."
This happened to her on two more occasions. When she told us this, our minds returned to the highest plane. Our dear Master would never leave us alone!

We disciples did not want to return to worldly affairs. The married devotees encouraged us. With their help, we rented a half-ruined house at Baranagore, near the Ganga. This was the first monastery or Math. Unanimously, I was made the first Head. It was now up to me to create a body of permanent monks. These would be dedicated to the service of mankind.

OLD BARANAGORE MATH

One evening, on Christmas Eve in 1886, all of us assembled at a place called Antpur. We assembled in a house which belonged to a disciple's mother. At night, we moved out into the field. With huge logs of wood we kindled a bonfire. The star-spangled night sky and the silence made us meditate. I have a passionate regard for Christ. I started to tell them the story of Lord Jesus. The parallel of Jesus, the Master, and the disciples struck us immediately!

Suddenly, the Master seemed to enter into me. I made an impassioned appeal to my brothers. I asked them all to become Christs, to renounce the world, and realize God. I told the brothers: "Our Master was like this Fire. Each of us should become a Firebrand to carry out the Master's mission! We should light the fires of Vedanta all over the world!"

When I finished, all the brothers rose to their feet. One by one, they took the oath to become a monk. The first task was accomplished. In hindsight, I see that each one of us represented one aspect of the Master. Get us together, and the Master was present!

DISCIPLES AT BARANAGORE MATH
(STANDING) SHIVANANDA, RAMAKRISHNANDA, VIVEKANANDA, PREMANANDA, D.MAJUMDAR, SHRI M, TRIGUNATITA, AND H.MUSTAFI
(SITTING) NIRANJANANDA, SARADANANDA, BRAHMANANDA AND ABHEDANANDA

A plan of action evolved. One brother, Ramakrishnananda, would remain in the Math as the guardian of the Relics.

SWAMI RAMAKRISHNANDA

The others would wander, one after the other, as mendicant monks. When one came back to the Math to rest, another would set out. Along with that, I decided that all of us must be on the same wave-length in religious thought. We went through the great philosophical books. The monks became aware of the great religious problems. They realized that the Truth was not limited to any particular school or race. All of this took two years. In 1888, the wanderlust came upon me.

It was only God who would explain to me what my Mission was. I set out in search of God. More as a beggar, I went to Kashi, Ayodhya, Lucknow, Agra, Vrindavan and the Himalayan Mountains. Each location was a seat of either religion or culture. I returned to the Math only when I fell ill. I had new experiences to relate to my brothers. In spite of their diversity, all the people of India whom I had met were spiritually united. This was true of Aryans, Moghuls, Christians and Dravidians.

I also told them of the famous saint of Ghazipur, Pavahari Baba. I had been very impressed by him. I wanted to learn Hatha Yoga from him. I was ready even to be initiated by him. But the sudden vision of my Master, with a sad face, on the eve of the initiation made me give up the idea. The brothers were horrified. They saw this readiness on my part to be initiated as a loss of faith in the Master. I convinced them that what is good is good, no matter what the source.

Again, in 1890, the Holy Mother gave me permission and blessings for a long journey. First, I went into the Himalayas for a religious retreat. Only God saved me from the ordeals of hunger and illness. Then, in 1891, from Delhi I traveled to the west, the south-west and the southernmost tip of India. Every day broadened my mind, and not only about religion. I saw that I had developed intellectual intolerance. Our way was the only right way, I had thought. This journey stripped me of my prejudices one by one. Let me give you an example.

Till now, I had considered monogamy the only right thing. Anything else was immoral! In the Himalayan Mountains, I found polyandry prevalent. In one family that hosted me, six brothers shared the same wife! Not only that, the wife was carrying her youngest husband, a toddler, in her arms! This repulsed me. I tried to explain the sanctity of monogamy. The family was scandalized! "This is sheer selfishness!" they said, "To keep one woman all to oneself?

Will only one man cultivate and enjoy the land which is in her name? What will happen to his brothers?"

They made me realize that the system was the only feasible one due to paucity of land. I meditated on this aspect later, and learnt two lessons. The first lesson was that virtue is relative. It is not black or white; I must think in terms of grey. The second lesson was that when you judge a race, take into account the standards, and problems, of that race in that age.

From the hills I traveled in the west to the state of Alwar. It was ruled by a Maharaja, Mangal Singh. I was the guest of a retired engineer at his bungalow. Some time later, the Chief Minister or Dewan of Alwar, Major Ramachandra, invited me to his bungalow. We had long discussions on various topics. The Dewan then said to me: "Swamiji, I wish you would have an interaction with our Maharaja Mangal Singh. It would be a good influence on him."
I asked: "Why, what is the matter with him?
The Dewan replied: "Between you and me, the Maharaja has become almost an Englishman in thought and actions."
"What does that mean? Please be clear."
With a lot of hesitation, the Dewan said: "This is a great kingdom. It requires a dedicated ruler. The Maharaja spends all his time with Englishmen and shooting trips."
I told the Dewan that I understood the problem. I would try to help if the occasion arose. The Dewan wrote about me to the Maharaja.

Soon, I was told that the Maharaja was coming to the Dewan's house. The Dewan invited me there. The Maharaja came to the house shortly after. He bowed to me, and urged me to remain seated. I was happy to see that he followed the Hindu tradition. Even a King must show respect to a monk! Maharaja Mangal Singh was tall, very fit and quite handsome. He also had a sardonic look about him.

The preliminary small talk about health and welfare was completed. Then the Maharaja fired the first salvo: "Swamiji, I hear that you are a great scholar. You are young and strong. You can earn a handsome sum every month. Why do you beg?"

MAHARAJA MANGAL SINGH, ALWAR

I copied his bantering tone and said: "Maharaj, you have a great kingdom to rule. Why do you neglect your duties to the state? Why do you waste your time with Englishmen and wild-game shooting?"

There were gasps and sharply drawn breaths from the audience. The King, however, seemed calm. He thought for a while and then said evenly: "No doubt because I want to."

I smiled and said: "What's sauce for the goose is sauce for the gander, your Highness. I, too, do what I want to do!"

For a while he was quiet. Then his sardonic smile returned, and he said: "Swamiji, I have no faith in idol worship. What is going to be my fate?"

I asked: "Why do you not like idol worship?"

The King said: "I really cannot worship wood, earth, stone or metal like other people. Will I be worse off in my next life?"

I said, "That I cannot say. A man should only believe in what he has faith in."

I saw the Dewan's crestfallen face. I continued: "I suppose you are strong enough to follow your own principles?"

"I think so. I hope so. Why, what do you mean?" asked the King.

One of his portraits was hanging on the wall. I pointed to it. I asked that it may be handed to me. I held it in my hands, and then laid it on the ground. This was sacrilege enough! The audience murmured its objections. They literally trembled at my next words. I told the Dewan and the assembled audience: "Please spit on this portrait! Any one of you may do so!"

There was pin-drop silence. The Dewan was thunderstruck. The people glanced at the Maharaja, at me and back at the Maharaja. I was implacable. I insisted: "Spit on it, I say! Spit on it."
The Maharaja's smile had vanished. His forehead was creased in a frown. His brows were contracted. In a panic, the Dewan cried out: "Swamiji, what are you saying? How can anyone do such a thing? This is a portrait of our Maharaja!"
"What is your objection? It is only a piece of paper, enclosed in glass and wood. Is the Maharaja physically present in it?"
The Dewan had, by now, caught the drift of my actions. Quite fluently he said: "By doing what you say, I shall be insulting my master?"
'In what way will you insult him?" I demanded.
"Swamiji, this portrait represents my master. I see him in it. I treat it with the same respect that I would show my master."

I looked at the Maharaja. "Do you see the paradox, your Highness? This image is not you. But still it is you. Do you agree?"
The Maharaja nodded. I continued: "The same thing holds good for idol worshippers. They see God in the idol. Have

you ever heard any devotee praying: 'O stone, I worship you, O metal, be merciful to me?'"

"No, I have not," said the Maharaja, "I had never looked at idol-worship in this light."

"There is only one Supreme Spirit. People worship Him according to their understanding and spiritual level. As man has got a form, it is natural for him to imagine God with form. It is logical for man to love and to be devoted to such a God with form. Hence you have the symbolic idols. As he advances, man starts to worship the God without form."

Mangal Singh thought for some time on this matter. Then he said: "I had not understood the symbolism of idol-worship. You have opened my eyes. What will be my fate for such ignorance? Will God have mercy on me?"

I said: "Maharaj, God is ever-merciful. Pray to Him."

I stayed for seven weeks at Alwar with the Dewan. I had the satisfaction of learning from him that the Maharaja had changed considerably for the better. Both the Dewan and the Maharani or Queen, were extremely happy to see him concentrate on ruling the state.

I wandered on to the hill station of Mount Abu. Here, on June 4, 1891, at the Summer Palace I met a special person. He was to be my dearest friend, my greatest benefactor and well-wisher. He was Raja Ajit Singh, of the princely state of Khetri. Days of discussion showed me how deeply sincere he was. The upshot of this was the deepest friendship between us. The Raja invited me to his state. It took us nearly a fortnight to reach Khetri. At Khetri, I stayed for nearly three months. It was a delightful period. There were lots of discussions on the scriptures. The ancient books in the library were a delight to read. I also taught people. And it was here that I was taught a lesson in humility by a most unlikely teacher!

One evening, Raja Ajit Singh arranged a special program for me. I came to the venue slightly before the appointed time. A number of musicians were tuning their instruments at the center of the hall. They saluted me, and continued their work. The Raja and the guests arrived shortly.

RAJA AJIT SINGH, KHETRI

I had expected a musical evening. I was totally unprepared for the entry of a lithe, slim girl. She had anklets on her feet. On her arms and wrists she had bracelets and bangles. She wore jewelry all over her person. She wore a Moghul sort of dress, with a veil over her head and face. She stood before the musicians at the center of the room. They started the music. The girl whirled on her feet into a dance pose. This was a dance-girl! She must be low-born, ill-bred and totally immoral! With scorn and anger, I stood up to leave the hall.

The musicians saw me and stopped the music. The girl stopped in mid-whirl, confused. The Raja got up, hurried to my side, and said: "Swamiji, what is the matter?" I said: "Maharaj, I did not expect a dance-girl. Such entertainment repels me. I am going to my room. I request you and the other guests to continue watching the performance."

As I moved away, the Raja followed me, and caught my hands. "Swamiji," he said, "This is no cheap entertainment. I will never do anything to demean your dignity. This was arranged especially for you. Please stay, I beg of you! Please remain."
His appeal moved me. I was in half a mind.

Then the dancer herself ran trippingly up to me. Her anklets and bracelets jangled and tinkled. She bowed before me. She said, in Hindi, in a low, sweet tone: "Brother, please stay and grace this humble performance of your sister!"
Her face was sad. There were tears in her eyes. I could not deny this appeal from a sister. I bowed silently to her, went

back to my seat, and sat down. The Raja signaled that the performance should proceed.

The girl sat down in the center of the musicians, facing us. The music struck up. After a while the girl started to sing in a melodious voice. She sang a devotional song written by the great blind poet-saint, Soordas. The purport of the song was like this:

Oh Lord, do not look upon my evil qualities. You are same-sighted.
A piece of iron may be an idol in a temple, another piece a butcher's knife.
When they touch the Philosopher's stone, both become gold!
A drop of water is in the sacred Jamuna River,
Another drop is in a foul ditch by the roadside,
But when they fall into the Ganga, both alike become holy!
So Lord, look not upon my evil qualities.

I was completely overwhelmed. Tears ran from my eyes down my cheeks as the song continued. The humble song affected me for life.

What was wrong with me? I was a monk. I should remain neutral to everything, totally unaffected by anything. Then how could I have held, and expressed, a judgment against anybody? And what was the object of my scorn? A poor, helpless female, who had been forced by circumstances into her trade! She was as much Brahman as

I was. What if she had been my own sister? Would I have had the same scorn for her?

A thousand emotions racked my mind. It was a supreme lesson in humility. A dance-girl had taught me anew that we are all equal in the eyes of God! My remaining prejudices vanished. I vowed upon my Master that I would never commit such a sin again. It took a long time for me to regain my equilibrium. After the concert was over, I went up to the dance-girl. I folded my hands to her and said: "Mother, forgive me. I am guilty of the great fault of trying to find fault in you."

A few days later, the Raja looked sad and downcast. I kept silent for some time. Then I asked him what the matter was. He replied, with a sigh, that it was a personal matter. I said: "Your Highness, sorrow is lessened only by sharing it. Consider me your friend, your brother. God willing, I may be able to help you."
He was silent for a moment. Then he said: "Swamiji, come with me, please."

He led me into the inner rooms of the palace. He took me to the women's quarters, where his wife, the Rani, resided. It was a mark of the deepest respect and trust. I was in an area where no outsider, and definitely not a male, is allowed. He seated me in a large room and went out. Shortly after, he re-entered the room. With him was his

Queen. She bowed to me with folded hands, and touched my feet. Both sat in front of me.

The Raja then said: "Swamiji, my wife and I have a secret sorrow. God has given us everything, excepting one thing. Till now, we have not been blessed with a son and heir."
The Rani added: "We do not know why God is so unkind to us."
I sympathized with them and said: "There is a time and a place for every event. Why be disappointed? You are a very God-fearing couple. You have done much for the welfare of your subjects. You have earned their blessings. I am sure that your prayers will be answered by God soon."

The Raja said: "Swamiji, we have prayed long and hard. I am glad to hear from you that my subjects have also blessed us. Only one thing is lacking. My wife and I request you to bless us. If you will do so, I am sure that our prayers will be answered soon."
I was much moved by their anxious longing. I meditated for a while. I prayed silently to my Master and the Divine Mother. I went into a super-conscious state, and blessed the royal couple. The Raja and Rani were very happy and cheerful after this.

****

THE RUBAIYAT OF OMAR KHAYYAM

We are no other than a moving row
Of visionary Shapes that come and go
Round with this Sun-illumin'd Lantern held
In Midnight by the Master of the Show;

Impotent Pieces of the Game he plays
Upon this Chequer-board of Nights and Days;
Hither and thither moves, and mates and slays;
And one by one back in the Closet lays.

The Moving Finger writes; and having writ,
Moves on; nor all your Piety nor Wit
Shall lure it back to cancel half a Line,
Nor all your Tears wash out a Word of it.

Ah Love! Could you and I with fate conspire
To grasp this sorry Scheme of Things entire,
Would not we shatter it to bits – and then
Re-mould it nearer to the Heart's Desire?

EDWARD FITZGERALD

CHAPTER 13

THE DECISION

The pleasant days at Khetri came to an end in October (continued Naren). I bade goodbye to Raja Ajit Singh. I did not know whether I would ever meet him again. My wanderings started anew. I moved on towards western India. The turning point for me came when I stayed with a family of untouchable sweepers. Their spirituality uplifted me, but their misery choked me. I asked myself: "What have we so-called men of God ever done for the masses?"
My Master's rough words came to my mind: "Religion is not for empty bellies!"

The burning question still remained; how could I help the masses? Suddenly, the thought flashed into my mind. I must appeal to the whole world! The rich culture and civilization of India must not meet the fate of ancient Egypt and Mesopotamia. At the end of 1891, an appeal from India to Europe and America began to take shape in my mind. I was traveling in Gujarat State then.

As if in response, I began to get positive signals. At Porbandar, an orthodox Pandit told me: "Your thoughts will be better understood in the West. Go to the West, take it by storm, and then return in triumph!"
This, from a person who normally held that crossing the seven seas makes you forever unclean and an outcast!

In the early autumn of 1892, at Khandwa in the Central Provinces, I heard, for the first time, about a Parliament of Religions. It was to be held in America, at Chicago, in 1893. My first thought was to take part in it.

The first person I broached the subject with was the Maharaja of Mysore, at Bangalore, in October 1892. I would spread the gospel of the Vedanta in the West. In return, the West would give me the means to improve the material conditions in India. The Maharaja immediately promised to give me the money to meet my traveling and other expenses. I refused for the present. I did agree, however, to have a phonographic record of my voice made. It is in the Maharaja's Palace.

MAHARAJA CHAMARAJA WADIYAR X, MYSORE

The Maharaja sent me to meet his Dewan, Sheshadri Iyer, at that heaven on earth, Mysore. I stayed for a week at Mysore at Niranjan Math, as a guest of the Dewan. We discoursed on many religious matters.

DEWAN K.SHESHADRI IYER, MYSORE

By the end of 1892, my mind was more or less made up. I was then in Kanya Kumari, the Land's End of India, the southernmost tip. Some distance in the sea was a large group of rocks. Having no money to pay the boatmen, I swam the distance, unmindful of the shark-infested sea, and reached the main rock. This was huge in size, like a platform. It could easily house three or four temples. There, on the rock, I meditated for three days. A blaze of energy submerged me. I felt numerous powers in me. I would blaze forth and revolutionize the world! I had seen the path I was to follow. I swam back to the landmass of India.

LAND'S END ROCKS, KANYAKUMARI

In the first weeks of 1893, at the Madras Presidency, I publicly proclaimed my wish to undertake a mission to the West. The response was electric! I was besieged by visitors in this intellectual city. I founded my first group of devoted disciples there. Everyone urged me to go to Chicago and represent Hinduism in the Parliament of Religions. My mind was also made up. But I required a direct command from a Divine Source to confirm my decision.

One night I had a dream. My Master walked from the seashore into the sea. He beckoned to me to follow him. The vision convinced me. Several nights later, my Master told me in a dream: "Go across the sea. Know that this conference is meant for you. Do not worry. People will be amazed hearing your speech."

This was a Divine command. I got ready to go to Chicago. But I still required the Holy Mother's permission and blessings. I wrote to Swami Saradananda at Calcutta. I

told him about the dreams. I requested him to get the Holy Mother's opinion. Back came the reply in a short while. The Holy Mother had had the same dream. She had said: "Please tell Naren that he should go to the West."
I was overjoyed when I received the Holy Mother's approval and blessings!

The Divine path was clear, but the material path presented obstacles. As usual, money remained the greatest problem. The Raja of Ramnad had promised ten thousand rupees for the trip. I did not accept it immediately. Later, the Raja flatly refused, saying: "I am unable to give any money for this purpose."

My hopes were dashed to the ground! I surrendered to the will of the Mother. I was going on behalf of the people and the poor. I asked my disciples to appeal to the middle classes for subscriptions. A heroic door to door campaign raised four thousand rupees. The disciples reserved a Second Class berth on the Pacific Orient Steamer "Peninsular." The balance money came to one hundred and seventy nine British Pounds, for safekeeping. I made several further arrangements for the journey.

RAJA BHASKARA SETHUPATHY, RAMNAD

Suddenly, one day, Munshi Jagmohanlal, Private Secretary to the Raja Ajit Singh of Khetri, came before me. I was very surprised to meet him. I asked him his reason for coming to Madras. His reply was simple: "To meet you, Swamiji."

"But why?" I asked him.

"Do you remember that the Raja Sahib had sought your blessings for a particular matter?"

"He sought my blessings for almost all matters. Please be specific."

"In this matter, both Raja Sahib and Rani Sahiba sought your blessings."

Thinking back, I said: "Yes, they requested my blessings for a son and heir."

"Your blessings have borne fruit! I am delighted to inform you that Rajkumar Jai Singh was born to the royal couple on January 26, 1893!"

I was delighted, and said: "Please convey my heartiest congratulations and good wishes to the royal couple, and my blessings to the young prince!"

"That will not do, Swamiji," said Jagmohanlal.

"What do you mean?"

"You will have to convey all those in person. Rajaji wishes to celebrate the event. He requests you to grace the occasion. The celebration will take place when you reach Khetri."

"Jagmohanlalji, I shall be sailing for America on May 31. Where is the time to visit Khetri?"

"Rajaji approves of your visit to the West. He learnt about the raising of funds. He will contribute the balance from his personal account."

"It is not a matter of funds. It is a matter of time."

"Leave off all your worry about the arrangements. Rajaji will himself take care of them. You must come even if for a day. Otherwise Maharaj will be devastated."

"But where is Madras, and where is Khetri? It will be impossible to return to Madras in time."

"Forget Madras, Swamiji! We will book the ticket from Bombay, close to Khetri."

This gave me pause. The idea was reasonable. Raja Ajit Singh was like a brother. I could never ignore his request. I departed for Khetri.

The celebrations at Khetri were a grand affair. I was on as much display as the baby Prince. Delightful Khetri

held me captive for nearly three weeks. It was here that I got my present name. You see, after my initiation, my Master wanted to rename me Kamalakshananda, the Lotus Eyed. I hated this sissified name, but kept quiet. My brother disciples began to pull my Master's leg with straight faces.
"Master, why not Kamalanayanananda?"
"Vaarijakshananda is even better."
"Pankajalochanananda is very suitable."
"Jalajaakshananda is the best."

All were variations of Lotus and Eyes. After some time, my Master caught their drift, and burst out laughing. "You rogues!" he said, "You seem to be describing dance-girls! All right, let Naren choose his own name."
I was not particular about any name. In the north, I called myself Vividishananda, or one desiring to know Brahman. In Madras, for my friend Alasinga Perumal, I was Satchidananda, or the three attributes of Brahman.

In Khetri, one evening I was sitting with Raja Ajit Singh. The topic of my name came up. The Raja said: "The name Vividishananda is difficult to pronounce. It is also not apt for you; your period of desiring to know is over. You should choose a new, simple name."
"What do you suggest?" I asked.
"I think Vivekananda is the best. It is quite common in India. It is easily pronounceable. And it suits your intellect," said the Raja.

What he said made a lot of sense. I agreed immediately. When my Madras devotees were printing visiting cards for me, I told them to print one hundred cards in the name of Swami Vivekananda.

It was time to leave Khetri and proceed to Bombay. The day before my departure I was taken to the women's quarters to bless the Raja, the smiling Rani and the infant Prince Jai Singh. The Raja arranged for Jagmohanlal to accompany me to Bombay. He also gave Jagmohan enough money to meet the balance of my estimated expenditure. He told Jagmohan to get my Second Class steamer ticket converted to First Class to ensure privacy. At Bombay, Jagmohan bought me all the silk robes, turbans and other dress items required for me in America.

S.S. PENINSULAR

Finally, on May 31, 1893, I boarded the steamer 'Peninsular' at Bombay. With Jagmohanlal and Alasinga, I went to the First Class cabin arranged for me. We checked that all my personal belongings had been stored safely there. Then we had dinner with the other passengers, who were Western. After dinner, the bell for departure rang. Jagmohanlal and Alasinga bowed to me and left the ship.

Slowly, the ship pulled out of the harbor. I stood on the deck gazing at my Motherland till it faded from sight. I sent my blessings to those who loved me, and to those whom I loved. My eyes filled with tears as I thought of my beloved Master and the Holy Mother!

****

ULYSSES

I cannot rest from travel: I will drink
Life to the lees: All times I have enjoy'd
Greatly, have suffer'd greatly, both with those
That loved me, and alone.....

For always roaming with a hungry heart
Much have I seen and known; cities of men
And manners, climates, councils, governments,
Myself not least, but honour'd of them all;
And drunk delight of battle with my peers,
Far on the ringing plains of windy Troy.

I am a part of all that I have met;
Yet all experience is an arch wherethro'
Gleams that untravell'd world whose margin fades
For ever and forever when I move.
And this gray spirit yearning in desire

To follow knowledge like a sinking star,
Beyond the utmost bound of human thought.

Come, my friends,
'T is not too late to seek a newer world.
To sail beyond the sunset, and the baths
Of all the western stars, until I die.

We are not now that strength which in old days
Moved earth and heaven, that which we are, we are;
One equal temper of heroic hearts,
Made weak by time and fate, but strong in will
To strive, to seek, to find, and not to yield.

ALFRED, LORD TENNYSON

CHAPTER 14

THE VOYAGE

"And so," said Naren, "that is how I happen to be here in Chicago."

"Oh no, you don't!" I exclaimed, "You can't finish the story of your journey in one sentence! I want to hear the whole story, and the places you visited. But first, let me have a look around."

I started around the station and the tracks again. The time was four a.m. There were still four hours to go before Naren's train was formed. I took half an hour for a detailed look-see. Everything was fine. I returned to Naren's bench.

"Ok," I said, "I'm ready for your story. Please don't leave out anything."

Naren smiled and started his narrative.

As I told you (said Naren), the 'Peninsular' sailed from Bombay on May 31, 1893. The next port for the ship was Colombo, the capital of Ceylon. It halted there for a day. I took the opportunity to visit the city. The city and the scenery are beautiful. The next stop was at Penang, in the Malay Peninsula. Most Malayans follow Islam. In the olden days the area had been infested by pirates. We passed through Sumatra to Singapore. There, I visited the Museum and the Botanical Gardens. It has a beautiful collection of palms.

The next stop was at Hong Kong, where the ship halted for three days. It gave me a very good chance to study the life-style of the Chinese there. I visited Canton too. I saw ladies with bound feet, hobbling rather than walking. People lived on boats, too. Every house was a shop. The inhabitants lived on the top floor. In Canton, an interesting incident occurred.

A few tourists and I wanted to see a monastery. We had a guide. The guide was reluctant to take us inside the monastery. Foreigners were not allowed. As we neared the monastery, three men with heavy clubs came towards us. The guide shouted: "Run, run!"
All the tourists ran away. I caught the guide and asked him what the Chinese phrase for 'Indian Yogi' was. He told me twice or thrice. I let him go, and faced up to the three men. I shouted loudly: "Indian Yogi." They slowed down and came nearer. I pointed to myself and again said loudly: "Indian Yogi."

To my surprise, the attackers dropped their clubs. They fell at my feet and said something in Chinese. I signaled to my guide and asked him what they were saying. He listened to them and said: "They are begging for an amulet or charm to protect them against evil."
I took a piece of paper out of my pocket. I tore it into three equal strips. I wrote 'OM' in Sanskrit on each piece and gave it to them. They touched the paper to their eyes with respect. Then they led me into the monastery.

From Hong Kong we sailed to Kobe, in Japan. It was a whole new world. In order to see the interior, I took the land route from Kobe to Yokohama, where I had to board ship again. I visited three large cities – Osaka, Kyoto and Tokyo. While visiting a match factory, I was pleasantly surprised to meet a fellow-Indian. He was a Parsee gentleman, Jamsetji Tata. He was also going to Chicago on business.

JAMSETJI TATA

Tata imports matches from Japan to India and gets a commission for his labour. While discussing numerous matters with Tata, I said to him: "By importing matches you are giving Japan money. You must be getting only a pittance as commission. Why don't you start a factory in India? You will get a profit, and provide employment to many Indians. The money will also remain in India."

Tata said he was seriously considering the matter. It appears that there are many difficulties in developing an industry in India. However, he was liaising with the

Government to smooth over the difficulties. He looks a very capable and enterprising person. His efforts could well produce good results.

SS EMPRESS OF INDIA

On July 14, we embarked at Yokohama on the SS 'Empress of India.' It was a six thousand ton ship of the Canadian Pacific Line. We were bound for Vancouver, Canada. It became terribly difficult to withstand the Northern Pacific cold. The Captain of the ship was kind enough to provide me with warm apparel from his own wardrobe. It was a quiet and uneventful journey in good weather. The 'Empress of India' docked at Vancouver, British Columbia, Canada, on Tuesday, July 25, at seven pm.

I stayed the night there, and boarded the Canadian Pacific train the following morning. I traveled Second Class through the wonderfully scenic country of Canada. I reached Winnipeg on Friday night. On Saturday afternoon, I caught the Great Northern train, arriving at St. Paul on

Sunday morning at 7.30 am. Half an hour later, I left by the Great Western train. I arrived at Chicago at 10.30 pm on Sunday, July 30. My odyssey was finally over!

Little did I know that my troubles were just starting! The Grand Central Station was absolutely bewildering. Confused, I did not know what to do, where to go, or who to ask. I had too much luggage. The other passengers were very amused at my outlandish dress. The redcaps charged me exorbitantly to take my luggage to the waiting room. There, a hotel agent took me to a good hotel. It had a marbled lobby and elevators. The bellhop deposited my luggage in my room. I sat down and heaved a sigh of relief!

THE 1893 WORLD'S FAIR

The next day I went to the World's Fair. I was an absolute child for twelve days. The power, the genius and the riches of America amazed me! It was totally intoxicating!

Then, almost as an afterthought, I went to the Information Bureau to enquire about the Parliament of Religions. As I have already told you, the information I got drove all the enjoyment out of my head. The Parliament would be held in September. It was too late for registering as a delegate. Registration would not be valid without official references!

That evening, in my room, I took stock of my position. I had heard vaguely of a Parliament of Religions in America sometime this year. None of my friends and well-wishers knew anything more about it. No one was aware of the formalities for registration. I was sure I had been divinely charged to make the attempt. I had just to appear to be given a chance. I did not foresee any difficulties. How simple, how naïve, and how foolish! And now how humanly impossible! It was nothing but a stupid adventure. To have come all the way from India for nothing! I almost broke down.

No use crying over spilt milk. The practical difficulties were that I had over a month to wait, and my purse was dwindling. The hotel charges were very high and everything was very expensive. How to get over these obstacles? I did not know. I surrendered to God's will.

A day later there was a knock on my room door. I opened it to find a very well-dressed couple, a gentleman with his wife. I invited them into the room. They introduced themselves as Mr. and Mrs. Phelps. Mrs. Phelps told me: "I was asked to address you as Swami. Is that the right pronunciation?"

"Yes," I said, "but who told you to do so?"

Mr. Phelps said: "In India, in Madras, there is a Mr. Varada Rao. Do you know him?"

"Of course! He is my very good friend. But how does he know you?"

"We met him at a religious gathering when we visited Madras. Of course, my wife knows him better, as she writes to him regularly."

Mrs. Phelps broke in: "Mr. Varada wrote to me about you. He said that Chicago was a new place for you. You might face problems. He has asked us to look after you till the Parliament of Religions starts."

"That is very good of him," I said, "but will it not cause you trouble?"

"Not at all, Swami. We would be delighted to have you. You might find better company in our house than in this hotel."

This was a godsend! I agreed immediately, checked out of the hotel, and went with them to their home at 1703, Indiana Avenue. The Phelps' belong to the highest Chicago society. They welcomed me warmly to their house. They were right about the company in their house. Many distinguished guests came to the house, and it was nice talking to them. I got new points of view about America and American culture. I utilized the time to cable one of the religious Societies of Madras to register me as an official member of the Society. I also requested proper credentials and a grant of money. Maybe Mr. Phelps could help me to register as a delegate at the proper time.

My stay and my dwindling purse had been taken care of. However, two things bothered me. The first was, how long could I stay in the Phelps' house? At some point, the stay began to embarrass me. The Phelps' have become my very good friends. It was not at all their fault; it just did not look nice for me to linger on and on.

The Phelps' were also busy society people. They were out of the house often enough. At such times, I began to feel like an interloper. The second thing was that the inaction was wearing me down. I am naturally a man of action. I like to do and see new things, to have new experiences. I felt that it was time to move on.

One day, I went to the nearby park and sat on a bench, watching the lake. On a bench nearby two middle-aged persons were talking to each other. I could hear them clearly. They were bemoaning the cost of living and the rising prices. They also felt that Chicago lacked in culture. One of the persons ended their conversation by saying: "You know, George, if you want a low cost life, and all the culture you want, Boston is the place to be in!"

It was like a clarion-call to me! It was like the Mother speaking to me! I got the view endorsed by many sources that Boston was indeed the place I had been looking for. I took the assent of the Phelps to go to Boston for a short time till the Parliament began. I set the date as August 13 for my departure. I sent a telegram to Varada Rao at Madras.

With my typical carelessness, I did not care to know what time the train would depart for Boston. I did what I always did in India. I bid goodbye to the Phelps last night, deciding to sleep in the station waiting room. But rules are different here, and so I am now on this platform, waiting for the Boston train.

Naren completed his narrative. It was now close to six am, and there was some bustle inside the station. The waiting hall also opened. I suggested to Naren that we move to the waiting room. He could freshen up before he boarded the train. I helped him with his baggage. In the waiting hall, I arranged his baggage near a door closest to Track 5. The Boston Express would depart from there. I took care of his baggage while he visited the rest-room. After he came back, I told Naren to relax. I would contact the Train Super, and make arrangements for the Boston journey.

"Thank you for everything, Jock. For being a patient listener throughout the night, for showing sympathy to a lonely stranger, and for all your help."

"You're very welcome," I said, "The pleasure is all mine. Very rarely, or rather not at all, have I meet a person like you at Grand Central."

Naren took out his purse and said: "Please tell me what the coach class fare is. I'll give the money to you."

I said: "Let me first see if I can help you reach Boston without spending any more of your money."

I left Naren there, and went in search of the Train Super. As I was passing the SM's office, I was surprised to see Bill Schumpeter sitting there! He was smoking one of his obnoxious cigars. I went in, and said to him: "Hello, Boss! What's up?"

"I'm up, that's what," he said. "One of my wife's blankety-blank relatives is coming from Utah. Thought I'd come early and wait for him. Now I hear that that train is running God knows how many hours late! How was your shift, anyway?"

I told him everything was fine, no problems anywhere. Then I told him about how one delegate to the Parliament of Religions had run short of money, and was looking for a ride to Boston. Schumpeter snorted and said: "Now we got to give deadbeats a ride at our expense, do we?"

He was curious, however, and asked me the details. I persuaded him to come with me to the waiting hall. I introduced Naren to him. I left them there and went to get some breakfast for Naren

I went to the station deli. I collected bread, jam, butter, doughnuts, and a large hot cup of coffee. When I returned to the waiting hall, I was not surprised to find Schumpeter eating out of Naren's hands! Naren was explaining the finer points of Judaism. The normally loquacious and opinionated Schumpeter was following every word, nodding at intervals. Much more surprising was the sight of Naren puffing away on one of Bill's cigar with evident enjoyment! I gave the eats and coffee to Naren, who said: "So much, Jock? And what do I owe you for these?"
Bill said immediately: "Nothing. Breakfast's on the house. Hope you like it."

We moved out of the waiting hall to let Naren have his breakfast. As we started towards his office, Bill was thoughtful. I joshed him, saying: "What was the deadbeat telling you?"
Bill looked at me obliquely, smiled his crooked smile, and said: "Jock, let's help the guy reach Boston. I'll do what I can."
Schumpeter could do quite a lot if he wanted to, of course!

It was close to 6:45 am. The station was filling up slowly. The Boston Express had backed on to the track. The cleaners were swarming through the coaches. The waiting hall was also filling up with passengers and their baggage. The porters were moving around, looking for customers. The shops in the station hall were opening one by one. The Ticketing and Information counters also opened.

My shift was over, but I wanted to see Naren off to Boston. I did not want any last-minute snags to occur. I came to Naren, and asked him if he had an address book. He took out a small red pocket diary. I asked him to note down my address. He wrote it on a blank page, asking for clarifications regarding some spellings. As a back-up, I gave him my station address also.

Around 7:10 am, Schumpeter sent for me. He told me: "Jock, I've squared it with the Train Conductor about the Indian gentleman. He will travel free to Boston. Help him with his baggage and bring him near Coach 3. I've told the Checker to let you through." "Ok, Boss!" I said.
I went to Naren and helped him up to Coach 3. It was 7:25 am. We sat down on a bench to await the opening of the train doors.

A little later, a slightly built middle-aged gentleman wearing a good suit and a fur cap on his head approached us. He was very fair and of medium height. He was carrying a briefcase. He came up to Naren, joined his palms, bowed low, and said: "Swamiji, do you remember me? My name is Lulloobhoy. We met briefly on board the ship *Empress of India* from Yokohama to Vancouver?"
"Of course I do, Lulloobhoyji. What a pleasure seeing you here. Are you also going to Boston?"

"Yes, Swamiji," said Lulloobhoy. "It will be a short visit to complete some pending business."
Naren introduced me to Lulloobhoy. Lulloobhoy sat down at the end of the bench. The two started a conversation about some matters not known to me. I left them at it. I saw Bill on the platform near the First Class coach, and strolled over towards him.

There was still time for the train to leave. Most of the passengers were standing on the platform talking to each other, or to those who had come to see them off. The porters and coach attendants were arranging their baggage in the overhead baggage racks. Schumpeter was standing near a tall, imperious looking lady. She was giving some instructions to another lady, obviously her subordinate. Schumpeter called me near and told me: "Bring the Indian gentleman over, and stand here."

I went over to Naren. We left Lulloobhoy in charge of the baggage, and went towards Schumpeter. Bill was now talking to the lady. She replied, and Bill turned and pointed towards us. The lady looked at us. Her glance merely flicked over me. When she looked at Naren, she stared at him. With his formal dress, topped by an orange turban, Naren looked regal. Keeping her eyes on Naren, the lady spoke to Bill. He nodded, and beckoned us to come nearer. We did, and heard him say: "This, Mrs. Cabot, is the Indian monk I was telling you about. He is a delegate to the Parliament of Religions. His name is...."

Bill paused and looked at Naren. Naren continued: "My name is Swami Vivekananda, Madam. It is a pleasure to make your acquaintance."

The golden voice obviously flustered the aristocrat. She gave a gulp, and then said: "Likewise, I'm sure. I am Mrs. Cabot from Boston."

Schumpeter spoke up: "Actually, Mrs. Cabot, Mr. V miscalculated the amount of funds he would require for the trip. He has traveled from Bombay to Vancouver via Japan. He has stayed at Chicago for some time. His funds are touching rock-bottom. There is still more than a month before the Parliament takes place. Seeing as he is a foreign guest, we have made arrangements for his travel to Boston in coach class. He requires some help for his stay at Boston."

Mrs. Cabot was once again her patrician self. She said: "Station Master, a delegate to the Parliament of Religions should not travel coach class. I'll provide him with the First Class fare. Let him travel comfortably. You can ask the Conductor to collect the fare from me. Regarding his stay at Boston, he will have to make his own arrangements."

Naren said: "Thank you for your help."

Mrs. Cabot continued: "But, I think I know just the right person who can help you even more."

She looked around at the other passengers. Then she called out: "Kate! Kate Sanborn!"

A lady with a large flowery hat was talking to another gent some distance away. On hearing Mrs. Cabot's call, she turned around and looked at her. Mrs. Cabot beckoned to her and said: "Come here, Kate. Here is something right up your street."
The lady started towards us, smiling. She was obviously on first-name terms with Mrs. Cabot. She asked her: "Morning, Sylvia. What's the matter?"

Mrs. Cabot told her about Naren and his predicament in a few words. Miss Sanborn looked at Naren and smiled warmly at him. She came up to him, and held his forearm. She said: "Oh, my goodness! You're a delegate to the Parliament everyone's been talking and writing about! What an honor to meet you! You have a problem of staying in Boston? You are very welcome to stay with me at my farm, Breezy Meadows. It's a lovely farm! It's very quiet and waiting for someone like you! You must tell me all about….."
She prattled on about this and that. Naren was visibly surprised at first, but then relaxed. Miss Sanborn's warmth, good nature, and bubbly humor were quite transparent. Even the aristocratic Mrs. Cabot smiled at the scene.

At that moment, the Train Conductor called out: "All aboard!"
The passengers started boarding the train. Lulloobhoy and I helped Naren with his luggage. Naren thanked Schumpeter warmly for all his help. Bill said: "The pleasure was all mine, Sir!"

Before getting into his coach with Miss Sanborn, Naren thanked me. He embraced me, and told me he would write to me. He entered the coach and sat down with Miss Sanborn. The Conductor blew the final whistle. The attendants closed the coach doors. The locomotive let out a shrill whistle. The train eased out of the station slowly. Schumpeter and I watched it disappear in the distance.

I never saw Lulloobhoy again; I never even heard of him, or from him, at any time in the future. Bill and I walked towards the offices. Bill sat down to wait for his relative. I went home to rest, and reflect upon all that I had heard during the far reaches of a fantastic night.

****

CHICAGO

Hog Butcher for the World,
Tool Maker, Stacker of Wheat,
Player with Railroads and the Nation's freight handler;
Stormy, husky, brawling,
City of the Big Shoulders;

They tell me you are wicked, and I believe them; for I have seen your painted women under the gas lamps luring the farm boys,
And they tell me you are crooked, and I answer: Yes, it is true I have seen the gunman kill and go free to kill again.
And they tell me you are brutal, and my reply is: On the faces of women and children I have seen the marks of wanton hunger.
And having answered so I turn once more to those who sneer at this my city, and I give them back the sneer and say to them:

Come and show me another city with lifted head singing so proud to be alive and coarse and strong and cunning.
Flinging magnetic curses amid the toll of piling job on job, here is a tall bold slugger set vivid against the little soft cities;
Fierce as a dog with tongue lapping for action, cunning as a savage pitted against the wilderness,

Bareheaded,
Shoveling,
Wrecking,
Planning,
Building, breaking, rebuilding,
Under the smoke, dust all over his mouth, laughing with white teeth,
Under the terrible burden of destiny laughing as a young man laughs,
Laughing even as an ignorant fighter laughs who has never lost a battle,
Bragging and laughing that under his wrist is the pulse, and under his ribs the heart of the people,
Laughing!

Laughing the stormy, husking, brawling laughter of youth; half-naked, sweating, proud to be Hog-butcher, Tool-maker, Stacker of Wheat, Player with Rail roads, and Freight-handler to the Nation.

CARL SANDBURG

CHAPTER 15

THE PREPARATION

Around 1835, Chicago was just a rough and muddy trading post. It belonged to the Indians. The white man purchased this trading post from the Indians. The remuneration – blankets, hatchets, kettles, beads, other knick-knacks and gee-gaws! It still grew very slowly.

Then, the Yankees from New England came and settled there. Working hard, shrewdly and ably, the Yankees turned the trading post into a profitable town standing at the crossroads of commerce. From the East, timber and manufactured goods made their appearance. From the West, grain and livestock poured in. The South sent all its wheat and cotton. All these were sold almost immediately. Millionaires were created overnight!

And then, disaster struck! The Great Chicago Fire of 1871 burnt almost all of Chicago to the ground! Everyone thought that was the end of Chicago. People scoffed at the rebuilding which started almost immediately. They had not reckoned with the burning ambition of its population to start making money again, and fast!

In less than ten years, Chicago became a commercial town again. By 1890, Chicago was a potpourri of greed, cardsharps, gamblers, swindlers, gangsters, vice and corruption. The first skyscrapers, grain elevators, stockyards and packinghouses came up. Immigrant labor poured in. This led to crowded slums. The bestial conditions imposed by industry led to bloody labor riots. Chicago had turned into a crime capital!

Astonishingly, the women of Chicago took the lead in cleaning these Augean Stables! Led by a society lady, Mrs. Potter Palmer, the women jolted the social conscience of the populace. Chicago was to become responsible. It had to have an elite and cultivated society. At the same time, the welfare of the poor was to be of prime importance. With these determined women and their work, Chicago fast became a metropolis.

A University came up; so did a literary club, the Fortnightly. The Art Institute came into existence; so did a Symphony Orchestra. The Auditorium hosted world-famous opera companies. To cap all this, Chicago decided to put on a glittering World's Fair. Along with it, they announced a World's Parliament of Religions. Both of these were extremely successful. Verily, a Phoenix had emerged from the ashes of twenty short years ago!

A few days after Naren left for Boston, I set out to discover what the Parliament of Religions was all about. I had not heard about it, but then I had no interest for such events. I imagined that very few people in Chicago would have heard about it either. I visited the Art Institute; I read the newspapers carefully. Imagine my surprise at the result of this inquiry!

The Parliament of Religions, far from being an obscure conference, was of immense interest to the public! The newspapers were also stoking the fires of sensationalism. There was a lot of controversy involved. Daily, there were great debates in the media about the Parliament.

CHARLES C. BONNEY

The World's Columbian Exposition of 1893 aimed to bring together the results of man's material progress. While hailed as a triumph, there were denunciations, too. Crass materialism was on display, true; but what about the progress of the mind and the world's thoughts? A famous lawyer, Charles Carroll Bonney, made a suggestion. A series of Congresses should be held. They should highlight the greatest themes of interest to mankind like Women's Progress, the Public Press, Medicine, Temperance, Religion etc. Moreover, they should invite representatives from all over the world to participate in them. A Steering Committee was formed, with Bonney as the President of the Committee.

The Parliament of Religions was the most controversial of these Congresses. Some claimed that the Parliament was an attempt to demonstrate the undoubted superiority of Christianity. Others said that it was an honest attempt to promote understanding and goodwill among all seekers of truth. Yet others said that no one was interested in religion at all; the Parliament would flop, and flop badly!

JOHN HENRY BARROWS

The many Christian organizations openly opposed the Parliament; it would only create discord. The

Archbishop of Canterbury said that it was heresy to equate the Christian religion with other religions; it was the One Religion without a second! With all this, 10,000 letters and 40,000 documents were sent out all over the globe. by John Henry Barrows, the Chairman of the Parliament's General Committee. They received a staggering amount of answers, and positive replies. The Press, with its sermons, articles, editorials and debates raised curiosity to fever-pitch.

The Fair managers had decided that the Parliament would function on Sundays also! This was blasphemy! Immediately, the Anglican Churches withdrew. So did Russia and Turkey. Ingersoll threw some more oil on the fires by writing in a newspaper: "No one can miss the paradox. The American Soul is profoundly ready for spiritual food. Alas, this attitude is acceptable neither to the Clergy nor to the bigots!"

All in all, the Parliament of Religions promised to be a humdinger!

A few days after he left Chicago, I got a letter from Naren, from Massachusetts.

Breezy Meadows,
Metcalf, Mass.
20 August, 1893.

My dear Jock,
This is to inform you that I reached Boston safely, in the very good company of Kate Sanborn. I am staying at

her farmhouse. I am very well, and I hope the same is the case with you.

We reached Boston on the evening of the 13th, and decided to stay there for four days, as Kate had some work to finish before going on to her farm at Metcalf. She put me up in a comfortable hotel in the heart of the city. After resting for the night, I decided to explore the city next morning on my own. It was a very mixed experience.

On the 14th, while loafing around, I saw a building with a sign saying "The Ramabai Circle." The Indian name roused my curiosity. There seemed to be something going on inside. I walked in, and found a meeting in progress. There were only American ladies there, and I found them discussing India! They saw me, and when they learnt I was an Indian monk, they asked me to speak about India. I agreed, and gave a lecture lasting one hour, on the "Women In India," which was well received. There were many questions. Later I learnt that Ramabai was a social reformer, working for the welfare of child-widows in India. Jock, I also realized that it was my first lecture in America!

The next day, I had a bad experience. Around noon, while walking around, I suddenly heard a noise behind me. Looking back, I found a large group of people following me. They started shouting at me. I walked faster, but they kept up with me. Suddenly, I felt a brick or stone hit my shoulder! I ran as fast as I could, and ducked into a dark alley. The mob rushed past. I ventured out cautiously, and hurried back to my hotel. I have not reported this incident to Kate Sanborn.

I think it was my mistake. I was wearing my formal outfit, and the colours seem to have excited the crowd. I took care to wear my normal dress, with the fur cap, for the next two days. I explored Boston without any difficulties.

It seems that Divine Providence has pushed me into the house of my mother! And what a lovable mother Kate Sanborn is! She is fifty years old. All the adjectives in the world cannot describe her personality, or her giving nature.

KATHERINE ABBOTT SANBORN

Her house was previously an old abandoned barn. Kate purchased it, and restored it. She has named it 'Breezy

Meadows.' Breezy it certainly is, too cold for my thin blood even in August! But what a peaceful abode it is! The house is a rambling comfortable barn. The roof is covered with creepers. The natural beauty of the place is astonishing. My sincere thanks to Station Master Schumpeter, and you, for helping me reach this place.

About Kate Sanborn (she despises all prefixes). She is a lecturer and authoress, and very energetic. She has a very good sense of humor. Her quick, sharp (though good-natured) repartee is well known. She is very observant, and has very warm feelings about humanity. She is amiable and gregarious. She reminds me strongly of my mother; with her around, I have never felt homesick. Her priceless contribution is this. She learns from me about India's men and women, culture, religion, vices and virtues. Then she compares it with what is prevalent in America today. This is helping me obtain a well-rounded view of the American scene.

Her one pride, or delight, is to make me dress up in my formal Indian dress, turban and all. She seats me in an open carriage drawn by a pair of trotting horses. We travel to various places so that she can "show me off." I am told the people mistake me, a penniless monk wedded to poverty, to be a Rajah! They gather around in large crowds wherever we stop. This is beginning to get highly embarrassing! Even with my meager purse I shall soon purchase western clothes. I shall save my red robe and turban only for my lectures.

Most important, thanks to Kate, I have been lecturing to various audiences on various subjects. The local newspapers are full of me (though they misspell my name horribly!). This ensures that the next audience is larger than the previous one. This is giving me invaluable experience for the future when (or if) I hope to address the august audience at the Parliament of Religions.

My participation in the Parliament still remains a nagging worry! But only God can help me in that matter. Meanwhile, the lectures are making it clear to me that the men and women of America are bright and articulate. They are not hesitant to question anything they do not understand. At one lecture, a small boy solemnly stood up. It had been about what I imagined a difficult subject. But the child asked a very pertinent question! I was astonished! There is a deep vein of spirituality in the American psyche which, if mined properly, will lead to worldwide repercussions. Maybe the people of Massachusetts are different, but I doubt it.

Kate took me to Boston. We stayed with her cousin, Franklin Sanborn. He was quite frigid, to begin with. As soon as the knotty questions of philosophy and religion began to be discussed and debated, he thawed. The upshot is that I shall soon meet my first American scholar and philosopher, Prof. John Henry Wright.

Prof. Wright is a Hellenist at Harvard. Franklin sent an undoubtedly inflated report about me to Prof. Wright, who expressed a keen desire to meet me. He lives in a small resort village on the Atlantic Seaboard, called Annisquam. He was to have come to Boston, and meet me at Franklin's house. That meeting did not materialize. However, Prof. Wright has invited me to spend a weekend at Annisquam. I am looking forward to going there.

My letter has gone on long enough, Jock. I shall end now. Who knows if I shall find so much time in the future to write such long letters?

With love,
Naren.

In the first week of September, I received a letter at the Grand Central station. The envelope was scented, the address written by a feminine hand. Everyone at the station seemed to know about the letter. There were smiles, winks and nudges amongst the railroad staff. They thought I had received my first love letter! I resisted all entreaties to open it at once.

In my room, I opened the envelope. It contained a letter six pages long. I glanced at the bottom of the last page. It was signed by a Mrs. John Henry Wright. I remembered the name from Naren's last letter. The letter was as follows:

Annisquam, Mass.
August 30, 1893.

Dear Mr. McClintock,

I have been charged by the Hindoo monk, Swami Vivekananda, to let you know that he had been here for the weekend, from Friday to Monday. He is well and in good spirits. He stayed with us at our house. That is all he requested me to write. However, I think you might be interested to know how his stay was.

Mr. McClintock, what a Lion you have let loose among us Daniels! What a queer time we have been having! He arrived in a long saffron robe that caused universal amazement. He is a most gorgeous vision! Apart from being handsome, he has a superb carriage.

We talked all day, all night, and began again the next morning. Chiefly, we talked religion. He is wonderfully clever. He is very clear in putting his arguments. He lays his trains of thought to a logical conclusion. You can't trip him up, nor get ahead of him!

We were very confused about his caste in the beginning. We took him to be a priest, therefore a Brahmin. Imagine our surprise when he partook of a plateful of hash with evident enjoyment! Someone raised a query at this. He replied in his deep bell-like voice: "Who told you I am a Brahmin or a priest? I am neither. I am a monk. I am bound by no rules in the matter of food!"
So that was that!

The Swami's style of argument is mostly Socratic. It starts with a story, or a simple uncontested fact. From these, he derives strange and unanswerable conclusions. His discourses are full of beautiful parables or legends.

All the people of that little place were moved and excited by him. It was not merely because he came from an exotic country or people. He has the unusual ability to bring his hearers into vivid sympathy with his point of view. All the people of all types were interested. The women's eyes blazed and their cheeks were red with excitement. Even the children of the village talked about what he had said to them. The idle summer boarders trooped in to hear him; all the artists wanted to paint him.

Lord! I could go on and on! Truth to tell, the Swami has shaken us all up! We cannot stop talking or writing about him! So much so, I almost forgot to write what finally occurred.

You know that the Swami has come to participate in the Parliament of Religions. He was deeply disappointed at all the legal obstacles standing in his way. He had almost given up all hope of speaking at the Parliament. Prof. Wright was deeply impressed with the Swami. He insisted that the Swami must represent Hindooism at that important gathering. He said: "Swami, this is the only way you can be introduced to the Nation at large."

The Swami said: "The date of registration is past. I have neither credentials nor references."
The Prof. exclaimed: "To ask you, Swami, for credentials is like asking the sun to state its right to shine!"
The Swami was much moved. He said: "Revered Teacher, it is enough that you have such regards!"
The Prof told him: "Swami, stop worrying about the Parliament. I shall take it upon myself to see that you are placed as a Delegate there. I know many distinguished people who are connected with the Parliament. Leave it to me to do what is required. It will be my little tribute to such a towering personality as you."

They both retired to the study. Prof. Wright immediately wrote a letter to the Chairman of the Committee for the selection of delegates. He wrote: "Here is a man more learned than myself; indeed more learned than all our Professors put together!" etc, etc. The Prof. gave the Swami letters of introduction to the Committee in charge of accommodating and providing for the Oriental delegates. Knowing that the Swami had very little money, the Prof. presented him with the fare to Chicago. He also provided sufficient funds to tide the Swami over during the intervening period.

The Swami was quite overcome. He said: "This is indeed a godsend! It is an indubitable manifestation of Divine Providence! Yes, the purpose for which I have come so far is to be fulfilled! But how it was to be fulfilled could never have been foreseen by me. I do not know in which manner to thank you and your dear wife, Professor! I shall never forget all the assistance you have rendered to me!"

The Professor and I were embarrassed by all this. My husband said: "Swami, the pleasure, nay the honor, is entirely ours."

So, Mr. McClintock, in our own little fashion we have been of some little help to your friend. We have no doubt that at the Parliament of Religions he will carry all before him! The Swami has asked me to end this letter with a question to you: "Do you see what I mean when I say that God will provide?"

With regards,
Mrs. John Henry Wright.

PROF. JOHN HENRY WRIGHT

MRS. JOHN HENRY WRIGHTt

I read the letter with great interest, amusement and awe. How neatly things had turned out for Naren! His decision to go to Boston was taken at random, on a whim. It resulted in circumstances that vaulted him into the Parliament of Religions as a Delegate! What a variety of actors had played their parts in getting him to this point! Even an unspiritual person like me could see one thing clearly. Mysterious forces, coincidences, were at play to place the final dramatic climax before the American public!

*****

BRAHMA

If the red slayer thinks he slays,
Or if the slain think he is slain,
They know not well the subtle ways
I keep, and pass, and turn again.

Far or forgot to me is near;
Shadow and sunlight are the same;
The vanished gods to me appear;
And one to me are shame and fame.

They reckon ill who leave me out;
When me they fly, I am the wings;
I am the doubter and the doubt,
And I the hymn the Brahmin sings.

The strong gods pine for my abode,
And pine in vain the sacred Seven;
But thou, meek lover of the good!
Find me, and turn thy back on heaven.

RALPH WALDO EMERSON

CHAPTER 16

THE RETURN

On Monday, September 4, I got a short letter from Naren:

166 North Street,
Salem, Mass.
September 2, 1893.

My dear Jock,

    I write this letter with great happiness. From Annisquam, I have come here to Salem as the guest of Mrs. Kate Tannatt Woods. This Kate is just like the other Kate (Sanborn). She is 58 years old, and an energetic lecturer and authoress. I am to stay here and deliver lectures at various places.

    The great news is that the arrangements for me to participate in the Parliament are well under way! Everything was made possible only due to the untiring efforts of Prof. John Henry Wright. I have written to him to tender my heartfelt gratitude.

    I have received a letter from one Mr. Theles of Chicago. He has confirmed my registration as a Delegate. He has given me the names of some of the other delegates. He has also given some other details about the Congress.

    Jock, this letter is to inform you that I shall be reaching Chicago in the second week. The Parliament is to open on September 11; I shall reach at least two days earlier. I shall be housed with the Oriental delegates. I hope to meet you in Chicago.

With love,
Naren.

Today was the 4th. The Parliament was on the 11th. So Naren might come anytime between September 8 and September 10. From Thursday 7th, I decided to keep a watch on the Boston trains. One came in the morning, the other in the evening. I also told Schumpeter about Naren. If I were absent for any reason, maybe Bill could help him in any way.

On the 8th evening, we received news of a pile-up near Milwaukee. A freight train had derailed and spilled over to the next track. Another oncoming freight train had hit the derailed wagons and also derailed. We collected a wreckage crew and readied a locomotive and a winch car to take us to the scene of the accident. We reached the spot fairly late, and started operations using lamps and flares. Taking turns to relax, we winched the derailed wagons either onto or away from the tracks. It was backbreaking work. It took us till the 9th evening to clear the tracks for rail traffic. We returned to the Grand Central late at night. I staggered back to my room for some well-earned sleep.

The next morning, September 10, I went to the Grand Central early. I asked the porters if they had seen anyone like Naren arrive on 9th evening by the Boston train. The train had been late, the crowd of passengers had been very large due to the Parliament, and no one remembered seeing Naren. Only one of the porters said that he had "seen a gent dressed fit to kill in yellow and red." This person was supposed to have exited the station after 9 pm. This porter was notorious for his tippling. I could not place full credence in his words.

I met the incoming Boston train, but Naren was not there among the passengers. Surely he was not thinking of arriving by the evening train, and attending the Parliament next morning? Had he missed this train? Where was he now? Was he making alternative arrangements to reach Chicago by road? All questions to which I did not have a clue. Only his God would have to take care of Naren.

I left the Grand Central, and went to the World's Fair. I searched out the Inquiry desk, and asked them about the delegates to the Parliament of Religions. They told me to go to the Art Institute on South Michigan Avenue, and enquire at the desk set up there for the purpose. I went there, and was informed that the Eastern delegates had been put up at a hostel on South Dearborn Street, closer to West Monroe Street. They gave me the address. It was around 11 am when I reached the hostel. No Swami Vivekananda was registered there.

I was seriously worried now. Was there some last minute slip between the cup and the lip? I went home since it was a Sunday. I had my lunch, and sat down to think.

Nothing came to mind. I decided that sitting still would not help. I got up, and started again for the hostel to have a second look. The Receptionist had gone home. There was a watchman looking after the premises. I persuaded him to let me have a look at the Registration Book. I opened it to the current page, and experienced a rush of relief and joy! Naren's name was registered there with his room number!

I wrote my name on a slip of paper, and requested the watchman to take it to that room, and hand it to the person there. The watchman asked me: "How come you're interested in any person here in this place?"
"Why not?" I asked him, "What's the matter?"
"Well," he said, "For one thing, they is all darkies here!"
I was very amused with the remark. He was a black person himself! I told him: "That's ok. I know this one. Please give this note to him."
He shuffled off with the slip. I sat back in my chair and waited.

Fifteen minutes later, a beaming Naren walked into the room. "Jock, I'm so glad to see you. Oh, what an adventure I went through yesterday! Only God's will brought me to this place without any mishap."
I asked him: "Naren, you had my address in your pocketbook. Why didn't you meet me? When did you come, anyway?"
"I arrived late on 9th evening. Unfortunately, I lost my little diary, and went through a lot of trouble. Let's sit down and I'll tell you the whole story."

We sat down. He started with the conversations he had had with Kate Sanborn in the train. He continued to the time he got into the train at Albany to come to Chicago.

It so happened (said Naren) that on the train I met a merchant. He promised to direct me to my proper destination as soon as we reached Chicago. The train had arrived late at Albany. The delay went on adding up. We had to give way for the freight trains at many places. So I reached Chicago late at night. There, the merchant was in a hurry to reach home. He forgot to tell me how to reach the office of Dr. John Henry Barrows, Chairman of the Parliament's General Committee. Added to this, I somehow contrived to lose my pocketbook, in which all the Chicago addresses had been written down. At Chicago I was swept with the other passengers out of the station.

I struck out in a random direction. I asked passers-by where the Parliament's offices were. Some responded that they did not know; others did not even bother to respond. Then I landed up in a part of the city where the people spoke a guttural language, probably German. We did not understand one another. Wandering through the warren of streets, I found that I had backtracked into the dark rail-yard of the Grand Central. I could not even make out where the station was. I was hopelessly lost. There seemed no point in going on.

But what to do next? Where to pass the night? Some boxcars were standing on a siding. One of them had an open side door. I felt inside, and encountered soft hay. God knew how clean it was! But God had given me a temporary home, I thought. I entered my home with my luggage, and arranged the luggage around me. As my eyes adjusted, I found the home quite comfortable. I lay down. Through the door, I could see the stars twinkling in the sky. It was quite warm in the boxcar. I piled some of the hay over me. The Lord will guide me, I thought. Trusting His guidance, I freed my mind from all anxieties, and fell asleep.

Just before I slept, a thought crossed my mind – had I come so far only to be reduced to this state; to sleep like an outcast, unknown, unaided, and perhaps despised? My soul immediately rejected the thought as unworthy. After all, was not I a true Sannyasi, a monk? Even in my land, did I not sleep where the evening found me? Why then crib? When I think of it now I was, by God's grace, extremely lucky! What if the boxcars had been attached to some freight train during the night? I might have woken up in the morning hundreds of miles away!

Morning came, and I arose smelling the scent of fresh water. I followed my nose and, in a short while found myself on Lake Shore Drive. It is, as you know, the most fashionable residential avenue in the city. Millionaires and merchant-princes dwell there. I had had no dinner, and was extremely hungry. So, like the monk I am, I started begging from door to door. I begged for food, and asked for directions. My clothes were strange and rumpled; my appearance was travel-worn. No wonder I was rudely treated! At some houses the servants insulted me. At others the door was slammed in my face. As I trudged on and on, my heart sank lower and lower.

Ultimately, exhausted, I sat down on the kerb opposite a fashionable house. I was determined to abide by the will of the Lord. After some time, the front door of the house opened. A regal-looking lady came out of the house onto the lawn. She looked across at me once and looked away. Again she turned towards me, and then came across the road to me. She said: "Excuse me, sir. Are you looking for someone?"

I stood up and bowed to her. I said: "Good morning, madam. I am actually searching for the way to the Parliament's General Committee."

"The Parliament's General Committee? Sir, are you a delegate to the Parliament of Religions?"

I told her I was, and introduced myself. I started to explain why I was here. She interrupted me and said: "But what am I doing, keeping you standing here on the street? Please come into my house. What an honor it is to meet a distinguished delegate like you! Let me help you with your luggage."

I entered her house. She immediately called a servant. She told him to take me to the Guest Room, and look to my needs. She introduced herself as Mrs. Hale, wife of Mr. George W. Hale.

MR. AND MRS. GEORGE HALE

I had a most luxurious bath. I came down to have a sumptuous breakfast. Mrs. Hale gave me company. She told me that she would personally accompany me to the office of the Parliament. I was grateful beyond words. A new spirit possessed me. I was convinced beyond doubt (Yes, Jock, I still have doubts!) that the Lord was with me. I awaited future events with equanimity. Much later, after finishing breakfast I met Mr. Hale and their children. We had some small talk. I then left with Mrs. Hale and called on the Officers of the Parliament.

I presented my credentials to them and was gladly accepted as a delegate. I thanked Mrs. Hale profusely, and saw her off. The officers then housed me here, along with the other Oriental delegates. Very soon, I shall be shifting to the residence of Mr. and Mrs. John B. Lyon at 262 Michigan Avenue.

MR. AND MRS. JOHN B. LYON

"With every passing moment, Jock, I feel that the Parliament of Religions will be the greatest test for me. I feel that it will be the most crucial experience for me," said Naren.

"Naren," I said, "I came here to see if you have reached here safely. I see now that you are in safe hands. There will be no more mishaps, I'm sure."

"For the present everything is comfortable. Tomorrow, of course, will be a different story. I am sure that my Master, the Holy Mother and the Divine Mother will take full care of me."

"Well, I'll leave you to take rest and to prepare for tomorrow's proceedings."

"Thank you for your concern, Jock. We'll meet tomorrow at the Parliament. If, of course, you decide to come."

"You bet I'll come! Nothing in the world can stop me! Goodbye till then."

"Goodbye, and God bless," said Naren.

And I left for my lodgings.

*****

AN ELDRITCH PHILOSOPHY

The difference I clearly see
"Twixt tweedledum and tweedledee –
That is a proposition sane,
But truly 'tis beyond my vein
To make your Eastern logic plain.

If "God is truth, all else is naught,"
This "world a dream," delusion up wrought,
What can exist which God is not?
All those who "many" see have much to fear,
He only lives to whom the "One" is clear,
So again I say,
In my poor way,
I cannot see but all's He,
If I'm in Him and He in me.

MISS MARY B. HALE

Then I heered th' han'some Hindu monk, drest up in orange dress,
Who sed that all humanity was part of God – no less,
An' he sed we was not sinners, so I comfort took once more,
While th' Parl'ment of Religions roared with approving roar.

AUNT HANNAH ON THE PARLIAMENT OF RELIGIONS

CHAPTER 17

THE PARLIAMENT OF RELIGIONS

The Parliament of Religions opened on the morning of Monday, September 11, 1893, at the Art Institute of Chicago. It was a permanent and newly constructed building on Chicago's Michigan Avenue. Behind the stone building fronting Michigan Avenue, there was a large open courtyard.

THE ART INSTITUTE, CHICAGO, 1893

In this open courtyard, two large halls were built. They were temporary wooden structures. To the north was Washington Hall; to the south Columbus Hall. It was in this great Hall of Columbus that the delegates of the Parliament were to gather.

HALL OF COLUMBUS, 1893, NOW REMODELED AS FULLERTON HALL

President Bonney had added some memorable touches. There was a New Liberty Bell on which was inscribed, "A new Commandment I give unto thee, that you love one another." At 10 o'clock, ten sonorous strokes of the bell would proclaim the opening of the Congress. Each stroke represented one chief religion – Judaism, Islam, Hinduism, Buddhism, Taoism, Confucianism, Shintoism, Zoroastrianism, the Catholic and Protestant faiths, and the Greek Orthodox Church. Of course, President Bonney had prepared this list.

Much before the bell pealed, there was a long line of people seeking entry into the Institute. I had come early in the morning, immediately after breakfast. The Institute doors were open and I entered. I got a vantage seat in the Hall of Columbus. I had a clear view of the Speaker's Platform. I also had a clear view of the audience. An hour later the Hall was three-fourths full. The door was closed to control the crowd for the remaining seats. Before 10 am, about four thousand people had crowded onto the floor and the gallery of the Hall. There were a large number of people standing along the sides. Outside, spilling onto the sidewalks of Michigan Avenue, a large crowd lingered.

In spite of the large crowd, there was a church-like hush in the Hall. From time to time, an organ played Christian hymns. The stage, or platform, was not as wide as the Hall. It was about twelve feet deep. My neighbor was quite talkative and gave me some pieces of information. Behind the platform hung two scrolls; one Japanese, and the other Hebrew. There were also two giant marble statues of Greek philosophers. To the right of these was a smaller bronze figure of the Greek Goddess of Learning.

Centered between the statues was a very intricate throne of iron; this was for Cardinal Gibbons, the highest prelate of the Catholic Church in America. On either side of this throne, about thirty ordinary wooden chairs stood three rows deep. These were for the delegates, officials and invited guests. There was a Speaker's rostrum at the front of the platform. Directly below this was a pit in which reporters and official stenographers sat at small tables to record the proceedings.

There was a stir in the audience just before the delegates entered the Hall. A wholly unexpected person was seen entering. This was the genial giant and arch-atheist, Colonel Robert Ingersoll. He had timed his appearance such that he arrived just before the delegates did. He had obviously asked a younger friend to reserve a seat for him. The youngster got up, offered his chair to Ingersoll, and stood at the side wall. Before the crowd could react, the Liberty Bell rang. Ingersoll was forgotten for the moment. He glanced around the room and his eyes met mine. He smiled and raised his right hand in greeting. I replied with a grin. My neighbor did not look happy.

As the Liberty Bell fell silent, the delegates entered the hall. They were in pairs. President Bonney and Cardinal Gibbons led the group. The procession walked down the center aisle to ascend the platform. The crowds cheered them till the last person sat down on the platform. What diverse persons formed the procession! The various colors of their dresses were like the sight of a fantastic rainbow! Strange robes, stranger headgear, ornate crucifixes and glittering crescents astonished the crowd. As Minnie Andrews Snell's Aunt Hannah put it:

I thought th' Fair was mixin' an' th' Midway made me crawl,
But th' Parl'ment of Religions was th' mixin'est of all!
I see the' Turks agoing round th' Midway in th' Fair,
But our Minister reproved me when he seen me peep in thair,
"Defilin' place" he called it, an' th' Turk "a child of sin,"
But th' Parl'ment of Religions took all them heathen in.

Cardinal Gibbons sat in the center, on the throne-like chair, and the delegates around him. Suddenly, the organ in the gallery started up with a familiar song, and the entire assembly rose to sing along:

Praise God, from whom all blessings flow,
Praise Him, all creatures here below,
Praise Him above, ye heavenly host,
Praise Father, Son, and Holy Ghost.

CARDINAL GIBBONS

DHARMAPALA, CEYLON, ARCHBISHOP DIONYSIOS LATAS, GREECE,

DR. CARL VON BERGEN, SWEDEN, KIRETCHJIAN, ARMENIA

KINZA HIRAI, ZENSHIRO NOGUCHI, JAPAN,

RABBI K.KOHLER, NEW YORK, NARASIMHACHARIA,INDIA

JAPANESE GROUP

GROUP OF REPORTERS

There were more verses. When the organ fell silent, Cardinal Gibbons raised his right hand. There was a deep silence. The Cardinal began the words of the Lord's Prayer: "Our Father, who art in Heaven….," and every voice joined his. It was seen that almost all the Eastern delegates, whatever their religion, joined this prayer.

The Parliament of Religions had begun!

It started with speeches of welcome from President Bonney and other officials. When the delegates started their replies, the crowd vociferously cheered each one of them. The Confucian Pung Kwang Yu, the Archbishop of the Greek Church, Mazoomdar of the Brahmo Samaj, Dharmapala from Buddhist Ceylon – all of them were greeted with cheers and a waving of hats and handkerchiefs. Many of the speakers had a need for interpreters. Through all this, Naren remained seated. The Chairman looked at him a number of times. Naren shook his head as if to say: "Not now, not now." The next delegate spoke instead.

In the afternoon session, four delegates spoke. Then the Chairman rose to introduce Swami Vivekananda "….who represents the Hindoo religion."

All eyes were on Naren. He slowly rose to his feet. He walked with measured steps to the speaker's rostrum. The previous speakers had read from prepared speeches. Naren's hands were empty. He placed his hands on either side of the rostrum. He leaned forward slightly. His face was glowing. His glittering eyes went over every person in the hall and the gallery. There was pin-drop silence. Then Naren suddenly smiled. In his ringing, resonant voice, rich as a bronze bell, he pronounced the simple greeting: "Sisters and Brothers of America!"

The words had an electric effect on the audience. Spontaneously, there arose a peal of applause. It built up to deafening proportions. The entire audience surged to its feet. The applause lasted for several long minutes. Even Ingersoll was on his feet, clapping vigorously. It was a tribute by the audience to something which I, at least, could not define. The whole phenomenon was extremely puzzling. The ovation could not have been inspired by

Naren's words alone! Somehow there was a combined effect of his bearing, his handsome and magnetic personality, and his magnificent voice. This combination had created an instant rapport between him and the audience. The audience was stirred as never before.

The applause and ovation initially startled Naren. Then as the ovation prolonged, he slowly smiled and waited for the applause to end. Twice he started to speak, but was drowned out by fresh applause. Naren smiled again, and looked around at the audience. He waited till all sat down. When there was complete silence, he began his address. It was short and met with applause after each meaningful statement and paragraph. The abrupt end again met with prolonged applause. The entire speech is as follows:

Sisters and Brothers of America, (Sustained applause)
It fills my heart with joy unspeakable to rise in response to the warm and cordial welcome which you have given us. I thank you in the name of the most ancient Order of monks in the world; I thank you in the name of the Mother of religions; and I thank you in the name of millions and millions of Hindu people of all classes and sects. (Applause)

My thanks, also, to some of the speakers on this platform who, referring to the delegates from the Orient, have told you that these men from far-off nations may well claim the honor of bearing to different lands the idea of toleration. I am proud to belong to a religion which has taught the world both tolerance and universal acceptance. We believe not only in universal toleration, but we accept all religions as true. I am proud to belong to a nation which has sheltered the persecuted and the refugees of all religions and all nations on the earth. (Applause)

I am proud to tell you that we have gathered in our bosom the purest remnant of the Israelites, who came to Southern India and took refuge with us in the very year in which their holy temple was shattered to pieces by Roman tyranny. (Applause)

I am proud to belong to the religion which has sheltered, and is still fostering, the remnant of the grand Zoroastrian nation. (Applause)

I will quote to you, brethren, a few lines from a hymn which I remember to have repeated from my earliest boyhood, which is every day repeated by millions of human beings: "As the different streams having their sources in different places all mingle their waters in the sea, so, O Lord, the different paths which men take through different tendencies, various though they appear, crooked or straight, all lead to Thee." (Applause)

The present convention, which is one of the most august assemblies ever held, is in itself a vindication, a declaration to the world of the wonderful doctrine preached in the Gita: "Whosoever comes to me, through whatever form, I reach him; all men are struggling through paths which in the end lead to Me." (Applause)

Sectarianism, bigotry, and its horrible descendant, fanaticism, have long possessed the beautiful earth. They have filled the earth with violence, drenched it often and often with human blood, destroyed civilizations and sent whole nations to despair.

Had it not been for these horrible demons, human society would be far more advanced than it is now. But their time is come; and I fervently hope that the bell that tolled this morning in honor of this convention may be the death-knell of all fanaticism, of all persecutions with the sword or with the pen, and of all uncharitable feelings between persons wending their way to the same goal.
Thank you. (Sustained applause)

That evening, after the end of the first day's session, the steps of the Art Institute were very busy indeed. Reporters swarmed around intellectuals and other important personalities. They wanted to get the various views of the day's proceedings. The maximum number of reporters had clustered around Robert Ingersoll. Questions flew fast and furious at him. He replied to each question seriously, with a disarming smile on his face, I shall never forget his answers.
"Col. Ingersoll, how is it that an arch-atheist like you has attended this Parliament?"

"My atheism, or more correctly agnosticism, has nothing to do with my presence here. The Parliament promised to be a clash of intellects, a feast of logic, reasoning and deduction. I have not been disappointed. As the British say, it has been a jolly good show!"

"But an atheist at a religious gathering?"

"If I am an atheist, then let me remind you that some of the delegates are also atheists. What have you to say to that?"

"What do you mean, Colonel?"

"Buddhism does not believe in God, but is it not still a religion? If Dharmapala can participate as a delegate, cannot poor Ingersoll at least be a spectator?"

"Who do you think deserves the greatest credit for this show?"

"Without a doubt President Bonney, to whichever religion he may belong."

"What did you think about the audience, Colonel?"

"I must admit I was most impressed! I expected the Hall to be filled mostly with idlers and sensation-seekers. I was wrong. The very cream of Chicago was present here, the very flower of womanhood. The audience was indeed most receptive to the delegates of the various religions who assembled on the platform today."

"Which delegate impressed you the most?"

"Need you ask? Without a doubt, Swami Vivekananda from India."

"What impressed you most about him?"

"The paradox that he represented nothing – and everything! You see, among the Indian delegates, Mazoomdar and Nagarkar represented the Theists of India. Dharmapala represented the Buddhists, Gandhi the Jains. Chakravarti represented the Theosophists. But Vivekananda, while belonging to no sect, represented India as a whole!"

"How do you assess his address, Colonel?"
Ingersoll thought for a moment, and then said: "It was a short but beautiful address. I rank it on par with the Gettysburg speech of President Lincoln. The political Lincoln defined Democracy in his speech. The spiritual Vivekananda defined Religion in his."
"What impressed you most about his speech?"
"One aspect attracted me immensely. Each of the other speakers spoke of his God, the God of his sect. The Hindu monk alone spoke of all their Gods, and embraced them all as leading to the Universal Being. Remember the quote about the different streams, and the different paths, all leading to God? Does any Christian preacher say this? More to the point, *can* he say it?"

"Col Ingersoll, how do you account for the great emotional ovation after his opening words?"
"Good question. All through the session I have been analyzing this overwhelming response to a very simple greeting. It happened because the Swami was certainly the first to cast off the formalism of the Congress. He spoke to the masses in the language they were waiting for. He received an immediate response."

"Did his personality have anything to do with it?"

"Of course! The combined effect of his dress, his bearing and his voice is devastating. At first sight everybody recognizes him as a Leader, the anointed of God, if I may be pardoned this blasphemy. The man is marked with the stamp of the power to command."

"Colonel, what do you think the future trends in the Parliament will be?"

"I think people will be extremely surprised by the Eastern brigade. You have seen them in action today. Did you ever think they would be men as learned as this? I am sure that today's audience came prepared to see the African delegates stamp out a rain dance, with the ladies grunting in accompaniment. They probably expected the Indian delegates to break out wicker baskets filled with snakes, and charm them with pipe music. Maybe they expected the Indian Rope Trick, too. Instead, they were fascinated by what they saw and heard here. As one of the eyewitnesses said to me: 'The heathen carried away the prizes of most value, while the agnostics and unbelievers cheered.' And you will hear hair-raising speeches in the future."

"Hair-raising? What do you mean, Sir?"

"Today Vivekananda spoke of One God for all. Tomorrow he will state that he, and we, are all God! I can imagine the bigots and rednecks foaming at the mouth about such blasphemy!"

"Any closing comments, Colonel Ingersoll?"

"I just want to bring to the attention of the people of this great land a very ironical fact. The Parliament of Religions could be convened only through a spirit of Christian evangelism. I prophecy that this same historic Parliament will become, in spite of itself, an instrument for the destruction of bigotry."

I hung around the Art Institute in the evening. I managed to get inside the hall meant for the delegates. There, Naren was getting ready to start for his lodgings. I congratulated him on his speech. I asked him: "How did you feel while addressing the vast audience?"
"Jock, you cannot imagine how nervous I was! True, I had addressed small gatherings. This Hall and gallery, packed with thousands of men and women, was overwhelming! They also represented the best culture of the country. On the platform were learned men of all nations on this earth! I was to address this august assemblage! My heart was fluttering. My tongue nearly dried up. I was so nervous that I could not venture to speak in the morning. I was lost in the amazement of all the proceedings. Like a fool, I had no prepared ready-made speech with me. When Dr. Barrows introduced me, I bowed down to Devi Saraswati, and stepped up to the podium.

As I surveyed the audience to calm myself down, a sudden scene of my Master flashed through my mind. He had been instructing the disciples on how to overcome nervousness before an audience. Jocularly he had said: 'When you face an audience, do not think of them as people. Imagine that you are addressing a gathering of earthworms!'

The image was so comic that I involuntarily smiled. My fears dropped away. I spoke the first words from the bottom of my heart."

"Naren," I said, "We in the audience did not notice any nervousness at any point of time. You looked supremely confident and in full control. The speech was a real hit!"

"After the first ovation," Naren said, "I wondered whether it could really be me they were applauding. Then, as I stood amazed at the reaction, I felt the spirit of my Master enter into me! If the speech was a success, it was the breath of my Master breaking down the barriers through my mouth. I made the small speech. When it was finished, I sat down almost exhausted with the exertion."

"And how do you feel now, Naren?" I asked him.

"Very relieved, Jock! I am also struck with wonder when I remember how my Master had told me in a dream at Madras: 'Go across the sea. Know that this conference is meant for you. Do not worry. People will be amazed hearing your speech.' Jock, what do I have to fear now? My Master is looking after my every step!"

****

DIVINE IMAGE

To Mercy, Pity, Peace, and Love,
All pray in their distress,
And to these virtues of delight
Return their thankfulness.

For Mercy, Pity, Peace, and Love,
Is God our Father dear;
And Mercy, Pity, Peace, and Love,
Is man, his child and care.

For Mercy has a human heart
Pity, a human face;
And Love, the human form divine;
And Peace, the human dress.

Then every man, of every clime,
That prays in his distress,
Prays to the human form divine:
Love, Mercy, Pity, Peace.

And all must love the human form,
In heathen, Turk, or Jew.
Where Mercy, Love, and Pity dwell,
There God is dwelling too.

WILLIAM BLAKE

CHAPTER 18

THE FLASH OF INTELLECTS

I had neither the time, nor the inclination, to visit the Parliament every day. The newspapers were copiously reporting whatever occurred there. By reading them I could gather that Naren had gone from strength to strength. In the papers I read that during the ensuing days, Naren spoke a number of times. Each time he spoke of a Universal religion. New arguments were revealed, but with the same force of conviction. There was no dogma. He emphasized the divinity inherent in man and his capacity for infinite evolution.

Day after day he spoke extemporaneously at the main sessions. He was allowed to speak longer than the usual half-hour. He was so popular that he was always scheduled last in order to hold the audience. On a warm day, when hundreds got up to go home, the Chairman would get up and announce: "Swami Vivekananda will give a short address before the benediction."
All would then sit down. Four thousand people, fanning themselves, would sit for hours, just to listen to Naren for fifteen minutes! And it would be time well spent!

Swami Vivekananda with other Religious Leaders at First Religions Parliament - Chicago, USA 1893

NARASIMHA CHARIA, LAKSHMI NARAIN, DHARMAPALA, AND V.A.GAMDHI

One more fact became rapidly clear. As Ingersoll had prophesied, not only Naren, but also all the Eastern delegates, proved to be extremely impressive. They demonstrated that they were not men of straw. In their attacks, they were devastating. In their manners they were devastatingly polite. With bland smiles on their faces, they would parry thrust after thrust hurled at them by the bigots. Suddenly, they would slip the poniard to the hilt when the occasion arose.

All of them supported one another in their lectures on one burning point – the intrusion, arrogance, ignorance, intolerance, selfishness, bigotry and failure of Christian Missionaries in the Orient! As can be deduced, this raised a hornet's nest among the bigots! The newspapers had juicy news for their readers.

What I could gather was this. The Christian speakers broadly made three points.
First, Christian missions were not at all a failure.
Second, any failure was due to the idiosyncrasies of the individual missionaries, not the whole group.
Third, Christianity was the only religion that assured salvation.

This was like showing a red cape to the Eastern bulls! Politely, but firmly, Pung Kwan Yu from China, Horin Toki and Kinza Hirai from Japan, Mazoomdar, Nagarkar, Dharmapala and Naren from India contested these statements. Speaker after speaker emphasized the false Christianity (rice Christianity, they called it) practiced by the missionaries. They showed how money was paid to the poor people to convert.

Rev. Joseph Cook said that to speak of a universe that is not created was nonsense. The Orientals politely said that for a universe to have a beginning was a self-evident absurdity. Bishop Newman said that insulting the missionaries was tantamount to insulting all the Christians in the United States. The Orientals calmly replied that the Bishop was an ignorant fool!

The internal schisms of the Christian denominations were also evident, and became the butt of jokes. As Aunt Hannah put it very pithily:

Then a Cath'lic man got up an' spoke, about Christ an' th' cross;
But th' Christians of th' other creeds, they giv' thair heds a toss,
When th' Baptist spoke, th' Presbyterians seemed to be fightin' mad,
'Tel the Parl'ment of Religions made my pore old soul feel sad.

Naren was particularly savage in debunking the notion that Christianity gave rise to prosperity. He said the most prosperous nations were invaders and cut-throats. At the end he said: "At such a price, the Hindu will not have prosperity. I have sat here today, and I have heard the height of intolerance. Blood and the sword are not for the Hindu, whose religion is based on the law of love!"

I particularly remember an exchange with the audience. Naren asked them: "Please raise your hands all those who have read the sacred books of the Hindus."
Only about five hands went up. Then Naren smiled, raised himself up to his full height, and said: "And yet you dare to judge us!?"
This was in the morning session. In the afternoon, Naren presented his 'Paper on Hinduism.'

I was there that whole day, because the newspapers had predicted a feast. I was a witness to the bloodbath in the morning. What a crowd there was; I got almost the last seat even though I went very early. The unique feature was that more than half the Hall was filled by ladies!

Naren presented his ideas with impeccable logic. His eloquence never clouded his logic with emotion. Everyone could see that he was in a super-conscious state, divinity pouring out of him. There was total silence; no one wanted to miss a word or any subtle nuance. To explain the Self (a tough enough subject!) in easy terms, to show it was a self-evident truth, to keep it logical, and to convince the audience – that is what Naren achieved! He showed how Hinduism soared up to the Divine, and achieved it. At the end of the speech, after the tremendous applause, I heard a neighbor say: "That man a heathen? And we send missionaries to his people? It would be more fitting that they should send missionaries to us!"

From the first speech on, the Press lionized Naren. His photographs appeared in every paper. The papers were not only local ones; several reporters were from the national papers at Washington, New York, San Francisco and other places. Their sensational reporting made a national hero out of Naren.

His adventurous odyssey across the oceans to reach Chicago found sympathy in the people of a land which loved adventure. He was called the "Warrior-Monk!"

Everyone in the country became familiar with his dress, his handsomeness, his eloquence and his bell-like resonant voice without even seeing him in person. Like Dayananda before him, he was a heroic figure stepping straight out of his legendary epics or Homer's 'Odyssey.'

A POSTER FOUND AROUND CHICAGO IN 1893

Life-size posters of him were put up at prominent places in the streets of Chicago. Even the Grand Central Station had two posters of him – one in the main station, and the other in the waiting hall. The words 'The Monk Vivekananda' were printed under these pictures. There was a byline in smaller letters 'See Him At The Parliament Of Religions.'' While entering, or leaving, the Art Institute he always attracted a crowd. Hundreds of women almost fought with each other to get near him and shake his hand.

He was dubbed "the greatest figure in the Parliament of Religions."

His tribute to America gladdened every heart: "Hail Columbia, motherland of liberty! It has been given to thee, who never dipped her hand in her neighbor's blood, who never found out that the shortest way of becoming rich was robbing one's neighbors, it has been given to thee to march at the vanguard of civilization with the flag of harmony."

When asked by the New York *World* for a "sentiment or expression regarding the significance of the great meeting," Naren unhesitatingly replied with two quotations:
"I am He that Am in every religion – like the thread that passes through a string of pearls."
"Holy, perfect and pure men are seen in all creeds, therefore they all lead to the same truth – for how can nectar be the outcome of poison?"

Throughout America, these were reported as "the lessons learnt through the Parliament of Religions!"

The Parliament of Religions was, no doubt, intended to be a serious Congress. The general sentiment, however, was that it was more like a carnival! Some sessions were no doubt tiring because of the warm weather; some were plain boring. But most of them were absolutely exciting! All sorts of new ideas were put forth, some clear and some cloudy. The strangest thing was that the revolutionary ideas came from totally unexpected quarters.

LAXMI NARAIN, DHARMAPALA, SWAMI, AND V.A. GANDHI

It *was* like a carnival – only substituting the word 'God' for the word 'fun.' Everybody talked about God very seriously. However strange the ideas expressed, nobody was prevented from saying whatever he or she wanted to say. It was therefore a lot of fun, too! This was reflected in the happy faces of the people who attended the close of the Parliament.

The day for the closing ceremony of the Parliament arrived. Much before the time announced for the function, masses of people collected before the doors of the Art Institute. Lines formed from the doors to Michigan Avenue, and extended half a block in either direction. The organizers of the Parliament had, on this last day, managed to combine the Halls of Washington and Columbus into one mammoth hall. As a result, nearly seven thousand persons had gathered there.

I, as usual, had managed to get a vantage seat again by unabashedly using Naren's good offices with the officials of the Parliament! It was a show I will never forget! Hundreds of Edison's incandescent lights filled the Hall of Columbus. The hall was jam-packed; every inch of space was occupied. In spite of this, there were no disputes or frayed tempers. The mood was absolutely festive. It had been, as Ingersoll had said 'a jolly good show.' It was right that it should end in a blaze of glory!

On the platform, the flags of all the nations were displayed. Under them sat the delegates, some in somber black, and some in splashes of color. I remember that photographs were taken twice during the evening. The gaslight and the electric lights were enhanced by the photographer using flashlight. The flash was a burst of gunpowder, which startled quite a number of persons in the audience.

At last the program started. There were short speeches by the President and the Officials. Then the delegates spoke one by one, thanking the organizers of the Parliament for bringing them closer to one another. Many of the Eastern delegates paid tribute to the purity of Christian ideals which had made this Parliament possible.

The organizers had so arranged the speeches that the last but one speaker should be Dharmapala, who had been most impressive throughout the Parliament. The gist of his speech is contained in this sentence: "If theology and dogma stand in your way in search of truth, put them aside. Learn to think without prejudices, to love all beings for love's sake, to express your convictions fearlessly, to lead a life of purity, and the sunlight of truth will illuminate you."

Dharmapala was so good in his speech that Aunt Hannah commented:

I listened to the' Buddhist, in his robes of shinin' white,
As he told how like to Christ's thair lives, while ours was not – a mite'
'Tel I felt, to lead a Christian life, a Buddhist I must be,
An' th' Parl'ment of Religions brought religious doubt to me.

Finally, the charismatic hero everyone had come to see and hear, rose and spoke. Naren started by thanking the organizers of the Congress for dreaming this wonderful dream and then realizing it. He thanked the other delegates and the enlightened audience. He even thanked the bigots by remarking: "A few jarring notes were heard from time to time in the harmony. My special thanks to them, for they have, by their striking contrast, made general harmony the sweeter."

He pooh-poohed the idea of religious unity coming about by the triumph of one religion and the destruction of the others. He decried conversion; a person belonging to one religion must "assimilate the spirit of the others, and yet preserve his individuality, and grow according to his own law of growth."

The last portion of the speech was delivered straight from the heart, with full emotion and sincerity, and it thrilled everyone in the hall:

"If the Parliament of Religions has shown anything to the world, it is this: It has proved to the world that holiness, purity and charity are not the exclusive possessions of any church in the world, and that every system has produced men and women of the most exalted character. In the face of this evidence, if anybody dreams of the exclusive survival of his own religion, and the destruction of the others, I pity him from the bottom of my heart, and point out to him that upon the banner of every religion will soon be written, in spite of resistance: 'Help and not Fight,' 'Assimilation and not Destruction,' 'Harmony and Peace and not Dissension.'"

No one had summed up so well the spirit of the Parliament, its limitations and its finest influence.

As expected, there was thunderous applause from the crowd. Immediately after was the really superb rendering of the "Hallelujah Chorus" by the Apollo Club. Waves upon waves of applause greeted this chorus. Then, slowly, in an orderly fashion, people began to leave the hall.

The Parliament of Religions had come to a triumphant end!

CLOSING SESSION OF 1893 PARLIAMENT OF RELIGIONS

****

THE CUP

This is your cup – the cup assigned to you from the beginning.
Nay, My child, I know how much of that dark drink is your own brew
Of fault and passion, ages long ago,
In the deep years of yesterday, I know.

This is your road – a painful road and drear,
I made the stones that never give you rest,
I set your friend in pleasant ways and clear,
And he shall come like you, unto My breast,
But you, My child, must travel here.

This is your task, it has no joy nor grace,
But it is not meant for any other hand,
And in My universe hath measured place,
Take it. I do not bid you understand.
I bid you close your eyes to see My face.

SWAMI VIVEKANANDA

SWAMI VIVEKANANDA IN AMERICA

CHAPTER 19

PLANNING FOR THE FUTURE

After the Parliament of Religions, Naren many times voiced his desire to become once again a wanderer. How peaceful it would be to return to a life of meditation! Of course, he rejected the thought as soon as it entered his mind. He had not been sent to America for his own salvation. To think in those terms was the rankest selfishness.

His main objective in coming to America was to improve the lot of the people of India. India remained in miserable poverty. The people toiled endlessly for a handful of rice. Sometimes they did not even get that. How to make them self-sufficient? India must regain the splendor of her lost glory. For this, he had to collect funds from America, where the people did not hesitate to spend millions for their personal comforts. How best to do this?

For some time, he considered the idea of making public appeals for collecting the funds. But, all said and done, would this not be begging? For himself it was all right, but only for food; he was a monk after all. But for his country? No, it would be despicable. Why would the American people part with their money for a distant land? What was in it for them? Naren was sensible enough to realize that no one would give something for nothing. That was the way of the world. So that idea was rejected as impractical.

Naren realized that he should lead from his strengths. What were his strengths? Well, his Master had trained him to be a great teacher in the Vedic mould. The Divine Mother had granted him the boon of a great voice. She had also given him a handsome, magnetic personality. When he spoke, all sorts of people listened and, more importantly, understood and appreciated what he said. During these occasions, the spirit of his Master entered into him, spoke through him, and turned the event into a magical interaction.

Also, he had stood his ground against his peers honorably in the Parliament of Religions – all America had paid tribute to this aspect. In the Parliament he had eradicated the erroneous ideas about India. Why not do so on a larger scale, making all America his canvas? Yes, that was something he could, and would, do!

He remembered his thoughts in India before he started for America – he would collect money for India from America, and give them the Vedanta in return. His thoughts crystallized, and he decided to tour America, speaking at various locations, earning through his own labor.

Before venturing on a macro-scale, it was sensible to get attuned to the micro-scale. Where better than

Chicago to get his training? The Parliament of Religions had made him a household word. People would come to see him, hear him. He would accept their contributions, and collect the funds in that manner. No sooner thought than done! There was great demand for his lectures, at least twice a week. He got $30 to $80 for his lectures. The experiment was going very well.

His headquarters became, more or less, the Hale home at 541 Dearborn Avenue. Mrs. Hale told me a charming story about the payments Naren got from contributions. He had no purse; so he would tie up the money in a handkerchief. He would hand it over to Mrs. Hale, who would teach him how to differentiate the coins, and count them.

Simultaneously, his spare time was spent in very useful endeavors. He actively searched for viable models for whatever he wanted to develop in India. He studied the working of schools, institutions, museums, universities and art galleries. He explored practical ways to adopt and adapt the industrial and economic models to the Indian way of life. He studied philanthropic and religious organizations too.

His lecturing helped him gather all kinds of information regarding the working of Western civilization. Everything was grist for his mill, and Chicago offered him a broad field of study. When he felt that he had gained enough experience, he accepted the invitation from the

Slayton Lyceum Lecture Bureau to make a tour of America.

The World's Fair and its Congresses gathered at Chicago some of the best minds of the day, the best thinkers of that age. Naren met them all, and they used their influence to further his quest. He met many rich and powerful people. He found, to his surprise, that they were in awe of him. Their wealth was of no importance to him, and they knew it.

Naren once had a short stay in the home of a partner or associate of John D. Rockefeller. One day, I casually dropped in to see Naren. Outside his door, I was almost knocked down by a man rushing out. He did not even look at me, let alone apologize for his behavior. He hurried away to his carriage. I had seen his photos in the newspapers. He was Rockefeller. When I met Naren, I found him quietly chuckling to himself. When I questioned him, Naren laughed and said: "Yes, Jock. He had come here to see me."
I said: "Is that all you have to say? Rockefeller looked furious. What happened?"

Rockefeller entered (said Naren) without being announced. I heard him enter, but I was writing. I really thought his entry had nothing to do with me, and kept on writing. I heard his footsteps come up to my desk. Then a hand clamped down on my left shoulder. A voice said: "You, Swami, I've come to see you! The butler had the

temerity to delay me, John D. Rockefeller! And you have the gumption to ignore me?"
I looked up into his angry eyes calmly, and said: "Even if you were the President himself, there is still a protocol, a courtesy, to be followed. Tell me, what can I do for you?"

Now, Rockefeller is a powerful man, a Karmayogi in his own way. He was angry, and his passions were roused. Because of my concentration in my writing, I was also in a heightened level of consciousness. His touch on my shoulder communicated the details of his life in a flash to me. I saw his past and future as in a play.

Rockefeller said: "My aim is to become the richest man in the world, and not care a damn about anything else!"
I told him: "You are going in the wrong direction. Anyway, that is not what awaits you in the future. No doubt, you will become the richest man in the world. But as for your not caring a damn for anything else, you will be damned if you don't!"
"Sitting there, how can you say all these things? You're just shooting your mouth off! What do you mean anyway?"
"Sit down and listen," I told him.

He refused the offer and continued to stand. I told him much of his past which only he knew about. Many of the facts were very unsavory. They caused him to squirm where he stood. I gave him some details of his future also. Finally, I told him: "Mr. Rockefeller, please understand that the money you have accumulated is not yours. You are only a channel. It is your duty to do something good for the world. Please realize that God has given you all your wealth for one purpose only. It is a chance for you to help, and to take active interest in the welfare of the people. That is the only path for your salvation!"

JOHN D. ROCKEFELLER

Naren said: "Rockefeller was angry to begin with, and he became angrier still. I had dared to talk to him in a way he was never used to. Worse, I had told him what to do. He ran out of here in a rage, and banged into you."
I asked: "Do you think your words will have any effect on him?"

Naren replied: "They should. I put enough power behind them. And if they don't, who cares?"

A week later, I was sitting with Naren in the study of the same house. Suddenly, the door of the study crashed open. Without any announcement, John D. Rockefeller strode in. He glanced at me as he marched to Naren's table. He had a sheet of paper in his hand. He threw it in front of Naren, and said: "There! This should satisfy you, I guess. You can thank me for it."
Naren did not move a muscle. He looked at Rockefeller for a long moment. He picked up the sheet, and quickly read it. He placed it back on the table. Then he told Rockefeller: "It is for you to thank me!"

Rockefeller strode out of the room as fast as he had come in. I was quite mystified by all this drama. I asked Naren: "What is it? What has he done?"
Naren said: "Jock, you had asked me a week ago if my words would have any effect on Rockefeller. See for yourself."
He held out the sheet of paper to me. I took it and read it. It gave the details of Rockefeller's intentions to donate an enormous sum of money towards the financing of a public institution. I reckon this was John D. Rockefeller's first large donation for philanthropic purposes.

I came to know of another incident through Schumpeter's wife, Hannah. I had been invited over for tea one evening. Hannah was an opera buff. Schumpeter, of course, avoided the opera like the plague. Hannah told me a story which was circulating in the operatic circles.

Madam Emma Calve was the most famous French operatic soprano of her time. She went from strength to strength in opera. Her dramatic interpretation of *Carmen* made her famous in France and England. In America, she was a huge success at New York and Boston. She then visited Chicago. Emma's only daughter was the light of her life. She accompanied Emma to Chicago.

One evening at the opera, Emma was singing at her best. Suddenly, a terrible depression came over her. She collapsed before the second act began. Through sheer will power, and the encouragement of her manager and the other singers, she managed to complete the show. When she returned to the dressing room, she received devastating news. Her only comfort, her daughter, had visited a friend of Emma's. The friend's house had burned down, and Emma's daughter was dead!

Emma collapsed. She thought constantly of suicide. Four times she was on the verge of killing herself. A friend begged her to meet Naren. She refused initially, but later agreed, and went to the house where he was staying. She sat in the living room. Soon, she heard a deep voice say from the study: "Come in, my child. Don't be afraid."
She got up, and went hesitantly into the study.

Naren was sitting at a large table-desk. He asked Emma to sit down. Then he said to her: "It is very necessary for you to be calm. Your state of mind is so troubled that it is vitiating the atmosphere around you. Control yourself."

Emma wanted to pour out her problems to him, and ask him how she could be calm in such circumstances. Before she could do so, Naren very quietly started to talk about the great loss she had suffered. He went on to reveal problems and fears which she had not revealed even to her bosom friends.

"How do you know all these things?" Emma cried, "Who has told you all these things about me?"

"Nobody need tell me, child. It is not even necessary. You are like an open book. It is so easy to read you," said Naren.

He then went on to take each problem, each fear, and tell her how she should resolve it. There were a lot of questions from her, which he answered patiently and convincingly. By the end of the discussion, Emma felt all her troubles slip away one by one. Even the deep grief at the death of her daughter was assuaged to a very great extent. The pain remained, but all her suicidal tendencies were extinguished. She felt deep relief. The hollow feeling within her vanished.

Before she left him, Emma asked Naren: "Swami, what do you suggest I do now?"

"My child, though it seems difficult to do right now, there are two things you *must* do. First, become gay and happy. This will help you to become healthier. Second, do not brood upon your sorrows. You are a great artist. Your art demands that you sublimate your grief, your emotions, into raising that art to new heights. Your spiritual health will improve beyond your own belief," replied Naren.

EMMA CALVE AS 'CARMEN'

After a few more questions, Emma rose to bid goodbye. Naren blessed her. His calming influence, and his empathetic suggestions, had ended Emma's desperation. It had driven out the dark demons from her heart and mind. With a supreme effort of will, she again became her former cheerful self. The grief at her daughter's death was converted into the passion and tragedy of Carmen. She soon became an unparalleled diva in the operatic field.

Another famous visitor to Naren was none other than my old acquaintance, Col. Robert Green Ingersoll! I happened to be visiting Naren that day. I was waiting in the living room when he was ushered in by the butler. He was his usual jaunty self. He wore a three-piece suit. The gold chain of his pocket watch ran across his waist-coat. He smiled at me and said: "Hello, Jock! So we meet again! Is the Swami meeting visitors today?"
I told him: "The butler informs me that the Swami is busy writing. He will be free soon. I, too, am waiting to see him."

We both sat in the living room, chatting about this and that. The butler came and ushered us both into the study. Naren stood, and welcomed us both. He addressed Ingersoll and said: "Your generous remarks in the Chicago *Tribune* were relayed to me. I am thankful to you for them. Please make yourself comfortable."
"You're welcome, Swami. In fact, it was a pleasure in two ways. It was a pleasure to hear such an able person as you represent Hinduism in its pure form. It was also a pleasure to see the way you stung the bigoted rednecks!" said Ingersoll.
He laughed his booming laugh, in which both of us joined in.

I was an interested onlooker as the two settled down to discuss many religious and philosophical matters. It was a revelation to see how well-read Ingersoll was! Perhaps an iconoclast has to be an expert on what he plans to demolish! I remember one part of their discussion. Ingersoll cautioned Naren: "Swami, you are too bold and outspoken for your own good. I must warn you to tone down your teaching of your new doctrines. Be very careful of how you criticize the way of life and thinking of the American people."

"Why do you say this, Colonel?" asked Naren.

"From long and bitter experience, Swami. Anything against, or deviating from Christian theology is considered blasphemy. Fifty years ago, a preacher such as you would have been hanged, burnt at the stake, or stoned," said Ingersoll.

Naren was surprised. "Surely you jest, Colonel. I cannot believe that the American people are capable of such bigotry and fanaticism. At least, I have not faced such problems till now. However, I shall keep your warning in mind."

Seeing them sitting together, I was struck by one fact. This great man of religion, and this great anti-religionist – how alike they were! Both were great orators, drawing huge crowds. Both had majestic and magnetic personalities. Both were blunt and direct, never minced words and both called a spade a spade. Both were against the bigotry of missionaries. The important difference was this. Ingersoll was antagonistic towards all religious ideals. Naren was tolerant of all religions and was even a devotee of Jesus Christ! Nevertheless, Naren and Ingersoll were highly compatible with each other.

Ingersoll now replied: "Swami, believe me. More damage has been done in the name of Christianity than was done in the wars. In the name of love and mercy and the compassionate Christ, instruments of torture were created. The thumbscrew, the collar of torture, the Scavenger's Daughter, and the rack were the arguments the Christians used, in the name of love and universal forgiveness."

ROBERT G. INGERSOLL

Naren said: "I imagine that every country has had a dark period when religion was at its worst. But what is your idea of religion, Colonel?"
"First, fear should not be the root of religion. Religion should not teach slave virtues to the devotee. It should not

be considered as a supernatural phenomenon. Most important, it should reform man. This it can never do, because religion is slavery. It is not real religion."

"And by real religion you mean……?" asked Naren.

Ingersoll said: "To stand erect and face the future with a smile. To rouse yourself to do all useful work. To increase knowledge; to develop the brain; to take burdens from the weak; to defend the right; to make a palace for the soul – this is real religion. It means the doing of justice, the giving to others every right you claim for yourself. It means the doing of duties of man to man, and in feeding the innocent. Real religion lies in saying what you believe is true."

Naren said: "I agree with you fully, Colonel. In fact, the Hindu religion goes much further along the road that you are traveling."

"How so?" asked Ingersoll.

"Our scriptures say that every soul is potentially divine. By work, or worship, or psychic control, or philosophy, manifest the divinity within. Do this by one or more or all of these, and be free. To be free, that is the whole of religion! Doctrines, dogmas, books, temples or forma are but secondary detail."

"That's wonderful!" said Ingersoll, "But again, how does it help others?"

"Colonel, a religion or God which cannot wipe the widow's tears, or bring a piece of bread to the orphan's mouth, is no religion at all. I do not believe in such a religion or such a God. Let us ourselves be Gods, and help others to become

Gods. BE and MAKE Gods! That is, as you say, real religion."

"Swami, I have great respect and regard for the Hindu religion. It is a dynamic religion. That is why the poverty and misery in India puzzle me. Why has this happened?" asked Ingersoll.

"Colonel, I consider our greatest national sin to be the neglect of the masses. That is one of the causes of our downfall. If we want to regenerate India, we must work for the masses. As long as touch-me-notism is your creed, and the kitchen pot your deity, you cannot rise spiritually."

Ingersoll said: "I could not agree with you more, Swami. There is one more thing. I have read your religious books to some extent. The sheer volume of the literature has defeated me. What would be the message of the Upanishads and the devotional works to an agnostic like me?"

Naren said: "Strength, strength is what the Upanishads speak to me from every page. Strength, O man, say the Upanishads, stand up and be strong!"

"Wonderful,' remarked Ingersoll, "And the devotional works?"

"You know," said Naren, "The sage Vyasa has written an ocean of devotional works, including our Epics. Once, centuries ago, a person like you asked him: 'Master, your works are voluminous, and my life is short. Please tell me, what is the gist of all your writings?'

The sage smiled and said: 'My son, the summary of all my works can be quoted in two sentences. They are: helping others is a virtue; hurting others is a sin.'
I have not found a better summary than this."

Col. Ingersoll actually clapped his hands and said: "Bravo! My faith in Hinduism has grown still further. But in America, such pearls are thrown mostly before swine. As for me, as an agnostic, I believe in making the most out of this world. I want to squeeze the orange dry! That is all we are sure of."
Naren had the last word: "I know a better way to squeeze the orange of this world than you do. I know how to get more out of it. Death is not the end for me, so I am not in a hurry. I know that there is no fear, so I enjoy the squeezing. Everyone is God to me. Think of the joy of loving man as God! Squeeze your orange this way, and get ten thousand-fold more out of it. Get every single drop!"
Col. Ingersoll and Naren met a number of times. I was present at only this one conversation. The two enjoyed each other's company. Probably it was a case of opposite poles attracting each other!

After his speaking engagements in Chicago were over, Naren left Chicago on the morning of November 20, 1893, to begin his tour of America with the lecture bureau. I lost touch with him, but the newspapers gave me details of where he was, and full reports of his speeches. He toured Iowa, Des Moines, Minneapolis, Detroit, Boston, Cambridge, Baltimore, Washington DC, and New York.

According to the newspapers, he was a sensation everywhere.

An incident which occurred in the Wild West badlands came to my knowledge under peculiar circumstances. Colored posters of Naren had been put up in the Grand Central Station during the Parliament of Religions. They remained there for a long time. One day, as I was working in the station, I saw a person dressed like a Western cowboy. He wore a Stetson hat, and riding boots with spurs on them. He was looking up at the poster of Naren, and mumbling to himself.

I was curious and came near him. He had taken off his hat, was slapping his thigh with it, and mumbling: "The son-of-a-gun, the-son-of-a-gun!"
I introduced myself to him. I found, to my surprise, that he was from a renowned university in the West. He and his friends, all university men, had taken to ranching. This is the story he told me.

This here Swami (he pronounced it 'Swam-me') came to our University. He spoke on Indian Philosophy to us in the faculty, and made it beautifully simple and logical. It was a lot of fun listening to him. He also spoke to the students about the power of concentration, which would help them in their tests and exams. Someone asked him what concentration did for him. He replied that it helped him to realize the Highest, which further heightened the concentration. This helped him to be balanced and unperturbed in any situation.

Some of my friends and I thought we should put him to the test. After all, pardner, the proof of the pudding is in the eating! We invited him to lecture in our town, and promised him a handsome donation for his country. Not that he asked for the donation or anything! He was quite happy just to speak.

On the day fixed, when he arrived, we took him to the town square. The speaking platform was a wooden tub, which we had placed bottom-up in the square. His dress was gorgeous, and he was the handsomest man we had seen, bar none. Soon, a large crowd gathered around him. He spoke on a subject quite dear to us ranchers. He told the crowd how Nature and God are synonymous. Nature should be nurtured, and not ravished. That was the way to God.

He quoted from Hindu philosophy about the subject. He moved on to philosophy proper in such simple and touching terms that the entire audience was fascinated. Even in the busy square, there was a hush as people strained to catch every word. It was the first time I had seen a rally in the square where people were so orderly and receptive. Even the town drunk was watching with mouth agape.

Suddenly, as we had planned beforehand, some cowboys rode into the square. They were whooping loudly, and firing their Colt revolvers in the air, and at the Swami. A number of bullets whizzed past the Swami's ears! A lot of dust was raised, and half the audience ran away. Soon the cowboys rode away, and the dust settled.

What did we see? The Swami's speech was going on as if nothing had happened! There had been no pause in his lecture. The audience had also come back and regrouped around him. The people closest to the Swami were our people, who knew of the prank. They told us later that at no time had the Swami paused, hesitated, or looked afraid. In fact, he was probably not even aware of the disturbance that had taken place! This meant that he walked his talk, that he put his money where his mouth was! His concentration had been so great that he had noticed nothing else!

"I kid you not," said the rancher, "That son-of-a-gun was a real cool fellow, cooler than ice, I swear! As his speech finished, all of us cowboys crowded around him to shake his hand. We pronounced him a right good fellow. If he had shown the faintest sign of being scared, we would have branded him a greenhorn and a tenderfoot. That's what we call an inexperienced newcomer to the cattle country of the Wild West. He wasn't that, for land's sake! He was the straightest-shooter we had ever seen!"

Much before this, the "straight-shooter" had created sensational news for the newspapers. He was attracted to, and much admired, America. But he could not be blind to its faults. He forthrightly damned the brutality and inhumanity he saw around him. The vices appalled him, and he condemned them roundly. In Boston, the artificiality of the audience enraged him. His subject went out the window. Instead, he called the audience a band of foxes and wolves! The scandal was terrific! The newspapers had a field day.

Religious hypocrisy, especially false Christianity, was also roundly criticized by Naren. The news reports printed statements such as these: "...Those who call upon Christ care for nothing but to amass riches! Christ would not find a stone on which to lay His head amongst you....You are not Christians! Return to Christ!"

Many clergymen condemned Naren in return, accusing him of blasphemy, and wrong-doing. They spread lies about him. All this was in the newspapers, too. Naren did not back down one bit. He committed all these buffoons, hypocrites and charlatans to the Devil! He never took sides with one sect or another. Slowly, surely, his moral character and his idealism shone brightly wherever he went. This attracted admirers and defenders from all quarters. These later became his first Western disciples.

Then he found that the Slayton Lyceum Lecture Bureau was cheating him, exploiting him and defrauding him! In the beginning, Naren got as much as $900 for a single lecture. As the tour went on, the amount started to come down. One lecture earned $2500; Naren got only

$200. Even the fiscally innocent Naren realized that he was being robbed. With the help of financial experts, he recalculated what he should have earned. He found that he had lost $5000!

Disgusted, outraged, he thought of abandoning his project and going back to India. In his short letters to me, he told me that he was also tired and fed-up with lecturing. In Detroit, he had the lecture contract scrutinized by several jurist friends. They opined that it was a shameful fraud, and could be annulled at any time he wanted. Naren requested his friend Mr. Palmer to try to annul the contract. By the time Naren returned to Detroit a second time, Mr. Palmer had been successful in his mission. The shameful contract had been annulled. There was considerable pecuniary loss to Naren, but the Lecture Bureau no longer controlled him. The Cyclonic Hindu, as he was called, was free to lecture independently again!

****

HOLD ON YET A WHILE, BRAVE HEART

If the sun by the cloud is hidden a bit,
If the welkin shows but gloom,
Still hold on yet a while, brave heart,
The victory is sure to come.

No winter was but summer came behind,
Each hollow crests the wave,
They push each other in light and shade;
Be steady then and brave.

The duties of life are sore indeed,
And its pleasures fleeting, vain,

The goal so shadowy seems and dim,
Yet plod on through the dark, brave heart,
With all thy might and main.

Not a work will be lost, no struggle vain,
Though hopes be blighted, powers gone,
Of thy loins shall come the heirs to all,
Then hold on yet a while, brave soul,
No good is e'er undone.

Though the good and the wise in life are few,
Yet theirs are the reins to lead,
The masses know but late the worth;
Heed none and gently guide.

With thee are those who see afar,
With thee is the Lord of Might,
All blessings pour on thee, great soul,
To thee may all come right!

SWAMI VIVEKANANDA

CHAPTER 20

THE GREAT BATTLES

In 1894, I was involved in the great strike against the Great Northern Railroad. The railroad cut the wages of its trackmen from a dollar and a quarter to a dollar a day. The trackmen walked out, and demanded from the ARU that a strike be called on the Great Northern. Debs requested arbitration with James J. Hill, the President of Great Northern, before calling a full-fledged strike. Debs always believed that strikes were bad medicine.

Before meeting Hill, Debs came to Schumpeter for statistics about the various problems the trackmen were experiencing. Though a management man, Schumpeter always had a soft corner for Debs. He compiled voluminous statistics. Debs saw the paperwork and groaned: "Bill, how am I going to read through all this? How am I going to remember it? Where's the time?"

Schumpeter thought a bit, and said: "Gene, take Jock McClintock with you. Once he glances through all this data, he's going to remember it forever, even the statistics. When you're with Hill, and you want to quote statistics, just tell Jock to trot it out. You'll get what you want."

Debs looked skeptical, but he had no choice. I spent the night studying the statistics in detail. By morning, I had compartmentalized them in my head for instant recall.

James Jerome Hill, President of the Great Northern Railway, was called "The Empire Builder." Hill had but one dream – the completion of the Great Northern's transcontinental line to the Pacific. In 1893, he fulfilled that dream. A joke about the rapid expansion made the rounds. People said: If the West was settled from the ox-cart, then the 'Hill Country' was settled from the box-car. Hill's method was unique. He laid the rails first. He then worked around the clock to create traffic for the trains.

Hill quickly saw that there were two things required for the success of his plans. First, he had to create colonies of settlers along the tracks. Second, he had to make the settlers stay in the colonies. To create the colonies, he sold land to anyone who wanted to settle there. To create stability for the settlers, he embarked on far-sighted schemes.

With the help of experts, he taught new techniques of farming, with improved methods, to the settlers. He introduced the ideas of soil-diversification, improved seeds, and experimental farms. He succeeded far better than he had hoped he would. The railroad mileage expanded rapidly. Mind you, all this was done only with the original grant of the Minnesota & Pacific! No other land grants or government subsidies were required! This was financial wizardry at its highest!

We went to meet Mr. Hill at St. Paul, Minneapolis. Hill's office was very large. The carpet was so lush that our feet sank into it. Hill was very impressive, too. He had a large head with a receding hairline. He had massive eyebrows, large bony nose and a thick mustache. His beard was very aggressive-looking. His right eye was made of glass.

There was a joke about the eye. Hill was notoriously tight-fisted. One day, a rising businessman came for a loan to him. After negotiations were over, Hill told him: "Here is the last test. I'll give you the check if you can tell me which of my eyes is made of glass."
The businessman looked at him keenly and said: "The right eye."
After giving him the check, Hill asked him: "How did you find out?"
With the check safe in his pocket, the businessman said: "That was the eye which looked kinder!"

Be that as it may, it was the first President of any organization that I had met. I was awed and impressed by the power that seemed to crackle from him. Hill greeted us very politely, and asked to sit down. The greetings over, he looked towards me enquiringly. Debs immediately said: "He is my record-keeper, Mr. Hill."
Hill nodded at me, and asked Debs what he could do for us. He treated Debs like an equal. They exchanged backgrounds, and found they were very much alike in their beginnings. Of course, Hill was a multi-millionaire now.

A very civilized discussion followed, and I was forced to recognize how intelligent Hill was. From time to time, I reeled out the statistics about the problems of the trackmen. Hill would very carefully listen, and then clarify some points with Debs. At the end of the discussion, Hill did not agree to the requests of Debs. Debs told Hill that he was left with no option but to call a strike. Hill just wished us good day, and ushered us out.

JEROME J. HILL

Reluctantly, Debs called the railroaders out on a strike. They responded with an enthusiasm that surprised even Debs. For eighteen days, the Great Northern stood still. The GN was an extremely important railway. It carried freight and passengers West through Milwaukee to the Pacific Northwest. Cessation of services meant a huge loss to the railroad every day.

Hill tried every method to break the strike and run the railroad. He offered inducements to a section of the workers if they went back to work. They did not. Hill then tried to get troops to run the railroad. He failed in that, too. Even judicial restraint failed to stop the strike.

The Members of the Chamber of Commerce of Minneapolis were hurting financially because of the strike. They decided to act on their own. They first requested Debs to come to Minneapolis, and tell them his side of the story. Debs took me again with the statistics and other records. Debs gave them a list of demands. If they were met, the railroad men would return to work.

Debs asked for a Mr. Pillsbury to be the Arbitrator. Pillsbury was a millionaire flour-miller and a member of the Chamber of Commerce. Debs said they would abide by his judgment if Pillsbury did the settlement.

In an astonishing decision, the Chamber granted ninety-seven and one half-percent of the workers demands! The strike was over! The one fall-out for me was that I got noticed favorably for my photographic memory. Both Mr. Hill and the members of the Chamber were impressed. Schumpeter was asked to promote me to a junior management position. Of course, my technical know-how was to be fully utilized in that position also. Debs was delighted by this, and so was Naren when I wrote to him about it.

Naren, in turn, happily informed me that in New York, in early 1894, he had gotten his first American disciple, Leon Landsberg. A Russian Jew by birth, he had an impressive intellectualism based on European philosophy and culture. He was intelligent and hardworking. He was a working journalist. What attracted Naren to him was the fact that he was unhesitatingly generous towards the poor and oppressed.

LEON LANDSBERG

But for Naren, in general, it was a period of despair. Almost a year had passed, and the target of his funds for India was being reached very slowly. True, America was going through a Depression. That was hardly the reason for Naren's financial doldrums. The target he had set for India was moderate by American standards. His rich acquaintances were not affected much by the Depression.

Naren's problem was not due to America's "poverty." For all that, the collecting of funds was a slow process.

Two more reasons caused Naren's despair. The first reason was the continued silence from India. Not a word had been uttered in Naren's official support till now. The Hindu community seemed to have given up on him. This provided fuel for the fire of slander against Naren.

Second, the fast emerging relentless campaign against Naren by his Christian and Hindu enemies was extremely attritive. They decried his work, and slandered his character. The Press printed everything that came their way.

By April, Naren was in deep distress. His main fear was that his American friends would lose faith in him. About the silence from India, he instinctively understood. The lack of support was due to the characteristic apathy of India and the Indians.

True, immediately after his triumph at the Parliament of Religions, the whole of India had been jubilant. Pamphlets from Calcutta highlighting extracts from local papers, cuttings from Indian newspapers – all of these had reached Naren. But neither were they official approval, nor had they been reflected in the American newspapers.

There was only one way for Naren to be declared as an authority on Hinduism. The Heads of various Hindu communities should unite, declare him their authorized representative, and thank America for receiving Naren handsomely on behalf of India. The Heads of the communities were not bothered to take up this aspect. This was typical, too. In many cases, the Heads of the communities did not even see eye-to-eye with each other!

Regarding the enemies, Naren had three sets. The first set was, naturally enough, the Christian missionaries. The exposures by Naren, and the other Oriental delegates, at the Parliament of Religions had dealt a financially crippling blow to the missionaries. Contributions, especially to the Indian missionary funds, came down annually by almost a million dollars!

The missionaries were livid! Their way of negating Naren's influence was to declare him a charlatan. Why, they said, what Naren preached as Hinduism was totally rejected by Hindus themselves! What more proof was required than the fact that not a word of official support had been heard from India regarding Naren's 'adventure'!

The second set of enemies was the Theosophists. They allied themselves with the missionaries, and trumpeted the same propaganda.

The third set was the worst, the most vicious, a stab in the back for Naren. This set provided the ammunition for the slander of Naren by the missionaries. This enemy was the Brahmo Samaj, and the calumny was propagated by their leader, Pratap Chandra Mazoomdar!

PRATAP CHANDRA MAZOOMDAR

Yes, it was the same Mazoomdar who had been a fellow-delegate of Naren at the Parliament of Religions! He had been brilliant, too, at the Parliament. But it was like, as Naren's Master had remarked about Keshab, holding a candle before the sun! The green demon of jealousy captured Mazoomdar. Even in Chicago he had been hinting that Naren was a non-entity in India, a pseudo-monk and a cheat. Won over by him, Dr. Barrows was barely decent to Naren. In the Parliament, the brilliance of Naren nullified all these nigglings.

In India, Mazoomdar returned to the attack openly. His main allegation was that Naren was leading an active sexual life in America. His celibacy was a sham! The brother monks of Naren were horrified. Some wanted to launch a counter-attack. Naren advised them: "Ignore what he and the other enemies say. Remember the words of the Master, 'the dog barks, but the caravan carries on!'"

Mazoomdar was hoist on his own petard very soon. During one lecture, he was eloquently slandering not only Naren but also Naren's Master. One of the members of the audience got up. He handed Mazoomdar a published article, and asked him: "Excuse me. But did you not write this?"

Fifteen years ago, Mazoomdar had been a disciple of Ramakrishna! He had written glowingly about the Master's celibacy, his love of God, his holiness and his endless wisdom! Now he was slandering the same Master! This exposure of his hypocrisy literally struck him dumb!

The final blow to Mazoomdar came from another brother-delegate, that too in the heart of Calcutta!! It was totally unexpected, completely unsolicited and the brother-delegate did not even know that he was defending Naren against anything! The brother-delegate was the Buddhist Dharmapala.

Dharmapala was lecturing at the Minerva Theatre in Calcutta. He went into rhapsodies about Naren in his lecture "Swami Vivekananda and Hinduism in America." He extolled Naren's worth and brilliance. This was followed by an equally admiring speech by His Holiness the Buddhist Archbishop of Japan.

ANAGARIKA DHARMAPALA

This impartial Buddhist assessment of Naren's work in America silenced Mazoomdar for good. The final nail in his coffin was hammered in by the public meetings held at Calcutta supporting Naren and his work. The speakers were all stars in their fields – Pandits, aristocrats, the Judiciary, and members of the high society of Calcutta.

Meanwhile, in America, events were assuming alarming proportions for Naren. In one of his letters to me, I remember this paragraph:

'As you know, Jock, at all times I have depended, for everything, only on the Lord, and my Master. It is certain that they have given me guidance at every step. They have unfailingly protected me at all times. The latest example occurred at Detroit. At a reception, I was offered a cup of coffee. I lifted the cup to my lips. Suddenly, I saw my Master standing beside me. He shook his head, and said in an urgent tone: "Naren, stop! Do not drink! This is poison." I was so delighted at seeing my Master that his words hardly registered! The cup fell unheeded from my nerveless fingers. It smashed to pieces on the floor.'

I was very alarmed. Writing to him to be even more careful, I enclosed cuttings from the Boston *Daily Advertiser*. This was an ultra-conservative newspaper. Still, it carried scurrilous reports by Naren's enemies. The reports said that he was only a singer and an actor; he had crossed the ocean, so he could not be a Hindu; more so because he was addicted to meat and the smoking of cigars; that he was a depraved man-about-town etc etc.

The *Advertiser* had only reported; there was no elaboration or editorial by the newspaper itself. I suggested that turning the other cheek had its limitations in such battles. Silence may well be taken for agreement with the slander! Could not Naren do something to counter these unrestrained allegations? Maybe something indirect, I proposed, adding that Ingersoll had suggested this course of action. Naren in his reply said: "I agree. With the Lord's help I shall take active and aggressive action to stop this flood of filth. I must explain the correct position to my friends in India and in America."

For Naren, to think was to act. He wrote to his Madras disciple, Alasinga Perumal. The plan he proposed was two-pronged. Alasinga would first meet and explain the problem to all Naren's admirers occupying the highest positions in India. These included the Rajas, the Princes, the Dewans, the Ministers, the Commissioners, the Civil Servants and the Religionists. Alasinga was to persuade them, in Naren's name, to hold public meetings. In these meetings resolutions should be passed, extolling the work done by Naren in America.

Next, Alasinga was to get glowing testimonials from all those who were very familiar and convinced about Naren's work, knowledge, and character. These included the Raja of Khetri, the Maharaja of Mysore, the Raja of Ramnad, and the well-known Dewans of the Princely states.

The letters were written to Alasinga. Then followed months of anguish from April to August. Letters took time to reach their destination; action by Alasinga, if any, would also be time-consuming. During this period, Naren was worried by just one thing. The printed rubbish should not turn his American friends against him, especially Prof.

Wright, the Hales etc. He need never have worried. Anyone who came in the ambit of his blazing intellect and sincerity could never be influenced by the newspapers. As the Raja of Khetri had put it: "At the time of evaluation, glass will always remain glass, but a diamond will forever be a diamond!"

By the middle of August, a one-letter telegram from Alasinga reached Naren: "SUCCESS!"

M. C. ALASINGA PERUMAL

The truly remarkable Alasinga, no doubt with the Divine assistance of the Lord, had delivered, and how! He had done all that Naren had asked him to do, and more. At the huge public meetings, it was made sure that reporters from America and England were definitely present. The resolutions passed thanked not only Naren but also "the American people for the cordial and sympathetic reception they have accorded to Swami Vivekananda."

Next came the flood of testimonials, in glowing terms, at special press-conferences arranged by the Raja of Khetri, the Dewan of Junagadh and other important personages. These attested to Naren's antecedents, his work, his character, his vast knowledge of Hindu philosophy and his burning desire to spread this knowledge to America and Europe.

The resolutions passed in the meetings at Calcutta, Madras, and Bangalore were printed in their entirety in the American newspapers like the *Boston Evening Transcript*, the *Chicago Interocean*, the *New York Sun*, and even the *Boston Daily Advertiser*! These were followed by the testimonials, also printed in full, in all the national American newspapers.

Naren was vindicated! India had spoken! She had declared two things. The first was that Naren was the accredited ambassador of the purest and best Hinduism; the second fact was that he was no less than India's soul! The American public totally discounted the missionaries' propaganda hereafter. Of course, the chatter of calumny and antagonism kept on for a time, like the reflex twitching of a dead snake, or a headless corpse. But the chief obstacle to Naren's mission was effectively smashed.

Naren continued his lecturing in Chicago, New York, Massachusetts, Maryland and Washington DC. A subtle change took place in his mind. True, he intended to speak about India, and earn money for her. At the same time, he longed to be spiritually creative too; to highlight the harmony of religions.

MISS SARAH FARMER

The Parliament of Religions had been an eye-opener for Miss Sarah Farmer. Influenced by it, she founded a retreat on the bank of the Piscataqua River, near Eliot, Maine. She named it Greenacre. The purpose of Greenacre was to emphasize that all religions led ultimately to God. Spiritual rejuvenation was the main goal. It attracted a lot of like-minded people who wanted to escape from the fetters of the orthodox religion into something providing more freedom for the intellect, and the soul. The Greenacre Religious Conferences were exciting, much-awaited revivals.

THE SWAMI AT GREENACRE

Naren, the first propounder of the main goal, was naturally invited to speak at a Conference. He came to give a speech, and remained to teach! He badly wanted rest, anyway. So he remained for two weeks, teaching a group of 'students' Raja Yoga and the mantra 'Shivoham.' Like in a

Gurukul, he taught under a pine tree, called "Swami's Pine." These were his first known classes, a step towards the spiritual creation he had longed for. Most important, it was at Greenacre that he met Mrs. Sara Ole Bull for the first time.

Mrs. Bull was in her early forties. She had been a widow for fourteen years. She was married when she was twenty, to a Norwegian violinist, Ole Bull, who was a widower of sixty. It had been love at first sight for both of them. The marriage had its cultural hiccups; Sara was very conventional, Ole Bull was highly unconventional, belonging to a free society. Sara's mother, Mrs. Thorp, compounded matters by trying to tame her volatile son-in-law. She failed; Sara went to Norway.

MRS. SARA OLE BULL

After that, life was a fairy tale for the Bulls. Sara became her husband's business manager. She managed his concert tours and his other social affairs. She took loans from her father, whenever required. She adored and worshipped her aging, erratic husband. The Bulls later settled down in Cambridge. Ole Bull died; Sara continued at Cambridge. She became quite famous; her house was the meeting place for intellectuals and thinkers.

Naren found her invaluable. Her spirituality was beyond question. She was also very welcoming to other spiritual people. Her warm-heartedness won over everyone who met her. But beyond all this, she had a quality very helpful to Naren.

Having been her husband's tour manager, she was very knowledgeable about gatherings, audiences, managers and costs. She gave Naren excellent advice regarding his work. Naren had full faith and complete trust in her, and followed her advice implicitly. He regarded Mrs. Ole Bull as his mother, and called her Dhira Mata.

In Cambridge, Naren delivered a beautiful and informative lecture on the Indian Woman. He emphasized the high regard in which they were held. For a Hindu woman, two things are paramount; a noble character and her role as a mother. A startling comparison was made by Naren.

In the West, he said, the husband and wife were equal companions in a family. In India, the mother was the central pillar of the Hindu home; almost akin to God! The mother's unselfish love and suffering for her husband and children could never be equaled by anyone, excepting God. Naren paid unstinting tribute to his own mother, and said that whatever he was now, he owed to his mother's conscious efforts.

The ladies of Cambridge and Boston were overwhelmed by this emotional tribute to his mother by Naren, coming as it did from the depths of his heart. As a group, they sent to Naren's mother a picture of the Virgin Mary and child. It was enclosed with a letter expressing their profoundest salutations and respect. When he heard about this indirectly, Naren was deeply moved, and experienced the greatest joy.

While lecturing on the 'Ideals of Womanhood' at the Brooklyn Ethical Association, a matter-of-fact statement by Naren ignited the fires of his last battle in America. Dr. Lewis Janes was the President of the Ethical Association. In the course of his lecture, Naren made a simple, innocent and totally non-controversial statement about women in India: "In India, woman has enjoyed property rights since thousands of years. In the West, a man may disinherit his wife. In India, the whole estate of the deceased husband will go to the wife, personal property absolutely, real property for life."

This statement caused an upheaval among the members of the Ramabai Circle of Brooklyn. It devastated them!

PANDITA RAMABAI SARASWATI

The Pandita Ramabai Saraswati had had a checkered life. Born in 1858 into a Maratha priestly family, educated by her father at home in Sanskrit till his death, wandering all over India serving as cook in several Brahmin families, she also picked up a lot of religious customs, and her title 'Saraswati' from a professor of the University of Calcutta who declared her a Sanskrit scholar,

Married at twenty-two, widowed at twenty-four, with an eight-month old daughter, she sold her house, sailed for England, became a Christian convert, and a Professor of Sanskrit in Cheltenham College. Her life-mission was to start schools in India for child-widows.

She came to America to study modern educational methods. She remained in America, and formed fifty five 'Ramabai Circles' all over America. The Circles had highly influential preachers and writers. Ramabai was a brave, determined, adventurous risk taker, and her motives were commendable.

What *was* wrong were her means and methods to raise the money for the schools. There was already a poor opinion of India in the American mind. Ramabai added freely and imaginatively to this degradation. In a nutshell, widows were left to starve and drudge, five million of them were below four years of age, thousands of child-widows were dying of sin and shame, and one-fifth of the women in India were widows used as beasts of burden.

Her book 'The High-Caste Hindu Woman' pleaded with Americans to imagine what would happen if their beloved girls were reduced to this state. Her solutions – open your purses, buy my book in large numbers, and help these child-widows of India! The restless American women, denied any part in politics and business, embraced Ramabai's pleas with fervor.

In the middle of all this plenitude, here was a wandering Indian monk standing up for the Hindu widows! Naren's statement, that Indian law provided more protection to Hindu wives and widows than American law, was a thunderbolt to the Ramabai Circles. Their propaganda, which was a source of their funds, was being questioned! The American ladies in the Circles would lose faith! The only way to counter this was to attack Naren.

The President of the Brooklyn Ramabai Circle fired the first salvo in the *Daily Eagle*. The gist of it was a rehash of all that Ramabai had been saying so far about child widows: Girls of age from 3-6 getting married to men of 50 or 60, becoming widows soon with shaven-heads, dirty white saris, starved, overworked, and committing suicide. Naren, of course, had been lying through his teeth in his lecture!

The *Daily Eagle* smelled a controversy, and enhanced sales of their paper. They contacted the Brooklyn Ethical Society President, Dr. Janes, for clarification. Dr. Janes succinctly pointed out that Naren had spoken only about the property rights of high caste widows. Hindu law was superior to the American law in this matter. Hindu widows got absolute possession and control of their inheritance.

He added a sting in the tail by saying that Ramabai's work solicited money from Americans. Naren, however, never asked for any money in repayment as a Teacher. Voluntary offerings by the people in the lectures were accepted. Admiring donations by strangers were returned with thanks, as in the recent case of a check for $500. So, said Dr. Janes, Naren was the more credible!

LEWIS G. JANES

The Ramabai Circle had not heard the proverb, 'Discretion is the better part of valor.' They continued to publish more letters in the papers; Dr. Janes continued to rebut them. The Ramabai Circles had stirred a hornets' nest; the hornets came back to sting them. Finally, there was silence on their part.

Naren spoke again in Brooklyn on 'India's Gift to the World.' It did not touch at all on Ramabai or the Indian child-widows. Reporters, however, will always be reporters. They raked up the issue during the question session. Naren spoke his final word on the matter: "Hindus marry at all ages; some, like me, do not marry at all. When the husband dies, all his possessions go to his widow. If the family is poor, then the widow is also poor. This happens in all countries. Old men sometimes do marry children. If the husband is wealthy, it is all the better for the widow the sooner he died. I, on my part, have failed to see a case of the ill-treatment mentioned."

Thus Naren's last great battle in America ended. He was mostly a spectator in this battle, on the sidelines, spending no time, energy, or money. At the end, all his enemies were finally silent. More important, India had recognized and felicitated his work. His mission must go on!

*****

ILLUSION

God and I in space alone
And nobody else in view.
"And where are the people. O Lord," I said
"The earth below, and the sky o'erhead,
And all the dead whom once I knew?"

"That was a dream," God smiled and said,
"A dream that seemed to be true.
There were no people, living or dead,
There was no earth or sky o'erhead
There was only Myself in you."

"Why do I feel no fear," I asked,
"Meeting you here this way,
For I have sinned I know full well,
And is there heaven, and is there hell,
And is this the judgment day?"

"Nay, those were but dreams," the Great God said,
"Dreams that have ceased to be,
There are no such things as fear and sin,
There is no you —you have never been —
There is nothing at all but ME!"

ELLA WHEELER WILCOX

CHAPTER 21

THE AMERICAN LESSONS AND MISSION

In November 1894, Naren was in New York. He spent almost a month there. He began to organize the Vedanta Society. It was to serve a dual purpose. First, it would manage the plans for his programs, and the finances required for them. Second, it would ensure the simultaneous flow of Vedanta out of the center, and the flow of funds in for the Indian works. He started the groundwork for the Society. Before actually settling down in New York, Naren visited Cambridge again. There he held classes, lecturing from December 5 to December 27, 1894.

Several bridges had to be built before he started the work in New York. The first was the problem of widespread poverty and misery in India. In speech after speech Naren emphasized one thing; India was unsurpassable in spirituality, both in knowledge and in adherence. This meant that the religion of India was far superior to the religion of the West.

This begged the question from the practical Americans. If Indian religion was supreme, why was India so materially backward? After all, they said, rise in spirituality automatically meant a rise in wealth. Why then the dichotomy? It had been Ingersoll who had first raised this question with Naren in Chicago.

Naren had to answer this question very carefully. What was obvious to him was not so to the Americans. They had to be convinced that the dichotomy was natural. Naren's answer was that it was wrong to assume that spirituality and material wealth were tied to each other. They were not; they were mutually exclusive. He proved that when a people concentrated on spirituality, their material life suffered. Why, this happened in America, too! He quoted the examples of the American philosophers, like Henry David Thoreau, who had chosen solitude to civilization. Conversely, when a people concentrated on material progress, their spirituality suffered. This was the case with India and the West respectively.

Did that mean that Naren was opposed to material progress? No, a thousand times no! The only thing he detested was the dollar-worship! Naren was second to no man in his admiration of America.

It had started with a gape-mouth admiration of the wonders of the World's Fair. His travels made him see the Americans with their innovative skills, their industry, their hardiness, their adventurous spirit, their receptiveness to new ideas, their organizational skills, their dignity of labor, their insistence on the equality of all men, their systems and cleanliness. He wished this material progress to be reflected in India. In fact, that was why he had come here to the West.

America should not decrease an iota in its material progress, but it should steadily build up its spiritual progress, too. India should never come down from its spiritual level, but definitely build up its material progress. But how to combine the two? Naren's solution, his theory was: "Unite the spirituality of the East with the materialism of the West. The energy of the lion should be combined with the gentleness of the lamb. This combination will produce marvelous results."

This was the first step of his mission, his greatest contribution to both religious and secular thought. The wealthy spiritual Americans agreed with his analysis. In spite of all their wealth, and the token worship of God on Sundays, they did lack something. There was a vacuum in their minds, hearts and souls; otherwise why should the spiritual words of this Indian preacher fill that vacuum? And he was not even advocating any change in their religion. He was just telling them to strive spiritually for their own contentment, their own salvation. Thus, the first bridge was built and crossed.

The second bridge was the great role that women play in human society. He admired the American women. Kate Sanborn, Mrs. Wright, Kate Tannatt, Mrs. Lyon, Mrs. Hale, Miss Sara Farmer and Mrs. Ole Bull – all these women had amazed him. They were highly spiritual, yet highly organized. They did work which the men could not do! Even the ladies of the Ramabai Circles, in their own misguided way, had been a powerful force to reckon with.

Naren poetically described these women as being "…..like Lakshmi in beauty, and like Saraswati in virtue…" And the contrast in India? Indian men no doubt showed absolute respect to women. But how were women treated, especially in religion and religious endeavors? "Girls becoming mothers below their teens," "…we call women 'despicable worms,' 'gateways to hell' and so forth." Women in India must play their part in the uplift of India. The starting point: The Holy Mother, Sharada Devi! Naren and the other disciples had recognized her divinity.

In America, Naren realized the fact that The Holy Mother had a great part to play in the elevation of women. The first action to take was to build a Math for the Mother. Naren would send 7000 rupees for the purpose. His reasoning: "Without Shakti, the world cannot be regenerated. We are holding Shakti in dishonor in India. Mother has been born to revive that wonderful Shakti….Hence her Math should come first…..First Mother and Mother's daughters, then Father and Father's sons……Mother's grace is a hundred thousand times more valuable than Father's!"
The planning for the second bridge had begun.

The third bridge was the most difficult. Mrs. Lyon once told me a funny incident with Naren. Shortly after the Parliament of Religions, Naren one day remarked to Mrs. Lyon, in a very thoughtful mood: "Mother, I have had the greatest temptation of my life in America."

"Uh-oh," thought Mrs. Lyon, "Here falls another eligible bachelor!"

Aloud, she said to Naren: "May I ask who she is, Swami?"

Naren looked startled for a moment, and then burst out laughing: "Oh no, no, no, mother! It is not a lady! It is Organization!"

Mrs. Lyon asked: "And why is organization a temptation?"

Naren replied: "Because we Hindus believe that organization brings new evils. I am convinced that what I have in mind requires organization as an essential part. Otherwise the work will be stalled."

The third bridge was obnoxious because it contained the dirty word: organization! A spiritual man, engrossed in his prayers and salvation, shunned organization like the plague. He would be part of a group to start with, but only so that he could eventually part from it to rise spiritually. Naren realized the power of organization soon after coming to America. It was required for his future work in India. It was also essential for the East-West culture that he had in mind.

Naren had seen two organizations in India. The first was the Brahmo Samaj. It had split into splinters because there were too many leaders, too many persons wanting to be leaders. Jealousy was the most damaging factor.

The second was the Arya Samaj. It had survived and grown from strength to strength, but it had depended on an almost dictatorial leadership of one man alone,

Dayananda. It was limited to some parts of India. And...and... the Master had found Dayananda wanting. Dayananda insisted that he alone was in the right, and therefore had the right to impose his will.

The Master had condemned this attitude of a leader. From his life with the Master, Naren had seen that the Master was iron-willed, but allowed latitude and democracy to his disciples. He had been a *gentle* dictator. Co-operation by all was his motto. That was what was required from the Order that Naren was trying to visualize.

The difficult task of convincing his brother-monks in India loomed before him. At Calcutta, the Alambazar Math was like a *serai,* a free guest house for travelers. It was also a much disorganized *serai*. Some of the monks lived there, performing ceremonial worship. Some monks came and went. Some monks were wandering around India. Some were practicing austerities in holy places. All these were in consonance with the teaching of the Master – seeking salvation through solitude, austerity and meditation. Only one maverick, Swami Akhandananda, on his own, was doing something different. At Khetri, he was working to remove the sufferings of the tenants of the Raja of Khetri.

These were the persons that Naren had to transform if the work of the Ramakrishna Order was to begin and go on in India. The only way to start the transformation was to write them letters for now.

Naren always wrote to Swami Ramakrishnananda. These letters were then circulated to all the other brother-monks. The first two letters were informative. In these, he gave them pointers about what he had in mind for them, and what they had to do. He also wanted to know from them what was going on in the Math at present. He received a reply from Calcutta regarding present day activities. Naren's third letter was a thunderbolt to the brothers in the Math.

He started by reminding them that the Master had been told specifically by the Divine Mother to serve humankind. The Master had also, in his speeches, emphasized that man is God; and must be served. This was what the Math and the Order was supposed to do. Naren roundly condemned ceremonial worship. He dubbed it madness and imbecility. These rituals must be rejected forthwith!

And what must the monks do instead? Naren was very clear about it: Most of you should spread the idea of the Universal aspect of God from village to village, door to door. This is the real work, to do the highest good to the world.

The next letter to Calcutta was even more explicit: Organize, make converts everywhere, start centers at places, create a sensation everywhere. Give up passivity and stand up, move around the country preaching. The end of the letter showed clearly to all that Naren was being directed by a Divine Force: "Arise! Arise! A tidal wave is coming! Onward.... There is no time to care for name, or fame, or Bhakti! We shall look to these at some other time...He is at our back. I cannot write any more. Onward!...Have faith! Onward! Great Lord! I feel as if somebody is moving my hand to write this way..."

Naren's letters created tremendous confusion in the Calcutta Math. His directions seemed divorced from reality. They were asked to serve others, feed the poor, and nurse the sick? They were to be teachers, preachers, and organizers? They must open centers all over? Each brother-monk asked: "Who, me?"

More to the point, how? They lived hand-to-mouth; where were the funds for all this? The Master had always led them along traditional paths; he had never told them what Naren was now telling them to do. These must be Naren's own ideas, under the influence of the West. The brothers did nothing; they did not try even one single idea.

The brothers, after all, had no idea how the Master was keeping Naren jumping through hoops in the West. Swami Akhandananda, in Khetri, was totally ignorant of what Naren had written. But he was doing the social work suggested by Naren in a small way. However, his was a voice in the wilderness. Naren's directions kept pricking the brothers' consciences nevertheless. He was their leader, after all!

SWAMI AKHANDANANDA

Letter after letter regularly followed. Organization was the emphasis in each. Expansion, motion and growth were stressed. Organization of the little society was important. Naren's motto was: "Expansion is life; contraction is death." Letter after letter hammered this point home. The brothers and other disciples at Calcutta, Madras and Mysore stirred, and began to take small hesitant steps. The third bridge had been proposed, and the blueprints prepared. Someday…someday, the bridge would become a reality.

In one of his infrequent letters to me, Naren wrote about how his Master guided and helped him. It was no stranger a tale than the tales he had told me at the Grand Central. It seemed that the Master was very clear about where he should go, and where not. After a day's lecturing and meeting persons, he would return to his room tired. What to prepare for the next day's lecture?

As he lay resting on his bed, a voice would begin to shout at him. Sometimes, there would be two voices arguing loudly. Whatever, he merely had to concentrate on what was said. The one voice would be his lecture for the next day; the two voices would be the lecture and the question and answer session. Naren said this was divine guidance; maybe this was how the sages who formulated the Vedas got their guidance!

The groundwork for the three bridges laid, Naren was now ready to settle down in New York. End January 1895 saw him lodged at 54 West 33rd Street. The area was poor and undesirable, the lodgings were sordid and shabby. Purposely so. Naren did not want people to come to him only because he was famous. He wanted sincere and spiritual-minded people to come. His teachings would be free of charge. The first course would be from February to June 1895. The instructions for the chosen disciples would be in Raja Yoga and Jnana Yoga.

The popular poetess, Mrs. Ella Wheeler Wilcox and her husband dropped in out of curiosity. She was the poetess who wrote the famous lines

Laugh, and the world laughs with you;
Weep, and you weep alone.
For the sad old earth must borrow its mirth
But has trouble enough of its own.

ELLA WHEELER WILCOX

The atmosphere in the class was so electric that they were spellbound. They attended the classes regularly for months. The winter was severe; for the American economy it was a winter of despair! Depression, failing banks and plunging stocks made businessmen suicidal. Mr. Wilcox would spend sleepless nights of worry and anxiety. After each lecture he would come out smiling and say: "It's ok. There is nothing to worry about."

For Naren, the financial scenario was bleak for another reason. His classes were free. His public lectures fetched him some money, enough to make both ends barely meet. But he was supremely satisfied. He refused donations from all sources, including from Mrs. Ole Bull. He felt free, and he taught like the sages of yore, as he liked, what he liked. He said "Live alone, walk alone…" He was at this time not raising funds for India.

Betty Sturges, a widow with two children, lived at Dobbs Ferry on the Hudson River. Her sister Josephine MacLeod lived with her. They accepted an invitation from a friend in New York to come see a wonderful holy man from India. They entered a room filled with about 25 people. All the chairs were taken. Betty and Jo sat on the floor in the front row. Naren, of course, captivated them. One of his sentences echoed in their minds: "Forget that you are American. Forget that you are women. Remember day and night that you are always children of God. Never forget this."

Some weeks later, Naren was speaking at a lodging house to about one hundred people. Jo attended the lecture, which was on the Gita. When Naren started the lecture, Jo had a vision. Naren vanished. In his place stood Krishna himself, explaining the Gita. Jo was overwhelmed. In the future, she was to prove one of Naren's most devoted friends and helpers.

Frank Leggett was an extraordinarily rich New York businessman in the high-quality grocery trade. He was courting the widowed Betty Sturges. Betty and Jo kept Naren a secret from Frank. One day, he invited Betty and Jo for dinner. They agreed on condition that it would finish soon, as they had an appointment later.

After dinner was over, Frank asked them what the appointment was. They replied that it was a lecture. Frank asked if he could attend it, too. Reluctantly, they agreed.

Frank went to the lecture and hung on to every word of Naren's. After the lecture, he went to Naren, shook his hand and requested him: "Swami, will you dine with me?"

As a businessman, Frank admired Naren from a totally different viewpoint. He said of Naren: "He has more common sense than anyone I've ever known."

FRANCIS AND BETTY LEGGETT

Naren had worked almost non-stop for almost two years in America. He was exhausted. Frank Leggett invited Naren to spend the Easter holidays at Ridgely, his country place in the Hudson River Valley, near the Catskill Mountains. Naren accepted gratefully.

It was a relief to get away from the noisy, grimy city. The countryside was green and filled with the flowers of spring. At Ridgely, the main house was the 'Manor.' A large play-house, equipped with tennis courts, gyms, and bowling alleys was the 'Casino.' There was also a well-kept nine-hole golf course on the premises. Naren rested at Ridgely. There was no teaching, but plenty of horse-play and acrobatics. He got on very famously with his hosts. Leggett, Betty, her son Hollister, Jo, and Naren occupied the 'Manor.'

JOSEPHINE MACLEOD

HOLLISTER STURGES

Betty's son Hollister admired Naren hugely. When he met me later, Hollister had two stories to tell about Naren. The first story was about golf. One day, Naren and Hollister were walking on the golf course. Naren saw the flag near the hole, and asked: "What flag flutters there?"
Hollister got a club, a ball and a tee-box. He explained the game to Naren, and concluded: "Good players require 4 strokes to put the ball in the hole. Beginners require more than eight strokes. You can use the club any way you want."
Naren measured the distance with his eye, and said: "With one stroke, I shall put the ball in the hole."

Hollister smiled and said: "Impossible!"
Naren asked him: "Want to bet on it?"
Hollister had fifty cents. Naren took out a dollar. Leggett arrived on the scene. Hollister told him about the bet.

Leggett pooh-poohed Naren's claim and said: "Even experts rarely achieve the hole-in-one."
Naren smiled and replied: "What is your bet?"
Leggett took out ten dollars from his pocket.

Naren asked Hollister to stand near the flag, but not too close. Naren pulled up the sleeves of his robe, looked fixedly at the flag, and swung the club. Shortly after, Hollister shouted: "The ball is in the hole!"
Leggett was astounded. He looked at Naren suspiciously and said: "Swami, I'm sure your yoga has something to do with this!"
Naren laughed and said: "Nonsense. Yoga has nothing to do with this. This is such a trifling matter."
"Then how did you shoot the hole-in-one?"
"I'll tell you in two sentences. First, I measured the distance by sight, and I know my strength. Second, I told my mind that I would be richer by ten dollars and a half. Then I swung."

The second story of Hollister was this. One day, Hollister walked past Naren's bedroom door. He heard peals of laughter coming from the room. Later, Hollister asked him: "Who were you talking to?"
Naren replied: "No one. I was meditating alone."
"But what was all that laughter about?"
Naren paused, and then said: "Oh Hollister, God is so funny!"

When Naren returned to New York, Leggett gifted him a large box of cigars – "a thousand cigars," as Naren put it. The holiday had done Naren a world of good physically and mentally.

On his return, Naren found the rooms empty. Leon Landsberg, his assistant, had absconded! Leon was a very contradictory person. A rootless person, he was victim to depression, a violent temper, self-pity, and paranoia. Many times, he not only tortured himself but was also an endless source of trouble to others. Naren met him and accepted him at a time when the contradictions were not apparent. Naren would always love Leon, and always give him the respect due to the first American disciple.

Till now, Naren and his living-companion had worked harmoniously. When the classes grew, many students claimed Naren's attention. Leon's latent faults ballooned. He became jealous of the students. He made enemies of many of them. Naren sought to pacify him, but he quarreled with him, too. During the entire period Leon was moping, sulking, complaining and criticizing. During Naren's absence, he fled. Naren took the matter equably, and said to me: "May the Lord bless Leon wherever he goes. He is one of the few sincere souls I had the privilege in this life to come across."

From a rooming house, Leon continued his preaching and teaching. He held classes on Karma Yoga. His classes did not clash with Naren's. He claimed that he did not bear any grudge against Naren; he loved him still. In the interest of peace, he had decided to keep away. Leon never returned to Thirty-Third Street to help Naren. But Mrs. Ole Bull, regularly corresponding with Leon, persuaded him to return to Naren's fold, at least in spirit. Leon agreed to this. Naren also accepted him gladly.

Naren's classes ended on June 1. People were leaving for the mountains and sea beaches to avoid the summer heat. The disciples, however, requested him to continue the classes during summer. But Naren felt that the summer heat would break the students' concentration. He also wanted the work to become permanent. The idea was to train a group of men and women to eventually carry on the work. How to do this, and yet avoid the enervating heat of summer?

The Lord provided a means for this, too!

***

DVAITA

GOD AND YOU

Water can never its own thirst sate,
No tree, for tasting, its own fruit ate,
When you and the Lord be different,
Then joyous love is most apparent!
If you say the Lord and you are one,
That joy, that love is instantly gone!
Ne'er pray that you and the Lord be one!!

If the diamond and setting be one,
Where remains the beauty of the stone?
We seek cool shade during burning heat,
If they are one, is comfort complete?
The loving mother and child are two,
If they are one, then who will love who?
When the parted child and mother meet,
What joy they find, it is bliss replete!
What joy will there be if both be one?
Ne'er say that you and the Lord are one!!

SANT TUKARAM

VISHISHTA ADVAITA

The Supreme Lord, is without name and form, attributeless? Oh, forsooth!
Brahman is Narayana, and with qualities infinite, in truth.

Transcendent, immanent, and pervading both nature and the living,
He pervades the universe; from Him it's born, into Him dissolving!

The sentient and insentient, the Supreme Self pervades yet both,
Brahman is Antaryami, the real self of all beings, on my oath!

SRI RAMANUJACHARYA

ADVAITA

Sarvam Khalvidam Brahma; All this is Brahman! The entire
Universe, with all its glories, seen, unseen, all we admire!
(Chandogya Upanishad-Samaveda)

Pragnanam Brahma; Brahman is Consciousness, Intelligence,
Wisdom, selfhood, awareness, subjectivity, sentience!
(Aitareya Upanishad-Rgveda)

Ayam atma Brahma; This Soul is Brahman! Thus our True Self,
The source of all consciousness, is nothing but Brahman itself!
(Mandukya Upanishad-Atharvanaveda)

Aham Brahmasmi; I am Brahman! The soul enshrined in mine
Body is the real Me! Ergo, I say I am Divine!

(Brhadāranyaka Upanishad-Shukla Yajurveda)

Tat twam asi; That thou art! If I, my Soul, am Brahman free,
It follows that what's true for Me, must hold also true for Thee!
(Chandogya Upanishad-Samaveda)

THE MAHAVAKYAS OF ADVAITA IN THE VEDAS AND UPANISHADS
Let me state in just half a couplet, what a million texts have weaved and spun,
Brahman alone is real, the world unreal; Atman and Brahman are one!

ADI SHANKARACHARYA

CHAPTER 22

THE AMERICAN DISCIPLES

One of Naren's New York disciples was a Miss Dutcher. She owned a cottage at Thousand Island Park on the St. Lawrence River. The cottage was three hundred miles from New York, near the Canadian border. She gladly offered the cottage to Naren for his use during summer. As many students as would fit into the cottage were welcome.

MISS ELIZABETH DUTCHER

The Park would be crowded in summer, but the cottage was some distance away. Quiet and secluded, it was an ideal summer retreat. Naren agreed with pleasure. He asked the interested students to proceed to the Park. He would join them a little later. He had an appointment with Frank Leggett at Camp Percy. This was Frank's fishing camp in the White Mountains of New Hampshire.

The short vacation at Camp Percy was a Godsend. Naren felt revivified. The woods, the lake and the quiet reminded him of an ashram. He had moments of solitude whenever he wished. The company was also very pleasant. Frank, Betty, Jo and Georgia Spence looked after Naren very well. The occasion was the betrothal of Frank and Betty, their engagement. They were to be married in Paris in September.

One morning, Naren told Jo: "Jo, I am going to sit under that pine, and read the Bhagawad Gita. See that the breakfast is sumptuous today."
Half an hour passed. Jo came to the pine to call Naren. She saw him sitting motionless. The book had fallen from his hand. He was not breathing. Jo was terrified, and ran to Leggett. She told him: "Come quickly. Swami Vivekananda has left us."
Frank, Betty and Jo ran to the tree. Leggett looked closer and said: "He is in a trance. I shall shake him awake."
Jo immediately shouted: "Don't touch him. It's dangerous for him."

All three watched and waited. After five more minutes, breathing resumed. Then Naren opened his eyes and said three times: "Who am I, where am I?"

Then he got up hurriedly, very embarrassed. He said to them: "I am sorry to have frightened you all. This state comes now and then. I shall not leave my body in your country. Betty, I'm hungry! Let's hurry!"

The Ashram-like surroundings had sent him into Samadhi!

By June 19, Naren was at the Thousand Island Park. The railhead was Clayton. From there, a steamer took him to the Park Dock. From the Dock, he went by horse and buggy to Miss Dutcher's cottage. It was a little two-storey house. Before Naren's arrival, Miss Dutcher had added a wing to it for more comfort. The students from New York, the future disciples, had already arrived there.

Miss Mary Elizabeth Dutcher was a devout Methodist. The Methodists were very orthodox, missionary-minded Protestants. Miss Dutcher was all that, prim and proper, but also a bit of a rebel. She went to New York, taught art and exhibited her paintings. She wandered into Naren's classes. What he said went totally against all her religious conditioning. The conflict was unbearable. She would disappear for two or three days at a time, but always wander back in. She held on, even to the extent of inviting this (according to her) deeply controversial monk to her cottage. She would play a leading role in Naren's mission in the future.

MISS DUTCHER'S COTTAGE

Miss Sarah Ellen Waldo, a distant relation of the philosopher Ralph Waldo Emerson, had studied his writings deeply. She had also read the works of Prof. Max Muller. She knew about Vedanta. She heard Naren first at the Brooklyn Ethical Association, and then attended his classes. She was tall, stout and domineering. She annoyed and irritated the others sometimes. But she was efficient, tireless and did most of the work.

SARAH ELLEN WALDO

Miss Ruth Ellis was a close friend of Miss Waldo, and of about the same age. She was gentle and retiring, and seldom spoke. She and a Dr. Wright had been attending lectures on philosophy, together with Miss Waldo, for close to thirty years. Dr. Wright was over seventy, but was as curious and enthusiastic as a young boy.

Walter and Frances Goodyear, a young, childless couple, came from New Jersey. They knew Naren, and had helped him in New York. Walter was the Treasurer of the New York Vedanta Society.

Two strange women had also come to the Park. The first was Miss Stella Campbell, a one-time actress. Her motive in coming seemed to be to become young and beautiful again by embracing spirituality. She rarely attended the classes. Fasting, and ascetic practices, were what she followed at the Park.

The second woman was a Frenchwoman, who was an American citizen. She was Mme. Marie Louise. She was a tall and very masculine looking person with a heavy voice. She was quite ahead of her times. She wore the robe of a monk, and she had come to learn Jnana Yoga. She was quite sincere, and she could speak well in public. While giving her sannyasa, Naren named her Swami Abhayananda.

SWAMI ABHAYANANDA (MARIE LOUISE)

Leon Landsberg had been asked by Naren through a letter to come to the Park. He did come. He was also initiated into monk-hood under the name Swami Kripananda.

SWAMI KRIPANANDA (LEON LANDSBERG)

Two latecomers to the Park were Mrs. Mary Funke and Miss Christine Greenstidel. Mary's husband Charles Funke was a wholesale grocer in Detroit. Mary was good-looking, optimistic and had a sense of humor. She had dreams of wearing the robes of a monk and residing in Himalayan caves. Naren disabused her good-naturedly and told her: "You are a householder. Find God in your husband and family. That is your path at present." Mary very sensibly followed Naren's advice.

Christine Greenstridel was also from Detroit. She was a teacher in the Detroit Public Schools. The day she arrived, Naren told her: "I am planning several initiations tomorrow. I don't know you well enough to initiate you too. If you permit me, I should like to read your mind to see if you are fit for the initiation."

Christine readily agreed. Naren's reading showed that she was tied to India with very strong bonds. The next day he initiated her as Sister Christine.

SISTER CHRISTINE (CHRISTINE GREENSTIDEL)

    The last person in the group was me, Jock McClintock. I was not there as a disciple, of course. I had not seen Naren for a long time. When Mrs. Hale told me about the Thousand Island Park, I decided to come over. Miss Dutcher was gracious enough to house me in the newly constructed wing.

The reason I was here was because the ARU was in trouble. Debs and the other leaders had been jailed. The Pullman Car Company strike was at its peak. Schumpeter thought a spell outside Chicago would not do me any harm. I attended all the talks, and spent my time going around the Park.

What a training we received in the Thousand Island Park! The classes started a day after Naren arrived. He arrived at the class with a Bible in his hands, and started with the Gospel of John. After this, day after day, started the progressively heavy doses of the Naradiya Bhakti Sutras, the Bramha Sutras, the Sri Bhashya of Ramanujacharya, the Bhashya of Madhvacharya, the Yoga Sutras of Patanjali, the Bhagawat Gita, the Brihadaranyaka and Katha Upanishads, and the extremely monistic Avadhuta Gita.

Miss Ellen Waldo transcribed all the teachings in longhand. Naren congratulated her on her accuracy, and for capturing the spirit of his thoughts. Relying on my memory, I also made written notes of some of the most interesting lectures, during the nights. It was heavy going. I stopped after a while, and gave my notes to Walter Goodyear, to do what he pleased with them. I don't know where they are now. Incidentally, Naren was emphasizing Advaita. Surprisingly, the students' favorite was Ramanujacharya, with his Vishishta Advaita.

What exactly did Naren teach at the Thousand Island Park? In Naren's hands, the subjects became very clear, very logical, at the time of teaching. The subjects were, nevertheless, tough. Let me attempt a simple sample of what Naren said as a preface. I have always been unspiritual. I have concentrated on the logical and common sense view. Any mistakes in the summary are mine.

All the great religions of the world (said Naren) have one book as their scriptures. Judaism has the Torah, Christianity the Bible, Mohammedism the Koran, and so on. But the Hindu religion is awash with oceans of Sanskrit literature. So what do we accept as the authority for correct knowledge of the Almighty? The various schools of Hindu philosophy decided on three benchmarks for basing their schools of thought. In Sanskrit, they are called the "Prasthana Traya" or Three Schools of Religion.

The first benchmark is the accepted highest religious authority by all Hindus, the Vedas. The Vedas are the authoritative utterances of inspired Seers claiming contact with transcendental truth. They are statements of their metaphysical experiences. Like Naren, possibly they heard a voice or voices, and passed the words uttered down to posterity. Nothing was written. The students heard, and remembered. The Vedas are therefore called the Shruti, the heard.

All the schools of philosophy are based on the last part of the Vedas, the Upanishads or Vedanta. The philosophers call themselves the Vedantins. There are many Upanishads, but 10 are recognized by all as the principal ones: Isha, Kena, Katha, Prashna, Mundaka, Mandukya, Aithareya, Taithareya, Chandogya, and Brihadaranyaka.

The second benchmark is the Brahma Sutra. These are cryptic one-line aphorisms in Sanskrit, collected and arranged by a Sage called Badarayana. The Brahma Sutra strings together the Vedanta texts like flowers in a garland. The study and understanding of these Sutras leads to the understanding of the nature of the Infinite Absolute God, Brahman.

The Sutras are like shorthand notes. This economy of words makes the sutras impossible to understand without commentaries. The main commentator of each school of religion interprets the shorthand in his own (logical) way. This is what has led to the difference in the schools of thought.

The third benchmark is the Bhagawad Gita, or simply Gita. Though it occurs in an epic, the Mahabharata, it is considered very different from the rest of the Epic, which deals with a great war. It blends the doctrines of Kapila, Patanjali, and the Vedas. It unfolds a philosophical system which has been accepted as the prevailing Hindu belief.

The Gita, or song, contains direct declarations of Krishna, accepted as an incarnation of the Lord by all the schools. Therefore it is equal to the Shruti, the Vedas, and the words of the Almighty. Here, too, only those stanzas that are in consonance with the Upanishads are taken to be true. Anything else is a later interpolation.

One more common feature can be seen among the schools of thought. The whole universe is divided into three parts. The first one is invisible, and is called God. The second visible part is the human being, within who is the Soul or Self. The third part is Nature.

Every school of philosophy tries to define the relationship between God, the Soul, and Nature. In Sanskrit we call them Brahman, Atman and Prakruti. The differing analyses form the difference between the schools. The three principal schools among the Vedantins are the Dvaitis or Dualists, the Vishishta Advaitis or Qualified Non-Dualists, and the Advaitis or Monists.

What do the Dualists or Dvaitis say? They say that God is Personal, is external, but has no physical body. He is the Creator and destroyer of the universe. He is perfection personified. He is changeless and eternal. He is a superhuman God, with none of the evil qualities men have. By God's Grace a Soul can be redeemed, never otherwise.

Nature is the physical universe. It is different from God and the individual Souls. It is eternal, but subject to change. It evolves only by the will of God.

The individual Soul is atomic in size, but pervades the whole body. It is a knower, knowing itself and others. It is a reflection of God. There are three types of Souls. The first type is fit for salvation. The second type will be eternally reborn. The third type is eternally damned.

All Souls ultimately come to salvation by the Grace of God, and by their devotion to Him. By salvation is meant that the Soul will remain eternally with God, in the same plane as Him, but separate from Him. Devotion is not secondary to knowledge; to love is to know, and to know is to love! Ninety percent of the people of the earth, who are theists, are Dualists.

The Qualified Non-Dualists or Vishishta Advaitis state that the whole universe is God Himself. He is the material of the universe. As the spider spins the web out of its own body, even so the universe has come out of the Being. God, Nature, and the Soul are one.

Think of it this way. If everything in Nature combines with all the human Souls, to form a cosmic body, then God is the soul of this body.

All Vedantins agree that the Soul is eternal. Bodies may come and go, but the Soul remains unchanged.

Similarly, the cosmic body consisting of Nature and the human Souls may come and go, but the soul of this body, God, is eternal. Like the Soul in the body, God is immanent in everything. There is not a particle in this universe, not an atom, where He is not!

God has Infinite qualities, no imperfections, and is Personal and internal. The Soul, on the other hand, is by its nature pure, but its deeds make it impure. Wicked deeds contract it, every good deed expands it. When any Soul expands to the point of becoming perfect, it lives with God forever. So a Soul is different from God.

The Non-Dualists or Monists or Advaitis say that God Himself is the universe. He is both the creator and the created! In reality, there is only one Existence, the Infinite and Ever-blessed one.

What we perceive as Nature and Man is caused by Illusion or ignorance or Maya. Maya makes us apparently see different forms of the Infinite God, and give it different names. If through knowledge, Jnana, this illusion is dispelled, the names and forms vanish, and only the Infinite Absolute remains.

The world we see, which is in reality God, is produced by our mind distorting a stimulus which issues from God, or Brahman. Let us call this unknown stimulus X. So the combination of X + Mind makes us see our external universe.

Our real Self or Soul, or Atman, within us issues the other stimulus. Let us call it Y. When we speak of ourselves as Mr. or Mrs. So-and-so, we are not speaking of just Y. We are speaking of Y+ Mind. So Y + Mind is our internal knowledge.

So it is the mind that distorts X and Y! The mind has limited X and Y and made them appear, and differ, as external and internal world. Control the mind, still the mind, and the mind and ego vanish. X and Y are one! The external and internal worlds become one. The God behind the universe, and the Soul within the body, are but One. The whole universe is One, Brahman. When God and man are analyzed, they are one.

So how have you, the Infinite Being, become broken into parts as men, animals, and so on? The answer is, all this division is only apparent. It has no reality, and never will have. It was not true at any time. It is but a dream. Know this and be free. That is the Advaitic conclusion: "I am neither the mind, nor the body, nor am I the organs. I am Existence-Knowledge-Bliss Absolute. I am He, I am He!"

This is knowledge; everything besides this is ignorance. Separate Souls are but reflections, and not real. This division is delusional. A pot dipped into a river fills up. The water in the pot and in the river is not different water; it is only the pot that creates the difference! Break the pot, and the water is but one.

Understand one thing clearly. It is not that there is a Soul in man. This concept is taken for granted initially in order to explain it. The man is all Soul. His senses perceive the Soul as the body. His thoughts visualize the Soul as the mind. But actually there are no three things – body, mind and Self. All is Atman. Man is the Soul – that is the conclusion.

Name and form are created by illusion. The illusion inside you makes you think when you say 'I,' that you are referring to the body. In reality, the body is only the house for the Soul. Due to ignorance or illusion, man forgets the Self, and pampers the body. When this illusion is destroyed by right knowledge, the Soul merges with the Brahman. Man becomes one with the Infinite Being.

These, then, are the salient points of the three steps which Hindu religious thought has taken in regard to God. It began with the Personal, the extra-cosmic, external God. It then went on to the internal cosmic body, God immanent in the universe. It ended in identifying the Soul itself with God, and making one Soul a unit of all these various manifestations in the universe. This is the last word of the Vedas. It begins with Dualism, goes through a Qualified Monism, and ends in perfect Monism.

However, there are very few in this world that come to the last, or even dare believe in it. Fewer still dare act according to it. Now, in modern society, all these three stages are necessary. No stage is denied, only looked upon as a lower one. Try to put man on a higher platform, but do not injure and do not destroy anybody or anything. All will come to the truth in the long run.

When Naren had come thus far, he asked the disciples whether they had any questions. Indeed they did. I have noted down the questions and answers.

AT THE THOUSAND ISLAND PARK

Q:- Monism is very attractive. But is it possible to realize this?

A:- It is! There are men in this world for whom delusion has vanished for ever. I can vouch for Monism from personal experience also.
Q:- After the great realization, why do such men continue their existence in this so-called illusory world?
A:- Because of their past Karma. They will live for some time till the past Karma is exhausted. Then the body and mind will fall, and the Soul will become free. Such a person is in the "Living Free" state while in the world.

Q:- Does the perfect soul, who is above the world, above idolatry, above all gods, become an atheist, or an agnostic?
A:- This is the greatest paradox. Once he has experienced the grandeur of the Brahman, the enlightened man is humbled. He becomes a great Jnani, and at the same time becomes the greatest devotee, a Bhakta. My Master is the greatest example to me. A greater example is Adi Shankara, the reviver and establisher of Advaita in India. He was a devotee par excellence. His devotional hymns to almost all the Gods in the Hindu pantheon are unmatched in their beauty.

Q:- What is this illusion or delusion you speak of?
A:- You experience illusion often, though you do not notice it. One Vedantic illustration is this. You see a rope lying around in the dark. In your imagination, you see it moving, and think it is a snake. When a light is brought, you see a rope. The darkness is ignorance, the snake is the illusion, and the light is knowledge. How did you see the snake, where did it come from? That is illusion. The Buddhists

have a very good example. Take a firebrand and whirl it around in a circle. You see a circle of fire. That is illusion. How do you dispel the illusion? The Buddhists say, by quenching the firebrand, Alaatashanti.

Q:- If existence is Brahman alone, then what is Maya? Is Brahman affected by Maya?
A:- Good question. Brahman has ever been in existence, He has no beginning and no end. If He can be compared to a great magician, Maya is the illusion born from Him. Just like the magician, Brahman is never affected by Maya. Maya began with Brahman, it had no beginning. But right knowledge dispels Maya, and it has an end.
Q:- But, Swami, when you talk of Maya and Brahman, you are admitting two existences in the universe. Does this not destroy Monism?
A:- No, because Maya is not an existence. Thousands of dreams come into your life, but do not form part of your life. Dreams come and go. They have no existence. Calling Maya an existence is sheer sophistry.

Q:- But still, Swami, delusion on such a grand scale that we see every day is very hard to accept, is it not?
A:- Good, good. You are thinking along the right lines. Let me tell you a personal experience to explain Maya clearly. In Western India, I was traveling in desert country for days on foot. Every day I saw beautiful lakes with trees around them. The trees were reflected in the water, and rippled there. I wondered why they called this desert country!

One day, when I was thirsty, I went towards one such pool for water. As I neared it, it vanished! It was a mirage. I had been seeing the mirage for months but did not know it. The next time I saw a lake and trees, I was not fooled, because of my knowledge.

So is the world a mirage through which we travel for years! A mirage in the desert is ignored quickly. But the mirage which hides the reality of God is not so easily overcome. This mirage is called Maya. Only the right knowledge can overcome Maya.

AT THE THOUSAND ISLAND PARK

Q:- Swami, I cannot accept that the world is unreal. If I am hit, I am hurt. What is unreal about it?

A:- Wonderful! Understand the difference clearly. You see the world only because Maya makes you see it so. But when I say the world is unreal, I only mean that it is impermanent and changes. Only Brahman is permanent and unchanging. You at age 10, at age 50, and at age 80, though the same person, have changed physically, mentally and intellectually. When you die, you are not even you, you are a dead body to others. This change is unreality.

Q:- Swami, what is this right knowledge you spoke of? How to get it?

A:- There are four paths of attaining right knowledge. The goal of each path, called a Yoga, is to overcome ignorance. It allows the soul to realize its own nature. Each yoga is suited to a different temperament. The two pre-requisites are that the traveler should develop non-attachment, and he should keep up constant practice.

The first yoga is called Karma Yoga. The mind is purified by means of work. The effect of the work is called the karma. Bad work creates bad karma and eternal bondage. Good work creates good karma and leads towards salvation. The work is done as a duty, without bothering about the fruits. This creates unselfishness, and creates enough good karma to break the fetters of ignorance and free the soul. This yoga is found in the Vedas.

The second Yoga is the Bhakti Yoga. Bhakti, or worship, or love is the easiest, most pleasant and natural to man. The object of Bhakti is God. It must be so intense that the devotee renounces all worldly acts. Such people experience God as a personal God, and attain union with him. The Naradiya Bhakti Sutra teaches this yoga.

The third yoga is called Raja Yoga. It can be used by all classes of men, even atheists. The chief parts are concentrated breathing practice called Pranayama, then concentration and meditation. For theists, a symbolic name such as OM or other sacred words are very helpful for meditating upon and repeating. This yoga is found in the Patanjali Yoga Sutras.

The last path is that of Jnana Yoga. It is the highest, but most difficult, yoga. First you hear the truth about the Atman, the Self, being the only reality. Everything else is Maya. Then you argue and reason about it. Finally, give up all arguments and realize the truth. This realization comes from being certain that Brahman is real, and everything else unreal. You give up all desire for enjoyment, control the senses, and the only motive is to be free.

This Yoga, found in the Upanishad part of the Vedas is very tough. Many persons get an intellectual grasp of it, but very few attain realization. As the sages say, walking this path is like walking on a razor's edge.

Q:- Swami, you say that meditation brings realization. What actually happens, and how?
A:- What happens is this. At the base of the spine, there is a great store of spiritual energy, called the Kundalini, which means coiled up. Hence its name 'Serpent Power.'

Philosophy says that to the left and right of the spinal column are the nerve currents Ida and Pingala respectively. The middle passage between these is called the Sushumna.

For a normal unspiritual person, the Sushumna remains closed. Spirituality, meditation and yoga open the Sushumna. The Kundalini uncoils and begins to travel up the Sushumna. It may reside in any of the seven centers of consciousness in every person.

The first and lowest center is roughly in the rectum, the second center in the sex organ, and the third center in the area of the navel. These are worldly centers, so the person may be pious and God-fearing, but still a victim to lust and greed.

The fourth center is based at or near the heart. Spiritual awakening takes place for such a person. The Kundalini does not go back to the lower centers. You will be above all lustful and greedy worldly passions.

The fifth center is at the throat. When the Kundalini reaches this far, man's mind is set free from ignorance and delusion. The man talks only of God, hears only about God, and cares for nothing else but God.

The sixth center is at the forehead, between the eyebrows. When the Kundalini reaches here, the mind has a direct vision of God at all times. But at this point, a little trace of ego is left. This acts like a barrier of glass, and allows only visions of God, but no direct contact. This ego is like the glass that protects the lantern's flame. This state is called Savikalpa Samadhi.

The seventh center is at the top of the head. When the Kundalini reaches here, the ego-glass shatters, and the mind achieves Nirvikalpa Samadhi. One achieves total realization, and becomes a knower of Brahman. In fact, one is united with Brahman.

To those with spiritual vision, each center appears in the form of a lotus. When the Kundalini reaches each lotus, the lotus blooms with unimaginable beauty and grandeur. The highest lotus, at the seventh center, is called the 'thousand-petalled,' the Sahasrara. One can only wonder how it appears to the person in Samadhi.

This is the process by which Brahman is realized.

Q:- Swami, have you attained this realization?

A:- Shiva, Shiva.... I have had a few glimpses of it, and stayed for a short time in Samadhi. It was enough for me to know that the teachings of Advaita are true. My Master was almost constantly in Samadhi or ecstasy. It was only by an effort of will that he kept his mind on an earthly plane.

Q:- Swami, surely you can tell us what Samadhi felt like?

A:- Words cannot describe the ecstasy. It can only be experienced. I can tell you that sugar is sweet. If you ask me 'what is sweet,' then I can only tell you to taste the sugar and find out.

Q:- Does this realization of God give you any supernatural powers?

A:- All efforts, by whichever yoga, give you some extraordinary powers. But all teachers tell you to ignore these diversions. God knows that the path is extremely difficult as it is, without being complicated by these obstacles.

I have given you an idea about how the classes were. But it was not all scholarship and learning at the Park. Everyone had a lot of fun, too. The supper table saw gales of laughter at a joke or a funny remark. Naren loved to joke. He roared with laughter at comic anecdotes. He used to entertain, no doubt, but the entertainment would contain certain truths. At times, the remarks would reach a sublime level. But it was like an extended picnic; nobody wanted it to end!

Naren's main motive was to train all the students in Advaita Vedanta, so that they could preach like he did. Of course, all the students did not have the same standard. Later criticism surfaced that Naren was not as discriminatory as his Master. His reply to the criticism was pure Vivekananda: "I gather the chaff and the wheat together. The morrow shall winnow the grain, and scatter the chaff to the winds."

On the last day at the Park, Naren, Sister Christine and Mary Funke gathered under an oak tree. Naren wanted to discuss something with them, and they started by meditating. Suddenly, Naren went into Nirvikalpa Samadhi. A thunderstorm with pouring rain and lightning started up, but Naren was unaware of it. Mary Funke tried to shield him against the rain with a small umbrella. We soon came rushing out with umbrellas and raincoats. Our panicked cries and shouts brought Naren down from his Samadhi. He looked around and said: "Once more am I in Calcutta in the rains."

IN MEDITATION

That night, after seven never-to-be-forgotten weeks, Naren, Miss Waldo and I boarded the steamer for Clayton on August 6. In the steamer, Naren raised his right hand and said: "I bless thee, Thousand Islands." He waved goodbye to his disciples with his hat.

At Clayton, due to the Pullman trouble, Naren did have some anxious moments in getting a seat in the train. However, I used my credentials with the Station Master to get Naren coach class accommodation to New York. Naren was so exhausted that he slept all the way to New York, even though the locomotive derailed at some point during the journey!

Naren spoke at all kinds of places in New York, Boston, and Detroit. He spoke to popular audiences; before the Metaphysical Society of Hartford; before the Ethical Society of Brooklyn; and before students and Professors of philosophy at Harvard.

At New York, under the Presidentship of Frank Leggett, he organized the Vedanta Society. It was to become the center of the Vedantist movement in America.

In New York he gave as many as seventeen lectures a week. Private classes were held twice a day. No lecture was prepared, everything he spoke was improvised. His power was overwhelming, and he was called the "Lightning Orator." His speeches were like an electric charge to some audiences. Some hearers came out exhausted. They had to rest for several days to get over the nervous shock. Naren used to concentrate all his power in thinking, writing and speeches.

All this seriously compromised his health. Naren required rest badly, and as quickly as possible. But any relaxation now would slow down his mission. Was there any way to combine the two – relaxation and the mission? It seemed a forlorn hope.
And then, the first glimmer of hope came from the enemy camp!

HOME – THOUGHTS, FROM ABROAD

Oh, to be in England
Now that April's there,
And whoever wakes in England
Sees some morning, unaware,
That the lowest boughs and the brushwood sheaf
Round the elm-tree bole are in tiny leaf,
While the chaffinch sing on the orchard bough
In England – now!

And after April, when May follows,
And the whitethroat builds, and all the swallows!
Hark, where my blossomed pear-tree in the hedge
Leans to the field and scatters on the clover
Blossoms and dewdrops – at the bent spray's edge –
That's the wise thrush; he sings each song twice over,
Lest you should think he never could recapture
The first fine careless rapture!
And though the fields look rough with hoary dew,
All will be gay when noontide wakes anew
The buttercups, the little children's dower
Far brighter than this gaudy melon – flower!
ROBERT BROWNING

CHAPTER 23

MEETING THE ENEMY

By now, Naren had received three invitations to visit England. Miss Henrietta Muller, a speaker at the Theosophical Congress of the Parliament of Religions, met Naren there. At the Parliament itself, she extended the first invitation to Naren to visit England.

In the latter part of 1894, Miss Muller's adopted son, Akshay Kumar Gosh, extended the second invitation on behalf of his mother. Akshay was also a disciple of Naren's.

An Englishman, Mr. E. T. Sturdy, had traveled in India, and met Naren's brother-disciple, Swami Shivananda, in the Himalayas. Sturdy was already in contact with Naren through letters. Miss Muller told Sturdy about her invitation. Immediately, Sturdy dispatched his own invitation to Naren to visit England as his guest.

A fourth invitation was given at this time by Frank Leggett. He requested Naren to accompany him on a sea voyage to Paris. Frank was to wed his fiancée Betty Sturges there. This plethora of invitations convinced Naren that it was a Divine call for further work.

But in his mind the question remained: "Should he hob-nob with the enemy?" The English had enslaved India, and were bleeding the country dry. They had also committed numerous atrocities against his countrymen, especially in Bengal. Naren had made his feelings clear to a few Americans regarding the British. Would it then be proper for him to accept their invitations to visit England?

Naren thought at length about this issue. He did not discuss it with anyone; he wanted to resolve the issue by himself. Finally, after a lot of thought and soul-searching, he came to a decision. He could not, indeed *should* not, mix his mission with his politics! The mission was Vedantic, and politics should not play any part in it, however patriotic he might be. This was to be one of the pillars of the Ramakrishna Mission later.

This would also be an opportunity to rest. A sea-voyage would be very useful for his health. Naren accepted all the invitations to visit England.

Much before this, as I already told you, the ARU had run into trouble. The success of the Great Northern strike had given the ARU membership an excessive sense of optimism and power. This would prove to be its undoing.

In 1894, a delegation of desperate employees, and their families, came from Pullman City to meet Debs. They appealed for support in their struggle with the Pullman Company. The company had laid off workers, and reduced their wages.

The problem was that the workers producing Pullman sleeping cars were not railroad workers. The ARU nevertheless sympathized with them, and advocated a strike. Debs suggested mediation before taking direct action. The ARU refused to listen to Debs. The Pullman Company refused mediation. Debs had no choice but to lead the ARU in a boycott.

Unfortunately, the situation had changed greatly. The Great Northern Company had had no support from anyone else during its strike. The Pullman Car Company had the support of all the railroad company owners. It also had the support of the Federal Government, the Judiciary, the National Guard, and the Press. All of them formed a solid front to break the strike, and destroy the Union.

The ARU got no support from the other unions, or from the American Federation of Labor led by Samuel Gompers. The result was a total disaster for the ARU. The strike was broken. There was considerable violence, and at least 30 workers were killed. Debs and the other ARU officials were sentenced to a year in jail. The ARU workers were blacklisted, and could not find any work in any of the railroads.

The ARU was finished, wiped out. It was during this period that Schumpeter had advised me to get out of Chicago. I had escaped the fate of the railroad workers since I had been promoted to a Junior Management position. But my sympathy to Debs and the ARU was well-known. Schumpeter was anxious that some unscrupulous person might accuse me of some misdemeanor or other. I had gone to the Thousand Island Park.

Around the middle of August 1895, I went to meet Naren casually. He told me about his impending trip to Paris for the Leggetts' wedding. London was, after all, just next door to Paris. He asked me if I was free to accompany him.

I told him about Debs and the ARU members who had been jailed for contempt of court. I had been, and was, the right-hand man of Debs for planning. I could not slip off to the Continent while Debs was in jail. Naren understood my position. He told me that he expected me to be extremely faithful, come what may. I should not hesitate for a moment in getting a fair deal for the railroad men.

Naren assured me that he would be writing to me whenever he found time to. And so, on August 17, Naren and Mr. Leggett sailed from New York by the SS Touraine, to reach Paris on August 24.

By the third week of September, I got a letter from Naren, from Reading.

High View, Caversham,
Reading.
September 24, 1895.

My dear Jock,

It has been more than a month since I left New York. As I had foreseen, the ocean voyage provided marvelous rest for me. We reached Paris as scheduled on August 24. At the St. Lazare Station, Betty Sturges and Jo MacLeod met us. They had been in France for a month.

One peculiarity of this modern city struck me very forcefully. Europeans, or at any rate Frenchmen, bathe with even less frequency than Americans! We stayed at the first class Hotel Continental. I was horrified to find that it had no bathrooms! After two days of suffering, I told Frank: "Dear brother, you are welcome to this royal luxury. I am panting to get out of here. Such hot weather and no bathing facility! If it continues like this, I shall turn mad like a rabid dog!" Frank had a dozen hotels looked into; none of them had bathing places. There are, of course, independent bathing houses. A bath costs Rupees 3-4.

I stayed in Paris till September 9, and I enjoyed my stay there. I visited the museums, churches, cathedrals and art galleries. The Omnibuses and trams are convenient modes of transport. I admire Paris. There were many discussions with scholars and spiritual people. Betty and Jo introduced me to their numerous Parisian friends. One such was the Countess of Caithness, better known as the

Duchesse de Pomar. Let me tell you of one incident that occurred in her company.

I was driving with her in the countryside. Suddenly, on a village road, the coachman stopped the phaeton. A little boy and girl, with a maidservant, came up to us. The coachman got down, and caressed both the little children very lovingly. Then he got back into his seat, took up the reins, and proceeded. The Duchesse was surprised, and asked the coachman: "Why did you do that? Those are a gentleman's children!"

The coachman explained: "Madame, I was the manager of the Bank ___ in Paris. The bank failed. I rented a house in the village. My wife, children and the servant maid live there. With the little money I had, I purchased these horses and phaeton. I work as a coachman to support my wife and children. Those were my children that I met on the road."

The calmness and dignity of the man impressed me. I said to the Duchesse: "This man is a real practical Vedantist! He has understood the essence of Vedanta. He has fallen from a very high estate to this low condition. He is nevertheless unmoved. Thank God for such powers of the mind."

It took me a little over two weeks to see all the important sights of Paris. Much time was also spent in discussions with philosophers, scientists, churchmen, and political ministers. On September 9, I witnessed the wedding of Francis Leggett and Betty Sturges, at the American Cathedral. Both were getting married for the second time. The ceremony was kept private and simple.

The Cathedral had a small, vaulted Chapel of St. Paul's the Traveler. The ceremony was performed there. A few friends, Betty's children Hollister and Alberta, and I were the only witnesses.

One of Frank's couriers persisted in addressing me as "Mon Prince." Bothered by this, I told him: "Look here, my man. I am no prince! I am only a penniless monk."
The man would not listen to me. He kept saying: "I have traveled with many princes. I know one when I see one!"
Well, Godspeed to him!

I sailed for England the next day, on September 10. I felt very apprehensive. I had very little expectations. After all, the English rule us and you know my feelings about them. How would the British public receive me? I was a Hindu, a part of their subject-race. Again, how would they respond to me preaching on my religion, and perhaps criticizing their religion? I was not yet free from biases, from prejudices.

Let me tell you, Jock, the very sight of London thrilled me! This was an emotion I had hardly expected to feel! Anyway, Mr. E. T. Sturdy met me at Paddington Station. He took me straight by train to Reading. It is 36 miles Southwest of London.

The borough of Reading is an ancient Victorian town. It is in the country of Berkshire, on the south bank of the River Thames. Edward Toronto Sturdy (to give his full name) was born in Toronto, Canada, in 1860. His father did not like Canada much. He returned to England, settling in Wareham, Dorset.

Edward studied at Blackheath and Bristol. He worked in the family business at London for 3 years. At the age of 18, he sailed to New Zealand to try his luck there. He did exceedingly well. Influenced by Theosophy, Sturdy read the Gita for long hours. He went around the world once in 1886. 3 years later, his father died, and Sturdy returned to England.

He was in the inner circle of Madame Blavatsky of the Theosophists, along with Annie Besant and Henrietta Muller. On Madame Blavatsky's death, there was a power struggle and a huge scandal. This disillusioned Sturdy. He went to Adyar at Madras. From there he went to Almora in the Himalayas. He met my brother-monk, Swami Shivananda, for long discussions. Sturdy lived like a Brahmin and was ready to take Sannyasa.

Returning to London, he became seriously ill. He is a vegetarian, and was nursed to health by a young hospital nurse, Lucie Black, on vegetables alone. He married her. She is still very fond of vegetables. Alas, she thinks it a very suitable diet for guests, too!

Edward T. Sturdy, ca 1902
EDWARD T. STURDY

Mr. Sturdy is a very nice gentleman. He is also a staunch Vedantist. He knows some Sanskrit. I am helping him study Sanskrit. A project dear to his heart is to translate the Naradiya Bhakti Sutras into English. He also wants to write the commentary for them. My time is spent in holding philosophical discussions with him.

Sturdy took me earlier this month to visit Miss Henrietta Muller at Maidenhead. She is another astonishing character. She was born at Valparaiso, Chile. She can speak fluent French, Italian, German and Spanish. She spoke at the Parliament of Religions, where she heard me speak, too. In Adyar, Madras, she adopted a young Indian of great promise, Akshay Kumar Ghose. This lad is my disciple too. At a time when she was shaken by the great scandal in the

Theosophical Society, Akshay suggested that she invite me to London.

MISS HENRIETTA F. MULLER

When Sturdy and I visited Miss Muller a second time, an amusing incident (amusing in retrospect!) occurred. The three of us were walking across the fields around Pinkney's Green. Suddenly we heard a loud bellow. A fierce bull came charging at us. Sturdy took to his heels, and reached cover. Miss Muller ran as far as she could, then fell to the ground. I was following her.

Reaching her, I turned around, folded my arms, and stood before her, facing the bull. To come to England to be gored by a bull! A goring by John Bull was acceptable, but to be killed by a real bull, really! A part of my mind was enjoying the irony. Another part was calculating how far the bull would toss me! Anyway, the animal suddenly stopped a few paces off. It snorted, pawed the ground and threw up its horns threateningly. Then, inexplicably, it turned round and ran off! Thank the Lord!

Another strange thing, Jock. You know how I hated everything English. That being so, I was surprised to find that the English received me warmly and gladly, with open arms. Contrast this with the behavior of some of the British in India.

That wonderful logic by which Americans identify every colored man with the Negro is totally absent here. Nobody stares at me in the streets; they are color-blind! I met several retired Generals from India who love India. I am more at home here than anywhere out of India! I am forced to greatly tone down my ideas about the British race.

I am still waiting for my English friends to arrange for public lectures in London. I am sure it will be different from what it was in America. From the moment I have set foot in the Old World, I have breathed a different atmosphere of intellectualism. I hope I will not be disappointed.

Meanwhile, my enforced relaxation is doing wonders for my health, in spite of the cold. How are things there? Are your friends still imprisoned? I offer my prayers and blessings to them, and to you.

With love,
Naren

"Oh ho!" I thought, "What's this?"
I had expected fireworks from Naren when he came into contact with the British. Instead, here he was, singing their praises! Well, stranger things have happened in life, I thought.

In November, I received a letter from Mr. E. T. Sturdy.

Reading,
29 October, 1895

Dear Mr. McClintock,

This short letter is to give you the latest news of Swamiji. He asked me to write to you. He has plunged into a round of lectures and discussions. He has created a set of devoted admirers around himself. He is busy in instructing them in Vedanta.

It was not until this month that we could arrange for Swamiji to give a public lecture in London. One reason why I moved slowly was the adverse publicity the Theosophical Society had received less than a year ago. The intelligent and the intellectual people have become wary of anything Eastern!

Finally, the opportunity arrived. Swamiji spoke on the 22nd instant evening at Prince's Hall, Piccadilly. I had the fortune, and the honour, of arranging the lecture. The Swamiji's lecture was "Self-knowledge." The large gathering had people from all walks of life. It also had some of the best thinkers in London. Needless to say, the lecture was a tremendous success! He electrified the audience by his grand and powerful oratory!

Following that lecture, Swamiji's success has been immediate. The Press expressed great admiration for him. He has been compared favourably not only with Raja Ram Mohun Roy and Keshab Chandra Sen, but also with Buddha and Christ. Aristocratic circles have welcomed him. Even the Heads of the Churches have shown their sympathy for him.

The Swamiji feels that his English trip has been worthwhile. He considers England as a fertile place for the teaching of the Vedanta. He wishes you and your friends well. He plans to start back for America by the end of November.

With warm regards, I remain
Yours faithfully,
E. T. Sturdy

In late November, Debs and the other ARU members were released from prison. A few days later, I got a letter from Naren.

Reading,
19 November, 1895.

My dear Jock,

By the time you get this letter, I shall have sailed for America. I could have informed you in person the contents of this letter. But I am so happy, that I could not wait that long. The good news is, I have found an English person who shows all the material for being a very good disciple. This person will help me no end in my Indian work at a later stage.

However, I am racing on to the end without having started my story. This is what happened. One Lady Isabel Margesson is the Secretary of a Club called the Sesame Club. She is a strong advocate of social and educational reform. She invited me to speak at her home at 63, St. George's Road, to a few selected friends.

The day chosen, Sunday, was a cold wet afternoon. The venue was a West End drawing room. There was a roaring fire in the hearth behind me. I was sitting facing a semi-circle of listeners. The group was well-read. They asked me question after question. One of the ladies, in particular, was weighing every word I said. She did not just accept what I explained. After each answer she would say: "Yes, Swami, but…."

She argued and resisted. I was absolutely delighted. I was reminded of my fights with, and resistance to, my Master. She may hesitate now. Once she accepts my ideas, she will be their most ardent champion. Her name is Miss Margaret Noble.

MARGARET NOBLE

Miss Noble is very interested in educational work. She is a Principal in a school of her own. She moves in quiet but distinguished intellectual circles. She is deeply interested in all modern thoughts and trends. She is Irish.

In her youth, she had met a preacher at her father's house. He told her that India would be the place to serve. This idea has got implanted in her soul. She needs a teacher who will push her to the decision. Once she is convinced, I feel that that she will be the most steadfast disciple. Let us see!

Jock, I feel very satisfied with this first visit to London. I have spoken at numerous Societies and Clubs. The work has been as hard as it was in America. I think I have established a sound foundation for any future work. I was welcomed alike by the Press, the Clergy, the Nobility, the Intellectuals and the public.

In America, enthusiasm for and acceptance of my ideas was immediate. In London, the public is more conservative in accepting what I say. The challenge is very refreshing. I have had to completely change my ideas about English men and women, at least about their spiritual depth.

Let me quote verbatim from a journalist: "It is indeed a rare sight to see some of the most fashionable ladies in London seated on the floor cross-legged, of course for want of chairs, listening with all the Bhakti of an Indian chela towards his guru. The love and sympathy for India that the Swami is creating in the minds of the English-speaking race is sure to be a tower of strength for the progress of India."
Need I add anything more?

Jock, you know how I felt about the English once! I have discovered now a nation of heroes, the true kshatriyas! They are brave and steady. Their tendency is to hide their feelings, and never show them. But there is a deep spring of feeling in the Englishman's heart! If once you know how to reach it, he is your friend forever. They have solved the secret of obedience without slavish cringing – great freedom, with great law-abidingness!

I shall be seeing you in a short time. I shall have much more to tell you. I shall have so much to hear from you, too. Till then, goodbye.

With love,
Naren.

I was truly happy for Naren. He had faced the enemy. He had found them honorable. With his weapons he had won a victory over them. More important, he had won them over. This was so different from the needless waste and degradation that accompanies a real battle or war. The greatest fallout was that they had won him over, too!

Of course, only Naren could have done all this simultaneously!

****

A THING OF BEAUTY IS A JOY FOR EVER

A thing of beauty is a joy for ever:
Its lovliness increases; it will never
Pass into nothingness; but still will keep
A bower quiet for us, and a sleep
Full of sweet dreams, and health, and quiet breathing.
Therefore, on every morrow, are we wreathing
A flowery band to bind us to the earth,
Spite of despondence, of the inhuman dearth
Of noble natures, of the gloomy days,
Of all the unhealthy and o'er-darkn'd ways
Made for our searching: yes, in spite of all,
Some shape of beauty moves away the pall
From our dark spirits. Such the sun, the moon,
Trees old and young, sprouting a shady boon
For simple sheep; and such are daffodils
With the green world they live in; and clear rills
That for themselves a cooling covert make
'Gainst the hot season; the mid-forest brake,
Rich with a sprinkling of fair musk-rose blooms:
And such too is the grandeur of the dooms
We have imagined for the mighty dead;
An endless fountain of immortal drink,
Pouring unto us from the heaven's brink.
JOHN KEATS

CHAPTER 24

THE CHRONICLER AND THE DISRUPTOR

By Friday, December 6, 1895, Naren was back in New York. He was in excellent health and spirits. His first action was to shift his headquarters to 228, West 39th Street. This lodging could accommodate upwards of 150 people at a time. Naren immediately started on a whirlwind program of classes.

Two classes were held daily on the four Yogas. Between classes, he handled a mountain of correspondence. Public lectures were also delivered. For the devotees a big problem arose. How to preserve these speeches, the class lessons, and the correspondence, for posterity? The Press was doing its best, but was it accurate and understanding enough? The New York Vedanta Society decided to do something in this matter. It would hire a stenographer to preserve all the talks and other material.

The first recorder had been Leon, or Kripananda as he was now called. He was a good typist, but a mere novice at stenography. He could not keep up with Naren's pace. There was also the danger that he might interpret some statements according to his own understanding.

The N.Y.V. Society hired another stenographer. He was very proficient in his work, but woefully lacking in the spiritual department. It was like the joke about a Russian translating: "The spirit is willing, but the flesh is weak." The translation read: "The wine is ok, but the meat has gone bad!" The Society, not too regretfully, let him go. They then placed an ad in the *Herald* and the *World*, which read as follows:

WANTED – A rapid shorthand writer to take down lectures for several hours a week. Apply at – 228 West 39th Street.

What the Society expected was a candidate who was intelligent, spiritual, an expert shorthand writer and typist. At the same time, the salary offered was considerably less than the going rate of $15 – 18 per week! It seemed a doomed expectation!

To their surprise, a candidate did apply. He was a young man, an Englishman with handlebar mustaches. He had more than a decade experience as an Editor for three newspapers, and as a Court reporter in England; his shorthand and typing were fantastic. His English was, well, impeccable, as it ought to have been. He was down and out, and any salary was attractive to him. He was overjoyed that his food needs would be taken care of. His name was Josiah John Goodwin. The only factor that remained to be tested was how he interpreted the spiritual lectures.

J. J. GOODWIN

One cold December day this handsome Englishman wandered into 228 West 39th Street. He took charge immediately. He checked and overhauled the typewriter. He kept ample supplies of shorthand pads and pencils.

For Naren's first lecture, Goodwin sat at a place where he could clearly hear him, and away from the audience. He transcribed the lecture, and the questions and answers. As soon as the lecture was over, Naren pursued his correspondence.

Goodwin typed up everything he had transcribed, and handed the typed sheets to Naren for going over ('perusal,' he called it). Naren was amazed! Barring a very few pardonable errors, the spiritual content was almost fully intact! Naren had finally found his scribe, the Ganesha to his Vyasa!

What a find Goodwin proved to be! He took his work very seriously. He transcribed Naren's utterances exactly. He worked late into the night, typing out the lectures. He prepared the manuscripts for the newspapers. He even prepared the material for the Brahmavadin in India. By the next morning, he would be ready before the classes started. He took a room directly across the street at 247 West 39th Street. Naren took Goodwin under his wing from the first day.

For the first time in his checkered life, Goodwin found someone giving him not only sympathetic treatment but also unconditional love and understanding. There was also unstinted appreciation of his labor, expressed in glowing terms! He became a changed man. Always poor, his meager salary barely made ends meet. But, as he told me once: "Income or no income, I am caught!"

The only liberty he took was to sit at Naren's table for lunch and dinner. Goodwin accompanied Naren to all his lectures. On his own, he started taking care of Naren's personal needs. He traveled to all the cities with him. Naren called him: "My faithful Goodwin." Without his tireless work, much of Naren's lectures and teachings would have been lost forever.

Meanwhile, Leon also made some disciples in Buffalo, Detroit and New York. When he had separated from Naren earlier, he had moved to an attic in 228 West 39th Street. Imagine his consternation, then, when Naren moved into the same house, taking over the bigger rooms!

To add to his misery, new upstarts also arrived at the scene. Whereas Leon had been all-in-all previously, he now found newcomers taking over his duties. Goodwin was the secretary and right-hand man. Sarah Waldo did the cooking, ran the house, took dictation and attended to odds and ends. Walter Goodyear kept the accounts.

All of Leon's responsibilities had been whittled away. Added to this were "….that omnipresent committee of petticoats!" These were the other workers. Leon hid away in the attic, brooded, licked his wounds, refused to eat with Naren and stole in and out of his room for his meals. His unreasoning jealousy plunged him into gloom, bitterness, resentment and despair. Nothing Naren could say to him consoled him. Naren rightly concluded that there was something wrong with Leon's head. He told the others to leave him strictly alone: "I am his father, and he my child. I shall always love him."

Before Christmas, Naren took a decision that was to drive his disciples and devotees to despair initially. He declared that the time had come for him to deliver public lectures. Good, thought the disciples, with visions of dollars dancing in their heads!

Then Naren punctured these visions by saying that the lectures would be totally free! His rationale was: "I am a monk. My religious teachings should be free. This is the age-old tradition in India. This is the pure way. To charge admission fees is distasteful!"

He added mischievously: "Free lectures attract big crowds."

IN NEW YORK

The Vedanta Society asked him: "What about the money to run the Society?"

Naren said: "That is your look-out. I do not prevent you from raising money by your own methods. But do not depend on me for money. I teach free."

Naren had set a precedent. The Vedanta Society had enough skills and brains to stand on its own feet. Also, his successors would not have the burden of earning money for the Society.

Just then, the fledgling Society had very little money. Naren paid, from his own savings, the rent for the rooms, the lectures, printing and advertisements. The classes were free; the public lectures would also be free. Leon once told me: "The Swami is starving himself!"

I did not believe him for a minute. Miss Waldo was too efficient for such a state of affairs to occur. Certainly, Leon himself was not starving! Others were contributing towards Goodwin's salary, and Naren's room rent. Still, Naren lived with the utmost frugality.

Mrs. Betty Leggett arranged a little dinner for Naren at the Metropolitan Club, known by New Yorkers as the Millionaires Club. One of the guests was a young Boston lady. Naren was speaking on the spirituality of the Hindu. The young lady spoke up: "But, Swami, you must admit that the common people of India are way below the cultivation of the same class in, say, Massachusetts."

Naren replied: "Yes, Boston is a very cultured place. I landed there once – a stranger in a strange land. I was wearing this same dress. On a busy street, I became

aware of a mob following me. I hurried, and they did the same. I felt something strike my shoulder. I ran, and to save myself ducked into a dark alley. The mob dashed past the alley. Yes, Massachusetts is a very safe place, indeed!"
The young lady persisted: "I am sure that a Bostonian in Calcutta would have met with the similar treatment."
Naren told her: "Impossible. It is unpardonable to show curiosity about a stranger within our gates. To be hostile to him is unthinkable."

Naren next commenced in New York a series of free lectures. These were held on Sunday afternoons at Hardman Hall. The twice-a-day classes also continued. The attendance at both venues increased beyond expectations. In Hardman Hall, there was sometimes not even standing room.

An enormous wave of interest and enthusiasm was aroused. The classes were crowded with doctors, lawyers, professional men and society ladies. The public lectures became so crowded that the Madison Square Garden was rented. It was a huge hall with a seating capacity of over fifteen hundred people. Even this was crowded to overflowing.

One result of these lectures was that Americans were using Sanskrit terms frequently. Shankaracharya and Ramanuja became familiar names. Libraries purchased a large number of books on Hindu philosophy, written in English.

Among the famous New Yorkers who met Naren, Nicola Tesla was one. The great electrical scientist was a genius, and unmatched in his field. He was my hero, too. I was lucky to be present when this handsome Croatian met Naren.

NICOLA TESLA

He was over six feet tall, slender, charming and highly cultured. He was the inventor of the polyphase alternating current system, which put the direct current system of Edison into eclipse. Direct current generators could send currents up to half a mile at most. Tesla's system sent high voltage electrical power for hundreds of miles. The Niagara Falls powerhouse had utilized that system successfully.

Tesla also discovered the principles behind the radio, remote control, fluorescent lighting, cosmic rays and improved X-rays. However, he lacked business sense, neglected to take out patents, or sold them to others for a pittance. Tragically, despite all his patents, he died in poverty and obscurity.

Of course, that was far in the future. When he met Naren, he was fascinated by the Samkhya philosophy with its Kalpas (cycles), Prana (life-giving force) and Akasha (Space). He told Naren he could prove them mathematically. Naren told him that if he could do that, Vedanta Cosmology would rest on the surest of foundations. I don't know whether Tesla actually provided Naren with the mathematical proof.

Another heavenly apparition I was fortunate enough to meet was the "Divine Sarah," the famous Sarah Bernhardt. She was a famous French actress. The meeting, for me at least, was marred by Naren telling me at frequent intervals, in an aside, to close my mouth! I was so fascinated by Sarah that I spent all my time looking at her. I never heard a word of what was discussed!

SARAH BERNHARDT

The last week of February 1896 was a busy period for Naren. He concluded the public lecture series at the Madison Square Garden. The last lecture was a thrilling one on "My Master." It was a glorious tribute to Shri Ramakrishna Paramahamsa. This is what Laura Glenn (Sister Devmata) wrote later about the lecture:

"As he entered the hall from a door at the side of the platform, one sensed a different mood in him. He seemed less confident, as if he approached his task reluctantly. Years after in Madras I understood.

SISTER DEVMATA (LAURA GLENN)

He hesitated at all times to speak of his guru. During his early wanderings through South India he refused to reveal his name even, believing he represented him so poorly. Only in Madras, when he came unaware upon his Master's picture, did the words burst from his lips: 'That is my guru, Shri Ramakrishna,' and tears streamed down his face.

So now was he reluctant. He began his lecture with a long preamble; but once in his subject, it swept him. The force of it drove him from one end of the platform to the other. It overflowed in a swift-running stream of eloquence and feeling. The large audience listened in awed stillness and at the close many left the hall without speaking.

As for myself, I was transfixed. The transcendent picture drawn overwhelmed me. The call had come, and I answered."

Then came the publication of his two great works, "Karma Yoga" and "Raja Yoga." They received very favorable reviews. The Vedanta Society was also re-organized, with Mr. Francis Leggett as its President. The main function of the Society, in Naren's own words, was "…..to create open doors, as it were, in which the East and the West could pass freely back and forth, without a feeling of strangeness, as from one home to another."

Naren then departed for Detroit for two weeks. His goal was to have two classes daily, more or less private. Word-of-mouth would attract the more serious students. Naren wanted to avoid any newspaper publicity.

Two years ago, the newspapers in Detroit had created a religious storm. Naren's enemies had gone all out to destroy him. Those newspapers, even now, did not know that public recognition in India had felicitated Naren, and offered tribute to him. Reluctant to stir another time-wasting controversy, Naren wanted to avoid the newspapers as long as possible.

Alas, he had not taken into account his impulsive disciple, Leon Landsberg, now Swami Kripananda! Leon was to have gone only to Buffalo. At the last minute, without informing anyone, Leon decided to go to Detroit.

The first thing he did after arriving there was to visit the principal newspapers! He had the details of Naren's arrival, and his schedule, published in them.

Scenting a good controversy, and more sales, one of them asked the Rev. J.M. Thoburn, a Christian missionary, for a comment. Thoburn went off like a rocket, slandering Naren. The paper had fine copy, which it printed. It was suspected that Leon had also given the newspaper a photo of Naren's Master. The photograph of the Master, scantily clad, was also published. The following day, all the newspapers reproduced the articles and the picture.

To his credit, Leon was horrified and shocked. He had never counted on such a reaction. He did not know of the controversies two years ago. He launched a counter-defense. This, in spite of the fact that he knew of Naren's dictum for such attacks: silence. Leon was trying to control the situation. He failed; the newspaper published a vulgar editorial.

Naren was a day late at Detroit. He arrived on the night of March 3, and checked into the Richlieu Hotel as arranged. No one met him; no one knew he was coming that night. He had no idea of the newspaper imbroglio.

Naren came down to the hotel parlor on the morning of March 4. He expected a few friends to meet him. To his surprise and shock, a huge crowd was awaiting him! There was only one familiar face in the crowd. The rest were all strangers!

On seeing the Master's sacred photograph on the front page of the newspaper, with a mocking article, Naren was furious. He said angrily: "Oh, this is blasphemy!"

To put it mildly, Naren was not pleased with Leon. Leon, on his part, could not see any wrongdoing. It must be that infernal Goodwin who had filled Naren's ears, he thought. Poor Leon, he must have been devastated to see all his hard work turn to ashes! Already psychologically weak, his mind became even more depressed. It led him to more serious mistakes.

Anyway, nothing much was lost. Naren brought the situation rapidly under control. When nothing "happened," the sensation-seekers vanished. Strangers became friends, and friends became more devoted than ever. Once Naren started lecturing, the crowd occupied the parlor and the hall, and overflowed up the staircase. Those who came on the first day returned again and again to listen in awe. The newspapers stopped their attacks shortly after as useless. They even printed admiring reports of Naren's speeches.

At the same time, Naren could not ignore the element of self-destruction in Leon. First Leon made wild accusations against the Vedantic Society. Then he wrote intemperate articles for the Brahmavadin in India, one of which was printed. It was insulting to the American public.

Naren immediately wrote to the Brahmavadin that no more of Leon's articles should be published.

Next Leon berated Naren in Detroit for showing indifference to him (Leon). It was the cry of a despairing soul, whose mind was betraying him. Naren rebuked him mildly for the sake of discipline, but always loved Leon for his compassion and generosity. Naren put it beautifully: "What difference can it make when one knows that the blamer, blamed, and praiser, praised, are one?"
However, Naren's disciples, especially Goodwin, felt that Leon was mad. He would be a loose cannon for the work if he were not tied down. As for me, I could never hate Leon. I would always respect him deeply.

Naren's last public appearance in Detroit was in the Temple of Beth El. His ardent admirer, Rabbi Louis Grossman, the pastor of the Temple, had arranged a lecture. Goodwin told me later that Naren had intended to speak on "India's Message to the West." It was to be a reply to the newspapers, to his enemies.

When he saw the devout crowd filling the temple, he changed the topic to "The Ideal of a Universal Religion." There was no question of rebuttal or vengeful reply. The spiritual crowd deserved an exalted subject and an exalted lecture. The world prophet changed the topic from India to religion. It was a stunning lecture. Goodwin told me that upwards of 5000 people were packed into the Temple. Those turned away threatened to batter down the main doors of the Temple. The authorities feared a huge riot. Even the newspapers reluctantly agreed that the Temple had been packed solid.

From Detroit, Naren and Goodwin traveled straight to Boston. It was a railroad journey of 750 miles. They arrived on March 18. The next day Naren, Mrs. Bull, Miss Emma Thursby, and Mrs. Antoinette Sterling were among the honored guests at the monthly reception of the Procopeia Club. Naren was to be the club's "Class teacher" for the rest of the month. He was to speak at the club itself.

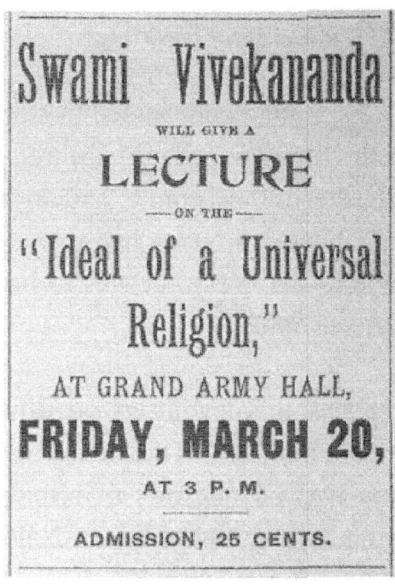

Swami Vivekananda
WILL GIVE A
LECTURE
— ON THE —
"Ideal of a Universal Religion,"
AT GRAND ARMY HALL,
FRIDAY, MARCH 20,
AT 3 P. M.
ADMISSION, 25 CENTS.

POSTER AT MEDFORD

The Club had heard, and read, about the crowds that had invaded his lectures at Detroit and elsewhere. They feared that the Club would be swamped if Naren spoke on its premises. The arena of the Allen Gymnasium was rented to accommodate this crowd. Even this proved too small; hundreds were turned away. Naren spoke 5 times for the Club. Naren also took this opportunity to renew his friendship with Professor and Mrs. John Wright.

Next, John P. Fox arranged for Naren to speak at the Harvard Graduate Philosophical Club. The Department of Philosophy had a brilliant galaxy of philosophers as its Professors – George Palmer, William James, Josiah Royce, Hugo Munsterberg and George Santayana. They were all stars. Naren's electrifying talk on "The Vedanta Philosophy," and his incisive, heated replies to questions made James remark: "That man is simply a wonder for oratorical power."

The professors felt that Naren's lucid lecture had helped the students understand what the professors had been teaching them the whole year! The discussions had been long and lively. The professors were so impressed that they offered Naren the Chair of Eastern Philosophy. Such invitations were not lightly given at Harvard. Naren respectfully turned down the invitation, saying that as a monk he could not accept such offers.

Naren's last lecture was delivered at the Twentieth Century Club. He then left for Chicago, his "almost hometown," on March 30. He remained there with his friends, giving private classes till April 10. On April 11, 1896, Naren was in New York, considering his next move.

****

HYMN OF CREATION

Nor Aught nor Naught existed; yon bright sky
Was not, nor heaven's broad woof outstretched above.
What covered all? What sheltered? What concealed?
Was it the water's fathomless abyss?
There was not death – yet was there naught immortal,
There was no confine betwixt day and night;
The only One breathed breathless by itself,
Other than it there nothing since has been.
Darkness there was, and all at first was veiled
In gloom profound – an ocean without light –
The germ that still lay covered in the husk
Burst forth, one nature, from the fervent heat.
Then first came love upon it, the now Spring
Of mind- yea, poets in their hearts discerned,
Pondering, this bond between created things
And uncreated. Comes this spark from earth
Piercing and all-pervading, or from heaven?
Then seeds were sown, and mighty powers arose –
Nature below, and power and will above –
Who knows the secret? Who proclaimed it here,
Whence, whence this manifold creation sprang?
The Gods themselves came late into being –
Who knows from whence this creation sprang?
He from whom all this great creation came,
Whether His will created or was mute,
The Most High Seer that is in highest heaven,
He knows it or perchance even He knows not.

F. MAX MULLER

CHAPTER 25

FRIENDS AND PHILOSOPHERS

In the spring of 1896, letters had come pouring in to Naren. They begged him to come to England again, and systematize the work he had started there. He felt the urgent need to do so. Thus, on April 15, 1896, at 12 noon, he sailed from New York on the Star Lines *SS Germanic* for England. He was to take up another season of strenuous teaching.

This time I was with him. This is how this came about. In the aftermath of the Pullman Car Company boycott, a number of ARU workers lost their jobs. They were blacklisted and could not find any other employment. They nursed a secret grudge against Debs. They were waiting for him to get out of Woodstock Jail. They wanted to physically assault him.

When Debs came out of jail, he was protected by his colleagues and friends. The disgruntled workers could not get to him. By mid-March 1896, the workers became pretty desperate. Rumor had it that they would not hesitate to kill Debs, and all those who supported him.

Schumpeter came to know, through his sources, that I was also a target. He called me immediately, and told me to keep out of sight for some time. He was seriously thinking of getting me transferred to Los Angeles.

At this juncture, Naren invited me to join him on the trip to England. The costs would be borne by his disciples. Schumpeter seconded the idea when I told him. He told me to pack immediately, and return only with Naren. I was not in want of money. My childhood Trust Fund would support me indefinitely. I accepted Naren's invitation to sail to England with him.

After reaching Liverpool, we traveled to Reading. Naren was once again a guest of Mr. and Mrs. Sturdy. The Sturdys' house proved to be quite crowded. Apart from us and the Sturdys, the house also hosted four more persons. They were Naren's brother-monk Swami Saradananda, Naren's brother Mahendranath Datta, Goodwin and John Fox from Boston. It was a very emotional meeting for Naren. He was meeting someone from the Order, and his family, for the first time in nearly three years. Saradananda gave Naren all the news from India.

Sturdy took this invasion of guests into his house quite stoically. Not so Mrs. Sturdy. She was always complaining about one thing or another. We could not blame her; after all, we did occupy her house! We tried to make amends by paying for most of the expenses. We also purchased the fruits and vegetables.

Mrs. Sturdy had a bee in her bonnet about Naren and Vedanta. She was sick of Sturdy's preoccupation with both. She got upset at the very name of India. She had, as

Naren put it: 'swallowed Sturdy." She was always on her guard lest Sturdy should become a monk, and escape to India or worse.

As soon as we reached London, I set about trying to get any job in the railways there. I could not sit idle, even while on vacation. I studied the railways in London.

Like our American railroads, the companies here were also owned by private individuals. There were about eleven large commercial railway companies. All were main line overground companies. All operated out of London termini stations to all parts of Great Britain. I visited their offices in Euston, Paddington, Marylebone, King's Cross, St. Pancras and so on.

I was most impressed by the Great Western Railway, and decided to try there for a job. The Great Western operated from London to the West Country. It covered cities such as Bristol, Cardiff, Exeter, Plymouth, and the most westerly town in Great Britain, Penzance.

Paddington Station was huge. Apart from the Station Master, there were hundreds of staff, including porters, lampmen, horse and carriage porters, letter sorters, cloakroom attendants, parcel porters, ticket collectors, Excess Luggage Collectors, Guards, station foremen, parcel foremen etc. Compared to this, even the Grand Central at Chicago seemed Spartan!

PADDINGTON RAILWAY STATION

My choice of the Great Western was also influenced by the admiration I had for the late Chief Engineer of the GWR, Isambard Kingdom Brunel. He was a Mechanical engineering genius. He started his career with the construction of the first tunnel under the River Thames. Then he designed a suspension bridge across the river Avon. He was Chief Engineer of the Bristol docks. He designed and built the docks at Monkwearmouth, Plymouth, Cardiff, Brentford and Milford Haven.

ISAMBARD KINGDOM BRUNEL

At the age of only 27, he was appointed Chief Engineer of the GWR. He built the first railway between London and Bristol. He used a much wider gauge of 7 feet. He was a workaholic, often working 18 hours a day. He would sleep in his office, or his Britzka carriage. Interestingly, he met his wife-to-be, Mary Horsley, in Kensington, while listening to Mendelssohn playing the piano. Brunel died in 1859.

I went to Paddington Station, and sought out the Station Master. He was a very cheerful and humorous man with the unlikely name of Cholomondeley, which he pronounced Chumley. He heard me out, and then took me to the Chief Administrative Officer of the GWR, Percy Larwood.

Larwood had me interviewed by the Engineer Angus McManus, who found me quite suitable for engineering work. Larwood then sent me to meet the Chief Mechanical Engineer, William Dean. Dean, for all practical purposes, was the chief of the railway. His chief assistant, George Churchward, was also a powerful figure. Both these technical men were very efficient. Dean was suffering from a wasting illness. This would soon put Churchward in his chair.

Both were intrigued by my story, and they did not want to waste my expertise. In principle, they agreed that taking me on would pose no problems for them. But my being an American would require the scrutiny by the

Chairman of the GWR, Viscount Emlyn. And so, I came face to face with the first Lord I would see in London.

DEAN AND CHURCHWARD

Viscount Emlyn was a surprisingly young man. He spoke in a very nasal accent, laced with numerous "I say" and "What." I could not understand a word of what he said. At one point, he asked me a question. I replied, seriously enough, that I only knew English! After a surprised look at me, he burst into laughter. God knows what he made of my remark! He told Dean to take me for any suitable job.

Dean told me the Viscount wanted him to incorporate the improvements, made in America, to the rolling stock here. In this way, I became an employee of the GWR. Dean was kind enough to ask me to come for the night shift, as far as possible. This suited me fine. I could spend the mornings with Naren, sleep in the afternoons, and come for duty at nights. The salary, in pounds, worked out more than the dollars I got at Chicago.

Naren's stay in Sturdy's house was short. To make Naren's work easier, Sturdy had rented Lady Isabel Margesson's house at 63 St. George's Road in South West London. The six of us stayed there – Naren, Saradananada, Mahendranath, Goodwin, John P. Fox and I. Miss Henrietta Muller also joined us.

Our relief at having escaped the prickly Mrs. Sturdy was short-lived! The thorny Miss Muller beat her hands down! In my opinion, the English were more moody and touchier than the Americans in small matters. Miss Muller, Mrs. Sturdy, Sturdy himself, and some others we met in high society were no exceptions. I found no such attitude at my work place, however.

Americans all over America were more easy-going and friendlier than the British. Or perhaps this was due to the cultural differences between the English and the foreign people they came in contact with. But Goodwin was no foreigner; he was an Englishman like them. Yet, he felt the lash sometimes.

Naren was very tolerant, but even his annoyance got the better of him sometimes. I once found him muttering about Miss Muller: "Nothing but quarrels! I wish she would go home for some time, cool off, and then come back."
Her strong opinions also drove him up the wall. One day, from outside his room, I could hear him telling Miss Muller: "The world is full of monomaniacs. Vedanta is my

monomania; whims are your monomania. We are all monomaniacs, Madam! Don't forget that!"

To which Miss Muller retorted: "You can out-shout me, and silence me, but you cannot convince me."

Miss Muller was not only opinionated, but one never knew when she would become touchy about anything. Let me give you a typical example.

Saradananda was a classic Hindu monk. He spoke little, and spoke softly. He was more of a listener, languidly interrupting with questions. He was very spiritual. Once, Miss Muller, dressed in a stylish sporting costume, was holding forth on the old cows in India. These cows, she said, suffered and were unproductive. Such cows, in England, would be done away with. Saradananda was horrified. He languidly, dreamily, offered the stock argument of the anti-cow slaughter group: "Do you do away with your parents, too, when they become old?"

What Saradananda did not know was that Miss Muller adored and took great care of her old mother. Miss Muller was stunned into silence, and glared at Saradananda. He, of course, never noticed this. Naren did, and cautioned Saradananda later to be careful in future: "Sharat, ladies in the West are different. Be polite to them. Get up when they come, and greet them."

Miss Muller was dissatisfied by the cooking of the elderly housekeeper Sturdy had provided. One day, grumbling away at him, she went home and returned with a cook. This cook's method of boiling rice was so comical that Mahendra and Saradananda went off into fits of silent laughter. Miss Muller caught them, and there was hell to pay!

Sturdy was a non-smoker. He bought inferior pipe tobacco for Naren at a bargain price. The tobacco was terrible and tasteless. After Sturdy left, Naren told Goodwin: "Throw this away. All day long I have to lecture, talk to people, have to think and write; I can't even smoke a little if I wish to? Get me some good tobacco."
When Sturdy came to know of this, he was very annoyed. He disliked Goodwin, who did everything so well.

In spite of all this, we had a good time. The parlor rang with the laughter of the jokes that Naren and the others made. The scope of the talks in the parlor was very wide. Sometimes Naren, sometimes Goodwin, sometimes me about the railways and sometimes John Fox about California – all were interesting to the others.

But Fox was a little confused. He confided in me alone: "Jock, I expected all the Swami's followers to be saintly as well. Look at them, just look at them! Miss Muller is a harridan. Mrs. Sturdy is a shrew. Sturdy is a damn fool! Goodwin, for all his efficiency, is narrow and dogmatic, always right! How un-Vedantic it all seems!"
John was a very good person, young and very naïve.

JOHN PIERCE FOX

The dislike between Fox and Miss Muller was mutual. She thought that Fox was a cadger, riding on Naren's coat-tails. The last straw came when she said that she wanted Fox's room for the new cook. Fox left immediately. He took a room at 137 Cambridge Street. Room and board cost 19 shillings a week. The food was very good, too.

Fox was very comfortable, and had more freedom. He could drop in on Naren whenever he wanted to. I had no problems with Miss Muller or Sturdy. But when Fox asked me to join him, I agreed and took Naren's permission. We got on very well together.

Goodwin fared no better with Miss Muller. He hated her, called her "that Chilean woman" since she had been born at Chile. But Goodwin was also a diplomat. He tactfully avoided any open conflict with Sturdy or Miss Muller.

Mahendra, on the other hand, proved to be a real problem. He wanted to be a barrister. Naren wanted him to be an electrical engineer. Mahendra had malaria, and got the fever frequently. Naren wanted Mahendra to go to America. Goodwin and Saradananda, when going to America, tried to force Mahendra to accompany them. They failed. Mahendra spent most of his time in the Reading Room of the British Museum. Miss Muller was ultimately successful in throwing him out of the house. Mahendra moved in with Fox and me. Now Miss Muller had Naren all to herself.

But enough digression. Naren had started regular Vedanta classes. The British were intelligent; Naren started directly with Jnana Yoga. He also gave public lectures at Piccadilly Picture Gallery, Prince's Hall, clubs, educational societies, Annie Besant's Lodge, and to private circles. Naren was at his ease with the English, and sure of them – their seriousness and their commitment.

Naren's classes on Raja Yoga were well attended, too. Once, he spoke about mental healing and it was fascinating. He said something like this: "A person whose mind has reached one-pointedness can heal mentally. The thought to heal joins the will. It is not any longer either mere thought or mere will. It is transformed into power, and issues out as the power to heal. You can direct this power to anyone. Jesus is the perfect example."

I believe this statement because I personally saw Naren in action. Naren and I were on the first floor. Mahendra and Saradananda were on the fourth floor. Mahendra was having one of his bouts of malaria. Suddenly Naren said: "Poor Mohin, he has suffered enough from this fever. I think he should be cured."
To think was to act. Naren sat absolutely still. Soon after, both Mahendra and Sardananda came running in. Mahendra cried excitedly: "Dada, dada (elder brother)! I am cured! My fever, my aches and pains are all gone! It is a miracle."

Naren kept quiet. I told them what had happened. Then it was Saradananda's turn. He, too, was suffering from malaria. He begged Naren to cure him also. Naren said: "All right. So be it."

MAHENDRA NATH DATTA

SWAMI SARADANANDA

Again the meditation, the stillness. At the end of it, Sardananda was cured of his malaria forever!

Naren had psychic powers, but he almost never used them. Once in London, he was speaking of the powers of the mind. His audience pleaded with him to demonstrate one such power. He refused. The audience begged for some simple proof. Naren relented, and said he would show them a small "parlor trick."

He did the trick he had told me about in Chicago at the Grand Central. Each student was to write a question on a slip of paper, and keep it in his or her pocket. Then Naren proceeded to answer each question, one by one. He also gave some details of the questioner's background, house, friends etc. Everyone was absolutely stunned!

One more phenomenon that I noticed in Naren was the change that took place in him when he lectured. Before the lecture he used to chat and joke with us in the cab, and at the lecture hall. Once he got up to lecture, everybody sensed a transformation in him. He seemed to fill the platform. His voice rang out melodiously. His gestures emphasized whatever he said. He spoke for hours without notes; he never paused; he never searched for a word!

IN LONDON

The total majesty of his bearing and his speech awed everyone. I felt that his Master, or the Divine Mother, had descended into him. There was a bright aura all around him. After he finished the lecture, he stood silent for a while. When he came down from the platform, and mingled with us, he was his normal self. Only his face would shine, and his eyes would glitter very brightly.

There was a memorable meeting between Naren and the famous Orientalist, Professor Friedrich Max Muller. Prof. Max Muller was professor of philosophy at Oxford University. He had heard that Sri Ramakrishna was an incarnation, and wanted to know more about him from Naren. In April 1896, Naren got this postcard from him:

2 April 96

Dear Sir,

Accept my best thanks for your interesting pamphlet. I believe you are a pupil of Rama Krishna Paramahamsa, whom I have always sincerely admired. I hope you will continue your work in America and make both Sankara and Ramanuja widely known.

Yours faithfully,
F. Max Muller

Naren had replied with great respect to this letter. Max Muller wrote again to Naren, telling him that he loved and worshipped the Master with his whole heart. He had not even known of his existence, but the Brahmavadin made him aware of the Master's teachings. He ended by saying that his great desire was to visit the spot where he had lived. Soon after, Max Muller invited Naren to visit him at his residence in Oxford on May 26, 1896.

Naren was delighted. Sturdy and I accompanied Naren to Oxford. It was a lovely summer's day. I went there only to have a look at Oxford. Truth be told, I had visualized a dry meeting between the Teutonic sage and the young Swami. No doubt there would be an exchange of platitudes and Sanskrit verses. I could not have been more wrong. The meeting was more emotional than two Frenchmen meeting after a long time.

The fire behind this emotion was, of course, the ghost of Sri Ramakrishna. The meeting began quite dramatically. Naren strode up to Max Muller, and bent down to touch his feet. Straightening, he said: "I hail you, great Sage, as the spirit of your race, the reincarnation of an ancient Rishi, and a soul that is every day realizing its oneness with Brahman!"

Max Muller was taken aback for a moment by this ornate greeting. He was visibly moved; his face shone with pleasure. He smiled and said: "It was so good of you to visit me."
Naren replied: "Guruji, I come not only to visit, but to pay my deepest respects to you. Whosoever loves Sri Ramakrishna, whatever be his or her sect, creed or nationality, my visit to that person I hold as a pilgrimage."

Max Muller then led us into his house, and introduced his wife to us. She was a very pleasant lady, always smiling. The day was nice and sunny. It was decided to move to the garden, and bask in the sun. What a pretty picture it all was! The neat little house, a true English cottage; the beautiful green garden where we sat and talked and laughed together; an unending supply of sandwiches and tea! Prof. Max Muller told us about himself.

Max Muller was born in Dessau in 1823. His father was a famous German poet. The patronage and advice of his father's friends had helped Max Muller immensely. He matriculated in the University of Leipzig. He first took up Sanskrit there. At the University Of Berlin he became a comparative philologist. At Paris, he was impelled to edit the Rig Veda and publish it. The difficulty was that he was poor, and copied manuscripts to survive.

F. MAX MULLER

In 1846, he came to England to try his luck there. Lady Luck at last smiled upon him. Two Englishmen, Bunsen and Prof. H.H. Wilson helped him. Bunsen introduced him to Queen Victoria and the Prince Consort. Wilson introduced him to Oxford University.

These introductions led to his fame and fortune. In 1848, the University Press printed his Rig Veda, in six volumes. Max Muller settled in Oxford. Oxford University soon found that he was no mere bookworm; he could bring his ancient subject alive. His magnum opus, History of Ancient Sanskrit Literature, was published in 1859

After some preliminary talk and tea, Max Muller turned to Naren and said: "I am very curious to know the power behind the sudden and momentous changes in the life of the late Keshab Chandra Sen."
Naren asked: "What changes do you refer to, Guruji?"
"Keshab was a Brahmo. Later he inclined to Christ. What made him become such an earnest student and admirer of the life and teachings of Ramakrishna?"

Naren told him, in a shorter form, what he had narrated to me about the interaction between Keshab and his Master. Max Muller hung on to every word, and then asked: "And what are your views regarding the incarnation of your Master? You were his closest disciple. Your views will be very important to me."

Naren again related, this time in greater detail, the life and death of the Master. He elaborated on his own life under the wings of his Master. He gave a summary of the teachings of his Master. He ended by saying: "Ramakrishna is worshipped by thousands today, Guruji."

The Professor immediately said: "To whom else shall worship be accorded, if not to such? You have told me things that I could not have gathered from any other source. But, I want to ask you, what are you doing to make him known to the world?"
Naren said: "When I have to speak about my Master to the masses, I feel great hesitation. A strange emotion fills my mind. I feel as if I am desecrating a sacred bond. I do not know what to do!"

Max Muller said: "I can understand that. The bond between Guru and pupil is sacred. May I suggest something?"
"Anything, Guruji, anything!"
"If you have confidence in me, I shall be glad to write a larger and fuller account of Ramakrishna's life and teachings."
"Would you, Guruji, would you? Oh, what an honor it would be to have my Master's life written by you!"
"But," said Max Muller, "I need more, many more facts and details. If you could provide them for me, I think I can do justice to the subject."
Naren said: "Guruji, let that burden lie on me. My brother-monk Saradananda will immediately write to India. We

shall collect as much as possible the facts concerning my Master's life and his sayings."

Out of this conversation was formed the article on Sri Ramakrishna entitled "A Real Mahatman," which appeared in the August 1896 issue of the Nineteenth Century. Later came the now famous book "Ramakrishna: His Life and Sayings." This book aided materially in giving Naren's mission a firmer hold on the English-speaking world.

Of course, all this was in the future. But what a wonderful morning and afternoon it was at Oxford! The philosophers were relaxed, discussing subjects near to their hearts, laughing like children, all thoughts of age, rank and learning forgotten. Sitting in this picture-postcard setting, being served light refreshment by the smiling Mrs. Max Muller, it was like a day in Heaven!

All too soon, the call for lunch came. It was a simple vegetarian lunch, tasty and wholesome. Later, we bade goodbye to Mrs. Max Muller. We went with the Professor on a tour of several colleges in Oxford. We visited the Bodleian Library also. The time came for starting back. Max Muller insisted on accompanying us to the railway station, saying: "It is not every day one meets with a disciple of Ramakrishna Paramahamsa."

Till the train arrived, Max Muller and Naren discussed many other matters about India and her past.

Naren asked Max Muller: "When do you plan to visit India? All of us in India would welcome you with deep gratitude."

Tears came to Max Muller's eyes. He said gently: "If I came to India, I would never return. You would have to cremate me there."

The train pulled in. Naren bent to touch the Professor's feet. He was blessed with a hand on his head. We got into our carriage. The train moved, and we waved to Max Muller till he was lost to sight. For some time we sat in silence. Then Sturdy sighed, and said: "Swamiji, what a lovely day we spent at Oxford today!"

Naren said: "We have seen today how the great Sage Vasishtha and his wife Arundhati must have lived in the Vedic times in their sylvan ashram! Today, we have met the Vedantist of Vedantists! I firmly sense that Guruji is a reincarnation of the 14th century Sage Sayana, who wrote a commentary on the Rig Veda. And what a love he bears for India! I wish I had a hundredth part of that love for my own Motherland!"

Sturdy said: "I agree, Swamiji. And look at the amount of work he has done in the field of Vedic Sanskrit."

Naren said: "It is truly astonishing. He learnt the language unaided. He interpreted manuscripts hardly legible to us Hindus. He spent days, sometimes months, in getting the meaning of a word correct. He cut a path through the forest of Sanskrit literature. This one man has done a thousand times more than what our forefathers or we could do to preserve, appreciate, and spread this literature throughout the world. Yes, Sturdy, it has indeed been a glorious day!"

Another memorable visit was to the memorial of that great Indian, Raja Ram Mohan Roy, at Bristol. At the Bristol Museum, there was a lovely portrait of Roy. He was man of great masculine beauty. He had delicate features, and large brown eyes. In the portrait, he is wearing a flat turban like a crown, and a shawl is draped over a brown robe.

Naren explained that it was Mohammedan costume, incorporating both cleanliness and comfort. This was due to Roy being brought up in the Court of the Great Moghul at Delhi. The epitaph on Roy's memorial runs: "A conscientious and steadfast believer in the Unity of Godhead: he consecrated his life with entire devotion to the worship of the Divine Spirit alone."
Naren said that if we used the language of Europe, the last words would be "of Human Unity." The meaning would remain the same. Naren spent quite some time meditating at Raja Ram Mohan Roy's grave.

In London, I met Miss Margaret Noble for the first time. She was a true English rose, with a blooming complexion. She had even features, bright dancing grey-blue eyes, light golden-brown hair, and a sparkling smile. Nobody could take liberties with her. She had the gift of keen repartee. Her Celtic ancestry was well reflected in her every action.

Margaret Elizabeth Noble was born in Dungannon, County Tyrone, Ireland. Margaret passed out of Halifax College. She was in a teaching post at Wrexham, North Wales, a coal-mining district. She met a young Welsh engineer there. They fell in love, but the young man died of illness before the engagement was announced. Margaret devoted all her time to education. The whole family shifted to Wimbledon, and she started a new school there. She, Lady Ripon and Lady Isabel Margesson formed a small coterie, the Sesame Club. Famous writers such as Bernard Shaw and Aldous Huxley spoke there.

During Naren's first talk in Lady Margesson's house, he met with a skeptic audience. They regarded psychology as the center of faith. Vedanta was impressive, but "there was nothing new." As time passed, Naren's words assumed newer meanings. A rigid mind was the wrong way to hear the message. They came for a second lecture, and yet another. They, especially Margaret, were not able to accept in toto whatever Naren said.

There developed a peculiar interaction. Margaret would do whatever Naren asked her to do, without hesitation. But any statement was questioned from a hundred angles. Naren was delighted. Just so had he fought with his Master! Once, in an argument, Naren attacked Margaret without mercy, and demolished her concepts. Her face crumpled, and tears came to her eyes.

After she left, I said mildly to Naren: "Your methods of teaching are no doubt time-tested. But have you not been too harsh with Miss Noble?"

"Jock, I can understand your sympathy, especially for a lady. But tell me, if you wanted to write something on a pat of butter, what would you use?"

"Well, I'd use a sharp pointed instrument."

"And if you wanted to write on soft stone?"

"A sharper, tougher instrument.

"What about hard stone, on which some drawings were already present?"

"Then, of course, I'd use a chisel and a hammer?"

"And why, pray?"

"Well, I'd first have to remove the already drawn characters, and then put down my own."

Naren said: "There you are, Jock. See, you and the Seviers are like a clean slate. You accept whatever I say, because the field is new for you. Margot is not that way. She is very learned in her field. She has many preconceptions about the way things should be done. To be useful to me, she has to come to my wavelength. She has to unlearn and then relearn. That is why I am rough with her. There is no other way. She goes home, broods over my words, argues it out in her mind, and then comes back and says 'Swami, you are right!'"

In this way, Naren built up a core group of strong, serious and intellectual men and women. They were Miss Noble, Miss Muller, Mr. Sturdy, and Captain and Mrs. James Henry Sevier. Naren felt that his work in England, though slower, was better and deeper than in the United States.

CAPT. SEVIER

MRS. CHARLOTTE SEVIER

July marked the end of the lecture season in London. The classes also drew to a close. To confirm Naren's presence during autumn, the members of the class readily subscribed to an advance fund.

All this was fine, but I noted one fact with dismay. Naren was terribly tired most of the time. After a lecture, he could barely drag himself home. Then he would collapse! I was very perturbed. Naren seemed on the brink of a breakdown!

****

THERE IS PLEASURE IN THE PATHLESS WOODS

There is a pleasure in the pathless woods,
There is a rapture on the lonely shore
There is society, where none intrudes,
By the deep sea, and music in its roar:
I love not man the less, but Nature more,
From these our interviews, in which I steal
From all I may be, or have been before,
To mingle with the Universe, and feel
What I can ne'er express, yet cannot all conceal.

GEORGE GORDON, LORD BYRON

CHAPTER 26

A CONTINENTAL INTERLUDE

I spoke to Miss Muller and the Seviers about Naren's condition. They had noticed it, too. They had been urging Naren to cut back on his work, and rest. He did not listen to them. I told them of Naren's love of traveling, and studying new cultures. I persuaded them to take Naren on a holiday tour on the Continent.

They thought it was a good idea, and went about it in an artful manner. They told him: "Swami, it is the holiday season. People are leaving for the seaside and mountain resorts. Instead of being idle in London, why not go to Europe? You can study the art and culture there?"
Naren was delighted; in fact, he was as happy as a child over the suggestion. He told me: "I would love to go to Switzerland. I long to see the snow, wander on the mountain paths, and cross a glacier."

I had more than enough money to pay my way, but Miss Muller would not hear of it. She told me: "You can take personal care of Swami. You are young and strong. You are not in awe of him. You are the only person he listens to without argument. And you can speak French and German perfectly."
All this was not strictly true, but no matter. Miss Muller detested Goodwin. She would probably have paid anything to prevent him from coming along. In the event, Goodwin

and Saradananda left for America. Goodwin would return after Naren's return from the tour.

We sailed from London on July 19. After breaking journey at Paris, we reached Geneva the next day. The clean, crisp air and the beauty of the place, especially Lake Leman, acted like a tonic on Naren. His strength visibly improved from day one. We did some sightseeing, and went up in a hot-air balloon. Naren was delighted; he said now he understood how the Gods felt when they see the earth from the heavens. He wanted to repeat the ride; I had to physically drag him away to the protected swimming pool.

At Chamonix, we were actually in the midst of snow. The Mont Blanc was impressive, and Naren wanted to climb it. The guide showed the appallingly steep route through a telescope. Naren discarded the idea remarking: "This is a climb only fit for a professional climber."

We did cross a glacier, the famous Mer-de-Glace. It was neither easy nor pleasant. There was a very steep ascent. Naren was attacked by vertigo. His foot slipped more than once. We were glad to reach the chalet on the summit, and have a mug of piping hot coffee.

Actually, I felt that a trip to Switzerland was quite bothersome. It required time, money and physical exertion. Everything was terribly expensive. Conveyance was a primitive affair. It was, however, worth all that to see

Naren's health improve day by day. He was free from his mental effort, his draining lectures.

Chamonix revived a long-standing dream of Naren's: "I have a cherished dream of establishing a monastery in the Himalayas. There, I can retire from the labors of my life, and pass the rest of my days in meditation. My Indian and Western disciples can live together there. I shall train them as workers. My Indian disciples will go out as preachers of Vedanta. The others will devote their lives to the good of India."

From Chamonix, we visited Little St. Bernard and then Zermatt. We saw the famous Monte Rosa, the Matterhorn and the Gornergrat. Miss Muller suggested that we stay at a little Swiss village of Saas-Fee, in the Upper Rhone Valley. It was so silent, so rural, and so peaceful, that we stayed for nearly two weeks. Naren completely revived in mental and physical health.

Then a letter came for Naren in this little village. It was an invitation from Dr. Paul Deussen, Professor of Philosophy at the University of Kiel. He was a famous German Orientalist. He had recently returned from India. He had read Naren's lectures, and wanted to discuss Vedanta with him. Naren immediately accepted. This was akin to meeting Prof. Max Muller at Oxford. Miss Muller fixed the appointment for September 10 at Kiel.

There was still time for Kiel, so we traveled to Lucerne. We crossed Lake Lucerne to visit the Chapel dedicated to the great patriot, William Tell. From Lucerne we went to Schaffhausen, then Heidelberg in Germany. We next visited Coblenz and had a steamer journey down the Rhine to Cologne. We moved on to Berlin. After a few days there we traveled straight to Kiel, reaching it by September 8. We informed Dr. Deussen about our having arrived.

That very evening we got a note from Dr. Deussen at our hotel. He requested our company at breakfast on the following day. We presented ourselves at his house the next morning. We were ushered into the library. There, Dr. and Mrs. Deussen received us very cordially. There was some small talk regarding Naren's travels and plans.

Naren noticed some volumes lying open on the table. They were books on Philosophy. Naturally, the conversation turned to serious topics. One of them was the versatility of Sanskrit in compressing the most profound thoughts into easily understandable couplets. Naren asked the Doctor: "Tell me, Dr. Deussen, how did you become interested in Sanskrit?"

"It's a long story," said Deussen, "When I was a student, my friends and I attended a lecture on a very new language and literature, Sanskrit. The lecturer was Prof. Lassen, and the lecture was free. Even now, unless the

University backs him, it is difficult for anyone to make a living by teaching Sanskrit."

"I have heard of Prof. Lassen. Was he not a pioneer in Sanskrit?"

"Yes, he was. He was the last of a band of heroic German scholars. Their only interest in Sanskrit was their pure and unselfish love of knowledge. Well, this veteran Professor was explaining a chapter in the Sanskrit play, Shakuntala. His exposition was wonderful, and the subject matter was fascinating. What cast a spell on me was the language itself. How wonderful it was, how strange, how sonorous the sounds uttered by the Professor! I was utterly captivated!"

"How fluent was the Professor in Sanskrit?"
"Very! My later studies showed that he did commit some mistakes. You see, he did not have a Pundit to correct his errors, as I did in India. Anyway, I returned to my lodgings, but could not sleep. A glimpse of an unknown land had been given to me; it was a gorgeous land of rich colors. My friends, and even I, had expected that I would soon enter a learned profession bringing me name, fame, a good salary and a high position. But then along came Sanskrit, a language unheard of by most European scholars, absolutely non-paying. My desire to learn it became irresistible."
Naren said: "I can understand that."
Deussen cocked an eyebrow at him and said: "You can? Many of my friends could not! Neither could my family."

"Doctor," said Naren, "I can understand it because even now in India this urge is prevalent. There are young and old pundits and sanyasis in places like Varanasi and Nadia. They are mad for knowledge for its own sake. They study by lamplight, spoiling their eyesight. They think nothing of traveling hundreds of miles, begging all the way. And their purpose? To read a particular manuscript, or seek a teacher! It is because of these scholars that India's greatness is undiminished."

"Yes, it is this type of thirst for knowledge that has made Germany one of the foremost nations of the world. It was a long uphill task to learn Sanskrit. I lived in Sanskrit. I even preferred to be called Devasena rather than Deussen!"

"Oh, something like Prof. Max Muller preferring to be called Moksha Moolara Bhatta!"

"Yes. Ultimately, my work was recognized. It was not due to my labor alone. It was also due to the intrinsic beauty of Sanskrit, especially so in the Vedanta. But first, I had to get over the damage caused by the Romanticists and the Reactionaries."

"Who were these people?"

"It was like this. The earliest Sanskritists in Europe had more imagination than critical ability. For them, Shakuntala was the high watermark of Indian Philosophy. These Romanticists were followed by the Reactionaries. They were a superficial band of critics and scholars. They knew no Sanskrit. They ridiculed everything from the East. These two groups were mere adventurers. The first real scholar of Sanskrit was Max Muller. He was the philologist par excellence. Undoubtedly, he was the pioneer."

"And what about you?"
"Following Max Muller, I revealed the metaphysical treasures of the Upanishads to the whole world. I never bothered with 'what would they say.' If Max Muller is the pioneer, I am proud to be his advance guard. For both of us, the truth is paramount."

"You were telling me about the intrinsic beauty of Sanskrit?" asked Naren.
"Just so. I consider the system of Vedanta to be the most majestic structure. It is founded on the Upanishads and the Vedanta Sutras. It is supported by Shankaracharya's commentaries. With all these, it is the most valuable product of the genius of man in his search for the truth."
"Doctor," said Naren, "I hope you will be as bold in showing us our defects and corruptions in our thought systems, so that we can improve our social needs."

Deussen was translating some of the Hindu scriptures, and showed his work to Naren. Some of the passages were decidedly obscure. How to interpret them? Deussen emphasized elegance of diction in unraveling the meaning. Naren delicately pointed out that the most important aspect of translation was the clearness of definition. Elegance of diction undoubtedly added beauty, but it was of secondary importance. He gave many examples of what he meant. Deussen was finally convinced.

Then Naren picked up a book of poetry, and was completely lost in it. He did not hear a question asked by Deussen. After Naren came out of his reverie, Captain Sevier repeated the question. Naren immediately apologized to Deussen, saying he had been concentrating totally on the poetry. Deussen was not fully convinced, but he gracefully accepted the apology. Imagine his astonishment when the talk turned to poetry; Naren quoted extensively from the same book, and interpreted the meaning. The conversation turned towards concentration as practiced by the Indian Yogis.

Dr. and Mrs. Deussen had spent time in India. They gave us a fascinating and animated account of their tour. They had especially enjoyed the old India, so rich in its historical associations. They discoursed on the Ganga, the temples, and the great hospitality that had been extended to them. Deussen especially appreciated the help given by the pundits to him in Sanskrit and Hindi. They had realized that he was a true searcher. The only thing the Deussens' had disliked was the beggars at every temple, monument and street corner.

As we finished tea, Deussen said that we would be much interested in an Exhibition being held at Kiel. The various arts and industries were on display there. He took us there himself, and we spent quite some time going through the exhibition.

DR. & MRS. PAUL DEUSSEN

Later, our host and hostess invited us to attend the birthday party of their daughter Erica. She was turning four on that day. It was charming to watch this little tot dispensing tea and cakes to her youthful guests. There was an atmosphere of joy and laughter.

Our host and hostess again pressed us to stay for dinner. They would not take no for an answer. We had another enjoyable session. It was delightful to see this young philosopher happily surrounded by a peaceful home, with devoted wife and darling daughter, honors, contentment and many genial friends. It was a very happy day for all of us.

The next day, September 10, was spent in sightseeing. For long periods, Naren and Deussen spoke in Sanskrit, in which both were fluent. This naturally turned Naren's mind towards his work at London. Deussen tried in vain to persuade him to stay at least for a few days. But Naren felt he had had enough rest, and was impatient to get back. Deussen understood his anxiety and told him: "Well then, Swami, I shall meet you at Hamburg, and we shall journey together to London via Holland."

We left Kiel for Hamburg and did some sightseeing there. Then Deussen joined us. We went to Bremen, then on to Amsterdam for three days. We then crossed the North Sea from Amsterdam to Harwich, and proceeded to London. The company of Dr. Deussen was excellent throughout. Naren was very grateful for the interest shown by this ardent Vedantist. He said: "I shall always keep a shining remembrance of my days at Kiel, Hamburg, Amsterdam and London, when Dr. Deussen was my companion."

I was privileged to see the two greatest Vedantists of Europe, Max Muller and Deussen. In my humble opinion, Max Muller was the greater of the two. He carried his knowledge lightly; above all, he was very humble. He listened, and was agreeable to, reasonable argument.

Deussen, on the other hand, was proud of his knowledge. He was touchy about being corrected. He was very patronizing. There were a lot of 'I's' in his talk. Any glory of ancient India was compared immediately to the progress in Germany. He liked Naren's company, but he found Naren himself very puzzling.

At his house, I accidentally overheard a small conversation between Dr. and Mrs. Deussen in German. He was telling her: "I can't make out the Swami. Look at the monks we saw in India. They were pale and half-starved; this Swami is roly-poly and eats well. Those monks were dry; this monk is laughing and joking all the time. Those monks were always fighting temptation; this monk loves to smoke. He is learned enough, but he feels he can correct even me!"
Mrs. Deussen murmured gently: "Monks can be different, dear. Be patient!"

It was a small enough incident, but it left a bad taste in my mouth. Max Muller wore all his feelings on his sleeve; I could never imagine him uttering such words about Naren! Well, philosophers can be different too, I guess! Of course, Deussen was still comparatively young.

He must have felt challenged by Naren, though Naren did nothing to foster that idea in him!

    After our return from Europe, we stayed with Miss Muller in her house, Airlie Lodge, at Wimbledon. One evening, there was knock on the door. I opened it, and found a Sannyasi in ochre robes standing there. He was young and extraordinarily handsome, with a kind of ethereal beauty.

"Does Swami Vivekananda live here?" he asked.

"Yes, he does. And you are....?"

"I am Swami Abhedananda, from Calcutta," he replied, in a strong but melodious voice.

SWAMI ABHEDANANDA

Naren had come into the hallway by now. When he saw the monk he cried out in a joyous tone: "Kali!"

He ran to Abhedananda, and they both embraced each other. After some time spent conversing in Bengali, Naren introduced me to Abhedananda.

"Have you come alone to Wimbledon?" I asked him.

"Yes," said Abhedananda very matter-of-factly, "I did not find anyone at the Docks. So I came to the city. From there, I found my way to Wimbledon."

I was terribly impressed. London was not an easy city to find your way about. It gave me a correct idea of what Abhedananda was capable of.

For the next two weeks, Naren and Abhedananda talked for hours at a stretch. Abhedananda had brought with him from India several books on the Vedas, the Brahmanas, the Sutras etc. The two worked over these Sanskrit tomes for great periods of time.

On October 6, Naren delivered a lecture at Airlie Lodge to a gathering of the town's residents. The very next day, he left for London to deliver a class-lecture there at 39 Victoria Street. Sturdy had rented this apartment, with three rooms knocked into one. It was ideal for the fall lectures. It was on the sixth floor, but had plenty of light. It was accessible through an elevator, or lift, as the English called it.

Victoria Street was ideally located, being close to Parliament Square, Westminster Abbey, both Houses of

Parliament, Victoria Station, and the Thames River. Naren did not return to Wimbledon. He took up residence at 14 Greycoat Gardens, two blocks away from the classroom. It was a basement flat, more or less underground, and Naren referred to it as "the Black Hole of London." But it was comfortable, conveniently situated and quite serene, almost like a monastery. Miss Muller was quite upset by Naren's move to London, and created a lot of fuss, but that too passed. The fall series of lectures commenced on September 9.

While all this was happening in England, all hell was breaking loose in America! What happened was this.

Summer lecture courses were to be held at Greenacre, Maine, by Mrs. Bull. She wanted Saradananda to deliver the lectures. At the same time, the Vedanta Society in New York also wanted Saradananda to come to New York for the Vedanta work. Both offered to pay the passage money of $50. Mrs. Bull, from Boston, actually sent the money to London. This established prior claim by Boston.

Add to this the fact that Goodwin disliked Miss Ellen Waldo and the other New York workers. He liked Mrs. Bull. When he and Saradananda arrived at New York, Goodwin took Saradananda directly to Boston. The New Yorkers were left high and dry without any information.

Swami Saradananda delivered the first lecture of his career at Greenacre; it was a runaway success. There was no reason why he should not have become popular; we had made him hold mock lectures in our house at London! Apart from this, he was so loving that he was inevitably loved. Naren had fretted about his success in America saying: "Sharat has nothing of that pluck and go which I have...Always dreamy and gentle and sweet! That won't do!"

But it did do very well in America! Nothing disturbed him; and his very presence tended to bring peace! Miss Waldo, with her friends, also attended the Greenacre Conference and they came to deeply appreciate Swami Saradananda.

So far so good! Naren had placed Mrs. Bull in charge of the American work. She took stock, and found the NY Vedanta Society without a head, with no headquarters, and little cooperation amongst Miss Waldo, Miss Phillips and Mr. Goodyear. She suggested dissolving the NYV Society; the group there could do co-operative work without an organization. She wrote to Naren about this; Naren replied that he should not be bothered with things like this. The Americans should work it out on their own.

So Mrs. Bull issued the Greenacre Circular. According to it, Saradananda would continue the Vedanta classes at New York, after finishing with Greenacre. A permanent room would be kept for him at New York. He was to be expected there by October 1. Everyone was satisfied; Miss Waldo and Miss Phillips also signed the declaration. They went away to New York to make arrangements for Saradananda. They also hoped that Goodwin would have control of the entire NY Center.

Mrs. Bull sent copies of the Circular to Naren in Switzerland for his approval. One portion of the Circular made Naren see red. It went: "….Mr. Sturdy will be asked to extend the leave of absence…..to Swami Saradananda from his London work…"
Naren tore up all the circulars and "threw them in the gutter." He wrote to Mrs. Bull: "…..Who is Sturdy….to permit (underlined three times) a Sannyasin? ……It was one piece of folly (underlined four times), nothing short of that…….Even so, I am no Master (underlined five times) to any Sannyasin in the world……."

Mrs. Bull was horrified; Goodwin was petrified. Both seemed to have exceeded their briefs. In a welter of indecision, they took a unilateral decision. Saradananda would remain in Boston through October and November, till Goodwin could go to England and return. They never bothered to inform the NY Center of this decision. In late September, Miss Phillips wrote to Mrs. Bull asking when Saradananda would arrive at New York. Goodwin replied: "….probably by the first of November….."

Did this mean that nothing was definite? Miss Phillips was outraged. What would she reply to inquirers? What was the changed plan? Would Saradananda alternate between Cambridge and New York, or what? Should she seek another Teacher, one J.C. Chattopadhyaya, also called Roy? Goodwin wrote back to not employ Roy for any reason. He was a Theosophist, given to speaking insultingly about Naren. But Goodwin's letter had not a word about Saradananda.

Shortly after, Goodwin decided to back away from the entire New York work. He would not take any responsibility for Saradananda. New York would probably see Saradananda during the New Year!

Miss Waldo was also fed up with Goodwin. She wrote a taunting letter praising Roy. This was all Goodwin was waiting for. He severed all connections with New York and wrote that he had advised Saradananda to remain in Cambridge this entire autumn. The day he wrote this letter, Goodwin passed quickly and silently through New York. He boarded the *SS Teutonic*, and sailed away to England. He left howls of outrage and despair behind him at New York.

Meanwhile, Miss Waldo cut through the Gordian knot. She wrote directly to Naren in London, asking for instructions. Naren wrote to her solving all the problems. Saradananda could alternate between New York and Boston. Miss Waldo should smooth over the jealousy between Boston and New York. She should not use Roy under any circumstances.

Swami Abhayananda (Mme Marie Louise) was doing excellent work in Brooklyn. Looking at that: "Why do you not begin to teach? Begin boldly. Mother will give you all power – thousands will come to you. Plunge in. No clinging to this fellow or that. Wherever Ramakrishna's children boldly come out, He is with them. You know a thousand times more philosophy than the boy Roy…plunge in bravely. Have faith you will move the world….I will be a thousand times more pleased to see one of you start than any number of Hindus scoring success in America, even be he one of my brethren. 'Man wants victory from everywhere, but defeat from his own children.' I will begin from today sending out powerful thoughts to you all. Make a blaze, make a blaze."

Miss Ellen Waldo filled in for Saradananda till he should come to New York. She started the work and did, in fact, do exceedingly well.

Naren also wrote to Mrs. Bull that Saradananda should work both at Boston and New York. On October 24, Saradananda visited New York. Miss Mary Phillips immediately started the Vedanta classes. The response was amazing, beyond all expectations. Even at just two days notice, the audience overflowed into the back parlor and hall.

During his short stay at New York, Saradananda managed to warm and uplift everyone who came into contact with him. His spirit of peace and loving understanding smoothed over the tangle of wills around him. During November and December, he lectured in and around Cambridge. In the first week of 1897, he moved to New York. He was escorted by John Fox, who noted that "the Swami was quite silent all the way in; perhaps America needs a new kind of non-attachment."

Saradananda held his classes at 509 Fifth Avenue, above Forty-Second Street. When the room overflowed, the kind landlord allowed the classes to continue in the ground floor hall free of charge. The landlord was also an admirer of Saradananda. The Swami held six lectures a week. Throughout the year, he moved dreamily between New York, Greenacre and Cambridge in a set pattern. All was well that ended well!

Meanwhile, in London, Naren was marching on triumphantly with his lectures. He spoke on the Isha Upanishad, and on Maya and its conquest. Then he took up the Katha Upanishad. Goodwin took Abhedananda around London and showed him the sights. Naren saw to it that he met people of all classes. He also coached Abhedananda in public speaking.

It was decided that Abhedananda should give a talk to a class. On October 27, Naren spoke in the morning on "God In Everything." Abhedananda was to speak in the afternoon. He got an attack of nerves, and said: "You know, Naren, I don't think that I will speak this afternoon. Some other time perhaps…"

Naren roared at him: "Kali, you must speak, or I will throw you out of that window!"

Abhedananda did speak to a small, well-chosen gathering. The meeting was friendly and informal. The audience was at first a little disappointed at not hearing Naren. But they quickly warmed to this handsome Swami's maiden speech. His voice was truly magnetic.

The vacation seemed to have rejuvenated Naren. He gave truly magnificent lectures. Not only that, the lectures seemed to get more and more innovative. Like in America, none of the lectures had any prior preparation. All were delivered on the spur of the moment. At one superb lecture, I saw Goodwin pause. He looked up in amazement before continuing with his shorthand. Later he told me: "Jock, Swami explained Vedanta in an entirely new way! He must have reasoned it out even as he was speaking!"

Naren's statements were backed by the tremendous power of his personality. Even though he was not in the best of health, he still transfixed the audience. Once Goodwin told me: "In his lecture on Maya, Swamiji rose to such heights that the whole audience seemed to be in a group Samadhi. I can only imagine how he must have been at The Parliament of Religions! No wonder people flocked to see him and hear him. Jock, you are a blessed person to have been a direct witness to such magic!"

Naren's magnetic personality was such that intellectuals from all walks of life fell for him like a ton of bricks. Members of the Psychical Research Society, non-conformist clergymen, and high clerics of the Church of England – none of these were immune to him.

Naren was now justifiably happy, and reasonably content, that the first steps of his work had been completed. His lectures were going famously. He felt confident that Abhedananda would carry on the English work very satisfactorily. The young Swami had delivered five successful lectures, and was gaining in confidence and public speaking skills day by day.

In America, the work was three-pronged. There was Saradananda, who in his dreamy, loving way was winning hearts, minds and souls between Boston and New York. There was Abhayananda, who in her thorough way illuminated the Vedanta classes in Brooklyn. Then there was the redoubtable Miss Ellen Waldo, who in her strict, efficient, no-nonsense way was carrying on at the New York Vedanta Center. Her first lecture on the mission of Vedanta in relation to Christianity and other religions, was a gem, and very successful. This was followed by other talks, well attended by earnest New Yorkers.

In this small way, the Ramakrishna Mission had begun. In America, Naren and the Mission became very well known in towns and cities far beyond New York. Now what was needed was for the work to be replicated in India.

In the midst of interviews, classes, public lectures, and writing, Naren still found time to give instructions to his brother-monks in Calcutta. These were regarding running of Maths on organizational lines. The structure of the organization was crystallizing in Naren's mind.

The first requirement was strict obedience and division of labor. The second was a long list of highly detailed rules. Naren said that rules were fetters; for a Sannyasin, they were positively evil! But for a fledgling organization rules were absolutely necessary to show the direction; laissez-faire would lead to anarchy!

I was astounded by the scope of the rules. Elections, management principles, daily routine, general conduct, even the furniture in each monk's room – all were covered. Naren said no mistakes could be committed now. As the organization grew, these faults would multiply in geometric progression, with no hope of correction. Hence all this care, all these details, chalked out with burning intensity. The foundation had to be strong for the structure to endure!

Naren's idea of a Math for women was vetoed by none other than the Holy Mother herself! Her desire was that a monastery should first be built to shelter the Master's Relics, carry on his work, and provide a home for his children.

All the American and English disciples knew of Naren's desire of starting a Monastery at Calcutta. Large sums of money were offered to Naren for the purpose. They wanted to see the work started. Mrs. Ole Bull wrote from America offering a substantial amount of money. She asked whether it should be sent to London. The London friends also offered equally large amounts. The combined sum would be more than ample for solving the problem. But Naren told them all: "Not now, please. Not immediately. The money will encumber me with additional responsibility. I shall start the Indian work on a small scale. After I find my bearings, I shall reconsider your offers."

A hardheaded person like me found this refusal difficult to swallow at first. Then I remembered Naren's dictum: "God will provide!" Of course He would! But Naren did accept contributions for another cause. In India, the monsoons had failed; a terrible famine was stalking the country. Naren wept openly, and sent everything that he had collected towards famine relief being collected by the *Indian Mirror*. One of his devoted supporters, Mrs. Emmeline Souter also gave him a generous amount for the purpose. Thus, the first token gesture of service, in the form of famine relief, was carried out by the Ramakrishna Order. In this small manner, the organization of the Order, and its duties, were started in London!

It was not all work and no play, however, and this Jack was never a dull boy! I remember a light-hearted evening that we spent in Cambridge. The 'Indian Majlis' of Cambridge gave a complimentary dinner honoring two Indian students. The first was Prince Ranjitsinghji, called Ranji by all. He was a fantastic cricketer. The second was Atul Chandra Chatterjee. Naren was invited to speak on the occasion.

RANJITSINGHJI (RANJI)

Naren started by saying that he had been probably invited to this dinner because he, by his physical bulk, bore

a striking resemblance to the national animal of India! All the students had a hearty laugh at this. They considered him a "jolly good fellow' for poking fun at himself. After his electrifying speech, one of the Masters commented to me: "He does resemble the national animal of India; he resembles the Lion!"

****

PATRIOTISM

Breathes there a man with soul so dead,
Who never to himself hath said,
"This is my own, my native land!"
Whose heart hath ne'er within him burn'd
As home his footsteps he hath turn'd
From wandering on a foreign strand?
If such there breathe, go, mark him well;
For him no minstrel raptures swell;
High though his titles, proud his name,
Boundless his wealth as wish can claim;
Despite those titles, power, and pelf,
The wretch, concentred all in self,
Living, shall forfeit fair renown,
And, doubly dying, shall go down
To the vile dust from whence he sprung,
Unwept, unhonour'd, and unsung.
SIR WALTER SCOTT

CHAPTER 27

HOMEWARD BOUND

November advanced, and the call of the Motherland grew stronger and stronger. Naren told me, a number of times, that he had stayed away far too long. Home-sickness was disturbing his concentration. Not just home-sickness; the eagerness to start the work in India as soon as possible also became stronger.

In the second week of November, Naren finished a class lecture. Then, suddenly, he called the Seviers aside. He told them: "Please purchase four tickets by steamer for India immediately."

Mrs. Sevier said: "Swami, you have not yet seen the classical side of Europe. May I suggest an alternative plan?"

Naren said: "So long as it culminates in my reaching India, I don't mind."

"Let us travel across the Continent till Naples. We will see all that lies on the way. Then, from Naples, we can take the first steamer for India."

"That will be all right. The tickets will be for you and Captain Sevier, Goodwin and I."

Capt. Sevier asked: "What are your immediate plans at India, Swami?"

"Well, I'm thinking first of founding three monastic centers at Madras, Calcutta, and the Himalayas. The two of you will manage the one in the Himalayas. Second, I want to start an institution for the education of girls, on national lines."

Mr. Sevier asked: "Swami, what will be the work of the monastic centers?"

"The main function of the monastic centers will be to train young men as preachers. The institution for girls will produce not only ideal wives and mothers, but also Brahmacharinis working for the betterment of the womanhood of India."

Mrs. Sevier asked: "Swami, the monasteries have no doubt been promised large sums of money. But how will the girls' institution be funded?"

"Miss Muller has gladly agreed to fund the girls' institution. I am seriously thinking of bringing Margaret Noble to India in due course. She will be in charge of my intended work for women."

Goodwin said: "Well, Swamiji, the prospects of launching a successful Indian campaign seems bright with promise!"

Naren said: "I am very happy that the dearest dream of my life, the rejuvenation of my Motherland, is going to be fulfilled at last!"

These plans suited me fine, too. I had already received a letter from Schumpeter that the trouble in Chicago had blown over. The disgruntled men had been taken care of. There was no danger for me. I could come back whenever I wished to, and the sooner the better. I decided that since Naren was going back to India, I would see him off, and then take the next ship back home.

None of us had reckoned with Miss Muller when charting out the journey to India! She had been in none of our plans. Suddenly, she insisted on going to India with Naren! Her behavior during this period was so strange that Goodwin suspected that she was going mad!

To avoid her, Naren first thought of going to America, and sailing from there to India. But this would be inconvenient and very expensive for the Seviers. The Seviers had seen the tempestuous behavior of Miss Muller during the Continental trip. They refused to sail with her.

Naren decided to bell the cat. He did some plain speaking with Miss Muller. She then decided to sail on her own to India with a companion. She also cast off her adopted son, Akshay Kumar Ghosh. Along with him, she also cast off, as Sturdy put it: "....all the nonsense and superstition that led her into that."

On Thursday, December 10, Naren delivered his last lecture on Advaita. The class was fully crowded; no one wanted to miss hearing him. After all, God knew when they would see him again. On December 13, Sturdy, on behalf of the English students, organized a farewell reception in Piccadilly at the Institute of Painters in Watercolors.

Scores of people from all over the city, and even from distant suburbs, poured into the hall. There was not even standing space. Abhedananda was present there; he had also made a name for himself in London. Musicians and singers performed on the stage at stated intervals. There were many speeches, and huge applause for them. Many in the audience were silent and sad; many were close to tears.

LAST LECTURE IN LONDON

Naren, dressed in glittering amber garments, was like a ray of sunshine in the cold hall. Finally, Sturdy presented his address to Naren. Naren's reply was in terms of great endearment and glowing spiritual fervor. He seemed to be saying to the audience: "I shall definitely meet you again."

Later, Sturdy told me: "Jock, I am heavy hearted at the loss of the noblest friend, and the purest teacher, I have met in this incarnation. I must have stored some exceptional merit in the past to receive such a blessing. What I longed for all my life, I have found in the Swami. One consolation is that his brother-Swami is a nice, attractive, ascetic-minded young man. He will undoubtedly continue the good work."
On his part, Naren was extremely satisfied with his English stay. In one of his letters to America he wrote: "The work in London has been a roaring success!"

On their part, the people of England and America had been ready to accept Naren's teachings unreservedly. I tried to analyze why this was so. Their whole religious culture was so decidedly different. Yet, they accepted Naren and all his disciples where Vedanta was concerned. I wondered why this was so! I shared this thought with Goodwin, and he took some time to analyze the question. After some time he reached his conclusion.

Goodwin put it very neatly: "Jock, the Westerners are practical people. The philosophy Naren teaches is grand and he is very eloquent. But then, so are the fire and brimstone preachers of the West. However, Naren's philosophy is practical. He is what he teaches. His life is his message. What does he teach? Some practices to improve your body, your health, your mind, your devotion, and your soul. And he is not even bothered about your religion! His message is 'At least become like me.'

"The Western thinking is 'if he could do it, why not I? I may not equal him, but at the very least, the practices will make me a better person.' Again, there is no fear, no sin; the Vedanta tells man to strive and become great. The Western people, you will no doubt agree, believe in working hard to achieve their goal. That is why they accept Naren and Vedanta."

This was a keen analysis, and as a Westerner, made complete sense to me.

Naren and the Seviers sailed for the Continent on December 16, 1896. I sailed for New York the next day. At Chicago, I took over my duties once again. Schumpeter, Lenglen and my other friends welcomed me. I told them about my work with the British Railways. Lenglen immediately tested me. He found that I had learned new things and processes from the British. He recommended my promotion to Junior Electro-mechanical engineer. The orders came through in a week. I took up my new job, definitely more interesting than my old one. I settled down to my routine.

By the middle of January 1897, I received a letter from Naren. It had been written just before he boarded ship at Naples for Colombo. Actually, it was typed, obviously by Goodwin on Naren's dictation.

Naples.
December 29, 1896.

My dear Jock,

A 'hello' and a 'farewell' from Naples, on the eve of my departure for India, and home. It was a vast relief when Josiah's ship arrived here on time today. I clapped my hands like a child and cried, "Now, at last, it will be India – my India!" We sail on the steamer Prinz Regent Luitpold tomorrow, December 30. We are scheduled to reach Colombo on January 15, 1897. So we shall spend the New Year on the high seas!

SS PRINZ REGENT LUITPOLD

Naples is a pretty little place. We spent almost a day visiting Vesuvius. The funicular railway took us almost to the crater. The volcano obliged us by hurling a mass of boulders forcefully up into the air! Another day was spent at Pompeii. I was impressed by the way the recently excavated houses have been left with their belongings exactly as found. The Naples Museum and Aquarium are also very good to visit.

After leaving London we passed via Dover, Calais and Mont Cenis into Milan. The long rail journey was spent in discussing with my companions the plans for my country. Also about the establishing of the Ashrama in the Himalayas. From Milan we went to Pisa, and thence to Florence. Imagine my surprise and absolute delight when I met Mr. and Mrs. George Hale there! They were also touring Italy! I spent many hours with them, reminiscing and telling them of my plans for my work in India.

Rome was a most remarkable and emotional experience. The glories of the ancient Roman world have always captivated me. Besides the ruins, there is the medieval and modern ecclesiastical Rome; there is also the fabulous Renaissance Rome of architecture, painting and sculpture. Suffice it to say that nothing disappointed me; everything in Rome interested me.

I was always absorbed in its many-phased past, especially Christian Rome. The Vatican and St. Peter's are especially grand! One cannot offer too much to God, no doubt; still, I became restless when attending High Mass at St. Peter's on Christmas Day. Why all this pageantry and ostentatious show? What a contrast between these splendours, and the great spirit of Sannyasa which Christ had taught!

Carping aside, the Spirit of Christ filled the air of Rome that Christmastide. I could not help drawing a comparison between the Christ child, and the child Krishna. The festival of the Bambino from Christmas Day to Epiphany reminded me of an Indian mela!

And now we are sailing for India. I am indeed happy! The long sea voyage will bring my health back to normal before I plunge into the maelstrom of India once again. The thought of visiting my homeland after three long years fills me with mixed emotions.

The thought of rejoining the Holy Mother and my brother-monks at Calcutta fills me with delight. It will be so good to meet them, tell them all that occurred here, and argue the Vedanta with them – all these are delightful prospects. Also the anticipation of visiting the old haunts of my Master at Dakshineshwar fills me with joy!

The thought of Calcutta also fills me with vigour. A noisy, quarrelsome city, with its argumentative people, orthodox and unorthodox, is also a pleasure to anticipate. To give public lectures, many of them at street corners, is something I look forward to. And of course meeting my beloved mother; I wonder how she will look upon all that I have achieved in the West!

The thought of the vast hinterland of India outside Calcutta fills me with apprehension. I have roamed all these areas, but in three years so many changes may have occurred! How will the people look upon me at distant Colombo or Madras? Barring Alasinga, does anyone else remember me? I can vouch only for the Raja of Khetri; the others are questionable identities. And what to say of the even more distant Himalayan towns?

Remember, I have vowed to spread the message of my Master all over India. It looks so daunting now!

I shall write again after I reach Calcutta. I will give you my correct address, to which you can write. Till then, my blessings and best wishes to you. I hope that you have joined your beloved railroad again. I pray that in the future you will not have to face the problems that you recently faced. Please convey my warm regards to SM Schumpeter.

Wish me luck, Jock! All my plans for action are in the realm of thought. All my plans for infrastructure depend on the money I have and shall, presumably, get. And who knows how I shall be received in India? Many months ago, in Detroit, I had told my disciples: "India must listen to me! I shall shake India to her foundations! I shall send an electrical thrill though her national veins! Wait! You shall see how India will receive me. It is India, my own India, that knows truly how to appreciate that which I have given so freely here, and with my life's blood, as the spirit of Vedanta. India shall receive me in triumph!"

Brave words, indeed! And now, I am so unsure of my reception!! Do we not have the words of the Holy Bible to support my apprehensions? Remember what Lord Jesus said to his disciples: "And he said, Verily, I say unto you, No prophet is accepted in his own country." There you have, in a nutshell, what might await me in my own beloved Motherland! Whatever I say, India is India! I expect that I shall, to a great extent, get the cold shoulder! And I am not even a Prophet; I am but a poor preacher!

Of course, these mountains of uncertainties and worries lie in the future. Shortly, I shall embark on a bracing and healthy sea voyage! I shall consign my anxieties to the deep and sing with old Omar Khayyam:

Ah, fill the Cup: -- what boots it to repeat
How Time is slipping underneath our Feet:
Unborn To-morrow, and dead Yesterday,
Why fret about them if To-day be sweet!

Why indeed?

With love,
Naren.

**** THE END ****

ABOUT THE AUTHORS

Sumana Shashidhar is a Clinical Research Manager at Stanford University School of Medicine. She grew up in India, where her exposure to the Vedantic teachings of Ramakrishna and Chinmaya Missions inculcated a lifelong love of all things spiritual. She now lives in San Jose, CA with her husband and daughter. She learned how to read when she was four and is incapable of passing by a book without itching to read it! This is her first novel, co-authored with her father.

Shashidhar Belwadi is an ex- Indian Police Service Officer, who started out his professional life as an Electrical Engineer, segueing into the Police Service, with stints in Industrial Security. The last ten years of his career were spent as a Life Skills Trainer with Software giant Infosys. He is a voracious reader, and a big fan of Swami Vivekananda, both of which contributed to his going through a very large body of literature on the Swami as research for this book. This is his first novel, co-authored with his daughter.

Connect with the Authors.

We really appreciate you reading our book. You can reach us one of two ways:

Friend us on Facebook: http://facebook.com/Writers Shashidhar

Correspond with us via email at: writers.shashidhar@gmail.com

Tweet us at: http://twitter.com@writeshashidhar

AUTHOR'S THANKS

We hope you enjoyed this book. Our new book ***The Flame*** will also be published shortly. Don't miss out on the future adventures of the Warrior Monk. Happy reading!!

****

Printed in Great Britain
by Amazon